A HIGH
SIERRA
CHRISTMAS

WILLIAM W. JOHNSTONE

with J. A. Johnstone

A HIGH SIERRA CHRISTMAS

PINNACLE BOOKS
Kensington Publishing Corp.
www.kensingtonbooks.com

PINNACLE BOOKS are published by

Kensington Publishing Corp.
119 West 40th Street
New York, NY 10018

PUBLISHER'S NOTE
Following the death of William W. Johnstone, the Johnstone family is working with a carefully selected writer to organize and complete Mr. Johnstone's outlines and many unfinished manuscripts to create additional novels in all of his series like The Last Gunfighter, Mountain Man, and Eagles, among others. This novel was inspired by Mr. Johnstone's superb storytelling.

All Kensington titles, imprints, and distributed lines are available at special quantity discounts for bulk purchases for sales promotions, premiums, fund-raising, educational, or institutional use. Special book excerpts or customized printings can also be created to fit specific needs. For details, write or phone the office of the Kensington sales manager: Kensington Publishing Corp., 119 West 40th Street, New York, NY 10018, attn: Sales Department; phone 1-800-221-2647.

ISBN-13: 978-0-7860-4213-5
ISBN-10: 0-7860-4213-3

First Kensington hardcover printing: July 2018
First Pinnacle paperback printing: November 2018

10 9 8 7 6 5 4

Printed in the United States of America

Electronic edition: November 2018

ISBN-13: 978-0-7860-4214-2
ISBN-10: 0-7860-4214-1

upstairs... be a bounty hunter. And he's ruthless, and fierce enough to bring down the deadliest outlaws of the day.

New fiction and they'll discover... Grizzly bears, savage... father-to-be... young man on his own... and as the front... Howlsatthe Lone... Louis thought killed in... nah...

THE JENSEN FAMILY
FIRST FAMILY OF THE AMERICAN FRONTIER

Smoke Jensen—*The Mountain Man*
The youngest of three children and orphaned as a young boy, Smoke Jensen is considered one of the fastest draws in the West. His quest to tame the lawless West has become the stuff of legend. Smoke owns the Sugarloaf Ranch in Colorado. Married to Sally Jensen, father to Denise ("Denny") and Louis.

Preacher—*The First Mountain Man*
Though not a blood relative, grizzled frontiersman Preacher became a father figure to the young Smoke Jensen, teaching him how to survive in the brutal, often deadly Rocky Mountains. Fought the battles that forged his destiny. Armed with a long gun, Preacher is as fierce as the land itself.

Matt Jensen—*The Last Mountain Man*
Orphaned but taken in by Smoke Jensen, Matt Jensen has become like a younger brother to Smoke and even took the Jensen name. And like Smoke, Matt has carved out his destiny on the American frontier. He lives by the gun and surrenders to no man.

Luke Jensen—*Bounty Hunter*
Mountain Man Smoke Jensen's long-lost brother Luke Jensen is scarred by war and a dead shot—the right

qualities to be a bounty hunter. And he's cunning, and
fierce enough, to bring down the deadliest outlaws of
his day.

Ace Jensen and Chance Jensen—*Those Jensen Boys!*
Smoke Jensen's long-lost nephews, Ace and Chance,
are a pair of young-gun twins as reckless and wild as
the frontier itself . . . Their father is Luke Jensen,
thought killed in the Civil War. Their uncle Smoke
Jensen is one of the fiercest gunfighters the West has
ever known. It's no surprise that the inseparable Ace
and Chance Jensen have a knack for taking risks—
even if they have to blast their way out of them.

Wide eyed, the little boy tipped his head far back to peer up at the gaudily painted vehicle looming over him in the Museum of Transportation.

"Whoa," he said in an awed voice that matched his gaze. "Is that a real stagecoach?"

"They probably just made it to look like one," the boy's mother said. "I'm not sure there are any real stagecoaches around anymore."

A tall, straight-backed man with silvery hair and a neatly clipped mustache approached them.

"Beg your pardon, ma'am," he said as he gave the woman a polite nod and reached up to pinch the brim of the brown felt cowboy hat he wore. "I couldn't help overhearing what the little fella asked. Son, that sure is a real stagecoach."

"You mean people used to ride it in the Old West?" the boy asked as his eyes got big.

"They did."

Ignoring the somewhat disapproving frown the woman gave him, the older man stepped closer to the stagecoach, which was painted bright red with brass fittings and a gleaming brass rail around the top. On the side, above the door and the windows, in gold paint were the words WELLS FARGO & CO. OVERLAND STAGE. *The rear wheels were bigger than the front wheels, but both sets were taller than the little boy, who wore a straw cowboy hat and a fringed vest from some playset.*

The man rested a fingertip on the side of the stage, just below the back window on this side, and said, "See this? It's been painted over a heap of times, so you can't hardly make it out anymore, but somebody scratched something into the wood here."

"I don't know," the boy said, frowning. "I can see something there, but I can't make it out. . . ."

"All right to give the lad a hand, ma'am?"

The woman sighed, tired from a day of sightseeing and eager to get back to the motel.

"Sure, go ahead," she said.

From behind, the man took hold of the little boy under the arms and lifted him so his face was close to the stagecoach.

"I see it!" the boy said. "It looks like somebody's initials. . . . B.B. . . . December . . . 1901." He turned his head to look at the man. "That was sixty years ago."

With only a slight grunt of effort, the man set the little boy on the floor again.

"It sure was," he said. "I happen to know that the fella who scratched those letters on there was riding in the coach when it was caught in a blizzard in Donner Pass back in oh-one."

"Wait, wait, wait." Another man approached, holding up his hands. This one was chubby, with dark curly hair. A pair of glasses kept slipping down his nose. "Don't fill the boy's head with nonsense."

"What are you talkin' about, mister?" the older man said as he looked around.

"No stagecoach would have been traveling through Donner Pass, at Christmastime or any other time of the year, in 1901. The Central Pacific Railroad was completed long before that and had been taken over by the Southern Pacific by then. There would have been no reason for a stagecoach to go through there."

"You know that for a fact, do you?"

"Yes, I do. I have a doctorate in history, and I wrote my thesis on the development and expansion of the American railroad system."

"So you're a college professor."

"That's right, I am."

"I reckon you set me straight, then." Clearly dismissive, the older man turned back to the boy. "Like I was saying, that stagecoach was on its way through the Sierra Nevadas that December when it started to snow—"

"No, you're wrong—"

"I'm telling the story here, amigo, not you." The older man's voice had taken on a flinty tone that made the professor step back nervously. "You're welcome to listen while I talk to the boy. Could be you'll learn something."

The woman said, "We have to go—"

"No!" the boy said. "I want to hear the story. Does it have cowboys in it?"

"A bunch of 'em," the older man told him with a smile. "And one of 'em was called Smoke. It all starts in San Francisco. . . ."

BOOK ONE

BOOK ONE

CHAPTER 1

San Francisco, December 1901

"Give me all your money and valuables, mister, and be quick about it!"

"No, I don't believe I will," Smoke Jensen said as he shook his head.

"I mean it!" the would-be robber said, jabbing the gun in his hand toward Smoke.

He had stepped out of an alley a moment earlier and threatened Smoke with the old, small-caliber revolver. Smoke was on his way to an appointment and had taken a shortcut along a smaller street, which at the moment was practically deserted.

A few people were walking along the cobblestones in the next block, but they were unaware of the drama playing out here . . . or ignoring it because they didn't want to get involved. It was hard to tell with big-city folks.

The thief wore a threadbare suit over a grimy, collarless shirt. Smoke couldn't see the soles of the man's shoes, but he would have bet they had holes in them. The man's dark hair was lank and tangled, his face gaunt, his eyes hollow.

"Opium?" Smoke asked.

"What?" The man looked and sounded confused as he responded to Smoke's question.

"That's why you've resorted to robbing people on the streets? So you can afford to go down to Chinatown and visit one of the opium dens?"

"That ain't none o' your business. Just gimme your damn money!"

"No." Smoke's voice was flat and hard now, with no compromise in it. "And you'd better not try to shoot that old relic. It'll likely blow up in your hand if you do."

The man turned the gun's barrel away from Smoke to stare at the weapon. When he did that, Smoke's left hand came up and closed around the cylinder. He shoved the barrel skyward, just in case the gun went off.

At the same time, Smoke's right fist crashed into the robber's face and sent him flying backward. Smoke was a medium-sized man, but his shoulders were broad as an ax handle and the muscles that coated his torso were thick enough to make his clothes bulge if the garments weren't made properly.

Smoke had pulled his punch a little. The robber looked to be on the frail side, and Smoke didn't want to hit him too hard and break his neck.

For many years he had been in the habit of killing or at least seriously injuring anybody who pointed a gun at him, but this time it seemed like enough just to disarm the varmint and knock him down. Smoke expected to see him scramble up and flee as quick as his legs would carry him away from here.

The man got up all right, but instead of running away, he charged at Smoke again with a wolfish snarl on his face. His hand darted under his coat and came out clutching a short-bladed but still dangerous knife.

That made things different. Smoke twisted aside as the man slashed at him with the blade. The knife was probably more of a threat than the popgun the man had been waving around.

Smoke tossed the revolver aside, grabbed the man's arm with both hands while the man was off balance, and shoved down on it while bringing his knee up.

The man's forearm snapped with a sharp crack. He screeched in pain and dropped the knife. When Smoke let go of him, he fell to his knees in the street and stayed there, whimpering as he cradled his broken arm against his body.

Smoke picked up the gun, took hold of the would-be robber's coat collar, hauled him to his feet, and marched him stumbling along the cobblestones until he found a police officer.

The blue-uniformed man glared at him and demanded, "Here now! What've you done to this poor fellow?"

"This poor fella, as you call him, tried to rob me," Smoke said. With his free hand, he held out the gun and the knife. "He pulled this gun on me and demanded all my money and valuables, and when I took it away from him he tried to cut me open with the knife. I'd had about enough of it by then." Smoke shoved the would-be robber toward the officer. "His arm's broken, so he'll need some medical attention before you lock him up."

"Wait just a blasted minute! I'm supposed to take your word for all this?"

"It's true, it's true!" the thief wailed. "Lock me up, do anything you want, just keep that crazy cowboy away from me!"

"Sounds like a confession to me," Smoke said. He started to turn away.

"Hold on," the officer said. "At least tell me your name and where to find you, so I can fill out a report."

"The name's Smoke Jensen, and my son and daughter and I are staying at the Palace Hotel."

The policeman's eyebrows rose. The Palace was the city's oldest, most luxurious, and most expensive hotel. The man standing in front of him wasn't dressed fancy—Smoke wore a simple brown tweed suit and a darker brown flat-crowned hat—but if he could afford to stay at the Palace, he had to have plenty of money.

Not only that, but the name was familiar. The officer recalled where he had seen it and blurted out, "I thought Smoke Jensen was just a character in the dime novels!"

"Not hardly," Smoke said. He was well aware of the lurid, yellow-backed yarns that portrayed him variously as an outlaw, a lawman, and the West's fastest and most-feared gunfighter. All of those things had been true at one time or another, but the fevered scribblings of the so-called authors who cranked out those dubious tomes barely scratched the surface.

These days he was a rancher. His Sugarloaf spread back in Colorado was one of the most successful and lucrative west of the Mississippi, not to mention the wealth that had come from the gold claim he had found as a young man. He could well afford to stay at the Palace Hotel. More than likely, he could have booked an entire floor and not missed the money.

Instead he had a suite, with rooms for himself; his son, Louis Arthur; and his daughter, Denise Nicole. He was on his way to meet the twins now, and he didn't want to be delayed.

"Is it all right for me to go on to the hotel?" he asked the policeman.

"Why, sure it is, Mr. Jensen," the officer said. He took hold of the thief's uninjured arm. "I'll tend to this miscreant. I'm sorry you ran into trouble here in our fair city."

"Don't worry about it," Smoke said. "For some reason, I tend to run into trouble just about everywhere I go."

Smoke had been to one of the banks in San Francisco where he had an account, to deal with some business regarding one of his investments. He had money in several different banks here and in Denver and Chicago, and over the years he had invested in numerous enterprises that had made him even more wealthy.

None of which affected the way he lived his life one bit. He had his ranch, his friends, his brothers and nephews, his children, and most of all his beloved wife, Sally, who at the moment was back on the Sugarloaf. Those were the only things that really mattered to him, not numbers written in some bank ledger.

From the bank, he had headed for the building where he was supposed to meet Louis Arthur and Denise Nicole. He hoped the encounter with the opium addict who had tried to rob him hadn't delayed him too much.

Of course, the twins were perfectly capable of taking care of themselves, especially Denny. She was a beautiful, genteel young woman—when she wanted to be—but as she had proved by strapping on a gun and going after a gang of outlaws who had raided the ranch, she wasn't shy about standing up for herself and her family, either.[1]

When Smoke walked into the office, which smelled vaguely of carbolic acid, he saw Denny waiting in one of the armchairs, but there was no sign of Louis.

"Where's your brother?" he asked.

Denny wore a dark blue traveling outfit with a hat of the same color perched on upswept blond curls. A pair of fawn gloves lay in her lap. She looked at Smoke and said, "He's already in with the doctor. He didn't want me to go with him, of course." She blew out a breath. "I don't know why. It's not like we've ever been that shy around each other."

"Yeah, but you're not kids anymore." Smoke took off his hat and sat down in the chair next to Denny's. "And even though he won't admit it, I think your brother feels like he's letting down the name Jensen by not being as tough as the rest of us. What he doesn't understand is that he's just as tough in other ways. How do you think Luke or Matt or I would have handled it if we'd had a bad heart and couldn't do all the things we've done?"

"I suppose," Denny said.

In truth, if Smoke or his brothers had been physically impaired like Louis, likely none of them would have lived to adulthood. Luke never would have made it through the war, let alone become a bounty hunter, and Matt probably wouldn't have survived the outlaw attack that had left his birth family dead. Smoke never would have headed west with his father after the war to clash with Indians and badmen and meet the old mountain man called Preacher who had taught him everything he knew about handling a gun.

And he never would have met and fallen in love with the beautiful young schoolteacher Sally Reynolds, so Denise Nicole and Louis Arthur wouldn't even be here.

Smoke was musing on those weighty thoughts when a door opened and a thick-bodied man with a beard stepped out. Pince-nez perched on his nose. He looked a little like President Theodore Roosevelt, who had taken office a few months earlier—and whom Smoke had met when he was a Montana rancher. Teddy was a good man for an easterner.

"Mr. Jensen?" the bearded man said.

Smoke got to his feet. "That's right."

"I am Dr. Hugo Katzendorf. If you would come back to my office, please."

Dr. Katzendorf had only a faint accent to indicate his Prussian origins. He was a heart specialist, reputedly one of the best in the country.

Years earlier, when Louis was a small child and

Sally's parents had taken him to Europe to seek the finest medical attention for him, Katzendorf was one of the doctors who had seen him.

Now, having immigrated to America and established a practice in San Francisco, Katzendorf had written to Louis and asked for the chance to examine him again after almost two decades, to compare his condition now to what it had been back then. Such knowledge might prove vital to physicians who specialized in treating heart problems.

Denny started to get up, but Smoke motioned her back into her chair. She glared at him. Denny hated being left out of anything, from a party to a fight. But she sighed and stayed where she was.

When Smoke and Katzendorf walked into the physician's office, they found Louis there, buttoning up his shirt after the examination. He had the same fair hair and slender build as his sister. He smiled and said, "Tell my father the good news, Doctor."

"I'm always ready to hear good news," Smoke said.

Katzendorf hooked his thumbs in his vest over his ample belly and frowned.

"Your son has a rather dry sense of humor, Mr. Jensen. The news is not . . . good." He held up a pudgy hand to forestall any response from Smoke and went on, "But neither is it entirely bad. Louis's heart is indeed stronger than it was when he was a child. But I fear it is also enlarged, and the valves in it are weak. He will always be in danger of it failing."

Louis laughed and said, "The good doctor doesn't understand. I fully expected to have dropped dead before now. I'm living on borrowed time, so I consider every day a blessing."

Smoke's hand tightened on the hat he held. Even though he had known it was too much to expect, he had hoped Katzendorf would declare that Louis was cured. The youngster's color was so much better than it had been, and he seemed stronger all the time.

From what Katzendorf had said, though, it sounded like there was only so much improvement that could ever take place.

"What's it look like over the long run, Doc?" Smoke asked.

Katzendorf spread thick fingers.

"Who can say? My experience and expertise tells me that the young man's life expectancy will be shortened, but by how much? That is impossible to predict. If he takes good care of himself, leads a healthy life, and avoids undue exertion and excitement, he may live another twenty to thirty years."

"See?" Louis grinned. "Not that bad."

Smoke was in his early fifties now. The doctor was saying he didn't think Louis would make it to that age. That angered Smoke, but some enemies couldn't be fought with fists or guns, or even outwitted. A bad ticker was one of them.

Louis went on, "This leaves me more convinced than ever that my future lies in the law. I'm thinking that next year I may try to attend Harvard."

"Your mother won't like you leaving home again," Smoke cautioned.

"Well, Denny will still be there on the ranch. If you're not careful, Father, she'll take over running the Sugarloaf from you. She'll be giving the orders before you know it."

"That'll be the day," Smoke said, but deep down, the prospect didn't displease him that much. One of these days, Denny might well be running the ranch, and Louis would be handling its business affairs.

When that happened, he could just sit back in a rocking chair and enjoy his old age. Yeah, Smoke Jensen in a rocking chair . . .

Nope, he thought. He just couldn't see it.

CHAPTER 2

Staghorn, Nevada

Two men rode down the main street of the bustling settlement, which served as the supply center for the mines that lay to the northwest and the ranches spreading across the range southeast of there.

Having both in such close proximity meant that clashes between the pick-and-shovel men and the cowboys were inevitable, but it also ensured that Staghorn was a busy, profitable place, with a lot of cash flowing into the merchants' coffers.

Because of that, the First Bank of Staghorn—which was the *only* bank in Staghorn, actually—usually had a decent amount of money in its safe.

The two strangers on horseback rode all the way from one end of Main Street to the other. Then, satisfied with what they had seen, they turned their horses and moved back along the street at a leisurely pace until they reached the hitch rail in front of the hardware store next to the bank. They swung down from their saddles and looped the reins around the rail, where three more horses were tied at the moment.

One of the men was a tall, rawboned hombre with a prominent nose and Adam's apple and straw-colored hair sticking out from under a battered old hat. He looked around the town again and commented quietly, "I figured we might see some o' them new-fangled horseless carriages here, but it looks like they ain't made it this far yet."

The other man grunted and said, "Good. From what I hear, they stink up the air something fierce."

He was shorter and stockier than his companion, with a face like a bulldog. His name was Warren Hopgood. The rawboned man was Deke Mahoney.

They had come here to rob the First Bank of Staghorn.

Mahoney glanced at a bench on the boardwalk in front of the hardware store. A man sat there reading a newspaper, or at least pretending to read a newspaper. He gave Mahoney an almost unnoticeable nod. That meant there were no lawmen or anybody else who appeared too threatening in the bank. Magnus Stevenson was the gang's lookout and horse holder, and he was good at his job.

A glance across the street told Mahoney that Otis Harmon was in position as well, leaning casually against one of the posts supporting the awning over the boardwalk. Harmon was the fastest gun in the bunch and the coldest nerved, as well. He wouldn't hesitate to shoot down anyone who caused a problem—man, woman, or child.

The bank sat on a corner, and on the other side of the cross street, the fifth member of the gang sat on the steps leading up to the boardwalk. Dark curly hair spilled out from under his thumbed-back hat, and he wore a friendly grin as he whittled on a piece of wood with a Bowie knife. Jim Bob Mitchell was an expert with the knife, and not just when it came to whittling.

Satisfied that everybody was in place, Mahoney nodded to Hopgood and led the way into the bank.

Two tellers stood behind a windowed counter helping customers. One teller had two customers in line, the other just one. Three more customers stood at a raised table filling out deposit or withdrawal slips.

A fat man in a suit sat behind a desk to one side, looking through some papers. Another desk was empty. The safe stood behind the desks. Its door was closed.

Mahoney's experienced gaze took in all of that in one quick scan around the room. He noted that four of the customers were men and the other two were women but didn't really pay attention to any details beyond that.

So, nine people in the bank and none of them looked particularly dangerous. Mahoney nodded to himself, satisfied that he and Hopgood could proceed.

He hauled the Colt from the holster on his right hip and clicked back the hammer. The ominous, metallic sound made silence drop like a curtain.

"Everybody stand still," Mahoney ordered in a loud, clear voice. He didn't shout. Yelling sometimes spooked folks into doing something stupid. "We ain't here to hurt anybody. We just want the money."

Hopgood had his gun out, too. The women gasped as he swung the weapon toward them.

Mahoney covered the tellers as he told the customers, "All of you move over there to the side, out of the way. Do it now if you don't want to get shot."

"See here," the fat man at the desk began.

"I ain't forgot about you, tubby," Mahoney said. "Stand up, slow and easy, and come over here with the customers."

"I'll do no such thing!" the man blustered. "You can't come in here and—"

Mahoney pointed the Colt at the man's face, which was turning red with anger. Staring down the barrel of the gun made the banker gulp and shut up, though. He tried to keep his hands raised, but he couldn't lift his bulk out of the chair without putting his hands on the desk and pushing.

Mahoney let him get away with that. He stepped back and tracked the banker with the Colt as the man crossed the room to join the customers.

Everybody except the tellers was grouped now under Hopgood's gun. Only a minute or so had passed since the two outlaws entered the bank. Things were moving along nicely.

Mahoney approached the counter and took a canvas bag from under his coat. It had the name of a bank in Kansas stamped on it and had come from a previous robbery.

Mahoney tossed the bag onto the counter in front of the teller on his left and said, "Fill it up. All the bills and gold coins from your drawer."

"Mr. Miller?" the teller asked tentatively as he looked at the banker.

The fat man sighed and nodded. "Do as he says. I don't want anyone to be hurt."

The teller scooped loot from the drawer and shoveled it into the bag. It wasn't long before he said, "That's all I have."

"Pass it over to the other fella," Mahoney ordered.

One of the female customers, a stout, older woman with gray hair under her hat, said, "I just deposited fifty dollars! You can't have it!"

"Sorry, Grandma," Mahoney said. "We're takin' all of it, includin' your fifty bucks."

"No, sir, you are not!" The woman reached into the big handbag she was clutching and pulled out an old percussion revolver.

The sight was so surprising that Hopgood didn't react immediately. But as the woman dropped her bag, held the heavy revolver with both hands, and pulled the trigger, he thrust his gun toward her and fired.

The shots blended together in one thunderous boom that shook the bank's front windows. Hopgood howled as the lead ball fired by the woman ripped a furrow across the outside of his upper left arm.

The woman stepped back against the wall and her eyes rolled up in their sockets as blood welled from the bullet hole in her chest. Her legs went out from under her, and she sat down hard.

"You killed her!" the banker cried in shock. He took a step toward Hopgood.

The wounded outlaw's face was twisted in pain.

The graze wasn't serious, but it hurt like hell. Furious because of that, and with gunfire having already broken out, Hopgood turned toward the banker and fired twice more.

The fat man grunted and doubled up as the slugs drove into his ample belly. Both hands clutched his stomach. Crimson welled between the fingers. He fell to his knees and then pitched over onto his side.

"Well, *hell!*" Deke Mahoney said. So much for any money that was left in the safe. There wouldn't be time for that now. He gestured with his Colt toward the second teller and yelled, "Empty your drawer! Now!"

Stunned by the deafening shots, the stink of powder smoke, and the brutal violence, the man didn't react quickly enough to suit Mahoney. He stood there gaping.

Mahoney lost patience and shot him just above the right eye, the bullet's impact snapping the luckless teller's head back. He collapsed.

"Get the money!" Mahoney shouted at the other teller, who instantly leaped to obey, grabbing greenbacks and handfuls of gold eagles and double eagles from the drawer and stuffing them into the bag.

After a moment, Mahoney said, "That's enough!" and leaned over the counter to grab the bag. Even in this frenzied moment, he could tell it had a nice heft to it, but even so, because of that stubborn old woman and her unexpected hogleg, the gang wasn't going to clear as much from this job as he'd hoped.

Waving his gun at the remaining customers and teller to keep them cowed, Mahoney told Hopgood, "Let's go!" and headed for the doors.

Hopgood snarled and looked like he wanted to shoot somebody else, but he followed Mahoney.

As they burst out on the boardwalk, Mahoney saw that Magnus Stevenson was up on his feet and had moved to the hitch rail to grab the reins of the gang's mounts.

Across the street, shots blasted from Otis Harmon's gun as he ventilated a couple of men who were running toward the bank, drawn by the gunfire.

On this side of the street, in the next block, a middle-aged man with a lawman's badge pinned to his vest rushed along the boardwalk. Jim Bob Mitchell tossed aside the piece of wood he'd been whittling on, rose lithely, and plunged the Bowie into the star packer's chest.

The lawman came to an abrupt stop as his eyes widened in shock and pain. Mitchell pulled the knife out and stabbed him twice more, the deadly blows coming almost too fast for the eyes to follow. The lawman's knees buckled.

Mahoney howled and sprayed lead around the street, being careful not to hit his partners. The wild shots made everybody on the boardwalks dive for cover. Harmon and Mitchell sprinted to the horses and leaped into their saddles.

Hopgood had holstered his gun and tried to mount as well, but he couldn't raise his wounded left arm to grasp the saddle horn as he usually did. He had to grab it with his right hand and swing up awkwardly. Stevenson gave him a shove to help him.

Mahoney made it onto his horse. Stevenson was the last man to hit the leather. All five outlaws yanked their mounts around and drove the spurs to them.

The animals leaped away from the hitch rail and thundered along the street at a dead run.

Mahoney, Harmon, Stevenson, and Mitchell kept up a steady fire, pouring lead into the buildings as they galloped past. That would keep everybody's head down and give the outlaws a better chance to get away.

They rode out of Staghorn headed for the foothills of the Sierra Nevada Mountains to the west. They knew that rugged country quite well and were confident they could give the slip to any pursuit.

Once they were clear of the settlement, Mahoney looked at Hopgood and called over the swift rataplan of hoofbeats, "You all right, Warren?"

"Yeah, I will be," Hopgood replied. "Arm just hurts like blazes, is all. But it's not serious." He grimaced. "We didn't get as much as we should have—again!"

Mahoney bristled at this challenge to his leadership. "Frank left me in charge! It was a good job. Ain't my fault it didn't pan out just like we expected!"

"Maybe," Hopgood said. "But Frank's going to be out of prison soon, and then we'll see how things pan out!"

Mahoney tried not to glare. He needed to concentrate on making sure they got away clean. A glance over his shoulder told him that the townspeople hadn't mounted any pursuit yet, and Staghorn was falling farther behind with each passing moment. By the time they got a posse together, it would be too late.

That was satisfying, but Mahoney couldn't stop thinking about what Hopgood had said. The wounded man was right. Frank Colbert was supposed to be released from prison any day now, and once he got out and returned to the gang, Mahoney's days of being the leader would be over. He wasn't sure exactly how he felt about that, but he knew he was going to miss calling the shots.

On the other hand, he wasn't going to argue too much with Frank taking over again.

Because defying Frank Colbert was just about the quickest way a man could wind up dead.

CHAPTER 3

The Sierra Nevada Mountains

Under gray skies, the westbound train chugged up the steep grade toward Donner Pass. At the controls of the big Baldwin locomotive was the engineer, Clete Patterson.

Huge clouds of steam billowed out into the cold air, which also caused a chill to go through Patterson. The locomotive's cab was partially enclosed, but air still whipped through it.

The fireman, Alvie Forrester, leaned on his shovel and looked out at the pine-covered slopes going by.

"Never thought I'd see the pass this clear in December!" he called to Patterson, raising his voice to be heard over the locomotive's booming rumble. "Why, there ain't but a dustin' of snow on the ground, and here it is, comin' up on Christmas!"

The florid-faced engineer waved a gauntleted hand at the sky. "Yeah, but just look at those clouds!"

he replied. "They've got plenty of snow in 'em, mark my words!"

"You been sayin' the same thing since the middle of November, Clete, and there ain't been a heavy snowfall yet!"

"Give it time!" Under his breath, Patterson muttered, "Good weather can't hold. Not at this time of year."

It never had, not in his experience, and he'd been making this run over the summit for nearly ten years. The snowsheds and the so-called Chinese walls and the tunnels built by the Central Pacific kept the snow off the tracks for the most part, but it always piled up in drifts many feet deep on both sides of the right-of-way. Every now and then, there was a blizzard bad enough to shut down the road, although it hadn't happened in several years.

Alvie was right, though, Patterson thought. This much bare ground in the Sierra Nevadas in December was just . . . unnatural, somehow.

It made Patterson wonder if when the snow finally started falling, it would ever stop.

Forrester's sudden shout cut into his reverie. The fireman yelled, "Holy hell, Clete! Look up there!"

Forrester was leaning out the window on the other side of the cab, pointing at something up ahead. Thinking there must be some sort of obstacle on the tracks, Patterson quickly stuck his head out on his side and peered at the iron rails as they cut through the rugged, rocky approach to the pass.

They were clear as far as he could see, going between cutbanks, along narrow ridges, and through stands of trees.

"I don't see anything!" he called to Forrester. "What's wrong?"

"I saw him! By jumpin' jiminy, I finally saw him, Clete. It was the Donner Devil!"

A feeling of disgust welled up inside Patterson. "Not that again," he said. "There's no such thing."

Forrester stared at him. "You didn't see it?"

"I didn't see anything except the tracks, and they look clear all the way to the summit."

"But he was there, I tell you!" Forrester smacked the side of his fist against the cab wall. "A big, hairy critter scamperin' across the tracks!"

"You saw a bear." *If you saw anything,* Patterson added to himself.

"This wasn't no bear, I'm dang sure of that! I've seen enough bears to know how they lumber along. This thing was kinda crouched over, but he was runnin' on two legs, sure enough! Like he was part man and part animal!"

"People have been saying they've seen something like that up here for years," Patterson said patiently, "but they never really seem to get a good look at it. Think about all the trains that have passed along this route, to say nothing of all the wagons and stagecoaches and fellas on horseback. If there really was anything that strange in these parts, don't you think more folks would have seen it by now? Or even shot and killed it?"

"The thing is canny," Forrester insisted. "It knows how to hide, and it don't let itself be seen except ever' now and then. You don't have to believe me if you don't want to, Clete, but I know what I saw!" A shiver ran through the fireman that had nothing to do with the temperature. "I don't mind tellin' you, it kind of spooked me, too."

"You'd be better off worrying about the weather," Patterson said. "One of these days, that sky is going to open up and dump snow on these mountains like you've never seen before. And when that happens, that Donner Devil of yours is liable to be up to his neck in the white stuff!"

Smoke sat in an armchair in the Palm Court of the Palace Hotel, waiting for his children to come down from the suite so they could go to dinner. The lounge was sumptuously furnished with potted palms, comfortable chairs and divans, and marble-topped tables. Seven stories of white-railed balconies rose around it.

Until the previous year, this area had been the hotel's grand entrance, where horse-drawn carriages could drive in off the street for guests to disembark, then turn around and depart. It had been remodeled into this luxurious lounge.

Smoke had his right ankle cocked on his left knee, and he held his Stetson on his right knee. He alertly observed all the comings and goings of the hotel's wealthy guests. It wasn't that rich folks interested him all that much; he was just in the habit of taking note of everything going on around him.

That caution was a big part of the reason he had stayed alive as long as he had, while living a very adventurous and perilous life.

Because of that instinctive wariness, he realized the man crossing the Palm Court was looking for him well before the hombre reached him. Smoke had a small pistol in his pocket, and his hand wasn't far from it as the stranger came up to him, holding a derby hat. The man's dark hair was parted in the middle, and he had a thin mustache that curled up slightly at the ends.

"Mr. Jensen?" the man asked. "Kirby Jensen?"

"Not that many folks remember my real name anymore," Smoke said. "What can I do for you?"

"My name is Peter Stansfield. I'm a journalist."

Smoke smiled. "An ink-stained wretch, eh?"

Stansfield returned the smile and said, "You've read Dr. Samuel Johnson, I see. That phrase is often attributed to him."

"And I've known some newspaper reporters," Smoke said. "The description generally fits."

"Indeed it does." Stansfield gestured with the derby toward another armchair nearby. "Do you mind if I sit down?"

"Nope. I can tell you right now, though, that if you're planning on interviewing me, I'm not interested. I've talked to more than my share of newspapermen over the years." Smoke added dryly, "It's been my experience that they don't pay real close attention to what I say and just write whatever they already had their minds made up on before they ever talked to me."

"I assure you, sir, I'm not like that," Stansfield said as he sat down.

"Yep, that's what most of 'em claim, all right."

"Speaking of someone having his mind made up."

Smoke inclined his head in acknowledgment of Stansfield's point. He said, "Speak your piece, Mr. Stansfield."

"I am a police reporter, Mr. Jensen. I was at headquarters earlier today when a prisoner was brought in . . . a prisoner with a broken arm. According to the report made by the arresting officer, the man was injured when he attempted to rob you."

"That's true, I reckon. A fella tried to hold me up. I took his gun away from him and didn't figure on hurting him too bad, but then he came at me with a knife. I took that away from him, too."

"And broke his arm in the process."

"When you attack somebody, you're just asking them to fight back," Smoke said, his voice hardening. "At that point, I figure whatever happens to you is on your own head."

"I wouldn't disagree with that. I just thought that perhaps a story about how frontier justice visited the streets of San Francisco . . ." Stansfield's voice trailed off as he stared across the Palm Court. After a moment he found his tongue again and said, "My word, what a magnificent creature!"

Smoke said, "I'd like it better if you called her a beautiful young woman, Mr. Stansfield, since that happens to be my daughter. Actually, I'd just as soon you didn't comment on her at all!"

The reporter swallowed hard and said quickly, "My apologies, Mr. Jensen. I assure you, I meant no disrespect. I was just surprised to see such a . . . rare flower."

Smoke's flinty gaze told him the reference wasn't that much better than what he had said before. As Smoke got to his feet, he said, "So long, Mr. Stansfield."

"Mr. Jensen . . . !"

Smoke ignored the man and walked away from the chairs to meet Denny. He said, "Where's your brother?"

"He'll be down in a minute." Denny nodded toward Stansfield. "Who was that you were talking to?"

"Nobody," Smoke said. "Here comes Louis."

The young man joined them, and the three of them walked past the bank of rising rooms toward the hotel's entrance. The rising rooms were sometimes called elevators and could be raised and lowered on cables so that guests on the upper floors of the hotel didn't have to walk up and down several flights of stairs.

Smoke had to admit that he didn't care much for being shut up in a little room that moved, but Denny and Louis had experienced many such modern things in Europe and didn't seem bothered by them.

Smoke put his hat on as they stepped out of the hotel. It was a cool, dank evening. Here on the coast, winter never set in with a fierce grip like it did inland. The weather had been on Smoke's mind, and as they walked along the street, he said, "Did either of you have anything else you needed to do here in San Francisco?"

"Not me," Louis replied. "Now that I've seen Dr. Katzendorf, I'm finished here."

Denny said, "I've already picked up the few things Mother asked me to shop for and made some purchases of my own."

Smoke smiled. "Are we going to need a baggage car on the train just for that?"

"You know me better than that," Denny replied sharply.

It was true. Smoke did know his daughter better than that. Denny appreciated fine clothes and jewelry and wore them well, but at heart she was just as happy in jeans and boots and a work shirt, sitting a saddle and riding the range.

"First thing tomorrow morning, I'll see about getting us on the next train to Colorado. We cut this trip a little closer than I'd like. Christmas is only a week away."

Louis said, "This was when Dr. Katzendorf could see me. And we have plenty of time to get back to the Sugarloaf before Christmas, don't we?"

"Sure. It'll only take a couple of days by train."

The warm yellow glow of lights ahead of them marked the location of the restaurant where they were going to have dinner. The place had a reputation as one of the best in San Francisco. It wouldn't be able to beat Sally's cooking, Smoke thought . . . but no restaurant he'd ever found was capable of doing that.

Why, this place probably didn't even serve bear sign!

A gust of wind ripped along the street just as Smoke, Denny, and Louis reached the restaurant. Smoke felt fingers of ice in it and frowned.

Winter might not be able to take hold of San Francisco, but there was a lot of high country between here and home. And he didn't like to think about what it might be doing up there.

CHAPTER 4

The warmth from the campfire felt mighty good
to the five men huddled around it. Not far away,
their unsaddled horses stood heads down and rumps
to the wind. The men felt sort of like doing the same
thing.

"I'm still not sure building a fire was a good idea,"
Warren Hopgood said, "but I've got to admit, we'd
be freezing our tails off without it."

"I kept an eye on our back-trail all day and never
saw no sign of a posse," Deke Mahoney said. "Anyway,
it feels like a storm buildin', and even if some of
those townies from Staghorn came after us, they're
bound to have turned back as soon as that first blast
o' cold air hit 'em in the face."

Hopgood nodded as he cupped his gloved hands
around a cup of coffee. "We can sure hope so."

The bulk of a bandage wrapped around his upper
left arm was visible under his coat sleeve. Earlier, as
soon as the outlaws were far enough away from the
scene of the bank robbery and murders to risk it,

they had stopped and Magnus Stevenson had cleaned and bound up the wound on Hopgood's arm.

Hopgood had lost quite a bit of blood and his arm would be stiff and sore for a while, but he could still use it. To help with the pain, he had spiked his coffee with a good slug of whiskey from a flask.

"You know," Stevenson said now, "I was paying attention while I was sitting there pretending to read that newspaper."

"Well, I should hope so," Mahoney said. "It's your job to be lookout, after all."

"No, I mean I was listening to what people were saying while they walked past me or stood around on the boardwalk, talking. You never know what you'll pick up that way."

In a voice almost as frigid as the wind, Otis Harmon said, "If you've got something to say, spit it out, Stevenson." The gunman had never had much in the way of patience.

"The telegrapher had left his office and come over to the hardware store to pick up something, and as he left he was talking to a friend of his he'd run into there. You know how those fellas aren't supposed to tell anything that's in the telegrams they send, but some of them just can't help themselves. They've got to drop a few hints to make themselves sound important."

Seeing the angry look on Harmon's lean face, Mahoney said, "Best get on with it, Magnus."

"There's a big money shipment coming in to the bank in Reno," Stevenson said. "The telegrapher in Staghorn had to pass along a message about it because of trouble in the lines somewhere else. I don't know why the money's coming, but it's supposed to be there before Christmas. I think one of those big mining tycoons is bringing it in. Maybe he wants to buy out another mine owner or something and needs cash for the deal."

Mahoney rubbed his beard-stubbled chin and frowned in thought. "Reno, eh? That's less than half a day's ride north of here."

"It's a bigger town than Staghorn," Hopgood pointed out. "More law. We wouldn't be able to hooraw everybody into ducking for cover."

"A job like that would take some good plannin', all right," Mahoney admitted.

"We'd need Frank for that."

"Frank ain't here. You said yourself he's supposed to get out of prison any day now," Hopgood cut in. "Hell, for all we know, he's *already* out. You got that letter from him six months ago. He told you to get in touch with him when the time came and let him know where we were so he could join up with us. But you haven't done that, have you, Deke?"

"I just ain't got around to it," Mahoney said, unable to keep a surly tone out of his voice.

In truth, he had been dragging his feet about contacting Frank Colbert because he didn't relish the idea of giving up leadership of the gang. They had pulled off a number of successful jobs while Colbert was in prison. Nothing spectacular, mind, and there had been some lean times as well, but Mahoney believed they had garnered a respectable amount of loot under his command.

Now Colbert intended to come in and take over again like he'd never been gone. At least, that was what Mahoney assumed was his intention. Nobody could blame him for not cottoning overmuch to the idea.

"There's a telegraph office in Reno," Hopgood said. "I think we should ride up there tomorrow and start getting the lay of the land. You can send a wire to that saloon where you're supposed to get in touch with Frank, tell him where we are and that we've got a line on a good job to pull, and maybe he can join us in time to figure out how to go about it."

"If the wires don't blow down in this wind," Stevenson said. "And if the weather holds and the pass stays clear enough for the trains to get through. Hard to say for sure about things like that at this time of year."

Hopgood said, "It's always hard to predict everything. What do you other boys say? Should we ride to Reno tomorrow?"

"Now, hold on there," Mahoney said as he leaned forward. "I've been makin' the decisions here. Frank left me in charge, and all of you know it."

"Times change," Hopgood replied. "I don't reckon it'll hurt anything to see what everybody thinks. That way you can make your *decision* better."

Anger boiled up inside Mahoney. He wanted to yank out his Colt and blast Hopgood for challenging him like this. All five of them knew good and well that Hopgood was actually calling for a vote on whether Mahoney was actually in charge of the gang anymore.

What stopped Mahoney from giving in to the impulse was his uncertainty over how the others would respond, especially Harmon, who was the fastest on the draw of all of them. If Harmon took Hopgood's side, he could have his gun out before Mahoney ever cleared leather. A bullet blasted through Mahoney's guts would settle things, sure enough.

So Mahoney kept a tight rein on his temper and said, "All right, fair enough. What do you boys think?"

Jim Bob Mitchell drew his Bowie and ran the tip of the blade under the dirty thumbnail on his other hand. With the usual pleasant smile he wore even when he was killing people, he said, "Goin' to Reno sounds like a pretty good idea to me. Hell, if nothin' else, you said we cleared near nine hunnerd dollars in that Staghorn job, Deke, and that'd be a good place to spend some of it on good whiskey and bad women."

"I can't argue with that," Stevenson said. "Based on what I overheard, it's worth checking out, anyway."

"I say we go," Harmon bit off in clipped tones.

Hopgood shrugged. "It's settled then. Unless you can come up with a good reason not to, Deke."

Mahoney knew that further argument would result in outright rebellion. And with him outnumbered four to one, there was only one way that would end. He had no doubt that eventually he would wind up in a cold, lonely grave. That was nearly always an outlaw's fate. But he didn't want it to be tonight.

"All right," he said with a nod. "Come mornin', we head for Reno."

Before any of them could say anything else, a sound cut through the night, carried on the frigid wind. At first Mahoney thought it was a wolf's howl, but then he realized there was something different about it, something almost . . . human . . . like the wail of a lost soul. But at the same time, it held the shivering ferocity of a wild beast.

"What the hell is that?" Stevenson exclaimed.

The cry died, shredded and whipped away by the wind. Harmon grunted and said, "Wolf."

"I don't know," Mitchell said, and for once he wasn't grinning. "It didn't sound exactly like any wolf I've ever heard."

Hopgood said, "It doesn't matter. It was some kind of wild animal, and that means it won't come anywhere near this fire. And we'll be taking turns standing watch all night, so if any varmint *does* come around, it'll get a dose of hot lead."

"Yeah," Mahoney said. "Nothing to worry about."

He wished he believed that. But between the near-mutiny of the other outlaws and the bizarre cry that had just swept over the foothills, his stomach had started to hurt.

Maybe being the boss *was* too much of a burden. Maybe it would be better to just turn everything over to Frank again, so he could stop thinking and worrying all the time. The more he thought about it, the more appealing that prospect sounded.

He sipped his coffee, peered narrow eyed into the darkness, and wished this night was over.

Donner Summit

Elmore "Juniper" Jones stepped out of the hotel onto the platform covered by a long snowshed and pulled his coat tighter around himself as the icy wind tried to bite into him. He had stepped away from his telegraph key for a moment to check the weather, and as he looked up into the night sky, he didn't like what he saw.

Nothing but blackness hung over Donner Pass tonight. Not even a hint of starlight penetrated the thick clouds. Jones sniffed at the air. He had been around the Sierra Nevadas, man and boy, for nigh on to fifty years. He could *smell* snow.

Of course, it helped when he could also *feel* the little crystals hitting his cheeks, like a couple of them did just now.

It was starting.

The westbound had come through earlier that day, stopping as usual at the Summit Hotel, and Jones had exchanged a few words with old Clete Patterson, the engineer. Patterson was worried that a big snowstorm was building up and might break any time. Jones had had the same feeling. The two old-timers had commiserated about the looming change in the weather.

But Patterson got to go on and was well out of the mountains by now. Jones was stuck here at the summit. If a blizzard came through, the hotel might be cut off from the outside world for days, even weeks.

James Cardwell had built the original hotel at the summit of Donner Pass a little more than thirty years earlier, when the driving of the Golden Spike at Promontory Point, Utah, meant the country was finally linked, coast to coast, by the steel rails. Cardwell had envisioned travelers stopping here in the high Sierras and making the hotel a successful resort. And so it had been until fire destroyed the place.

Cardwell had rebuilt, though, and the Summit

Hotel had carried on. The railroad tracks, covered by snowsheds, ran right past the platform at the hotel's front door. Telegraph wires linked the establishment to Sacramento, San Francisco, and Reno. It was a busy place during the summer, as folks came here to take in the spectacular scenery and enjoy the soothing mineral waters.

Not many people stopped in the winter. Now, with Christmas only a week away, the hotel was empty. Any travelers at this time of year were on their way to see their families and wouldn't risk getting stuck in the mountains. Because of that, the hotel had only a few employees working at the moment.

Jones worked for the telegraph company, though, not the hotel, and he couldn't abandon his post.

If they *did* get snowed in, the hotel had plenty of supplies and firewood. Nobody would freeze or starve to death. It was possible, though unlikely, that the telegraph wires would stay up, so they might even maintain contact with the outside world.

Still, Jones didn't care for the idea of the pass being closed. If anything bad happened up here, they would be on their own, with no way to get help.

The snow was falling faster now. He could see it swirling in the wind beyond the snowshed. A few flakes found little gaps in the shelter's construction and fell on the platform. Jones brushed another away from his face and turned to go back into the building.

Herman Painton, the manager of the hotel, called across the empty lobby, "How's it look out there, Juniper?"

"Startin' to snow," Jones replied. "It's already

comin' down pretty fast and heavy. The wind's stayin' strong, too. It'll pile the stuff up, sure enough."

"Do you think the tracks will stay clear?"

Jones shook his head, not in the negative but just to say that he didn't know. "It all depends on how long the storm lasts. Clete Patterson said his bones tell him it's gonna be a bad one." He headed for the little room off the lobby where his telegraph key was located. "I'm gonna let headquarters know."

"Is there anything we should be doing to get ready?" Painton had worked up here at the summit during a number of snowstorms, but no real blizzard had blown through during his tenure. The trains had always been able to run.

"Anything that could be done has already been done," Jones told him. "From here on out, we're at the mercy of whoever decides the weather." He smiled grimly. "So you might try prayin'."

CHAPTER 5

San Francisco

China Mike's First and Last Chance Saloon lived up to its name. Close to the waterfront on San Francisco's Barbary Coast, it was the first chance for sailors fresh off the boats to get drunk and enjoy the company of fallen women.

It was also the last chance for many of those women, and for young men as well who downed a drink, passed out, and woke up on a boat bound for Shanghai. That was why the proprietor had gotten his nickname.

There was nothing fancy about the place. The sawdust on the floor had soaked up gallons of blood, vomit, piss, and spilled beer. The bar was deeply scarred.

Thick clouds of tobacco smoke hung in the air and stung the eyes and nose. Tinny piano music and raucous laughter competed to see which could assault the ears worse.

There was no more wretched hive of scum and villainy to be found anywhere on the Barbary Coast.

Frank Colbert didn't mind any of that. Squalid and stinking though it might be, the First and Last Chance Saloon beat the hell out of prison.

Colbert's hard-planed face might have been carved out of the same wood as the bar. A thatch of dark hair drooped over his forehead. Under a hawk nose, a thick mustache decorated his upper lip. His cheeks were gaunt, and there were harsh lines around his deep-set eyes.

During the past five years, life behind bars had honed away any softness in the man . . . not that there had ever been much to start with.

He sat at a table in a rear corner, his back to the wall, playing cards with two brawny sailors, an idiot cowboy on his first visit to the big city, a frock-coated professional gambler, and a woman with red hair and an enormous bosom displayed to full advantage in a low-cut emerald gown.

"I call," Selena Charlton said as she laid down her cards. The young cowboy and one of the sailors were the only other players left in the hand. Colbert, the other sailor, and the tinhorn had already dropped out.

The sailor grimaced and threw in his cards, admitting defeat. They landed faceup, showing that he had tried to fill a straight but failed, then attempted to bluff with it.

The cowboy was more reluctant to admit defeat, spreading his cards faceup on the table and studying them, his eyes going back and forth between his hand and Selena's as if hoping that by staring at them he could force the markings to change.

Finally, he sighed and said, "Dadgum it."

"That's all right," Selena said as she leaned forward to rake in the pot. "I'll give you a chance to win it back."

She was also giving him an eyeful, and the youngster had trouble tearing his gaze away from the impressive cleavage. But then he began to frown, and he said, "Hold on a minute. I'm confused about somethin', ma'am. You had a full house just then, right?"

"That's right," Selena said.

"Three queens and two eights."

"Yeah. What are you getting at?"

The cowboy tipped his hat back, scratched at the hair above his left ear, and said, "It seems to me that there was two queens played before now. There's one of them, right there."

He pointed to the sailor's busted straight.

"So?" Selena asked.

"I threw away another one on the draw," the cowboy said. "You can look in the stack if you want."

Selena stared at him. "You threw away a *queen*?"

"I didn't figure I could use it. That sure enough makes five of 'em. That seems like one too many."

Selena looked around. Everyone else at the table knew what was going to happen next. She would summon one of the bouncers, and the young cowboy who had all but accused her of cheating would be dragged out of here and beaten within an inch of his life . . . if he was lucky.

If he wasn't lucky, he would be beaten within an inch of his life and then tossed in the water to drown.

Of course, Selena *had* cheated the cowboy, and

Colbert and the others knew that, too. But the sailor had never had a real chance to win the hand, and the others had already folded before that, so they didn't care.

A kid like that was just asking for trouble by coming into a place like this. The cowboy wasn't a total greenhorn, though. He knew he'd been dancing on the knife edge of danger.

He started to come up out of his chair. The gun on his hip whispered against the leather of its holster as he drew. He was fast, no doubt about that.

Unfortunately for him, Frank Colbert was faster.

One of the first things Colbert had done after being released from prison, before he ever went looking for a drink or a woman, was to arm himself. He had a knife shoved down his boot, a gun in one coat pocket, and a long leather sap in the other pocket. The sap was filled with lead shot, and Colbert wielded it expertly.

He brought it around as the cowboy's gun cleared leather. The sap smacked across the young man's wrist and broke several bones. He cried out in pain and dropped the gun, unfired, as he stumbled back a step.

Colbert surged up and backhanded the cowboy with the sap. This blow shattered the youngster's jaw, knocked out several of his teeth, and dropped him senseless to the floor. He lay there with blood and spit drooling out of his mouth into the sawdust, forming a pool in which lay the broken teeth.

"Well, it looks like you haven't slowed down any, Frank," Selena said.

"Damn right."

"Why didn't you shoot him? I know you're packing iron."

"This was easier and safer. No bullets flying around. And more entertaining."

Selena motioned curtly for some of China Mike's men to drag the unconscious cowboy out of the saloon. The brief but brutal flurry of action had caused a momentary hush to fall over the room, but the hubbub rose to its former level by the time the bouncers got the unfortunate youngster outside.

Colbert neither knew nor cared what would happen to him out there.

Selena gathered up the cards. "Another hand?" she asked the remaining players.

"Sure," Colbert said. "With no extra queens this time."

For a second, the redhead's green eyes glittered with anger. Then she threw back her head and laughed.

"You've still got your sense of humor, Frank."

Colbert just grunted. Selena could cheat anybody else she wanted to, as long as she didn't try to pull any fast ones on him.

As she shuffled and dealt, he said, "You're sure there haven't been any telegrams for me lately?"

"We've been over this," Selena replied with a touch of irritation in her voice. "If a wire came for you, Frank, I'd know about it. Mike gives me a pretty free hand running this place. I'd have given it to you right away. What sort of important news are you waiting for, anyway?"

"That's my business," Colbert replied.

"And my business is cards," the tinhorn said. "So let's get on with it, shall we?"

Colbert started to get mad but then decided it wasn't worth the time and effort. He picked up the hand Selena had dealt him and studied it. A pair of fours was the best he could do.

His thoughts strayed to the gang he had left behind when he'd been arrested in Truckee. He had been alone that day, by chance, and if the others had been with him they probably could have shot their way free.

As it was, he'd been tried and convicted for robbery—they hadn't been able to prove any of the murder charges levied against him—and sent to prison for five years. Five *long* years.

Before going away, he had gotten word to Deke Mahoney to keep the gang together, and since then they had traded a few discreetly worded letters. Mahoney knew approximately when Colbert was getting out and was supposed to be in touch so Colbert would know where to rendezvous with them.

But he had been free for almost a week and hadn't heard a word so far. It was damn frustrating. Colbert wanted to get back in harness, to lead his men again, to hold a gun in his hand and feel the power that always coursed through him when he took the money—and sometimes the lives—of the pathetic sheep that made up most of humanity. There was nothing else quite like that in the world.

But until then, he would make do with sipping whiskey and playing cards and taking Selena upstairs now and then. These days, she might not be on the

line anymore, but she was still a whore at heart and
Frank Colbert knew how to treat whores. She liked it,
too, or at least she knew she'd damn well better pre-
tend to.

"You in, Frank?"

The question broke into Colbert's reverie. He looked
at his cards again and threw three of them into the dis-
card.

"Yeah," he said. "I'm in."

It was easy to tell that Christmas was fast approaching. As Smoke and his children walked toward the
restaurant where they planned to have dinner, they
passed numerous decorations commemorating the
season. Wreaths of holly with red berries hung on
the buildings, and strings of silver bells stretched between lampposts.

It was all very festive and made Smoke wonder if
Pearlie and Cal had fetched in a Christmas tree for
Sally, back on the Sugarloaf. He suspected they had,
because Sally loved to decorate and celebrate the
holiday.

The Crimson Arch was one of the finest eating es-
tablishments in San Francisco, and the prices on the
fancy, gilt-printed menu reflected that.

"They must set a lot of store by the cows these
steaks came from, judging by the prices they're asking for them," Smoke commented after he, Denny,
and Louis had been greeted by an elegantly dressed
maitre d' who ushered them to a table covered with a
fine linen cloth and set with sparkling china, silver,

and crystal. A string quartet played softly in a corner. "You could buy a dozen meals in Big Rock for what one costs here."

Louis laughed and said, "Father, we should take you to Paris and let you dine there."

Denny frowned dubiously and shook her head. "Smoke Jensen tangling with a French waiter? I don't think that would be a very good combination."

"I get along all right with most folks," Smoke said.

"You've never met a French waiter."

Smoke inclined his head in acknowledgment of that point and went back to studying the menu.

Best not to worry about the prices, he told himself. He could afford to pay them. Anyway, the next morning he and the two youngsters would be on the train, heading back to Colorado, so he wouldn't have to be annoyed by these fancy, expensive surroundings for much longer.

He suddenly found himself annoyed by something else as he glanced over the top of the menu and spotted a familiar face several tables away. The man sitting there was partially concealed behind a potted palm, but Smoke got a good enough look at him to recognize him.

Smoke set the menu down and stood up. "Excuse me," he said to Denny and Louis. "I'll be back in a minute."

"Something wrong?" Denny asked.

"No, I just see somebody I know and want to have a word with him."

Smoke made his way to the other table, weaving around several tables in between. By the time he reached his destination, the man sitting there had lifted his menu to cover his face and pretended to be studying it.

"You're a mite late for that, Mr. Stansfield," Smoke said as he came to a stop beside the table. "I already saw you."

Peter Stansfield lowered the menu and tried to act surprised to see Smoke. "Ah, Mr. Jensen, this is a surprise."

"I'll just bet it is," Smoke drawled. "You followed me and my children here, didn't you?"

Now the journalist attempted to look offended. "After you explained to me that you preferred not to be interviewed? Why would I do such a thing?"

"I don't know. Maybe you thought somebody else would try to rob me and you could get a story that way."

"It just so happens that the Crimson Arch is one of my favorite places to eat. I take my meals here fairly often."

"I wouldn't have thought an ink-stained wretch could afford to frequent a restaurant this expensive."

Stansfield scowled but didn't say anything.

"Listen, Mr. Stansfield," Smoke went on, "it's a free country, so you can eat wherever you want to. You can even skulk around and follow me and my kids. But you'll be wasting your time, and if you make too much of a pest of yourself, I won't take it kindly."

"You can't threaten the press," Stansfield said.

"I don't make a habit of threatening folks. I just tell 'em what I'm going to do if certain things happen . . . and then I do it." Smoke's impressively broad shoulders rose and fell. "Seems simple enough to me, and fair enough, too."

"I assure you, you have the wrong impression about me, Mr. Jensen. I have no intention of troubling you."

"Good." Smoke nodded to the reporter. "Enjoy your evening, Mr. Stansfield."

He went back to the table and sat down. Denny said, "What was that all about? Who was that man?"

"Nobody you need to worry about," Smoke said. He reached for the menu again. "Now, let's figure out what we're going to eat that doesn't cost an arm and a leg."

CHAPTER 6

The jail cell stunk from all its previous occupants. The hard, bare mattress on the narrow bunk had vermin living in it. The small chamber was dank and uncomfortably chilly this morning. During the night, the fog that nearly always came in and blanketed San Francisco had crept through the single barred window and hung in the air, making the place even more unpleasant.

The cold and the damp caused Gordon Lewiston's broken arm to ache even worse than it would have otherwise. He had spent a miserable night, able to sleep for only a few minutes at a time before the pain woke him.

More than ever, he needed the blessed relief that the smoke of the lotus would have provided for him.

The day before, a doctor at the hospital where the police had taken him had set the broken bone, splinted the arm, and wrapped it tightly in bandages.

"This man should remain here in the hospital under a physician's care," the medico had told the police, but the officers didn't pay any attention.

"He's charged with attempted armed robbery and assault," one of them had told the doctor. "He's going to the lockup, busted wing or no busted wing."

Lewiston supposed he should have been grateful they'd gotten him as much medical attention as they had. But it didn't really matter.

If he remained behind bars for very long, he would die from lack of opium. He couldn't live without the stuff. Never had been able to, ever since he'd come back from Cuba and the war against the damn Spaniards.

At least they had put him in a cell by himself, not one of the larger holding cells. The men they threw in there would have seen that he was injured and couldn't defend himself, and there was no telling what might have happened to him overnight. It wouldn't have been good, though.

Footsteps echoed in the corridor outside the row of cells. Lewiston remained sitting on the bunk with the thin, gray, scratchy blanket wrapped around him. He hadn't been able to find a position lying down where his arm didn't hurt like blazes, so any sleep he had snatched during the night was done sitting up. He didn't raise his head to watch the jailer approaching.

But then the footsteps stopped and the man said, "Lewiston, you've got a visitor."

A visitor . . . ? Who in the world—

Lewiston raised his eyes, saw the woman standing there, and groaned.

"Alma," he said. "How did you find me?"

She said, "Once I'd poked through every opium den and joss house in Chinatown and you weren't in any of them, I knew you had to be either in jail or lying dead in an alley somewhere. So I came here next."

"Hoping that you'd find me here?" Lewiston asked with a faint smile. "Or that you wouldn't?"

"Don't be like that," Alma snapped. "If I'd wanted you dead, I would have killed you myself a long time before now."

"Lady," the jailer said, "that probably ain't the wisest thing to be sayin' in front of somebody who works for the law."

"Oh, go away and give me a minute with my husband," Alma told the man as she glared at him.

Nobody could stand up to Alma when she looked like that, as Lewiston knew all too well from experience. The jailer muttered, "All right, all right," and retreated to the far end of the corridor. Alma turned back to the bars and gripped them.

Lewiston's spirits couldn't help but rise for a moment as he gazed at her. Life had been hard on Alma. Being married to *him* had been hard, and he could admit that.

She was twenty-eight years old but appeared to be six or seven years older than that. She was still a fine-looking woman, though. Her blond hair had a shine to it, even in these dingy surroundings. Maybe especially in a place like this. Her eyes had lines around them, but they were still like blue pools to her husband. There were lines around her mouth, too, but Lewiston wanted to kiss her, anyway.

"Alma, you shouldn't have come." Emotion choked his voice as he stood and moved slowly over to the bars. "You should get far away from me and forget you were ever married to me. You deserve better, and it won't be long until you're free to find it."

"What are you talking about, Gordon?"

He waved his uninjured arm at his surroundings. "I won't live long behind bars. You know that. You'll be a widow, and you can find yourself a husband who can take care of you like you deserve."

"Stop being an idiot," she said. "I'll get you out of here, and we'll go someplace where you can get better—"

"There's not any such place," he interrupted. "And you can't get me out. There's no money for bail."

"I've put aside a little you didn't know about—"

He was too tired to even be bothered by the admission that she'd been hiding money from him. Good for her. He said, "But there's not enough, is there?"

"Well . . . no. But if the man you tried to rob were to drop the charges against you, they'd have to let you go, wouldn't they?"

"I don't know. They might. Why would he do that, though?" Lewiston shook his head. "I did try to rob him, you know. I threatened him with a gun, and then I tried to cut him with a knife." He laughed, but there was no humor in the sound. "What a fool I was. That man Jensen, he was just playing with me. I couldn't have actually hurt him in a hundred years."

"Jensen," Alma repeated.

"Yeah. He gave his name to the officer who arrested me. Smoke Jensen."

"Did he say where he lives?"

Lewiston frowned. "Why? Alma, what in the world are you thinking of?"

"I thought that if I talked to this man Jensen and told him that you're not really a criminal, not a bad sort at all, he might see his way clear to dropping the charges."

"No!" Lewiston said. "I don't want you getting mixed up in this, Alma. You've already had way too much trouble in your life because of me. Anyway, it wouldn't do any good. Jensen's a cowboy. A real hard-bitten type. The policeman acted like he's some sort of famous gunman. There are dime novels about him."

"He's still a man," Alma insisted. "He must have a spark of decency in him. I'll tell him about how you were wounded in Cuba, and about the laudanum and the opium—"

"He guessed already about the opium," Lewiston said, wanting to hang his head in shame. "I don't think he cared."

"I'll *make* him care. I've always been able to convince men to do what I wanted, ever since I was fourteen years old. You know that, Gordon."

Lewiston didn't doubt it. Alma's beauty might be faded a little, but she was still one hell of a woman. He didn't know everything she had done over the past couple of years to help them get by, and he didn't *want* to know. But this time it wasn't going to work.

"Not Jensen," he said. "I'm sorry, Alma, there's just nothing you can do for me."

"Where can I find him?" she insisted.

From the far end of the corridor, the jailer called, "Time's up, lady. You're gonna have to go."

Alma gripped the bars harder and said, "Tell me, Gordon."

Lewiston swallowed. He supposed it couldn't hurt anything for her to try.

"The Palace Hotel," he said. "Jensen told the officer he was staying at the Palace Hotel."

She reached through the bars and stroked his gaunt,

stubble-covered cheek. The jailer yelled, "Hey! Get your hand out of there! No touching or reaching through the bars."

Lewiston caught hold of her hand with his good one and pressed his lips to the back of it for a second. Then Alma stepped back as the jailer stomped angrily toward her.

"Don't give up, Gordon," she said.

He managed a weak smile and a nod, but he didn't believe it.

He had been in the process of giving up for too long to stop now.

Smoke always traveled light, but the same couldn't be said of Denny and Louis. Denny had added to her load with her shopping excursion, too. Because of that, the cart that a porter wheeled out of the Palace Hotel that morning was piled high with bags. A second porter helped load them into a wagon.

Smoke ambled out of the hotel's front entrance and watched the loading. He didn't like having anybody taking care of chores for him, but he fought the urge to step in and heft some of the bags himself. That was the porters' job, and they might be insulted if he acted like they weren't doing it correctly. He would give both men a good tip when they were finished.

While he was standing there, he looked up and down the street, halfway expecting to spot Peter Stansfield lurking around somewhere near the hotel. There was no sign of the reporter this morning, though, so Smoke hoped he had found somebody else to write about . . . and to bother.

A carriage was parked in front of the wagon, waiting to carry Smoke, Denny, and Louis to the train station. Denny wasn't the sort of young woman to spend hours and hours getting ready to go anywhere, but she was enough of a female that she usually wasn't as prompt as her brother, either. When Smoke heard a footstep behind him and glanced over his shoulder, he wasn't surprised to see Louis.

"Is your sister almost ready?" Smoke asked.

"When I knocked on her door, she said she would be down in just a few minutes." Louis shrugged. "Don't ask me what that translates to in actual time."

"Are you talking about me?" Denny asked from behind him.

"Of course not," he said smoothly as he turned to smile at her.

"Yeah, you need to take up the law, all right," she said. "It's the natural profession for anybody who lies that easily."

Smoke flipped open the turnip watch he had just taken from his pocket to check the time. "We'd better get going," he told his children. He snapped the timepiece closed. "We don't want to miss that train."

He cast an eye toward the distant mountains. The sky was overcast this morning, as it often was in San Francisco, and the clouds were a dark, ominous gray in the direction of the Sierra Nevada Mountains.

Denny wore a dark brown traveling outfit today, and Louis was in a brown tweed suit. The cold air that swept along the street made both of them shiver as they started toward the carriage.

Smoke had traded in his town clothes for garb more suitable to riding the range. He wore a sheepskin-lined jacket over a flannel work shirt and jeans. The authorities in San Francisco frowned on wearing guns openly, so he hadn't strapped on his shell belt and holster this morning.

But there was a Colt Lightning .41-caliber double-action revolver tucked into the waistband of his jeans, out of sight under the coat but where he could get to it quickly if he needed it. He didn't anticipate needing the gun, but he had carried one for enough years that it didn't feel right to be unarmed.

As his old friend Pearlie had once said, "I been packin' iron for so long that if I don't have one on me somewheres, I walk slant-wise."

Smoke felt the same way.

They climbed into the carriage and the driver slapped the reins and got the pair of horses hitched to it moving along the street. The wagon with the bags rattled along behind them.

Since the carriage was the open type, the driver was able to turn his head and say over his shoulder, "They tell me those horseless carriages are gonna take over and fellas like me will be out of a job. You believe that?"

"They're the coming thing," Louis said. "I read the other day that there are already several hundred automobiles in service in the United States."

"Maybe out on flat land," the driver said. "You reckon one of those rattletraps could make it up and down hills like we got here? That takes a good team o' horses!"

"Maybe you're right, sir. I'm a young man, but I've already seen enough in my life to know that it's difficult to keep things from changing. Sometimes everything seems to change while we're not even looking!"

The driver just *harrumphed* and kept his team moving.

The carriage and the wagon arrived at the depot a short time later. More porters came out to unload the bags, place them on carts, roll them inside, and load them into the baggage car of the eastbound train that would be departing shortly.

Smoke, Denny, and Louis had round-trip tickets good any time—one of the advantages of being an investor in the railroad—so they didn't have to stop at the ticket windows in the lobby. A conductor met them beside the steps leading up to one of the cars.

"Mr. Jensen," the blue-uniformed man said as he tugged on the brim of his cap. "Good to see you again. You, too, young Mr. Jensen and Miss Jensen."

"How's the weather along the route, Mr. Kanigher?" Smoke asked. "I don't mind saying, I don't really like the look of those clouds over the Sierras."

"And well you shouldn't," the conductor agreed. "Word came last night from the Summit Hotel in Donner Pass that it had started snowing heavily up there. Juniper Jones, the telegrapher, said it was snowing fit to bust, in fact. But I reckon the snowsheds and the Chinese walls are doing their job. Last I heard, the tracks were still clear and open and the telegraph wires were still up. We'll make it through if anybody can."

"That's good to hear," Smoke said, "because I'm planning on being home for Christmas."

CHAPTER 7

At the touch of a hand on his shoulder, Frank Colbert instantly came fully awake. His eyes opened, he saw the shadowy figure above him, and his reaction was lightning fast.

He grabbed the figure by the neck with his left hand and rolled to the left as his right hand snatched the knife from the little table close beside the bed.

Colbert pinned the person who had awakened him to the pillow while the tip of the blade rested just under that unwise individual's jawline, ready to plunge in and rip across the throat in a killing stroke.

Selena Charlton gurgled and sputtered but couldn't form any coherent words with Colbert's fingers locked painfully around her throat, cutting off her air and threatening to crush her windpipe.

Her green eyes were huge with surprise and fear, though. Those emotions were quite obvious.

So were her breasts, since the silk dressing gown she wore had come open when Colbert flung her down on the bed.

In the murky light that came through a gap in the curtains over the window in the room on the second floor of the First and Last Chance Saloon, Colbert gradually became aware of the red curls in disarray on the pillow, the soft flesh of her throat in his grip, and the abundant milky flesh on display. His breathing slowed, and his pulse didn't hammer quite as hard inside his head.

He took the knife away from her throat, let go of her, and said, "For God's sake, Selena, I could have killed you."

She had to gasp for air, hauling in deep, ragged breaths for several seconds before she was able to say, "What the hell . . . is *wrong* with you?"

"You don't come up on a sleeping man who got out of prison only a few days earlier and touch him," Colbert rasped as he tossed the knife back onto the bedside table and stood up. He stretched and shook his head as if trying to dislodge the cobwebs of sleep from it.

He wore only the bottom half of a pair of long underwear. His bare torso was fish-belly white but covered with slabs of hard muscle.

Colbert went on, "You should have known better. Anybody who sneaks up on you in prison probably wants to stick a shiv between your ribs, or cut your throat with it."

Selena sat up, sniffed haughtily, and pulled her dressing gown closed. "For your information, I *tried* to wake you up without touching you, Frank. I said your name a couple of times. But you were sleeping like a dead man." She smirked. "I guess I wore you out good and proper last night."

"I would have said it was the other way around," he snapped, unwilling to let her get the better of him.

"Anyway, when you didn't wake up, I figured I ought to try harder, because I knew you'd want to see this."

She reached into the gown's pocket and pulled out a piece of paper.

Colbert recognized it as a yellow telegraph flimsy and leaned forward to snatch it from her fingers. He scanned the block-printed words.

JUST ARRIVED RENO STOP PROFITABLE
WORK HERE STOP ALL FRIENDS SAY
HELLO STOP LOOK FORWARD TO SEEING
YOU BEFORE CHRISTMAS STOP DM

"Is that what you've been waiting for?" Selena asked.

"Reno," Colbert said instead of answering directly. "The train goes there, doesn't it?"

"Yeah, I think so."

"Is there one this morning?"

"How the hell should I know?"

Colbert ripped the curtain aside to let in gray light. "What time is it?"

"Around ten o'clock. Awfully early for somebody in my line of work, that's for sure. But one of the bartenders came up and said there was a wire for you, and I knew how anxious you'd been for it, so I had him bring it up to me." She paused. "Did I do the right thing, Frank?"

"Yeah. You did."

She massaged her throat where he had grabbed her. "And in return you tried to choke me to death or cut my throat." She smiled coyly. "I think you should come over here and give me a proper thank you."

Colbert turned to the wardrobe and jerked it open. "No time for that. I need to get to the depot and see if I can catch a train."

He knew the telegram was from Deke Mahoney, at last. The whole gang was in Reno waiting for him, and "profitable work" could mean only one thing.

Deke had a big job lined up, one that would net them a lot of loot. And whatever it was, it had to be pulled off by Christmas.

This was going to be a holiday worth celebrating after all, Colbert thought as he hurriedly began getting dressed and ignored the redheaded whore who sat pouting at him.

Jerome Kellerman strode into the railroad station carrying a carpetbag in his left hand and a smaller, flatter case made of fine leather in his right hand. A stocky, middle-aged, well-dressed man with white hair under his black bowler hat, he walked directly to the nearest ticket window and asked the clerk, "When is the next eastbound train leaving?"

"You're in luck, mister. It was supposed to pull out twenty minutes ago, but there was a problem with the engine and it's a little behind schedule. Should be ready to go in just a few minutes, though. You need a ticket?"

"Would I have asked if I didn't?" Kellerman said, not bothering to conceal the impatience he felt.

The clerk sniffed a little and asked, "How far?"

"All the way through to Chicago."

That ought to be far enough, Kellerman thought. And Chicago was a big city, big enough to get lost in so that no one would ever find him.

If he changed his mind later, he could always travel on to Philadelphia or New York or Boston. He could afford to go anywhere he wanted now.

When the clerk named the price, Kellerman pulled out a pocketbook made of expensive leather, like the case, and paid for the ticket. He was vaguely aware of someone standing behind him but didn't pay attention until the man said, "Hurry it up. I've got to get to Reno."

"So do I, my good man," Kellerman said as he put away his pocketbook and reached down to pick up the carpetbag he had set momentarily on the floor. "So do—"

He fell silent at his first sight of the man glaring at him.

The man was tall, with dark hair and a mustache, and as Kellerman looked at him, he was reminded instantly of a wolf or a panther or some other sort of predator. The man was dressed in a cheap suit and was the sort of individual Kellerman would have kept a close eye on, if he had ever walked into the bank where Kellerman worked.

Where Kellerman *had* worked. He would never set foot in the place again. Those days were over forever.

Now there were nothing but better days ahead of him.

As he stepped aside and the dark-faced, menacing-looking man moved up to the ticket window, Kellerman smiled and nodded to the woman who was also standing in line to pay for her fare. She was blond and reasonably attractive, though a little time and care worn. He briefly considered approaching her on the train. She might be pleasant company.

But then he discarded the idea. For one thing, he could afford to do better now, and for another, she wore a wedding ring. He knew that such vows of fidelity meant very little to some women, but the woman being married might well be an obstacle to overcome and she wasn't *that* good looking.

Without looking back, he walked across the cavernous, high-ceilinged lobby toward the platform where the train that would carry him to a new life was waiting.

Smoke, Denny, and Louis had a private compartment on the train. The two young people sat on a padded bench and watched their father pace back and forth as best he could in the cramped quarters.

"Really, Father, it's just a minor delay," Louis said. "Nothing to worry about. The conductor assured us that the train would be ready to roll any time now."

"I know." Smoke stopped his pacing and looked out the compartment's single window, but he couldn't see anything from there except part of the depot. "Earlier, though, he told me it was snowing up in Donner Pass. You two haven't spent enough time out here to know what it can mean when a bad snowstorm blows in, up there in the high country."

"Donner Pass," Louis repeated with a slight frown. "Why do I know that name?"

A bark of laughter came from Smoke. "You're bound to have heard of the Donner Party. That's how the pass got its name. Before that, it was called Stephens Pass, after one of the fellas who first explored it, but once the story got out, nobody ever thought of it as anything except Donner Pass."

"What story?" Denny asked with a note of impatience in her voice.

"Back in forty-six, there was an immigrant trail that ran through the Sierra Nevadas over that route. The California Trail, folks called it. Thousands of settlers traveled over it safely, but that year one group of them, led by a man named Donner, got too late a start. The approach to the pass isn't too bad on this side, but on the east it's a real ripsnorter, with lots of cliffs and very rugged country, so it was slow going. The Donner Party didn't make it through the pass in time. A blizzard dumped so much snow in it that the trail was blocked until the spring thaw. Donner decided that he and his people would camp there on the eastern slope and wait it out."

"I take it that was a bad decision," Louis said.

"There were more than eighty people in the group. Come spring, not much more than half of them made it out alive. The ones who died had frozen or starved to death." Smoke shrugged. "But if it hadn't been for them, even more of the settlers wouldn't have survived."

"Why not?" Denny asked.

"Because once some of them started to die, the others didn't starve as fast."

Denny and Louis both stared at Smoke in confusion for a second; then expressions of horror and loathing began to creep over their faces.

"You don't mean . . ." Denny said.

"Surely they wouldn't . . ." Louis said.

Smoke nodded solemnly. "Yep. That's what they did, all right. It was that or certain death."

"I would have died first!" Denny said.

"As would I," Louis added.

"It's easy to say that," Smoke told them. "Fact of the matter is, though, most folks never know what they're capable of until they have a life-or-death situation staring them in the face. When they do, some of them rise to the occasion. That's why there's the old saying about how heroes are made, not born." Smoke shrugged. "And sometimes, when the chips are down, people fail. It's not always a reason to be ashamed. You can't really blame folks for wanting to save their lives."

"You can blame them for crossing a line like that," Denny said. "You're talking about people, not animals. When you get right down to it, there's such a thing as right and wrong, good and evil. You *do* believe there are evil people in the world, don't you?"

"I've traded lead with enough of 'em," Smoke said. "There's no doubt about it."

"Damn right," Denny muttered. "And some of them deserve to be shot."

"I can't say as I disagree with you."

Smoke lifted his head as he heard a clanking noise and felt vibration shiver through the floor under his feet.

"I reckon we're about to get moving at last," he said. "And not a moment too soon to suit me."

Louis was frowning in thought. He said, "You don't think . . . in this day and age . . . if this train was to get stuck in the mountains people would resort to such drastic measures?"

"Let's hope we never find out," Smoke said.

CHAPTER 8

Reno, Nevada

Deke Mahoney had to admit that he liked the looks of Reno. It reminded him a little of Staghorn, where he and the rest of the gang had just hit the bank, because there were several lucrative industries in the area. Mining, ranching, and logging all poured money into the town. The railroad had helped it grow, too. A successful town meant the bank would be worth robbing, even under normal circumstances.

According to the conversation Magnus Stevenson had overheard, the circumstances were soon going to be anything but normal here in Reno. The outlaws didn't know how big that cash shipment coming in was going to be, but considering how much money flowed through Reno to start with, it might be as large as a hundred thousand dollars. Maybe even more, although Mahoney wasn't sure he ought to allow himself to dream that big.

Warren Hopgood was waiting for him when he stepped out of the telegraph office.

"Get it sent?" Hopgood asked.

"I sure did," Mahoney replied. "Don't know how long it'll take Frank to get it, but I bet he'll be on his way here before the day's over."

"If he got out of prison on time," Hopgood reminded him. "Maybe something happened and they decided to extend his sentence and not let him go."

Mahoney shook his head. "Not Frank. You know how smart he is. Once his time got short, he would've been on his best behavior. He wouldn't do nothin' to risk gettin' out of there when he was supposed to."

Hopgood grunted and said, "Yeah, you're probably right about that." He looked up at the overcast sky. Every so often, a tiny snowflake would fall, more like a little frozen pellet of moisture instead of a crystal. Hopgood lightly ran his right hand over his left upper arm. "I don't like this weather. Makes that bullet graze hurt even worse."

"Maybe once we get our hands on all that dinero, we ought to go some place where it stays warm all the time. Hot sun, hot food, and hot little brown gals."

"Not me," Hopgood said. "I don't want to spend the rest of my life with nothing but stinking greasers for company. I was thinking I might go to New Orleans and buy a saloon or something like that."

Mahoney slapped Hopgood on the shoulder, being careful to avoid the left one and clap his hand on the right, instead.

"How about a whorehouse?" he suggested. "I can just see you becomin' a whoremonger."

"Blast it, I'm serious," Hopgood insisted.

"Damn, Warren, you mean you're actually gonna become an honest businessman? I can't hardly imagine that!"

"To tell you the truth, neither can I." Hopgood let out a bitter chuckle. "You know what'll happen, more than likely."

"No, what?"

"However much money we get from this job, we'll blow through it in some spree of debauchery, and then we'll be back to scrounging around, looking for some bank or store to rob. You ever hear tell of an outlaw who actually turned his back on it, walked away from that sort of life and never went back?"

Mahoney sighed. "No, I can't say as I have. And now you've got me feelin' all gloomy again, just like the weather. Where'd the other fellas go?"

"They were going to hunt up some place to have a drink."

"Sounds like a good idea. What say we go find 'em?"

Donner Pass

Juniper Jones stifled a yawn as he stepped out onto the railroad platform next to the Summit Hotel. He had snatched a little sleep on the cot in his office during the night, but he hadn't gone up to his room to get some real sleep because he didn't want to be away from his key for that long.

In bad weather, a telegrapher had to be on the job around the clock, unless he had a relief man to spell him, which Juniper didn't. Important messages could come through at any time of the day or night, and he had to be on hand to relay them.

Also, every hour on the hour, he checked in with the offices in Reno to the east and Sacramento to the west, to let them know that the lines were still up and working. The wind was still blowing hard enough to swirl the snow in mad patterns, but the telegraph wires had stood up to it so far.

Earlier, Herman Painton had taken a pair of snow-shoes with him just in case and walked the tracks from one end of the pass to the other.

He came back brushing snow off his coat and shaking it out of his hair and reported that the tracks were clear, although the drifts were getting worri-some close in places.

"If it doesn't get any worse, I think we'll make it," he had told Jones, who dutifully relayed that infor-mation to his superiors without being convinced of it himself.

Now, as he stood on the platform with a biting wind trying to work its way inside his coat, he looked at the snow and frowned. It seemed to be falling faster and thicker now. The clouds were so dark and solid it might as well have been night. Juniper couldn't see more than fifty feet past the end of the platform.

He needed to go back inside and let Painton know he thought it was getting worse. A bad feeling gnawed at Juniper's guts. His experience and in-stincts warned him that they might not dodge this bullet after all, despite Painton's earlier optimism.

He was about to turn away when he caught a flicker of movement from the corner of his eye and stopped. Squinting, he peered toward the spot at the far end of the platform where he thought he had seen something.

Nothing was there. Juniper blew out a disgusted breath and shook his head, then turned away again.

Only to freeze and jerk his head around in that direction again as more movement darted at the side of his vision. He frowned and called over the howling wind, "Is somebody there?!"

There was no answer, of course. How could there be? The wind would have whipped away any words. And nobody would be out there in that white maelstrom, anyway.

Nobody sane.

A memory tickled the back of Juniper's brain. During the decades he had spent in these mountains, he had seen things . . . heard things . . . he just couldn't explain. Half-seen glimpses of what most people would claim was a bear or some other animal. Long, ululating cries raised on cold, lonely nights, like that of a wolf. Things easily explained away . . . by someone who hadn't been there to see and hear them.

But the sheer, eerie *strangeness* of them had gripped Juniper and never truly let him go.

It had been years since he had run across anything so odd, and he had told himself that if there ever had been something unnatural in the Sierra Nevadas, it was long gone. Eventually he had stopped even thinking about it.

But now those memories came flooding back. Whatever he had just caught sight of—if there was really something there—had darted through the snow with a weird, hitching gait. Not like an animal, but not truly like a man, either.

Juniper took a step toward the end of the platform and shouted, "Dadgummit, if somebody's out there, you damn well better answer me!"

Nothing. Just the wind and the snow . . .

Then what sounded like the tiny fragment of a laugh, and memory whispered a name in his ear.

Donner Devil.

Juniper backed toward the door to the hotel, suddenly aware that he wasn't armed. Inside his office, he kept an old Remington .44 revolver, in case anybody ever tried to rob the hotel—something that had never happened—but the gun wasn't going to do him any good out here. He backed a few more steps, head jerking from side to side as he peered futilely into the thick white curtains of snow.

Then his nerve broke and he turned and ran.

Just as he yanked the door open and threw himself inside, he caught a whiff of a scent.

Something feral.

Then he slammed the door and it was gone. Juniper pressed his back against the panel and tried not to shudder.

"Still snowing out there, Juniper?" Herman Painton called from across the lobby.

"Yeah," Juniper replied, his voice weak. "It's still snowin'. And it looks like it's gettin' worse."

Alma Lewiston approached the conductor and said, "I was told that a man named Jensen is on this train. Smoke Jensen. Do you know him?"

The man frowned at her. "Employees of the line don't make a habit of gossiping about our passengers, ma'am. You understand, I'm sure."

"Of course," Alma said easily. She smiled, knowing that when she did, it made the lines around her eyes and mouth disappear almost completely and the years of hardship and disappointment fall away from her. "But Smoke and I are dear old friends. I'm sure he'd want to see me again."

She made it sound like she and Jensen were more than just friends, but as soon as the words were out of her mouth, she saw the disapproval in the conductor's eyes and knew she'd made a mistake.

"Mr. and Mrs. Jensen have traveled on my trains many times, ma'am."

"I'm sure they have." Alma tried to salvage the situation. "Why, Mrs. Jensen and I are friends as well."

"Is that right? You know Mrs. Jensen, do you?"

Alma realized the man was waiting for her to provide the first name of Jensen's wife. She hadn't even known the man was married, let alone what his wife was called.

All she could do was summon up another smile and say, "Well, if you see him, tell him I was looking for him, would you? I'll be in the club car."

Maybe when Jensen heard that an attractive blond woman was looking for him, he would be curious enough to seek her out. Most men would be.

In the meantime, she would try to come up with some other way to locate him.

"Ma'am, if you'd tell me your name . . . ?" the conductor said as Alma turned away. She ignored him and kept moving.

She walked forward to the club car. She needed to think, and she might as well be comfortable while she was doing it. She knew she would look a little out of place there. Her traveling outfit had been a nice one when it was new, but time had dulled the dress's luster . . . just like it had done with her.

It had taken most of the money she had squirreled away just to purchase her ticket on this train. She had booked her passage through to Reno. That was as far as she could afford, and she figured she would have found Jensen by then and persuaded him to drop the charges against Gordon. If she hadn't accomplished her goal in that amount of time, chances were she never would.

She had a little money left over. Enough for a drink, anyway. And there was always the chance she wouldn't have to pay for it. Men still tended to want to buy her a drink . . . especially when she smiled.

She took a seat at the bar in the club car and looked around. Most of the booths were occupied, some by couples, the others by men either alone or in small groups. One man sat by himself at the counter, several stools away, his hands wrapped around a cup of coffee.

Alma glanced in his direction, then had to look again. He was a big man, with a hard-planed face and dark hair and mustache. His suit was a little on the cheap side, just like hers. Muscles bulged the coat's shoulders.

She judged by the man's grim expression that he was brooding about something. But he must have sensed Alma looking at him, because his head turned and his eyes swung to meet hers.

"Hello," she said. She held her left hand so that he couldn't see the wedding ring she wore. She should have slipped it off before she came in there, she thought, on the chance that she might meet a man like this.

She hadn't always been so shameless. Well, actually, she had been, she supposed, but she had tried to be faithful and true to Gordon. He knew quite a bit about her past but hardly everything, and he had told her it didn't matter. Grateful for that, she had tried to put it behind her.

Then he had gone off to fight in that war against Spain and come home still recovering from his wounds and addicted to laudanum. With a thriving Chinatown nearby, it was easier to get opium, so he had turned to the smoke of the lotus and had never been the same since.

But she still loved him and would do whatever she had to in order to save him from going to prison. He was right: if he was locked up for very long, he would die in there.

So if helping Gordon meant playing up to some stranger on a train, Alma was more than willing to do it.

Especially if he possessed the hard, cruel, primitive appeal that this one did.

The big man nodded curtly to her and said, "Ma'am."

"Is that coffee good?"

"It'll do," he replied with a shrug. He was trying not to show it, but she could tell that she had caught his interest. His dark eyes kept sliding over to study her.

"I'll have a cup," she told the man working behind the counter.

"It's on me," the stranger offered, just as Alma expected.

"Really? Why, thank you. That's very kind of you. People need kindness on a cold, snowy day like this, don't you think?"

The man's grunt told her he had never given that thought much consideration, one way or the other.

He was on the hook now, and she didn't want him to wiggle away. Still smiling, she said, "I believe I saw you back there in the depot. You were just ahead of me at the ticket window. My name is Alma Lewiston."

She didn't add the *Mrs.* Let him work that out for himself, if he wanted to go to that much trouble. As soon as he wasn't looking and she had the chance, she would slip off the wedding ring and put it in her handbag.

"Frank," he introduced himself. "Frank Colbert."

"It's very nice to meet you, Mr. Colbert. If I may be so bold as to ask, are you traveling for business or pleasure?"

"Business," he answered without hesitation. "But that's no reason the trip can't be enjoyable as well."

Alma liked the sound of that. She picked up the cup of coffee the counterman set in front of her and said, "To success in business . . . and pleasure."

CHAPTER 9

By noon, the storm over the Sierra Nevadas had strengthened into a true blizzard. A man caught out in it wouldn't have been able to see his hand in front of his face and would have been hopelessly lost if he went more than two steps from shelter.

In Donner Pass, the snow drifted so high against the sides of the snowsheds that it began to pile up on top of the structures. The drifts grew deeper and deeper until the sheds were completely covered and looked like a huge snake winding along underneath the thick carpet of white.

The sheds were sturdy structures, built to withstand a great deal of weight. But a storm such as this came along once in a decade. Maybe even less often. As it dumped more and more snow on the sheds, the timbers supporting the roof began to groan under the burden.

Then, half a mile east of the Summit Hotel, one of those timbers gave way with a rending crack. The roof sagged, and then another support timber broke.

The roof split apart. Tons of snow poured through the jagged opening. More boards splintered. The collapse spread until snow and debris were piled six feet deep on the tracks for more than a hundred yards.

The rumble generated by that catastrophe echoed from the surrounding mountains, even though those slopes couldn't be seen in the blizzard. The echoes were a long time dying away, and before they did, they caused a shiver to run through some of the deep drifts high above the pass.

Inside the hotel, Herman Painton came to the little room where Juniper Jones sat hunched over his telegrapher's key and said, "You sent for me?"

A few minutes earlier, Juniper had looked out into the lobby, seen one of the maids going by, and asked her to find Painton. He stood up now and handed the hotel manager the message he had copied down when the key began to chatter.

Painton read the printed words and looked up with a worried frown on his face. "The line wants me to check the tracks again."

"Yeah," Juniper said dryly. "I know."

"I just checked them a few hours ago!"

"The storm's gotten a lot worse since then. The line has an eastbound that'll be pulling into Sacramento pretty soon. They need to know whether it can get through."

"Your telegraph is still working. That means the storm isn't *too* bad."

"Just because the lines are up don't mean the tracks are clear," Juniper pointed out. "You know that, Herman."

Painton's frown deepened. He was in a bad spot,

Juniper thought. Although technically an employee of the hotel, during the winter when there was only a small staff up here, Painton also served as the railroad's superintendent for this station. If the line wanted him to check the tracks, he had little choice but to carry out the order.

"Why don't you come with me?" Painton asked.

"Me?" Juniper said. "I work for the telegraph company."

"But you're also my friend, aren't you? A man doesn't need to be out in weather like this by himself."

Juniper grimaced. Painton was right about both of those things. Juniper knew it, but he didn't have to like it.

He liked it even less because of what had happened earlier that morning, when he thought he had seen something out there in the storm . . . something that shouldn't have been there.

But Painton looked so miserable that Juniper sighed and said, "All right, I'll come with you."

He wasn't going unarmed, though. He turned back to the desk, opened a drawer, and took out the long-barreled Remington.

"What do you need that for?" Painton asked, puzzled by his friend's actions.

"I'll just feel better havin' it along," Juniper said. He shoved the gun in his waistband. It was awkward carrying it there because of the long barrel, but he didn't have a holster for the revolver. He reached for his heavy coat, which was hanging on a nail.

A few minutes later, the two men left the hotel and started walking east along the tracks. They were bundled up against the cold and wore caps with fleece-lined flaps that pulled down over their ears. Each man carried a pair of snowshoes.

Juniper hoped they wouldn't need the snowshoes. If they had to leave the tracks, they were pretty much dead, anyway. They wouldn't survive long in this howling storm.

Painton carried a lantern, too; otherwise it would have been pitch black inside the snowsheds. The drifts were high enough to cover them and cut off any light from outside. A dusting of white that had sifted through cracks in the structures covered the tracks here and there, but that much snow wouldn't cause any trouble for the locomotives.

Juniper stuck his hand inside his coat so he could reach the Remington if he needed to. The circle of light cast by the lantern upraised in Painton's hand didn't seem to extend very far. The flickering glow moved along with them, which meant darkness closed in behind them.

Juniper looked over his shoulder and saw a speck of light that marked the location of the railroad platform adjacent to the hotel. It seemed lonely in the murk.

"Everything looks fine," Painton said as they followed the tracks that made a long, gentle curve through the pass.

"So far," Juniper said.

"You really are spooked today, aren't you? What put a burr under your saddle?"

Juniper hesitated. Painton had been around the mountains long enough that he'd probably heard of the Donner Devil, too, but what would he think if Juniper admitted that he believed he had seen the creature? Would he decide that the telegrapher had gone mad, maybe from being stuck up here at this isolated post?

Juniper didn't want his friend to think he was crazy. Yet, he felt a compulsion to share his suspicions. Maybe Painton had noticed something odd, too, and was just as wary of talking about it. . . .

Before Juniper could say anything, Painton stopped short and exclaimed, "Oh, dear Lord!"

Juniper saw the same thing. A couple hundred yards ahead of them, faint gray light filtering into the snowshed revealed a wall of snow blocking the tracks. Broken beams stuck out of the barrier like toothpicks.

"There's your answer for Sacramento and Reno," Juniper said. "Won't be any trains gettin' through that for at least a week."

"It's going to take more like a month to clear that away and rebuild the shed," Painton said with devastation obvious in his voice. "Juniper, this is terrible—"

He didn't get any farther because Juniper grabbed his arm and said, "Listen!"

Both men heard the rumble that was slowly but steadily growing louder. They stared at each other, eyes growing wide with terror, and yelled the word that everyone who lived in the mountains during winter dreaded above all others.

"Avalanche!"

They turned and sprinted toward the hotel. Both cast aside the snowshoes so they could run faster. The rumble turned into a roar. The ground trembled beneath their feet.

It wasn't easy running on railroad tracks. They had covered fifty yards and the noise around them was deafening when Painton's foot caught one of the ties and sent him sprawling forward. He dropped the lantern. It bounced ahead of him and somehow didn't break. It even stayed lit.

Juniper saw the mishap from the corner of his eye and slowed for a second. He didn't know if Painton was hurt or just stunned, but the hotel manager wasn't scrambling back to his feet like he should have been. Juniper stumbled to a stop and swung around.

His heart was pounding so hard from fear it seemed like it was about to burst from his chest. Every instinct in his body screamed at him to keep running. Unguessable tons of snow were about to come crashing down on the shed at any second.

But Painton was having trouble pushing himself even to hands and knees as he shook his head groggily.

Biting back a curse at his own foolishness, Juniper sprang to Painton's side, reached down to grasp his arm, and hauled him upright.

"Let's go!" Juniper yelled over the roar that was like the world ending.

And that was what it seemed to do as the two men staggered and ran toward the hotel. The snowshed's roof exploded inward, and a huge wave of white swallowed everything.

It was midafternoon when the train reached Sacramento. Because of geography, the route from San Francisco went down the coast, then back north

again on the other side of the bay for a considerable
distance before turning west toward California's capital city. Sacramento was the last major stop before
the tracks began the climb into the Sierra Nevada
Mountains, although there was a small depot at Fol-
som, west of Donner Pass.

Smoke, Denny, and Louis had eaten their midday
meal in the dining car, then returned to their compartment. Louis complained of being very tired.
Weariness was one of the symptoms of the heart ail-
ment that had plagued him ever since he was born.
Smoke had advised his son to rest, while he and
Denny walked up the train to the club car.

They got cups of coffee and sat down in one of the
booths. Smoke sipped the strong black brew and
said, "I worry about your brother."

"So do I," Denny said, "but it would be better if
you don't let him know you're worrying. Louis is determined to live as much of a normal life as possible."

"I don't blame him for that. Determination's a good
quality to have." Smoke chuckled. "Although your
mother has been known to say that in me it's more like
mule-headed stubbornness."

"I come by it honestly, then."

That brought an outright laugh from Smoke. "You
said that, not me."

Denny grew more serious as she went on, "Louis
doesn't want to be coddled."

"I don't do that, do I? I always figured it was best to
just let him do whatever he feels like he's up to. He
ought to know what he can and can't do better than
anybody else."

"Yes, but sometimes he can be mule headed, too."
Denny shook her head. "I'd rather break a horse or
pull a cow out of a mud hole or even swap lead with
rustlers than try to deal with somebody's feelings."

"You mean like the feelings you and Brice Rogers
have for each other?" Smoke said, cocking an eyebrow quizzically.

Denny's face instantly flushed a little. "What are
you talking about? Brice Rogers is a pain in the rear
end, and I'm sure he feels the same way about me. It
can't get much simpler than that."

"Maybe so," Smoke said, thinking about how Denny
and the young deputy U.S. Marshal had worked together to break up the gang of outlaws responsible for
him being wounded and laid up earlier in the year.[2]
"Seemed like the two of you got along all right when
you needed to."

"Yeah. To keep from getting killed. But it doesn't
go any further than that."

"Oh," Smoke said, nodding. He wasn't convinced
by what his daughter was saying, though. Not for a
second.

Denny was saved from having to explain herself
even more by a new arrival. A small boy who was
walking through the club car stopped beside the
table in their booth and stared at Smoke. He was
about eight years old, slender, with brown hair and a
few freckles. He wore a suit and a shirt with a stiff collar, but from the way he moved his head around uncomfortably and pulled at the collar, he didn't care
for the garb.

"Howdy, son," Smoke said to the youngster. "Do I
know you?"

Instead of answering directly, the boy said, "You look like a cowboy. Are you a cowboy?"

"I am. I have a ranch and I work with cows all the time."

"My pa was a cowboy. But he's dead now."

"I'm mighty sorry to hear that. What's your name, son?"

"Bradley," the boy said. "But I'd rather folks call me Brad."

A woman came along behind the boy and said, "Bradley, stop bothering those people." She smiled at Smoke and Denny. "I'm sorry, my son doesn't seem to see anything wrong with coming up to complete strangers and annoying them."

Denny said, "He wasn't annoying us. I think he's adorable."

Smoke got to his feet, pinched the brim of his hat, and said, "We were just having a talk about cowboys, ma'am. No harm done at all. You've got a nice polite boy there."

The woman smiled. "Well . . . I'd like to think he is, most of the time."

She was young, probably in her midtwenties, and quite pretty, with light brown hair and a nicely shaped body in her dark gray traveling dress. She went on, "My name is Melanie Buckner."

"I already told 'em my name," the boy said.

"I'm Smoke Jensen," Smoke introduced himself, "and this is my daughter, Denise. We call her Denny. At least I do. Her mother still calls her Denise most of the time."

Brad said, "Would you rather be called Denny?"

She smiled at him. "Most of the time."

"But Denny's a boy's name."

"Well, I like to ride horses and rope cows and shoot guns, so a boy's name suits me just fine."

Brad's eyes got wide. "But you're a *girl*."

"I know. And it really annoys some of the hands on my pa's ranch that I'm better at those things than they are."

Melanie Buckner put her hands on her son's shoulders and said, "I think we'd better go now, Bradley. It was very nice meeting you folks, and again, I'm sorry if Bradley made a pest of himself."

"Don't think a thing in the world of it, ma'am," Smoke assured her.

He sat down as the woman and the little boy went on their way. "Friendly little shaver," he commented.

"I wonder what happened to his father," Denny said.

"I didn't reckon it would be polite to ask."

"No, probably not."

A couple of minutes later, the conductor came through the club car and announced, "We'll be rolling into Sacramento very shortly, and we'll be stopped here while I check on the weather and track conditions up ahead."

Smoke looked out the window and saw that the snow was coming down at a faster rate now. He had been over the Donner Pass route several times and knew that the snowsheds and the barrier walls could handle quite a bit of snow.

But avalanches were always possible, and as the train bumped and jolted a little as it slowed for its stop at the Sacramento depot, he knew that he didn't have a good feeling about this journey.

CHAPTER 10

Smoke's misgivings grew stronger as half an hour passed and the train hadn't started moving again. He and Denny returned to the compartment to find Louis awake after a nap that had left him looking refreshed and stronger.

"You have a copy of the railroad schedule, don't you, son?" Smoke asked.

"I do," Louis responded with a smile. "I'm very organized, as you know." He reached inside his coat and found the folded schedule, which he held out to Smoke.

"We met the cutest little boy in the club car," Denny said. "When Pa just called you 'son,' it reminded me of him."

"I remind you of a little boy?" Louis frowned. "I wonder if I should be insulted."

"Not at all, silly. I didn't say *you* reminded me of him. It's just that Pa called him 'son,' too. . . . Never mind. The boy was very interested in cowboys. He said his father had been one . . . but was dead now."

"That's terrible. How old was he?"

"Seven or eight, I'd say."

"So his mother couldn't have been very old."

"A few years older than us, I suppose." Denny said. "It depends on how old she was when she had him. Why are you curious about that?"

"I was just thinking . . . I mean, if there's a young, pretty widow on the train . . . I assume that she *was* pretty?"

Denny pointed a finger at him and told him disapprovingly, "You're the one who's terrible."

"Twenty minutes," Smoke said as he slapped the schedule against the palm of his other hand.

Both his children looked at him and said, "What?"

"Twenty minutes," Smoke repeated. "That's how long the stop here in Sacramento was supposed to be. And since we were late leaving San Francisco, I reckon normally the engineer would try to move faster at every stop and shave a few minutes off of that time, to get us back closer to being on schedule. This delay will throw us behind even more."

Before Louis or Denny could comment on that, a knock sounded at the door of the compartment. Smoke swung around and opened it to find the conductor standing there.

The man touched a finger to the brim of his cap and looked uncomfortable as he said, "Sorry to have to tell you this, Mr. Jensen, but there's a problem."

"Donner Pass is blocked, isn't it?" Smoke asked.

The conductor looked surprised. "How'd you know that?"

"Because I can tell how hard it's snowing here,

and if it's coming down like this in Sacramento, it's likely to be a lot worse up in the mountains."

"The storm started last night," the conductor said, nodding, "and it's just gotten worse as the day's gone on. A telegram came through a little while ago saying that there'd been an avalanche. Some of the snowsheds were destroyed, and the tracks are completely blocked."

"Oh, no!" Denny said. "Was anybody hurt?"

"I don't think so, Miss Jensen. The telegrapher and another fella who works up there at the Summit Hotel were almost caught in it, but they made it to safety by the skin of their teeth."

"The hotel's all right?" Smoke asked.

"As far as I know. The snowsheds collapsed just east of there. They're buried for at least a quarter of a mile. That's how wide the avalanche was."

"Then the train could go that far," Smoke pointed out.

"Yeah, but what would be the point?" The conductor spread his hands. "The bosses can't even start thinking about getting a work train and a repair crew up there until the storm stops, and who knows how long that will be? Sometimes those blizzards settle in and don't budge for days. Once they *can* start clearing the track, it'll take a week or more to get it in good enough shape to use again." The blue-uniformed man shook his head. "The line has decided that this train's not going any farther. It's going to pull onto a siding and sit right there in Sacramento for the time being."

"But it's nearly Christmas!" Denny exclaimed. "People need to get home to their families."

"Believe you me, I know, Miss Jensen. I've been hearing an earful about it since I started passing along the news. But blizzards and avalanches don't stop for holidays."

Smoke's face was grim as he said, "What about some other way to get through the mountains?"

"Not by train. I hate to say it, but you folks are stuck here. The railroad is offering free passage back to San Francisco. For those who'd rather wait and see just how bad the situation is, they're willing to put folks up in hotels for a few days—"

Smoke stopped him with a gesture. "I'm not worried about that. My children and I can get rooms here in town. I just don't like the idea of being away from home for Christmas. My wife will be expecting us."

"You can get a wire through to her and let her know what's going on," the conductor suggested. "The wires are still up, or at least they were a little while ago. Might be a good idea to go ahead and do it, though. With a storm like this, you can't ever tell what else might happen."

Smoke nodded and said, "All right. Thank you." He managed a smile. "I know this isn't your fault."

"You know what they say—everybody talks about the weather, but nobody does anything about it!"

The conductor moved on to deliver the bad news to more of the passengers. Smoke turned to his children. Louis said, "Mother's going to be disappointed. This was going to be the first Christmas that Denny and I were home to stay."

"I know. Your uncles and your cousins were going to be there, too."

"Spending Christmas in a Sacramento hotel room," Denny said. "That doesn't sound very festive at all. But I suppose we'll have to make the best of things."

"I suppose," Smoke said, but a frown creased his forehead. The wheels of his brain had already started to turn.

The conductor had said that unless they wanted to return to San Francisco, they were stuck here in Sacramento for the foreseeable future. But that might not be the case. Accepting that meant giving up, as far as Smoke was concerned.

And Smoke Jensen had never cottoned much to giving up.

There had to be some other way. . . .

Alma Lewiston stood outside the door of the compartment and took a deep breath as she gathered her courage. A big part of her would rather have been sitting in the club car, talking and flirting with Frank Colbert.

But Fate had dropped Smoke Jensen practically into her lap. She had barely been able to believe it when the tall, broad-shouldered man in the cowboy hat had stood up and introduced himself to that young mother, giving the name of the very man she was looking for! She couldn't allow this opportunity to help Gordon slip away from her.

Anyway, Frank had turned surly and mean once he found out the train wasn't going on through the mountains after all. Alma didn't care; she didn't have any business on the other side of the Sierra Nevadas.

Judging by Frank's reaction, though, he had something waiting for him over there, and it was important.

Not as important as saving her husband, Alma thought. She took a deep breath, then lifted her hand to knock on the compartment door.

It opened before she could do so. The man she wanted to talk to stood there with a small carpetbag in his left hand.

He looked like he had been about to step out of the compartment, but he stopped short when he saw her. He cocked an eyebrow as Alma slowly lowered her hand.

"Can I help you, ma'am?" he asked.

"You're Mr. Jensen, isn't that correct?"

"It is. I'm Smoke Jensen, if that's who you're looking for."

"My name is Alma Lewiston. Mrs. Gordon Lewiston."

Clearly, the name didn't seem to mean anything to him. Jensen raised his right hand to his hat brim and ticked a finger against it politely.

"My pleasure, Mrs. Lewiston. How can I help you?"

"You know my husband," Alma said.

Jensen frowned slightly and shook his head. "Gordon Lewiston, you said? I'm sorry, but I don't recognize the name."

"You met him yesterday in San Francisco."

"Not that I recall." His frown deepened. "Wait a minute. Are you talking about—"

"You broke his arm," Alma said.

Jensen's air of polite affability vanished. His face hardened as he said, "That was his choice, not mine. Fact of the matter is, I did my best *not* to hurt him, until he came at me with a knife. I figured it was best to take it away from him as quickly and efficiently as I could."

"And now he's locked up. He's going to be sent away to prison, and . . . and he'll die there."

"Because he's addicted to opium," Jensen said flatly.

"You know that about him, and yet you'd condemn him to death for nothing more than a botched robbery!"

A younger man appeared at Jensen's shoulder and asked, "Is something wrong, Father?"

"No, just having a talk with this lady here." Jensen addressed Alma again. "Did you follow me onto this train?"

"Yes," she answered bluntly. "I had to talk to you."

He shook his head. "There's nothing I can do. I've already given my statement to the police. It's out of my hands."

"No, it's not," Alma insisted. "If you sent a telegram to the authorities in San Francisco right now and told them that you want to drop all the charges against Gordon, they would probably let him go."

"Maybe, maybe not. He's been accused of a couple of crimes, and the law can go ahead with the case against him whether I press charges or not."

"But the case is based entirely on your statement." Alma couldn't keep a note of desperation out of her voice. "If you took that back . . . if you told them you were wrong about what happened . . ."

"That would be lying," Jensen said. "I'm sorry, Mrs. Lewiston. I'm not going to do that."

"You don't understand. Gordon's not really a criminal. He's not even a bad man. He only did it because of the opium, and he wouldn't be using the damn stuff if he hadn't gotten himself shot in Cuba!"

"He was in the war?" Jensen asked.

"That's right. He wasn't one of Teddy Roosevelt's fancy Rough Riders. He was just a soldier who signed up because he wanted to do the right thing."

Jensen looked at her for a long moment, then said, "I won't take back the statement I gave to the police, but I'll tell you what I *will* do. I know a very good lawyer in San Francisco. I'll send him a wire and ask him to look into your husband's case and represent him if he thinks it would do any good. I'll pay his fee, too."

Alma caught her breath and said, "Do *you* think that will do any good?"

"It can't hurt anything," Jensen said. "Maybe instead of putting him in prison, they could send him somewhere else. Some kind of hospital, maybe."

"Do such things even exist?"

"I don't know," Jensen admitted honestly. "But it's worth a try, don't you think?"

Alma swallowed hard. She wanted to hate this man standing in front of her, but somehow she couldn't. Her instincts told her that Smoke Jensen was a good man, that he genuinely cared about Gordon's situation and wanted to help.

Whether that was actually possible or not remained to be seen.

"Thank you, Mr. Jensen," she said.

"I've got to send some wires anyway. If you want to come along with me to the telegraph office, I'll get in touch with that lawyer I told you about." He turned and handed the carpetbag to his son. "You and Denny go on to the hotel and get rooms for us, all right? I'll see you there."

A young, very pretty blond woman came up behind Jensen, too. "Are you sure about this, Pa?" she asked. "I mean, that man *did* try to rob and kill you."

"When I first met Monte Carson and Pearlie, they were working for men who wanted me dead," Jensen said. "They got second chances and turned out to be two of the best friends I ever had. Not saying it's the same thing here, but this fella Lewiston struck me as a pretty poor excuse for a badman." He glanced at Alma. "No offense, ma'am."

"None taken," she assured him. "You're right. Gordon's a pretty poor excuse for just about everything. But I love him."

"Sometimes that's all a fella needs to justify helping him—the love of a good woman."

CHAPTER 11

Frank Colbert debated whether he ought to get drunk. That seemed to be about the only way he could accomplish anything, since the train wasn't going on and he couldn't make it to Reno before Christmas.

He wished Deke had been a little more forthcoming in that telegram, so at least he would know what job he was missing out on.

He understood, though, why the man he had left in charge of the gang hadn't wanted to reveal too many details to the telegrapher. Deke wasn't the smartest fella in the world, but he was canny and had a good sense of self-preservation. He wouldn't do anything to attract the attention of the law unless it couldn't be helped.

Colbert decided that he needed to let Deke know he wouldn't be rendezvousing with them after all. If there was loot to be had in Reno, the boys ought to go ahead and go after it themselves, instead of waiting for him.

That knowledge left him with the sour, bitter taste of defeat under his tongue. Some whiskey might wash it out, or at least dull it a little. He would hunt up a saloon, as soon as he sent that wire to Reno.

He was on his way across the depot lobby toward the telegraph office when he spotted the woman he'd been talking to in the club car earlier. She appeared to be headed for the same destination, but from a different angle.

A tall man in a sheepskin jacket and cowboy hat was with her, his hand lightly touching her arm now and then as they made their way through the noisy crowd in the lobby. With the railroad coming to an unexpected standstill because of the weather, there were a lot of angry, frustrated people in the depot this afternoon.

Alma, that was the name the woman had given him, Colbert recalled. Alma Lewiston. He didn't know if that was really her name. Something about her struck him as shady.

Maybe he sensed a kindred spirit in her. If the train had continued on, there was a good chance he would have tried to get to know her better before they reached Reno. That would have helped to pass the time.

Besides, after five years in prison, even the time he had spent with Selena back in San Francisco hadn't completely taken the edge off his needs.

However, it looked like Alma Lewiston had found herself a different beau, he thought. A big, gallant cowboy. Well, that wasn't surprising, Colbert mused. Cowboys always had a soft spot for whores, and he had sensed right away that deep down Alma was a whore.

For some reason Colbert couldn't understand, he felt a little resentment toward the tall man. What did it matter? Alma meant nothing to him.

But he had set his sights on her, even if only briefly, and Frank Colbert hated to lose. To anybody, at anything.

The two of them walked up to the telegrapher's counter ahead of him. Colbert hung back and moved behind a pillar that would conceal him if she happened to look around. He didn't want to attract Alma's attention and maybe cause some sort of scene.

Those cowboys could be mighty touchy.

Alma Lewiston stood to one side while Smoke printed out the telegram to Claudius Turnbuckle, the San Francisco lawyer he had mentioned to her. Turnbuckle was one of the top attorneys in the city. In the whole country, for that matter. If anyone could do any good for Alma's husband, it would be him.

Smoke figured she was destined to be disappointed, though. Chances were, Gordon Lewiston was going to wind up in prison no matter what Turnbuckle or anyone else did, and it wasn't likely that someone such as him would survive in there for very long. If the lack of opium didn't kill him, some brutal convict would.

With the telegram sent, Smoke turned to the woman and said, "All right, I've gotten in touch with the lawyer. I told him to reply to me at the hotel where I'll be staying. Why don't you stay there, too, so I'll know where to find you when I hear anything?"

"If it's fancier than a flophouse, I can't afford it, mister," Alma said. "I'm not sure how I'm going to scrape up enough money for a ticket back to San Francisco."

Smoke shook his head and told her, "Don't worry about either of those things. I'll pay for the hotel and your return ticket."

She narrowed her eyes at him. "When a man starts offering to pay for a woman's hotel room, it usually means he wants something in return."

"I'm sure some men are like that," Smoke countered, "but I'm not."

"As simple as that? You just say it, and it's true?"

"That's the way I've always lived my life."

She stared at him for a moment, then laughed. "Damned if I don't believe you, Mr. Jensen."

"You can call me Smoke. And I might add, I'm a happily married man. Been one for a lot of years now."

"Then your wife is a lucky woman."

He smiled. "I'm not sure she'll think that when she gets the telegram I'm about to send her. The kids and I were supposed to be back home for Christmas, but now it looks like we might not make it."

"That's not your fault. You can't control the weather."

"No, but she'll still be disappointed, just like I am. Hang on a minute while I take care of sending that wire, and then we can share a buggy to the hotel."

Alma shrugged. "You'll be paying for it, so I'll wait as long as you need me to."

Smoke picked up the pencil he'd been using earlier and got another telegraph blank from the stack.

DONNER PASS CLOSED BY BLIZZARD STOP
WILL TRY TO GET HOME SOME OTHER
WAY STOP ALL MY LOVE AND MERRY
CHRISTMAS SMOKE

"Some other way?" Alma said. "Sorry, I shouldn't have been reading over your shoulder. But what other way is there to get across the mountains?"

"People used to make it to California before there were trains running all the way. Thousands of them, even before the Gold Rush made thousands more head this way. They came by horseback, wagon, and stagecoach."

"Good luck riding all the way on a horse in weather like this. I don't know much about frontier life—I'm a city girl and always have been—but I can't imagine driving a wagon across the Sierra Nevadas, either. Anyway, the pass is blocked."

"There are other routes that don't go through Donner Pass. The old McCulley Cutoff is lower in elevation and safer, and it might not be blocked by snow. I'm betting that a stagecoach with a good strong team could make it."

"How do you know that? Have you been over every foot of ground west of the Mississippi?"

"Nope. But between me; an old friend of mine named Preacher; my brothers, Luke and Matt; and my nephews, Ace and Chance, we've covered just about all of it at one time or another. I know about the McCulley Cutoff because Preacher was one of the first mountain men to go through the Sierra Nevadas that way, back when California was still part of Mexico, and he told me all about it. I've been over that trail myself since then."

"That doesn't do you any good, though, unless you have a stagecoach."

"Well," Smoke said with a smile, "it just so happens I know where I might be able to put my hands on one."

Colbert stayed where he was until Alma and the cowboy she called Mr. Jensen had moved away from the telegraph office window and left the depot. He had been close enough to overhear them talking, although the hubbub in the lobby had kept him from catching every word of the conversation. Despite that he had heard enough to realize something important.

Jensen thought he knew a way to get across the Sierra Nevadas and reach Reno before Christmas. Something about a stagecoach. Colbert wouldn't have thought that any stagecoaches were still running these days, but maybe he was wrong about that.

Traveling all the way to Reno in some cold, drafty, rough-riding coach wasn't the most appealing prospect, especially compared to riding in a comfortable railroad car, but if it would get him there in time to ramrod that mysterious job and claim his share of the loot, Colbert was willing to give it a try.

He had also heard Alma and Jensen talking about

the hotel where they were going to stay. Jensen claimed he wasn't trying to get anything out of Alma, but Colbert didn't believe that for a second. Why would any man help a woman like that without expecting some favors in return?

But since he knew where they were staying, he could keep an eye on the place. That way, whenever Jensen made his move to get across the mountains, Colbert could make sure to cut himself in on the deal. And if Jensen didn't like it, well, that was just too damn bad.

Colbert's spirits definitely were higher now as he wrote out the message to send to Deke Mahoney in Reno. One way or another, he promised Mahoney, he would be there for that big job.

Despite the cold outside, it was warm in the hotel, which boasted of steam heat and a radiator in every room. Even so, it wasn't warm enough to explain the beads of sweat covering Jerome Kellerman's face as the stout, white-haired man walked along the corridor toward his room.

He carried both his carpetbag and the smaller case, but he stopped and set the carpetbag down before he reached the room. He pulled a handkerchief from his pocket and used it to mop some of the dampness from his ruddy features.

"Are you all right, mister?"

The high-voiced question made Kellerman jump a little. He looked around and saw a boy standing in the open doorway of one of the rooms.

"Were you talking to me?" Kellerman asked.

"Yeah. I mean, your face is awful red, the way mine gets when I've been playing too hard and it's hot outside. Sometimes that makes me feel like I'm gonna be sick. Are you gonna be sick, mister?"

Kellerman muttered a curse under his breath and stuffed the handkerchief back in his pocket. "I'm fine," he snapped. "Leave me alone, child."

"I didn't mean anything—" the boy began.

A woman moved up behind him and put a hand on his shoulder. "Are you annoying people again, Bradley?" She gave Kellerman a weak smile. "I apologize, sir. My son is very talkative, and, well, you know that old saying, 'He never met a stranger'? That describes Bradley perfectly."

"It's quite all right, madam," Kellerman said. He couldn't manage a smile, not as upset as he was right now, but at least he was able to keep his voice civil, even polite. "The lad just inquired as to my health."

"Well . . . not that it's any of my business," the woman said, "but you do look a bit overheated."

"They keep it too warm in this confounded hotel. I wouldn't even be here if not for that da—for that blasted railroad."

"And that confounded blizzard," the boy said. He looked up at the woman, who evidently was his mother. "I like that word. Confounded."

"I'm sorry again," she said hurriedly.

Kellerman held up a hand in a gesture meant to tell her not to worry about it, then grasped his carpetbag's handle and picked it up again. He started once more toward the door of his room.

"I hope you get to feeling better, mister," the boy called behind him.

Kellerman ignored that, unlocked the door, and went into the hotel room. He closed the door and made sure it was locked. The curtains were open, but the sky was so overcast outside that the room was as gloomy as twilight.

The pilot light of a gas lamp in a bronze wall sconce gleamed a dull blue. Kellerman set the carpetbag on the bed and turned up the lamp until it lit, then closed the curtains.

He took off his hat and threw it onto the bed. When he was a child, his mother had told him that having a hat on the bed was bad luck, but that old biddy had been wrong about everything else, so why not that, too?

He turned to the dressing table near the wall lamp. A gilt-framed mirror hung above the table. Kellerman could have watched himself set the case down flat on the table if he'd wanted to, but he had no urge to do that. Instead he took out the handkerchief and wiped his face again.

This is a disaster, he thought, *an utter disaster.* He couldn't afford to be stuck here in Sacramento, still so close to San Francisco. The precautions he had taken ought to ensure that what he had done wouldn't be discovered for several days, but he couldn't guarantee that. Flukes, strokes of bad luck, were always possible. He had planned to stay on the move until he was far away.

This way, if the shortage were uncovered, it wouldn't take them long at all to track him down and arrest him.

The thought made a shudder go through him. He went to the carpetbag and rummaged in it until he found a silver flask. He unscrewed the cap and took a long drink, the muscles in his throat working as he swallowed.

The liquor's fiery bite strengthened him and stiffened his spine. He drank more of it and then felt well enough to go back to the case on the dressing table.

He laid his hand on it but didn't open it just yet. Instead, another thought intruded on him.

He had been upset by the situation and annoyed by the little boy, but despite that, he had noticed how attractive the woman was. Fluffy, light brown hair; a tantalizing face; a slender but feminine body . . . And despite being the child's mother, which meant she wasn't totally unsullied, she had possessed an air of wholesome innocence that greatly appealed to Kellerman.

Of course, such a woman would never pay any attention to a man like him, older, portly, yes, even pompous, he had to admit that. None of those were qualities that attracted lovely young women.

But money did.

Kellerman laid his hands on the case and unfastened the catches. He raised the lid and gazed upon the contents, still in awe at what he had managed to do.

Neat stacks of crisp bills bound together with paper wrappers filled the case.

Fifty thousand dollars.

Enough to live like a king for the rest of his life . . . if only he could get far enough away from San Francisco, fast enough.

Jerome Kellerman looked up, and this time he did smile at himself in the mirror. With that much money, any woman he wanted could be his.

Even that sweet little brown-haired beauty down the hall.

But only if they didn't catch him and throw him in prison for the rest of his life. That wouldn't happen, Kellerman vowed to himself. He would never let them take him back.

Kellerman's hand closed around the other object in the case and lifted it out, the smell of gun oil strong in his nose as he tightly gripped the Smith & Wesson.

CHAPTER 12

Denny and Louis hadn't been able to get a suite at the hotel, but they had secured rooms for themselves and Smoke. When Smoke reached the hotel, the clerk at the desk told him he would be staying in Room 212. Louis was next door in 214, while Denny was directly across the hall from her brother in 215.

After making arrangements for Alma Lewiston to have a room as well, Smoke headed upstairs. He was glad this hotel didn't have any of those fancy rising rooms like the Palace in San Francisco. He preferred climbing the stairs with his own two feet.

Smoke's room and Louis's were adjoining, and the door between them was open when Smoke came in. Both of the younger Jensens were waiting for him there, seated in overstuffed armchairs near the window.

On the other side of the glass, snow still fell, not heavily but steadily.

Smoke took off his hat and placed it on the dressing table. Louis asked, "Did you send that wire to

Mother letting her know we won't be back for Christmas after all?"

"I sent her a wire telling her that Donner Pass is closed," Smoke said. "But that's not the only route, and I told her we'd try to get back some other way."

Denny said, "That's what Louis and I were just talking about. In the morning, we can catch a train for Los Angeles, go down there, head across to El Paso, and then up through New Mexico into Colorado and on to Big Rock that way. They had some train schedules down in the lobby. The connections aren't as good as they might have been. We'll lose some time to layovers that can't be avoided. But we should be able to make it, barely, if we don't run into any more trouble."

"Which we might, traveling through the mountains in New Mexico at this time of year," Smoke pointed out. "Those passes get blocked by snow sometimes, too."

"Well, do you have a better idea, Pa?" Denny asked.

"Maybe," Smoke said. "The railroad is still open between Big Rock and Reno. We'll meet your mother and the others and celebrate Christmas there."

Louis raised his eyebrows. "In Reno? Away from home?"

"We've been away from home for Christmas plenty of times over the years. The most important thing is being with family, not where you are."

"But we can't get to Reno, either," Denny said. "The train can't get through, remember?"

"Of course I remember," Smoke said. "That's why we're going by stagecoach."

Both youngsters stared at him for a moment. Then

Denny said, "Are you telling me there's a stagecoach that runs from here to Reno and *it* can get through where a train can't?"

"There's not a regular stagecoach route anymore," Smoke said, "but there used to be several that went through the Sierra Nevadas. The Dutch Flats Wagon Road followed pretty close to the same route the railroad uses now, up through the pass. But we can swing south on the McCulley Cutoff through easier terrain that's less likely to be blocked, then turn back north toward Reno on the other side of the mountains."

Denny frowned and said, "I suppose we could do that . . . *if* we had a stagecoach."

"Do you remember Fred Davis?"

Louis and Denny looked at each other. Louis shrugged, and then Denny shook her head and told Smoke, "That name doesn't mean anything to me."

"Fred used to own a number of stage lines that ran where the railroads don't and kept the small communities in touch with the rest of the world. Twenty-some-odd years ago, after your mother and I had started the Sugarloaf but before you two were born, I did a favor for Fred and rode shotgun on one of his routes when he was being plagued by a gang of road agents.[3] We've kept in touch ever since. He's retired now, but he stayed in the stagecoach business up until just a few years ago, keeping a small line going here in California. He lives here in Sacramento and told me in one of his letters that he has the last of his stagecoaches in storage here."

Louis said, "So you're going to just . . . what? *Borrow* a stagecoach?"

"I don't see why not," Smoke said.

"Mother would say you've lost your mind," Denny told him.

"I don't know about that. She's always had a pretty adventurous nature. She married me, after all." Smoke smiled. "But just in case, that's why I didn't tell her what I had in mind. I'll go and talk to Fred in the morning, and if we can work out a deal, I'll wire your mother then and ask her to meet us in Reno."

"Wait a minute," Louis said. "Who's going to *drive* this stagecoach, assuming you can even find one?"

"I can handle a six-horse hitch if I have to." Smoke shrugged. "It might be better if we could hire somebody with experience, but I don't know who's available or if there even are any *jehus* left around here from the old days."

"Any what?" Denny asked.

"Old Spanish word. It translates roughly to stagecoach driver. That's what we called them sometimes, back in the old days."

Louis shook his head dubiously and said, "I'm not sure you'll find anyone willing to sign on for a risky trip like that, especially at this time of year."

"What about you two?" Smoke asked bluntly. "Are you willing to risk it?"

"Taking a stagecoach over the mountains in the middle of winter, not knowing what sort of trouble we'll run into?" Denny laughed. "Actually, it sounds exciting to me."

"It would," Louis said.

"If you think it would be too much of an ordeal for you, son—" Smoke began.

"That's not what I said at all. I just meant I'm not surprised Denny thinks it sounds exciting. She's always been willing to tackle just about anything if it strikes her as an adventure."

"I can't help it." She pointed at Smoke. "I inherited it from him."

"I have the same legacy," Louis said. "If you think we can make it across the mountains in a stagecoach, I guess that's what we'll do!"

Smoke smiled at his children, pleased that neither of them lacked for sand. It *was* a wild idea, and he knew it, but with luck and determination they could see it through.

Before they could continue the discussion, a soft knock sounded on the hotel room door.

Smoke opened the door to find a freckle-faced bell-boy standing there with a small envelope in his hand.

"I have a wire for you, Mr. Jensen," he said.

Smoke took the envelope and handed the boy a dime. "Thanks, son." He took a folded yellow telegraph flimsy from the envelope and read the words printed on it. When he turned to Denny and Louis, a grim cast had settled over his features.

"What's wrong, Pa?" Denny asked, sensing right away that the wire contained troubling news.

Smoke snapped the middle finger of his other hand against the paper he held and said, "This is a reply to the wire I sent Claudius Turnbuckle a while ago. He went to the jail to talk to that fella Lewiston, like I asked him to."

"The opium addict who tried to rob you yesterday," Louis said.

"Yeah. But when he got there, he found out that Lewiston was dead."

"Dead!" Denny exclaimed.

Smoke nodded. Bleak lines formed trenches in his cheeks.

"He managed to tear up the blanket in his cell, make a rope out of it, and hang himself. I reckon he decided there was no way his wife could help him, and he couldn't face the likelihood of going to prison."

"That lawyer, Turnbuckle, is certain of his facts?" Louis asked.

"Says he saw the body himself. They hadn't taken it to the morgue yet."

Denny said, "Well, that's just terrible. His poor wife is going to be devastated. Were you going to drop the charges against him, Pa?"

"More than likely," Smoke said, "but I don't think it would have done any good. The police had my statement, so they could have gone ahead and charged him whether I wanted them to or not. Turnbuckle might have been able to talk them out of it, but there's no guarantee of that."

"What are you going to do?"

Smoke shook his head. "Not much I can do other than go and tell Mrs. Lewiston what happened. I got her a room here. She's up on the third floor."

Denny got to her feet. "I'll come with you."

"That's not necessary—"

"It might be better to have a woman along when you're breaking bad news that way."

That sounded exactly like something Sally would say, Smoke thought. He nodded and said, "Good idea. Thanks."

"I'll stay here and rest a bit," Louis said. "When you get back, we can get some supper."

Smoke reached for his hat.

A few minutes later, he and Denny stood in front of the door to Room 327. Smoke grimaced and said, "I think I'd rather take on a gang of owlhoots or an Apache war party than tackle a chore like this."

"Let me tell her," Denny suggested.

He shook his head. "It's not your responsibility. I'm the one the fella tried to rob."

He knocked on the door.

Alma Lewiston opened it a moment later. She had taken off the hat and jacket from her traveling outfit, leaving her in the long skirt and high-necked white blouse. She had taken her hair down, too, which softened her rather severe look.

As soon as she saw Smoke and Denny standing there, she caught her breath and took a step back. Her eyes widened and she started to shake her head. With an obvious struggle to speak, she said, "You wouldn't be here . . . looking like that . . . unless . . . unless . . ."

Smoke took off his hat and held it in front of him with his left hand.

"I'm mighty sorry, ma'am," he said. "I heard back from that lawyer I wired in San Francisco. He was willing to try to help your husband, but when he went to the jail—"

"Let me guess," Alma interrupted him. Her voice was brittle with grief now. "Gordon found some way to kill himself, didn't he?"

Smoke didn't figure she needed to have all the details right now. He just nodded and said, "I'm afraid so."

The woman surprised him by laughing, but it was a cold, humorless sound.

"He's been trying to do that ever since he got back from the war, first with the laudanum and then the opium. It was taking a long time, but that's what he was doing, all right. Since he couldn't get any of that stuff in jail, he figured out something else. Hanged himself, more than likely."

Since she was the one who had put it into words, Smoke nodded.

"That's what the telegram from Turnbuckle said."

Denny moved forward a little, as if to give Alma Lewiston a hug, but the woman stepped back again and said, "I don't need your sympathy. You don't know what I've gone through."

"No, but I'm sorry for your loss," Denny said.

"I've been losing Gordon for two years now. Do you think I ever really believed this would end any other way?"

"We're very sorry," Smoke said. "I'll pay for your ticket back to San Francisco and see to it that your husband is laid to rest properly."

Alma shook her head. "There's nothing there for me to go back to. As for Gordon, they can put him in Potter's Field. He didn't have any family besides me. Nobody's going to mourn him, and there's no point in pretending otherwise."

"I really don't mind—"

"You've already done enough." Alma gripped the edge of the door. "Thank you for letting me know. Good night."

"If there's anything we can do—" Denny ventured.

"There's not."

The door closed in their faces.

Smoke saw the anger flaring in his daughter's eyes

and took hold of Denny's arm to steer her along the corridor, away from the door.

"What a cold-blooded woman," Denny said. "Doesn't even want to go back and make sure her husband gets a decent burial."

"Like she said, she's known for a long time what was bound to happen sooner or later. Or at least, what the odds were that it would. I reckon she's already done all the grieving she had inside her."

"Well, it still seems wrong to me."

"Folks have to handle losing loved ones in their own way."

Smoke's mind went back, ever so briefly, to his first wife, Nicole, whose name he had given to this beautiful young woman beside him. Nicole and their infant son, Arthur, had been murdered, and Smoke had handled that loss by going after and killing all the men responsible.

He couldn't help but wonder if Alma Lewiston blamed him for what had happened to her husband.

And what she would do about it if she did.

CHAPTER 13

By the next morning, a thin layer of white lay over the capital city. It had stopped snowing sometime during the night, but from the looks of the clouds looming over the mountains in the distance, the terrific blizzard that had buried Donner Pass was still going on up there.

From the letters Smoke had exchanged with his old friend Fred Davis, Smoke knew the name of the street where the man lived, and a helpful desk clerk gave him directions to the neighborhood. Smoke found a livery stable several blocks from the hotel and rented a horse and tack.

It felt good to be in the saddle again, he thought as he rode toward Davis's house. He spent too much time sitting behind the desk in his office at the Sugarloaf.

Calvin Woods handled the foreman's duties these days, and Pearlie, although retired from that job, was still around to give Cal a hand with advice or whatever else needed doing.

Smoke had to take care of all the ranch's paper-work, though, and it seemed like the longer he lived, the more of that pestiferous stuff there was.

One of these days—and it wouldn't be that long from now if Smoke had his way—Louis would be wrangling all those papers, and Denny could make the decisions regarding the day-to-day running of the ranch. She was smart enough to rely heavily on a top hand like Cal, and Smoke knew his daughter's own instincts were good to start with.

That would leave Smoke and Sally free to enjoy life without any real responsibilities for the first time in years. They could ride up into the high country, just the two of them, along with their mounts and a packhorse, and spend some time surrounded by beautiful isolation.

He might even take an ax with him, Smoke mused, so he could fell some trees and build a small cabin by hand, just like in the old days. He was only in his fifties, still the prime of life as far as he was concerned, and could handle that without any problem.

As long as the world was big enough for him and Sally, that was plenty big enough as far as Smoke was concerned.

Fred Davis lived in a residential area a good dis-tance away from the capital and the businesses in the middle of town. Davis was a widower, Smoke knew, but the small house where he reined in was neatly kept, with flower beds in front of the porch even though they were empty at this time of year.

Smoke swung down from the saddle and wrapped the rental horse's reins around one of the gateposts.

The jowly, elderly man who opened the door to

Smoke's knock had thinning gray hair and wore a simple shirt and trousers with suspenders. A pair of spectacles had slid down on his nose until they seemed to perch at the very end of it. He looked over the top of them and said, "Yes, what can I do for—" He stopped short, pushed the spectacles up with one finger, and exclaimed, "Good Lord! Is it really . . . Smoke Jensen?"

"It is," Smoke replied with a grin. He had taken off his gloves as he waited for Davis to come to the door. He stuck out his right hand and went on, "It's been a long time, Fred."

"By God, it sure has!" Davis gripped Smoke's hand with the strength of a man who had hitched and un-hitched thousands of teams of stagecoach horses, and then the two of them roughly embraced and slapped each other on the back. "What in blazes are you doing here? Wait, never mind that right now. Come on in here out of the cold!"

Davis ushered Smoke into the house, which was as neat inside as it appeared from the outside. He took Smoke's hat and sheepskin jacket and hung them on a rack inside the door.

"There's coffee on the stove," he offered.

"With snow on the ground, this is a mighty good morning for it," Smoke agreed.

When the two men were sitting in the parlor with their coffee, Smoke in an armchair and Davis in a rocker, the older man said, "How many years has it been?"

"Since we shook and howdied? Ten, I'd say. And a little more than double that since I rode shotgun for you."

"You sure saved my bacon that time," Davis said. "Hell, you saved the whole hog! What brings you to Sacramento? Just passing through? I'm sure you didn't come all the way from Colorado just to see an old pelican like me."

"Well, I might have. We had some high old times back then that would be good to revisit." Smoke sipped his coffee. His expression grew more serious as he went on, "But to tell you the truth, Fred, I actually was just passing through, on my way home from San Francisco. You remember me mentioning my boy, Louis, in my letters, I'm sure. Well, he has some health problems, and we were seeing a doctor in San Francisco about them. His twin sister, Denise, is with us, too."

"Sorry to hear about the boy having trouble. Doesn't seem right, any son of Smoke Jensen not being as hale and hearty as his pa."

"Sickness doesn't care who you are or where you come from. It can ambush anybody."

Davis nodded solemnly and said, "Aye, that's true. It took my Emily without much warning."

"You know how sorry I am about that, Fred."

Davis waved a hand. "We don't need to make a gloomy day even darker. You said you were on your way home. Trying to get there before Christmas, I expect."

"That's right," Smoke said, "only we ran into trouble."

"Donner Pass."

"I'm not surprised you guessed it. You had to deal with it often enough during winters past."

"I surely did! Nothing more unpredictable than a Sierra Nevada snowstorm. I hadn't heard that the pass was closed, but I've been smelling snow in the air for the past couple of days."

"The telegraph lines are still up, or at least they were yesterday," Smoke said. "Word from the Summit Hotel is that an avalanche collapsed a long section of snowsheds and blocked the pass. Christmas will be over before it ever gets cleaned up enough for the trains to get through."

"So you can't get home to Sally. That's mighty bad luck, all right."

"It's not just Sally. My brothers and nephews are supposed to join us for the holiday."

"And now you're stuck in Sacramento, so you decided to pay a visit to an old man." Davis cocked his head a little to the side. "Don't try to fool me, Smoke. That's not the only reason you're here. You've got something else on your mind."

"I never thought for a second I could fool you, Fred," Smoke said with a smile. "What I've got in mind is the McCulley Cutoff."

Davis's bushy gray eyebrows rose. "Nobody uses that anymore. No need to."

"But it was a good road in its day. Better for stage-coaches than Dutch Flats ever was. The only reason the stage lines used Dutch Flats was because it was shorter and faster . . . when it wasn't covered up with snow."

Davis chuckled. "Always struck me as funny how the highest trail over the mountains got named after some flats, but that's the way it worked out. I'm sure you know there's no stagecoach running through the Sierra Nevadas anymore, not over Dutch Flats or McCulley or anywhere else."

"No . . . but there could be."

That left Davis frowning in puzzlement even more. "What are you getting at, Smoke? Spit it out, boy."

"You've got a stagecoach," Smoke said as he spread his hands. "I need to get to Reno."

Davis's eyebrows climbed higher this time. "You're talking about that old coach I couldn't bear to part with because I'm a foolish, sentimental old man?"

"I'd take good care of it and make arrangements for it to be brought back to you," Smoke promised.

"It's just been sitting in the barn out back for a couple of years. And I don't have a team."

"I can rent or buy a team. Fact is, I ought to have two teams, so I can switch them out and keep them fresh. There are no stage stations along the way to get relay teams."

"These days, there sure as blazes aren't." A calculating look appeared on Davis's weather-beaten face. He was starting to really consider the idea and not finding it as far fetched as he'd thought at first, Smoke told himself.

"You think it could be done, don't you?"

"Don't know. Probably been a lot of snow even on the cutoff, but it never was bad about drifting too much through there. If a man had two good sturdy teams and didn't get in too much of a hurry . . . You say you want to get to Reno?"

"By Christmas," Smoke said.

"You'd be cutting it close, but you might could do it. Not without a good driver, though."

"I can handle the teams."

Davis shook his head. "Under good conditions, you sure could. I don't doubt it for a second. But setting out across the Sierra Nevadas in the middle of winter, even on an easier route, would be plumb foolish without an experienced hand on the reins."

"You know where I can find one?"

"Happens that I do. You remember old Salty Stevens?"

The name brought back memories, all right, and surprised a question out of Smoke. "That old codger is still alive?"

"And kicking."

Smoke chuckled and said, "Well, he would be, if I recollect what Salty was like. He's here in Sacramento?"

"Yeah. He got into town a while back. I know because he came to see me. Of course, it wasn't just a social call. He wanted to borrow money. Sort of how you came looking for a favor today."

"You're right, Fred. If I hadn't been caught up in trying to get home before Christmas, I would've made time to stop and visit with you."

"Remember that next time," Davis said.

"What's old Salty been doing?" Smoke asked.

"He went up to Alaska, of all places, to hunt for gold. Ran into some gunfighter while he was there and partnered up with him for a while. The way Salty tells it, they had some wild times. The other fella had to go off on his own to take care of some business, though, and that left Salty by his lonesome again, so he decided to hunker down here for a while."

"In Sacramento?"

"He kept talking about how he wants to go on down to Mexico and spend the rest of his life there, but he ran out of time this year. He swears he'll get there next year, though."

"Salty was as good at handling a team as anybody I've ever seen," Smoke said. "But he's got to be getting on up in years by now."

Davis grunted. "Aren't we all? He doesn't seem like he's aged much since the last time I saw him, though, and I've got a hunch he can still do it. Plus, it would probably be a good idea to give the old rapscallion some honest work before he gets himself in trouble!" He leaned forward in the rocker and clasped his hands between his knees. "I'll make a deal with you. Get Salty to sign on as jehu, and you can have the loan of my stagecoach. He can even bring it back when you're done with it. I don't reckon he'd mind spending some time in Reno until the weather gets better. How does that sound to you?"

"It sounds like you've got a deal," Smoke said as he stood up. Davis got to his feet as well, and the two men shook hands again to seal the agreement.

Davis pointed over his shoulder with a thumb and said, "The coach is in the barn out back. I'll go over it and make sure everything is in top shape. When do you want to leave?"

"As soon as possible," Smoke said. "Which means I'd better go hunt up Salty right now. Do you know where I might be able to find him?"

"I can give you a pretty good idea," Davis said dryly. "There's a saloon not far from here called the Rusty Hinge. Salty spends a lot of time there."

"You reckon he'd be in a saloon this early in the day?"

"I'd say there's a good chance of it. He's sweet on a gal who works there."

It was Smoke's turn to lift his eyebrows. "He's still chasing women at his age?"

"You know Salty. He's always been determined to live up to his name!"

CHAPTER 14

Being the state capital, Sacramento was full of politicians and bureaucrats, or as Smoke thought of them, confidence men and paper pushers. They had their own places downtown where they drank.

The Rusty Hinge, however, was more the sort of drinking establishment where men who actually worked for a living congregated.

Even though it wasn't noon yet, the saloon had a good number of customers. Some of them gathered around the free lunch that was already set out at the end of the bar, while a poker game was going on at one of the tables and a roulette wheel had several players standing around watching it spin.

The wheel was being operated by a middle-aged woman who was still handsome and displayed signs of having been a real beauty in her youth. Her graying blond hair was done up on top of her head, and though her figure was a tad on the stout side, the dark blue gown she wore showed it off to her advantage.

Smoke recognized one of the men playing the wheel. He was short and scrawny, with long white hair and a white beard. The battered brown hat he wore had seen better days, with a permanently pushed-up brim that was a little ragged here and there. A fringed buckskin jacket over a cowhide vest and flannel shirt, patched jeans, and high-topped, moccasin-style boots completed his outfit.

Actually, Salty Stevens didn't look a day older than he had the last time Smoke saw him. He was one of those men who had always appeared older than he really was, up to a certain point, and then he just stayed at that point, seemingly as unchanging as the mountains.

"Let it ride, Eloise, honey," he was saying as Smoke stepped up beside him.

"Are you sure about that, Salty?" the blonde asked. "I think you've been pushing your luck on red."

"No, ma'am, it's gonna come up again," Salty insisted. "I can feel it in my bones, and there ain't nothin' I trust more than the feelin' in my bones."

"I trust his bones, too," Smoke said as he reached out and placed a twenty-dollar gold piece on red. He wasn't a man who normally gambled for enjoyment, but he could afford to risk a double eagle now and then.

Salty glanced over at him, curious who was betting the same as him. Then the old-timer looked again, sharply, and said, "Smoke? Can't be! Smoke Jensen?"

Smoke grinned at him and said, "That's right, Salty."

"Well, I'll be a ring-tailed horned toad!" Salty

grabbed Smoke's hand and pumped it enthusiastically. "Dadgum, son, it's good to see you!"

"You too. I'll admit, I was a little surprised when Fred Davis told me you were still alive."

"What sort of a thing is that to say to a fella? Durned right I'm still alive! Feelin' mighty spry, too. Even better now, seein' you again after all these years!"

One of the other players said, "Have your reunion some other time, pop. Some of us are here to win money."

"Keep your pants on, sonny," Salty snapped. "You don't know who this fella is."

"I don't care if he's Billy the Kid or Wild Bill Hickok come back to life." To the blonde, he added, "Spin the damn wheel, lady."

Salty's face flushed with obvious anger, and Smoke wondered if the blonde was the woman Davis had mentioned, the one Salty was sweet on. It seemed possible, given the old-timer's reaction to the other player's rude comment.

Salty was about to say something to the man when Eloise announced, "All bets are down. Here we go, gentlemen."

She spun the wheel.

Salty's eyes were drawn to the colorful blur of motion. All the men around the wheel watched it, including Smoke. There was something compelling about the motion and the uncertainty of its result.

The wheel slowed gradually as the little ball bounced, and after a few more turns, the ball gave a last hop and came to rest on one of the red spaces.

"I told you!" Salty exclaimed. "My bones always know where it's gonna wind up!"

The man who had complained a moment earlier let out a frustrated curse and thumped a fist on the edge of the table. He snapped, "Tell your bones to shut up, old man!"

"Take it easy, friend," Smoke told him. "It's not Salty's fault if you lost. Just bad luck. That's why they call it gambling."

"Nobody asked you to butt in either, mister. Keep your damn trap shut."

Salty said, "Best tread lightly there. You don't know who you're talkin' to."

The man thrust out an already pugnacious jaw. "You said that before, and I told you, I don't give a damn who he is." He turned to Eloise. "I just can't get a break today, can I? I've been losing steady, lady. Give me a chance next time, all right? Stop that wheel where I'll win for a change."

Eloise frowned. "What are you saying, mister?"

"Look, I know how these things work. That wheel's got a brake on it so you can stop it wherever you want. You've got it rigged so this old man wins every time. Who is he, your pa?"

"Why, you mouthy polecat!" Salty exploded. "Are you accusin' this here fine lady of cheatin'?"

The man sneered and said, "I'm saying nobody wins as much as you do without some help, grandpa."

Salty balled up his fists and took a step toward the man. "I ain't your damn grandpa. No son or daughter o' mine would ever spawn a whelp like you—"

The tirade was cut off abruptly by the meaty thud of fist against flesh as the man punched Salty in the jaw.

Smoke saw the blow coming and tried to get in

front of Salty to block it, but there wasn't time. The impact knocked Salty backward. Smoke was able to catch him and keep him from sprawling on the floor.

Then as Salty shook his head groggily, Smoke gave him a shove into the arms of the blonde and stepped up to meet the attack.

The man cursed him and said, "I'll teach you to mind your own business!"

"You hurt a friend of mine, and that makes it my business, mister," Smoke said.

The man snarled and threw another punch. His shoulders were heavy with muscle and the blow might have done some damage if it had landed.

But Smoke was cat-quick and weaved aside from the big fist. The miss made the man lose his balance. Smoke hooked a left into his ribs and then rocketed a straight right to the face. The impact shivered satisfyingly up his arm.

The man flung his arms out and went backward. Eloise gave a little scream as she clutched Salty and dragged him out of the way. The man struck the roulette table and fell onto it on his back.

Smoke figured that would finish the fight almost as quickly as it had begun. But his opponent was tough and put a hand on the table to shove himself back up. He shook his head to clear it of cobwebs and lunged at Smoke.

The man was surprisingly fast. He grabbed Smoke around the torso and tried to butt him in the face. Smoke jerked his head back to avoid that, but he couldn't stop the man's arms from locking around him with rib-crushing force. Smoke's hat flew off as the collision knocked him backward.

Boots driving against the sawdust-littered floor, Smoke braced himself and stopped the man from forcing him off his feet. He cupped his hands and smacked them against his opponent's ears.

That brought a howl of pain from the man and caused him to loosen his grip a little. Smoke hit him under the chin with a short, sizzling uppercut that made the man's head snap back like it was on a hinge. Smoke put both hands on his chest, shoved, and broke free.

The man couldn't get his arms up in time as Smoke hit him twice, a left and right that jerked his head first one way and then the other. Smoke bored in with a pair of punches to the body that rocked him even more.

Then a roundhouse right lifted the man off his feet and sent him flying. He crashed down on a table that broke under him and left him sprawled on the floor, tangled in debris. The man moaned but made no attempt to get up.

Smoke was breathing a little harder than he would have been after a fight like this twenty years earlier, but he felt good as he grinned, picked up his hat, and turned to Salty and Eloise, who stood beside the roulette wheel. Despite the man falling on it during the fight, the apparatus didn't seem to be damaged.

"Reckon that finishes that," Smoke said as he brushed sawdust off his hat and then put it on.

"It would have," Eloise said, "if Thad Stoermer's brothers weren't here."

Smoke saw that she was staring apprehensively at something behind him. He turned his head to look over his shoulder and saw three men who had been gathered around the free lunch platters when he came in.

Now they were advancing toward him with clenched fists and angry glares. Smoke saw the resemblance between them and realized their faces were very similar to the blood-smeared visage of the man he had just knocked out.

"Brothers?" he said.

"Yeah," Salty replied, gulping a little. "And they stick together."

The saloon's other customers started backing off, clearly wanting no part of what was about to happen. The bartender leaned over the hardwood and pleaded, "Boys, take it easy. You don't need to bust the place up."

The Stoermer brothers ignored him, and Smoke could tell from the bartender's nervous expression that the man wasn't going to do anything to put an end to the confrontation. Some aprons would have hauled out a sawed-off shotgun from under the bar or grabbed a bungstarter and waded into the fracas themselves, but not this one.

"Reckon it'd do any good to tell 'em who you are, Smoke?" Salty suggested tentatively.

"You can give it a try if you want." Honestly, though, Smoke didn't believe it would help.

Salty stepped forward and held up his hands as he raised his voice and said, "Hold on there, fellas. This here is Smoke Jensen, the fastest, deadliest gunfighter there ever was. They's been a bunch of dime novels written about him. You're bound to have read 'em."

"We ain't much on readin'," one of the brothers said.

"And he's an old man," added another.

"He ain't even packin' iron," the third put in.

The Stoermers weren't armed, as far as Smoke could tell. They were all stocky, beard-stubbled bruisers, but they didn't look like gunmen.

He reached behind his back and drew the .41-caliber Lightning, which officially had been dubbed the Thunderer by Colt, but most folks called it by the same name as its .38-caliber sibling. The Stoermers came to an abrupt halt at the sight of the double-action revolver.

"That ain't fair," one of the brothers protested. "We ain't got no guns."

"But you consider three to one to be fair odds," Smoke said with an edge of contempt in his voice.

"Three to two," Salty said as he stepped up beside Smoke. "You got into this mess because o' me. I ain't gonna let you face it by yourself."

Smoke laughed. "Salty, compared to a lot of the trouble you and I got ourselves into over the years, this isn't really much of a mess."

"Yeah, you're right about that." The old-timer grinned contemptuously at the Stoermers. "More like shooin' away some bothersome gnats."

"You talk mighty damn big, you old coot, when you've got a man standin' beside you with a gun in his hand!" one of the men yelled.

"Well," Smoke said with a reckless grin of his own, "we can do something about that."

He set the Lightning on the roulette table.

The gun was barely out of his hand when the Stoermer brothers charged.

CHAPTER 15

It was plumb foolishness to be getting mixed up in a saloon brawl at his age, Smoke thought as he braced himself to meet the attack.

But it was going to feel mighty good giving some swaggering bullies what they had coming to them.

The Stoermer brothers were used to winning fights on sheer strength and superior numbers. They were clumsy and had no technique. But one of their punches might take a man's head off if it landed right.

Smoke leaned away from the first one and snapped a jab to the nose of the man who had thrown it. It was a clean hit. Blood spurted hotly over Smoke's knuckles as cartilage crunched. The man howled and staggered back a couple of steps.

That made him bump into one of his brothers, and while they were trying not to get their feet tangled up, Smoke moved in and caught the second man with a left to the cheek, then sunk his right fist into his belly.

From the corner of his eye, Smoke saw Salty duck under an attempt by the third man to catch him in a bear hug. Quick as a flash, Salty got behind the man and leaped onto his back. He wrapped his legs around the man's waist, got his left arm around the man's neck, and started walloping him in the head with a bony right fist.

The man stumbled around, bellowing curses as he tried to throw Salty off.

The one whose nose Smoke had flattened had caught his balance by now. Despite the blood streaming from that damaged appendage, the man bored in and hammered a punch to Smoke's shoulder. The blow was aimed at Smoke's face, but he slipped aside just in time.

Even so, the punch packed enough power to rock him back a step and make his left arm go numb. He couldn't raise it to block the Stoermer brother's vicious follow-up. Smoke leaned away so that the iron-hard fist glanced off the side of his head. That was still enough of a jolt to set off red skyrockets behind his eyes.

The other man had recovered some, too. He circled to grab Smoke from behind and pin his arms.

"I'll hold him, Bart!" he yelled to his brother. "Pound the son of a bitch!"

The bloody-faced Bart closed in, fists cocked and ready to beat Smoke within an inch of his life.

He didn't get the chance. Smoke yanked both legs up and straightened them in a double-barreled mule kick that landed on Bart's chest and knocked him all the way to the wall on the other side of the saloon. The back of Bart's head thudded against the wall, and when he bounced off, he pitched forward to land on his face and didn't move again.

The kick also sent Smoke's would-be captor flying back the other way. The small of his back rammed against the bar, causing him to cry out in pain and lose his grip on Smoke.

Smoke's boots hit the floor. He had to take a second to catch his balance and gather himself, but when he had, he whirled around and brought a looping, thunderbolt right-hand punch with him. His fist crashed into the man's jaw. The powerful blow twisted his head so far it looked like it was about to pop off his neck.

The man's eyes rolled up in their sockets, and he went down like a pile of cow dung dropped off a shovel.

The feeling was back in Smoke's left arm. His knuckles ached a little, but otherwise he was fine. He turned to check on how Salty was doing and saw that the old jehu still clung to the remaining Stoermer brother's back, yelling like he was riding a bucking bronc as he battered his opponent with punches to the head.

Eloise was getting in on the fight, too. From somewhere, she had picked up one of the trays the saloon girls used to deliver drinks and was clouting the last of the brothers with it.

The man finally got hold of Salty, tore him loose, and flung him into Eloise. Both of them wound up lying on one of the tables. Before the man could go after them, Smoke caught hold of his shoulder, hauled him around, and delivered a punch that dropped him to his knees.

The man stayed there for a couple of seconds,

swaying back and forth like a tree trying to make up its mind whether to fall, then toppled over on his side and stayed there.

Salty scrambled off the table and helped Eloise to her feet. He had lost his hat during the fracas, and his long white hair was a wild tangle as he jerked his head back and forth, looking around for more enemies.

"Did we get all of 'em?" he asked Smoke. "Is that all o' the varmints?"

"That's all of them," Smoke said. Lightly, he rubbed the bruised knuckles of his right hand.

"Whooo-eee! That was a dandy fight! Best ruckus I've had in a month o' Sundays!" Salty reined in his exuberance and turned to Eloise with a worried frown. "Are you all right, darlin'?"

"I'm fine," she said as she brushed herself off and straightened her gown. "And I appreciate you defending my honor, Salty. But you really didn't have to."

"Durned right I did! That no-good polecat claimed you was cheatin'! I couldn't let him get away with that, no sirree."

She leaned toward him and kissed his leathery old cheek. That made him gawp and open and close his mouth like a fish.

"Aw . . . aw, shucks!" he managed to say.

"You sit down," Eloise told him. "I'll get you a cup of coffee from behind the bar."

"Well . . . all right. I'm obliged to you."

"It's the least I can do," she assured him.

Salty sat down while Smoke followed Eloise over to the bar. He took another double eagle from his pocket and slid it across the hardwood toward the bartender.

"For the damages," he told the man quietly.

"The Stoermers ought to pay for that," Eloise said.

"Maybe, but I think Salty and I got our money's worth in excitement," Smoke said with a smile. "I'll bet he feels younger right now than he has in quite a spell."

"You're probably right about that." She looked around and smiled fondly in Salty's direction, then told the bartender, "Hank, get me a cup of coffee, all right?"

"Sure, Eloise," the man said. He went through a door behind the bar to what was probably a small kitchen where a coffeepot would be sitting on the stove.

While the bartender was gone, Smoke said in a voice so quiet only Eloise could hear him, "You do have a brake on that wheel, don't you?"

She darted a nervous glance toward him. "What makes you say that?"

"I saw the little move you made with your foot on that last spin, just before the wheel stopped. There was a little hitch in the wheel just then while it was turning, too. Then the ball landed on red for Salty."

"Look, don't say anything, all right, mister?" she asked, her voice scared now. "I don't want to lose this job. Anyway, is it really that bad when you're just trying to help an old-timer feel better about himself?"

"Is that what you were doing?"

"You don't think I was getting anything out of it for myself, do you?" Eloise sounded a little offended by the idea. "Salty started coming around a while back, and he was so sweet. I could tell he was smitten by me. But he's terrible at roulette."

"Is he?" Smoke said.

"One of the worst I've ever seen. I don't know how much money he has, but he would have wound up broke if he kept going the way he was. The worst part about it was that I could tell he was just doing it trying to impress me."

"So you made sure he started to win."

"Not all the time," Eloise said quickly. "And not a fortune, either. Just enough to keep him breaking even, or maybe making a little."

"And your boss doesn't know about this."

"Oh, Lord, no. Look, Mr. Jensen, most of the time I run an honest game. I'm only supposed to . . . help the odds a little . . . if it looks like somebody's going on a really lucky streak that might cost the place a significant amount of money. That's it."

Smoke nodded as the bartender returned with the cup of coffee for Salty. Eloise started to turn away from the bar, but Smoke stopped her by saying, "You don't feel the same way about Salty that he does about you, do you?"

"Well . . . not really. But I like him. I think he's a very sweet old man."

"I wouldn't want to see him hurt."

"And I'd never hurt him," she insisted.

"I reckon we see eye to eye on that, then," Smoke said. "You might not have to worry about his roulette skills much longer, either."

"What does *that* mean?"

"I'm going to offer him a job."

Eloise frowned in puzzlement, but she didn't ask Smoke anything else. She carried the coffee over to the table and set it in front of Salty.

"There you go, hon."

"I'm much obliged to you," the old-timer said. "Smoke, why don't you join me?"

Smoke pulled back an empty chair at the table, sat down, and said, "Actually, I was hoping you'd join me."

Salty took a sip of the coffee, smacked his lips over it, and said, "Eh?"

"I've got a proposition for you, Salty. I need a top-hand stagecoach driver, and I don't reckon I'd find a better one if I looked all the way from the Rio Grande to the Milk River."

"You need a stagecoach driver? What in tarnation for?"

"Why, to drive a stagecoach, of course. Specifically, Fred Davis's old stagecoach, which he's agreed to loan to me if you'll agree to handle the teams. Seems like he trusts you to bring the coach back safely."

"Well, I should hope to smile he does! I drove hundreds o' runs for ol' Fred's lines and never lost a coach, a passenger, a mail pouch, or even a horse! But what in blazes do you need a stagecoach for, Smoke?"

Smoke had to wait a minute to answer that question because the Stoermer brothers were regaining consciousness. Their moans and groans and curses created quite a racket.

The one called Thad, the first one Smoke had clashed with, got to his feet first and helped one of his brothers up. Then they got the remaining two onto unsteady feet.

Smoke stood; picked up the Colt Lightning from the roulette table, where it still lay; and turned to face the brothers.

Bart, the one with the broken nose and bloody face, held up his hands.

"No more, mister, no more," he declared. "We're done here. We just want to go on our way without any more trouble."

"Fine by me," Smoke said with a curt nod. He didn't return the revolver to his waistband at the small of his back until all four of the Stoermers had stumbled out of the Rusty Hinge, though.

Then he sat down again and told Salty about how Donner Pass was blocked by an avalanche and how he had come up with the idea of taking a stagecoach around the McCulley Cutoff to Reno so he, Denny, and Louis could meet Sally and the others there for Christmas.

"The McCulley Cutoff, eh?" Salty scratched at his beard as he frowned in thought. "I didn't figure anybody ever used that old trail anymore. You reckon it's still in good enough shape for a stagecoach?"

"There's only one way to find out," Smoke said. "I suggested I could drive the coach myself, but Fred wanted a more experienced hand at the reins."

"When it comes to handlin' a six-horse hitch, there ain't nobody more experienced than me!" Salty blinked as a thought occurred to him. "Where you gonna get the horses? You'll need two teams, so's you can switch 'em out."

"I thought the same thing. You know horseflesh, and Fred can probably help us locate some animals, too. I'll rent them, or buy them if I have to."

"You'd spend that much just to meet up with your family for Christmas?"

"The holiday means a lot to Sally," Smoke said. "I don't want to disappoint her if I can help it.

"How about it, Salty? One last stagecoach run through the Sierra Nevadas?"

The old-timer drew in a deep breath, then blew it out and nodded. He thrust a knobby-knuckled hand across the table to shake with Smoke.

"Some people'd say we're plumb crazy to try it," he said, "but I reckon it's time I done somethin' plumb crazy again!"

CHAPTER 16

It looked like they would be staying another night in Sacramento, which would make the time remaining to reach Reno before Christmas that much shorter. But finding enough reliable, sturdy horses to make up two stagecoach teams was a lengthy process, even with the help of Fred Davis and Salty Stevens, and it had to be done.

Smoke's wealth helped, because he wound up having to buy all the livestock. Fred Davis could sell them for him once Salty got back to Sacramento with the coach.

The stock included a couple of good saddle mounts for Smoke and Denny. They might need those mounts if any of the coach horses got scattered for some reason and had to be rounded up.

Smoke could tell that Denny wouldn't really mind if that happened. She was always on the lookout for some sort of adventure.

She came by that honestly, too.

During the busy afternoon, Smoke managed to

swing by the telegraph office and send a wire to Sally explaining the plan and asking her to meet him in Reno for Christmas.

When he got back to the hotel that evening, after making all the arrangements to have the horses brought to Fred Davis's house first thing the next morning, he found her reply waiting for him.

Some wives would have chided their husbands for coming up with such a scheme, would have called them reckless, foolhardy, even harebrained. Sally Jensen had never been a typical wife.

A GRAND AND DARING JOURNEY STOP
WILL SEE YOU IN RENO STOP LOVE TO
DENISE LOUIS AND MY DARLING
HUSBAND STOP MERRY CHRISTMAS STOP

Smoke grinned as he read the telegram. He knew that if Sally said she would be there in Reno, he could count on it. Now all he had to do was complete his part of the trip.

He was having dinner in the hotel's dining room with Denny and Louis that evening when one of the waiters approached him with a folded piece of paper.

"A boy just delivered this message for you, Mr. Jensen," the man said as he held out the paper.

Smoke took it and reached for his pocket to pull out a coin, but the man shook his head and gestured for him not to do that.

"Not necessary," the waiter said. "My boy is a loyal reader of the dime novels about you. I hate to think about how many coins he's put in the pockets of Mr. Beadle and Mr. Adams!"

"And those publisher fellas keep those dimes and don't give a penny to me," Smoke responded with a grin. "Doesn't hardly seem fair, does it?"

"No, indeed. But I was wondering . . . perhaps I could prevail upon you to sign one of them for him . . . ?"

"You know I don't write them, don't you?"

"Of course, sir. But you *are* the dashing hero whose exploits fill their pages."

Smoke chuckled. "Sure, I'll sign one of them. First time I ever recall anybody asking me to do that."

"I'll stop by your room later this evening, if that's all right."

"Sure," Smoke said.

With that taken care of, the waiter left and Smoke unfolded the paper. A frown creased his forehead as he read the scrawled words.

"What's wrong, Father?" Denny asked. When they were out on the range, or when she was excited or upset about something, she called Smoke "Pa." In more elegant, genteel surroundings like this hotel dining room, however, he was "Father."

Smoke tapped a fingertip against the paper and said, "This note is from Salty. Says he needs to see me. Some problem with the stagecoach."

"Oh, no," Denny said. "Once I got used to the idea, I started looking forward to this trip."

Louis said dryly, "You're just hoping for some excitement."

Smoke said, "Getting across the Sierra Nevadas in a stagecoach in the middle of winter will be enough excitement all by itself. Salty says for me to pick him up at the Rusty Hinge and we'll go on out to Davis's place."

"Are you going to?" Denny asked.

"Reckon I'd better see what it's all about," Smoke replied with a shrug.

He had finished his supper anyway, so he laid his napkin aside and stood up.

"You two take your time," he told his children. "If I don't see you later tonight, be ready to leave early tomorrow morning. We can't afford to lollygag around here in Sacramento any longer than we have to."

"We'll be ready," Denny promised.

Smoke had left his hat and the Colt up in the room when he came down to supper, so he made a quick trip up there to retrieve them and his sheepskin jacket before he left the hotel.

He hadn't expected to need a saddle mount again tonight, so he had left the horse he'd rented at the livery stable. When he stopped there now, he found that the same horse was in its stall, so he paid the hostler to use the animal again.

He rode to the Rusty Hinge. The streets in this part of town were hard-packed dirt, not cobblestone or brick, and enough snow remained on the ground to muffle the horse's hoofbeats as Smoke approached the Rusty Hinge.

His eyes narrowed as he saw a flash of movement up ahead. Someone had leaned out of the dark mouth of an alley beside the saloon, then pulled back quickly into the shadows.

Several thoughts flashed through Smoke's mind in rapid succession. Plenty of times in his life, enemies had tried to ambush him. The warning bells

going off in his brain told him this might well be another of those bushwhack attempts.

He was here tonight only because of that note
from Salty he had received. Maybe the note was genuine, but more than likely it wasn't. Smoke knew he
could trust Salty, but it was possible the old-timer had
been forced into being the bait in a trap. If that was
the case, it meant Salty was probably in danger.

The rented horse had drawn even with the alley
mouth while Smoke was thinking these things. Earlier, when he had shrugged into the sheepskin jacket
in the hotel room, he had tucked the Lightning into
the waistband at the front of his jeans, where it would
be easy to get to. His hand closed around the revolver's butt.

The alley was to his left. Smoke heard shoe leather
scrape on the ground from that direction and flung
himself out of the saddle to the right as he yanked
the gun free.

A shotgun boomed from the alley, along with the
crash of a couple of revolvers. Garish orange muzzle
flame bloomed in the darkness.

The rented horse screamed and bolted ahead.
Smoke hit the ground and put his left hand down to
catch himself and power into a roll. He came up on
one knee, facing the alley, with the Lightning thrust
out in front of him.

More Colt flame spurted from the shadows. Smoke
felt the wind-rip of a slug passing close to his face. He
triggered a return shot. Another muzzle flash. A bullet
thudded into the ground just to his left. He fired
again.

Echoes of the gunfire filled the street, but Smoke's

keen ears heard a familiar clank and recognized it as the sound of a double-barreled shotgun being closed after reloading. He aimed toward that sound and blasted two more rounds into the alley.

The shotgun clattered to the ground before the man wielding it could pull the triggers. Its twin barrels poked from the shadows. A man yelled a curse as he emerged from the alley, scooped the shotgun from the ground, and lunged toward Smoke.

With only a split second to save himself from a deadly blast, Smoke put a bullet in the man's head. In the bad light, it was a remarkable shot, but no more impressive than many other shots Smoke Jensen had made.

The would-be killer's head jerked back. He dropped the shotgun and spun off his feet.

Smoke had one bullet remaining in the gun. He waited to see if he needed to use it.

But the alley was dark and silent now as the gun thunder gradually faded away.

Then a raspy voice called thickly, "Smoke! Smoke, you all right, boy?"

That was Salty. The words came from farther back in the alley. Smoke straightened to his feet and took a step in that direction, the Colt still ready in his right fist.

"Are they all down, Salty?" he asked.

"Yeah, you plumb ventilated the whole bunch. But be careful! I ain't sure all the skunks are dead. Lord have mercy, that was some shootin', Smoke!"

As he stepped into the alley past the body of the man he had shot in the head, Smoke used his left hand to take a match from the shirt pocket where he usually carried several of them. He struck it on the wall and held it up so the yellow glare filled the narrow passage.

Three more bodies littered the dirty ground. None of them moved. Two were lying facedown. The other man was on his back. Smoke recognized him as Thad Stoermer, the one who had taken offense to losing at roulette and accused Eloise of cheating.

That meant the other three were the remaining Stoermer brothers. Smoke held the Colt ready and used the toe of his boot to roll them onto their backs. The eyes of all three men glittered lifelessly in the light from the match.

Satisfied that the ambushers were no longer a threat, Smoke went quickly to Salty, who sat with his back propped up against the wall of the building that housed the Rusty Hinge.

The old-timer's ankles were tied, and judging by the way his arms were pulled back in what had to be a painful position, his wrists were lashed together behind him.

A rolled-up bandanna was around Salty's neck, and a wadded-up piece of cloth lay on the old-timer's chest. Smoke figured the Stoermer brothers had gagged Salty to prevent him from shouting a warning about the ambush, after taking him prisoner and tying him up.

The match was about to burn down to Smoke's fingers, so he dropped it and lit another one before he knelt beside Salty.

The old man said in a miserable voice, "Lord, I'm sorry, Smoke! You don't know how sorry I am. The damn sorry buzzards didn't give me no choice!"

By now the gunfire had drawn people from the saloon. Several of them clustered at the alley mouth. A man called, "What the hell's going on here?"

Another exclaimed, "It's the Stoermer brothers! They're all dead!"

Smoke ignored them and said to Salty, "Are you hurt?"

"Naw. They pushed me around a mite, but they didn't do any real damage. They said they was gonna cut my throat, though, once they'd bushwhacked and killed you. No good sons o' bitches couldn't stand the thought that we'd whipped 'em. They . . . they grabbed me and said if I didn't write that note to you, they'd kill Eloise. I couldn't let that happen, Smoke!"

"Of course you couldn't," Smoke said as he put the gun away and pulled a Barlow knife from his pocket. He opened it with his teeth and used the razor-sharp blade to cut the ropes around Salty's ankles. Then the old-timer leaned forward and Smoke cut the bonds around his wrists as well.

The glow from a lantern filled the alley. A uniformed policeman held up the light and came toward Smoke and Salty as Smoke helped the jehu to his feet. A couple more officers examined the bodies of the Stoermer brothers.

"Ye gads, what a massacre," the policeman with the lantern said. He put his other hand on the butt of his holstered revolver as he glared at Smoke. "Are you responsible for this, mister?"

"Hold on there!" Salty said. "This here is Smoke Jensen, and those varmints tried to bushwhack him!"

"This ain't the Wild West anymore, old-timer," the officer said. "We don't have gunfights in the streets."

"And I don't cotton to doing nothing while somebody tries to kill me," Smoke said coolly. "Those men assaulted and kidnapped my friend here, threatened to murder a woman, and very nearly shot me. So I think whatever happened to them, they had it coming."

"Wait a minute. There are four of them and just one of you. Are you sayin' you gunned down all of them while they were shooting at you?"

"I told you," Salty said, "he's Smoke Jensen."

"Well, I never heard of . . . Wait a minute. There used to be some famous gunfighter named Jensen."

Salty crossed his arms over his chest, nodded emphatically, and said, "Durned tootin'. This is him."

The policeman sighed and said, "All right, Jesse James. Come along, both of you. There's going to be lots of questions that need answering, so we might as well get started."

CHAPTER 17

Eloise was among the curious crowd that had gathered in front of the Rusty Hinge. When she saw Salty come out of the alley, she threw her arms around him, hugged him, and cried, "Oh my God, Salty, are you all right?"

"A whole heap better now," Salty replied, beaming, "but if you was to hug me a mite tighter, it'd probably help some."

"What?" She drew back, frowned, then said, "Oh, you!" But she laughed and hugged him again, just like he asked.

Smoke started walking along the street, causing the policeman with the lantern to say, "Hey, you! I told you, I've got questions to ask you."

"Then come along with me and ask 'em," Smoke said. "I'm responsible for the horse I was riding, and I want to make sure it wasn't hurt too badly."

The exasperated officer followed him, and Smoke was glad for the lantern light. It helped him locate the rented horse, which had stopped about a hundred yards along the road.

The still-spooked animal tried to shy away, but Smoke was a top hand when it came to horses. He spoke softly in a calm, soothing voice and soon had hold of the horse's headstall.

"Bring that light closer," Smoke told the officer. He pointed to a red streak on the horse's rump that was visible in the lantern's glow. "Either a bullet or a piece of buckshot grazed him when those boys threw down on me. You can see it's a fresh injury. I reckon that proves my story about them shooting at me first."

"Maybe," the policeman admitted grudgingly. "Or maybe they were just shootin' back at you after you attacked them."

"You said yourself there were four of them and one of me. Do you believe I'd deliberately go after four armed men?"

Of course, that was exactly the sort of thing Smoke would—and had—done many times in the past. But the policeman didn't know that, so he shrugged and said, "It ain't very likely, I guess."

With Smoke leading the horse, they returned to the saloon. The other officers were standing there keeping the morbidly curious bystanders away from the corpses. One of the uniformed men said, "We've already sent for the wagon, Sarge."

The man with the lantern grunted and said, "Good." He jerked his head toward the door and told Smoke, "Let's go inside out of the cold air."

Once in the saloon, Salty and Eloise joined them,

and it didn't take long to lay out the whole story for the police sergeant. When they were finished, the officer told Smoke, "It sounds like you're not going to be in any trouble for this, since it's a pretty clear case of self-defense, but you'll have to stay in town for the coroner's inquest."

"Sorry," Smoke said. "Salty and I are leaving for Reno first thing in the morning."

"You can't do that," the sergeant insisted. "Not only is there the matter of the inquest, but I've heard that the pass through the mountains is closed. The train can't get through."

Salty grinned and said, "We ain't takin' the train. We're takin' a stagecoach around the old McCulley Cutoff!"

The officer stared at him as if Salty had lost his mind. Smoke said, "We'll write out official statements and swear to them, Sergeant. Any more questions can be referred to my attorney in San Francisco, Claudius Turnbuckle."

The officer didn't like that, but he agreed to pass the information along to his captain.

"I may get in trouble for not taking you into custody," he said, "but it's pretty obvious you didn't do anything except defend yourself from four would-be murderers. The coroner's jury will likely see it the same way."

Salty said, "If anybody needs to talk to Smoke later, they won't have no trouble findin' him. He's just the owner of one o' the biggest ranches in Colorado, after all!"

"Well, the law's the same for him as it is for anybody else." The sergeant paused. "But if I'm bein' honest, I can't say that I'll get too worked up about somebody ridding these parts of those damn Stoermer brothers. They've been in trouble with the law plenty of times, and even though we were never able to pin any of it on them, it's likely they were mixed up in plenty of strong-arm stuff. Robberies, a protection racket, and even a few killin's. So you've done the neighborhood a favor, Jensen."

"I was just trying not to collect any bullet holes in my hide," Smoke said.

There was nothing wrong with the stagecoach currently sitting in Fred Davis's barn. The note that had been delivered to Smoke at the hotel was pure fiction, dictated to Salty by one of the Stoermer brothers while they held him at gunpoint.

Even that, along with more roughing up than Salty would admit to, hadn't been enough to get the old-timer to cooperate. He hadn't given his captors what they wanted until they had threatened to kill Eloise.

"I knew they'd do it, too," Salty told Smoke later, after the police sergeant was gone. He looked toward the bar, where the blonde was talking to the bartender. "As for some o' the other things they said they'd do to her first . . . well, I ain't ever gonna talk about that, and I sure as shootin' won't tell her. But even so, I feel like I done let you down, Smoke."

"Don't give that another thought," Smoke said. "I would have done the same thing if I'd been in your place, if someone was threatening Sally."

"Yeah, maybe. But more'n likely, you would've found some way to turn the tables on those bastards and kill 'em all before it ever got that far."

That was exactly what Smoke would have tried to do, but there was no way of knowing how that would have worked out, so he didn't see any point in dwelling on it.

He said his good nights to Salty and Eloise, once she had returned to the table, then told Salty they would meet at Fred Davis's place at eight o'clock the next morning.

Smoke rode back toward the hotel, stopping a few blocks away at the livery stable to return the horse.

"There was a little bit of trouble," he told the hostler as he pointed out the minor wound on the horse's rump. "You'll want to daub something on that, but it ought to heal up just fine."

"I dunno, mister," the hostler said as he scratched his head. "That's extra trouble, and the owner's liable to be upset, you bringin' back a mount injured this way. . . ."

Smoke handed the man a five-dollar gold piece.

"You reckon that'll soothe the owner's feelings and cover your extra trouble?"

The coin disappeared instantly into a pocket of the man's overalls. Smoke knew the owner would never see any of the money. The hostler said, "Oh, yeah, I reckon that'll make everything just fine."

It would be nice if every problem in life could be taken care of so easily, Smoke mused as he walked the remaining short distance to the hotel.

When he walked into the lobby, he was surprised to see Louis sitting in one of the chairs with a folded newspaper in his lap. Louis stood up and moved to meet him.

"What was wrong with the stagecoach?" Louis asked.

"Nothing," Smoke replied with a shake of his head. He hadn't told Louis and Denny about the earlier brawl with the Stoermer brothers, and neither of them had seemed to notice his bruised knuckles. Explaining what had happened tonight would take too long right now, he decided. He could tell them about it later. "Just a misunderstanding. What are you doing still up? I figured you would have turned in by now."

"I thought you might like to see the late afternoon edition," Louis said as he held out the newspaper.

Smoke took the paper and scanned the headlines, his eyes stopping at one that read: LEGENDARY PISTOLEER TO UNDERTAKE EPIC STAGECOACH JOURNEY—NOTORIOUS GUNFIGHTER RISKING LIFE AND LIMB TO CELEBRATE CHRISTMAS WITH FAMILY—HISTORIC CROSSING OF THE SIERRA NEVADAS IN WINTER. Each succeeding section was in slightly smaller type. Below them in dense print was the story.

> Smoke Jensen, the hero of a thousand fights and fast-draw artist par excellence, who at various stages of his checkered career as a Westerner and frontiersman has been both outlaw and lawman and is now one of the leading cattle barons of Colorado, has come to Sacramento to embark upon an unheard of journey across the majestic mountains that form the veritable spine of the great Golden

State. Mr. Jensen, accompanied by his grown children, Mr. Louis Arthur Jensen and Miss Denise Nicole Jensen, will attempt to travel from this fair city to the bustling settlement of Reno, Nevada, by the outdated conveyance known as a stagecoach.

Such stagecoaches, now rendered all but obsolete by the glittering steel network of the railroads, once traversed trails far and wide across the West, but no one uses them in these more modern times. Mr. Jensen's perilous attempt is motivated by the desire for he and his children to reunite with his wife in time for Christmas, with the rendezvous to take place in Reno, which is approximately halfway between here and Mr. Jensen's sprawling ranch, known as the Sugarloaf, located near the town of Big Rock, Colorado.

The wisdom of such an undertaking is open to great debate, given the current uncertain state of the weather and the arduous conditions under which the stagecoach will be forced to travel. Two nights previous to this, a great blizzard precipitated an avalanche in Donner Pass that inflicted great damage to the railroad tracks and blocked the pass. It will be several weeks before trains will be able to travel through the pass, at the very earliest.

Mr. Jensen claims to know of another route and has accordingly arranged for the use of a stagecoach belonging to Mr. Frederick C. Davis, formerly a successful operator of several stage lines. Mr. Jensen has also engaged the

services of an experienced driver for said
stagecoach.

It remains to be seen whether such an am-
bitious undertaking can be concluded suc-
cessfully, but this reporter intends to travel
with Mr. Jensen and his family members on
the historic journey in order to maintain a
journal and produce a volume telling the story
of this adventure, in the great literary tradition
of Mr. Mark Twain's "Roughing It" and other
such stirring tales.—Peter Stansfield.

Smoke's grip on the newspaper had tightened as
he read. He was breathing a little harder by the time
he finished, but from anger, not exertion.

Louis said, "I can tell you're not pleased, Father."

"Not pleased is putting it pretty mildly." Smoke
rolled up the newspaper and smacked it against the
palm of his left hand. "How in blazes did that scrib-
bler find out about this?"

"And perhaps more importantly, do you intend to
allow him to come with us?"

"Not hardly," Smoke snapped.

"How are you going to stop him?"

"It's a private coach, or what amounts to it," Smoke
pointed out. "It's not like when Fred Davis or anybody
else was running a regular stage line, where folks who
could afford to buy a ticket had a right to ride. I can
tell this persistent varmint Stansfield to—"

Smoke stopped short, since he wasn't inclined to engage in language that was too colorful or profane . . .
and that was certainly what he was feeling at the moment.

"You can tell him that, of course," Louis agreed, "but if you do, he's just going to write more newspaper stories that make you look bad."

Smoke snorted. "You reckon I care about that?"

"I know you don't. But Mother might."

"Your mother would tell him to go climb a stump. And then she'd grab a shotgun and threaten to dust his butt with birdshot if he didn't leave us alone."

"It's a new century," Louis argued. "Some would say a whole new world. The newspapers reach a lot more people than they used to. They mold public opinion." He gestured toward the paper still clutched in Smoke's hand. "In that story, he paints you two different ways. He calls you a hero . . . but he refers to you as notorious as well. He makes you sound like a good family man, but he points out that you were once considered an outlaw, too."

"That was a long time ago," Smoke said.

"Very true, but does the average reader of this newspaper know that? And it's certainly possible that the story will be picked up and run in other places in the country as well. It could spread all the way to the East Coast."

"Like I said before, I don't care."

"Read between the lines," Louis said, "and you can see where Stansfield makes it sound like this is going to be a very dangerous trip. He all but says that you're putting your children's lives at risk unnecessarily. I hate to say it, Father, but that's not good for business. And since you want me to handle that end of the ranch's operation at some point, I'd like to think that you'd give my opinion some weight."

"Are you saying you think I don't trust you?"

"I'm saying if you let this reporter come along, then he'll see what sort of man you really are, and that's what he'll write in the future." Louis shrugged. "It really can't hurt anything."

Smoke wasn't so sure about that. But Louis was right about one thing: if Smoke was going to put his faith in the youngster to handle the ranch's business affairs, he had to learn how to pay attention to him.

Smoke brandished the newspaper and said, "Stansfield says he wants to come with us, but he hasn't shown up and asked me yet. If he does before we leave in the morning, I'll think about it. But if he's late, I won't wait for him. As soon as that team gets there and we've got them hitched up, that stagecoach is rolling for Reno!"

CHAPTER 18

Smoke was up early the next morning and made sure that Denny and Louis were, too. After coffee and breakfast in the hotel dining room, Smoke had all their bags loaded onto a buckboard to be taken to Fred Davis's house, where they would be placed in the canvas-covered boot on the back of the stagecoach.

Louis looked askance at Denny's outfit as they stood near the hotel entrance, waiting to leave. She wore boots, jeans, a flannel shirt, and a sheepskin jacket. Her long, curly blond hair was tucked up under a brown Stetson.

"You and Father look more like twins than you and I do, at least in your attire," he said. "What possessed you to bring along such garb on a trip to San Francisco?"

"You never know when you might need to do some riding," Denny said. She smiled. "I left my gun belt and Colt in one of my bags, but I can get them out and wear them, too, if you think I ought to."

Louis held up a hand and said, "No, no, that's all right. I don't expect you'll need to be armed."

"The time you think you don't need a gun might be the time when you need it the most."

"Yes, you *sound* like Father, too."

"I'll take that as a compliment."

Louis shrugged and said, "As well you should." He sighed. "There are times I wish that *I* reminded people of Father. Perhaps then he wouldn't be disappointed in me."

Denny frowned and told her brother, "I've never once heard him say to anybody that he's disappointed in you. Not ever, as far back as I can remember."

"Maybe not, but he has to feel that way sometimes, don't you think?"

"Not for a second," Denny said. "You need to put that kind of thinking out of your head. And for damn sure, don't ever say it where he can hear it." She nodded across the lobby. "Here he comes."

Smoke was indeed striding toward them. If he noticed the solemn looks on the faces of his children, he gave no sign of it. He grinned and said, "Ready to go?"

"We sure are," Denny said. "Isn't that right, Louis?"

"Absolutely," he replied. "We're setting off on a grand adventure."

"I've had more than my share of adventures," Smoke said. "I just want to make it to Reno in time for Christmas with the rest of the family."

Smoke checked his watch after they had climbed into a waiting carriage in front of the hotel. He wanted to be away from Davis's place by eight o'clock, and they were on schedule to accomplish that.

There had been a few breaks in the clouds over Sacramento the day before, allowing shafts of sunlight through, but the sky was completely overcast again this morning and a chilly breeze swept over the capital city.

To the east, above the Sierra Nevada Mountains, thick, dark clouds still roiled and clustered, at times taking on the sinister aspect of a black-fanged mouth looming wide and waiting to close on unwary travelers. No snow fell over the city this morning, but Smoke had a hunch it might still be coming down heavily in the mountains.

Before the carriage's driver could flap the reins and get his team moving, a woman came out of the hotel and hurried over to the vehicle. She placed a gloved hand on the sill of the window beside Smoke and said, "Mr. Jensen! Could I talk to you for a moment, please? It's very important."

Louis was sitting on Smoke's other side. He leaned forward, looked past his father, and said, "Mrs. Buckner? Is that you?"

The name jogged Smoke's memory. This nice-looking young woman was the mother of that talkative boy Brad. He nodded politely and said, "Mornin', Mrs. Buckner. I'm sorry, but we're in kind of a hurry—"

"Just a minute of your time," the woman said. "Please."

Smoke was too much of a gentleman to be rude. He called up to the driver, "Hold on for now," then asked Mrs. Buckner, "What can I do for you?"

"Take Bradley and me to Reno on that stagecoach with you," she answered bluntly.

Smoke had had no idea what the woman wanted,

but he wouldn't have guessed she'd make that request. He started to ask her how she knew what their plan was, but then he realized what must have happened.

"You saw that newspaper story, didn't you?"

"Yes, and it was like . . . deliverance. My son and I really need to get to Reno, Mr. Jensen. My mother lives there and is very ill. This will almost certainly be her last Christmas. She wrote to me and asked me to come see her, and to bring Bradley with me. She . . . she's never met him, you see."

"Never met him?" Smoke repeated. "The boy's got to be at least eight years old."

"He is indeed eight. But when I married his father, my mother greatly disapproved of the match. She said I was too young . . . only fifteen . . . and . . . well, she wasn't fond of my late husband. She thought he was too wild and reckless. She said that if I insisted on marrying him, she wouldn't have anything more to do with me. So I haven't see her since then, and she's never seen Bradley, and now she . . . she's dying, and . . ."

The words had come out of Melanie Buckner's mouth in a rush, but now they trailed off and tears began to roll down her cheeks. Louis quickly took out his handkerchief and leaned past Smoke to hand it to her.

"Here, Mrs. Buckner," he said. "Please don't worry. I'm sure everything will be all right."

She managed a weak smile as she took the handkerchief and dabbed at the tears.

"Thank you, sir."

"Louis," he reminded her. "My name is Louis."

"Ma'am, I'm sorry," Smoke began, "but I hadn't intended on taking anybody else with us on this trip—"

"Why not?" Louis said. "Oh, I understand why you don't want that annoying reporter along, but surely it wouldn't cause any problem to provide some humanitarian assistance to Mrs. Buckner and her son."

"This might not be an easy trip. We're talking about several days in a stagecoach, and we won't know what sort of shape the trail is in until we get there. The weather could be pretty rough, too."

"I'm willing to risk all that, Mr. Jensen," Melanie said, "to see my mother again and especially to make sure Bradley knows her before she's gone."

Smoke frowned. He'd been honest when he told Melanie of the dangers inherent in this journey, but at the same time, if he didn't believe they could make it through, he wouldn't be setting out with Denny and Louis accompanying him.

"We won't be able to take it easy," he warned. "We'll be setting a fast pace."

The young woman summoned up a smile. "I want to reach Reno before Christmas just as much as you do, Mr. Jensen."

Smoke glanced across at Denny, on the opposite seat of the carriage, but couldn't read her expression to tell whether she approved or disapproved of the idea.

His first instinct was to refuse Melanie Buckner's plea. At the same time, he recognized the genuine suffering in her eyes. He wasn't in the habit of turning his back on folks who needed help.

"All right," he said, reaching a decision. "You can

come with us, ma'am, but only if you can get ready pretty quick-like. We need to get started."

A brilliant smile appeared on Melanie's face. She said, "I can be ready very quickly, Mr. Jensen. I already packed, because I had faith in you. I just need to get Bradley and our bags. I'll be back in five minutes! Maybe less!"

She turned and hurried back into the hotel, leaving Smoke with a rueful smile on his face. He had never been the sort to second-guess himself, but this was one of those rare occasions when he hoped he had done the right thing.

As soon as Melanie had disappeared into the building, Denny leaned forward and punched Louis in the shoulder.

"You hypocrite!" she said. "Humanitarian assistance, my hind foot! You just want us to take that woman along because she's a widow and you think she's pretty!"

"Denise, you wound me deeply," Louis said with a grin. "The only thing I feel for that poor woman is compassion. You heard her story."

"Yes, and it was like something out of a cheap melodrama. How do you know she wasn't lying and has some other reason for needing to get to Reno?"

Smoke commented, "It seemed to me that she was telling the truth."

"Well . . . maybe," Denny admitted, clearly not wanting to question her father's judgment. "But that doesn't change the fact that Louis has his eye on her."

"I have a bad heart, remember?" Louis said.

Denny scoffed and said, "That never stopped you from chasing half the girls in Europe, once you got old enough to figure out they were different from boys."

"Mrs. Buckner is older than me," Louis pointed out. "She has an eight-year-old son, after all."

"And if she had him when she was fifteen, that would make her just two years older than us. Two years doesn't add up to a lot of difference, Louis." Denny paused. "Remember the Countess Belloq in Paris?"

Louis's expression tightened at the mention of the countess, prompting Smoke to look at his son, raise an eyebrow, and drawl, "I don't reckon I've heard that story."

"And there's no need to bring it up now," Louis snapped. "That was an entirely different situation."

"Not so different," Denny said. "You saw something you wanted, and you went after it—"

She stopped as Smoke said, "Here comes Mrs. Buckner and the boy." He frowned. "But who's that with them?"

A stocky, white-haired man bundled in an overcoat, wearing a bowler hat, and carrying a carpetbag and a flat leather case hurried along beside Melanie and Brad as they headed for the carriage.

"She didn't say anything about anybody other than the boy being with her," Denny said.

"I guess we'll find out," Smoke said.

The older man came up to the carriage, set the carpetbag down, and extended his hand through the window to Smoke, who took it out of politeness.

"Mr. Jensen," the man said as they shook, "my name is Jerome Kellerman. I ran into Mrs. Buckner in the hotel—our rooms are near each other—and she told me that you're traveling to Reno by stage-coach. I would very much like to purchase a ticket for this trip."

"I'm sorry, Mr. Kellerman, but this isn't a regular stagecoach run," Smoke said. "I reckon you could call it a private coach. I made the arrangements for it, and I'm not selling tickets."

"Maybe you should, Pa," Denny said with a mocking smile on her face.

"Perhaps I phrased that badly," Kellerman said. "I'm accustomed to approaching everything on a business basis, you understand, since I work in a bank. But I simply must reach Reno in the very near future, and I'm prepared to do whatever is necessary to accomplish that."

"I don't think I can help you—" Smoke began.

"Mrs. Buckner told me you agreed to take her and her son along."

"That's a favor, to help her out with a family matter."

"Then I must throw myself on your mercy and appeal to your sense of family as well, sir. My wife is in Reno, and I would very much like to spend Christmas with her if at all possible." Kellerman paused. "We're moving there, you see, and I sent her on ahead, but then that confounded train couldn't get through the pass. . . ." He took a deep breath. "It would mean a great deal to me, Mr. Jensen, and I'm ready to depart at this very moment. I won't delay you, nor will I be any burden during the journey. I give you my word on that."

"That confounded train," Brad said with a grin.

Smoke looked at Denny and Louis. Melanie and

her son were at the door on the other side of the carriage, ready to get in. Smoke assumed they had already put their bags on the buckboard that would follow them to Fred Davis's house.

"It's about to get crowded in here," Smoke said to his children. "What do you think? Are you willing to put up with it all the way to Reno?"

Louis shrugged and said, "I don't mind the company."

"Fine with me," Denny said coolly. "If I get to feeling too crowded on the stagecoach, I'll just get out and ride one of those saddle horses. Might do that most of the time, anyway, as long as the weather's not too bad."

"All right, Mr. Kellerman," Smoke said. "Climb in. I don't suppose it'll hurt anything, and I wouldn't keep a fella away from his wife on Christmas." He smiled. "That's one reason I came up with this idea, after all, so I wouldn't be away from *my* wife."

A moment later, with the three newcomers in the carriage, making the quarters rather cramped, the vehicle rolled away from the hotel. Smoke looked at his children and added, "But if we get to Fred's place and find a line of would-be passengers waiting, I'm liable to call the whole thing off!"

CHAPTER 19

As it turned out, there wasn't a line of would-be stagecoach passengers waiting when the carriage got there.

Only three.

However, Smoke definitely wasn't glad to see two of them in particular.

Fred Davis had been busy this morning getting everything ready. The stagecoach was parked in front of the barn with a six-horse team already hitched into the traces.

The other team of six horses were linked together by lead ropes. The two saddle mounts were there as well, their reins fastened to one of the brass rails at the back of the coach.

Davis stood nearby, his breath fogging in the cold as he rubbed gloved hands together. Salty Stevens was with him, as well as a tall, lean, mustachioed man Smoke recognized as the reporter Peter Stansfield.

The sight of the journalist couldn't help but irritate Smoke. If not for Stansfield's sensationalistic story in the previous day's newspaper, the stagecoach might already be rolling toward its destination.

Smoke had hoped he wouldn't see Stansfield this morning and so would be justified in leaving him behind in Sacramento. That was what he had told Louis he would do.

The woman standing near Davis, Salty, and Stansfield was the other person Smoke recognized, but her presence here came as a complete and not very welcome surprise. Alma Lewiston was dressed in black, as befitted her status as a recent widow.

Next to her stood a man Smoke didn't know, although something about him seemed vaguely familiar. Smoke wondered if he had seen the man in the hotel, or maybe on the train.

Although he wasn't happy about whatever new developments these people represented, Smoke was happy to see that Salty appeared ready to go.

As the carriage came to a stop, Smoke swung down from it and strode over to the two old-timers.

"I hope you haven't gone and opened a ticket office, Fred," he said. He glanced back at Denny, who was climbing down from the carriage, and remembered her mocking comment about selling tickets.

"I swear to you, Smoke, I didn't do anything of the sort," Davis replied as he held up his hands, palms out. He nodded toward Stansfield. "It was all this fella's doin'." A slightly shame-faced look came over Davis's rugged countenance. "Although maybe I did talk a mite too freely when he came around here yesterday afternoon asking questions."

"You followed me here, didn't you, Mr. Stansfield?" Smoke said. "In fact, I suspect you've been on my trail all the way from San Francisco. Not to brag on my own skills, but a fella's doing pretty good when he can keep me from realizing that I'm being followed."

Stansfield said, "I take that as a high compliment from a man of your caliber, Mr. Jensen . . . no witticism or comment on your reputation as a gunman intended. It's true I've been hoping for a chance to speak with you again before you set out on this historic journey."

"So you can ask me if you can come along and write about the trip," Smoke said. "I read that story of yours, too. The answer is no."

By this time, the others had gotten out of the carriage and followed Smoke over to the stagecoach. Stansfield looked past him at them and said, "It appears you've already taken on some extra passengers."

"All we've got room for. And it's none of your business who else goes on this trip."

"On the contrary. I've looked into it, and a stagecoach of this size can carry nine people in relative comfort, three on each seat and three more on the bench in the middle." Stansfield made a show of counting, pointing out each of them including Alma Lewiston and the man Smoke didn't know. "I believe there are exactly nine of us, not counting our intrepid driver."

Salty spoke up, frowning and blustering, "Are you callin' me old, mister?"

"Not at all, sir. Intrepid means courageous, valiant, daring. I believe the word you're thinking of is decrepit."

"Oh," Salty said. "Well, in that case, go on."

Before Stansfield could say anything else, Smoke turned aside from the reporter and touched a finger to the brim of his hat as he nodded to Alma Lewiston.

"I didn't expect to see you here today, Mrs. Lewiston."

"I told you, there's no good reason for me to go back to San Francisco," she said. "Gordon can be laid to rest whether I'm there or not. I did my mourning for him a long time ago. I don't have any more tears to shed. And there's nothing else to hold me there. So I've decided to start a new life somewhere else . . . in Reno."

"With this fella?" Smoke asked bluntly as he nodded toward the hard-faced man with the drooping black mustache.

"Frank Colbert," the stranger introduced himself. He didn't offer to shake hands, and neither did Smoke. "And don't assume too much, mister, especially when it means you'll be insulting a lady if you do."

Smoke inclined his head in acknowledgment of that point and said, "I apologize, Mrs. Lewiston. I meant no offense. You just took me by surprise by showing up here, is all. The two of you want to come along to Reno with us, is that right?"

"Some of my business associates are waiting for me there, and it's vital that I reach them as soon as possible," Colbert said. "A great deal of money may depend on it."

"There are other ways to get there," Smoke pointed out. "Other routes that the railroad takes."

"That go all the way around by way of Texas." Colbert made a slashing gesture with one hand. "I can't risk not getting there in time."

"Mister, this whole trip is a risk."

"Maybe, but I'm willing to chance it."

Smoke and Colbert stood there, two big, tough men sizing each other up. Smoke didn't like the looks of the hombre, but despite the fact that he still felt no responsibility for Gordon Lewiston's death, he did have some sympathy for the man's widow. He thought it was a little cold-blooded of her to have taken up with Colbert so soon, which she had obviously done . . . but her personal life was none of his business.

He turned his head to look at Salty and asked, "What do you think? Will the extra weight slow us down?"

The old-timer frowned in thought for a moment, then said, "No, I don't reckon so. I looked over all them horses, and they's good, strong animals. We got plenty of food. If we run into any patches where there's ice on the trail instead of snow, havin' some extra weight in the coach might even come in handy and keep us from slippin' and slidin' around as much."

Smoke heaved a sigh. "All right. Since Salty doesn't think it'll be a problem, I suppose it won't hurt anything. You other folks can come along."

"Does that include me?" Stansfield asked quickly.

"If we don't take you, you'll probably try to follow us, and then you'll freeze to death somewhere along the way. So yeah, you can come too, mister." Smoke's voice hardened. "Just don't get on my nerves too much, or I'll pitch you out and leave you in the middle of the Sierra Nevadas."

He wouldn't actually do such a thing, of course, but he wouldn't mind if Stansfield worried some about the possibility. It might make the reporter a little less obnoxious . . . although probably not.

Smoke turned away from the stagecoach, waved an arm at the vehicle, and told the gathering, "Load up your things and climb aboard. I want to get on the trail before anybody else shows up asking for a ride to Reno!"

BOOK TWO

BOOK TWO

CHAPTER 20

Gila Crossing, Arizona

A curtain of beads hung across the entrance to the cantina in this little border settlement. The beads swung back and forth and made a faint clattering noise as Luke Jensen brushed them aside and stepped into the building.

The thick adobe walls kept the air in here cool despite the bright sunshine and heat outside. Winter might be in full swing elsewhere in the country, but here, less than a mile from the Mexican border, the days were still sultry.

Luke paused to let his eyes adjust to the dimness. He wasn't expecting trouble—well, not too much, anyway—but in his line of work, a man always had to be careful.

After all these years of manhunting, he didn't want to do something stupid and get his light blown out now.

He was closing in on sixty, too old for this job, really, but what else did he know? Ranching held no appeal for him, and clerking in a store would be pure misery, and he damn sure didn't want to go sit in a rocking chair on some porch and wait for death to kindly stop for him.

So he would keep hunting men who had a price on their heads, and if the risks inherent in that caught up to him someday . . . well, hell, it was the life he had chosen, wasn't it?

Or at least, the life fate had chosen for him.

Luke was a tall man, still ruggedly built despite his age. His craggy, deeply tanned face showed the wear and tear of decades spent mostly outside. His dark clothes were gray from trail dust. He wore two long-barreled .44 Remington revolvers, butt forward in their holsters.

The guns were old, like him, but could still kill a man just fine. Also like him.

Luke's keen eyes needed only a second to account for everyone in the cantina, six men and two women.

A man and a woman stood behind the bar, both of them short and fat, the woman looking more Indian than Mexican. The other woman, more of a girl, really, since she couldn't be a day over fifteen, stood in front of the bar.

Despite her youth, her shape was womanly already, with her full, brown breasts mostly exposed by the low-cut blouse she wore. The daughter or granddaughter of the couple behind the bar, Luke thought.

Two men stood at the bar with mugs of beer in front of them. Cowboys from one of the local spreads, by the looks of them. Neither wore a gun where Luke could see it.

At a table sat two more men, older, maybe *vaqueros*, maybe bandits from across the border. They had glasses and a half-empty bottle of tequila on the table. Gun belts were strapped around their waists, with holstered revolvers attached.

Luke wasn't after them, but they were unknown quantities. They might try to kill him if they decided he posed a potential threat. Or they might just feel like killing him.

He would need to keep an eye on them.

It was the sixth man in the cantina who interested him, the man sitting at a table in the corner, slumped forward, snoring. Luke couldn't see his face, just silvery hair askew.

That was the man Luke was after . . . if the information he'd been given in Tucson was correct.

The fat man behind the bar spoke to the girl. She hesitated, and the man gave her an emphatic, imperative nod. She picked up a round wooden tray from the bar and came toward Luke, holding the tray in front of her.

"Something to drink, señor?" she asked him.

"Perhaps later, señorita. Right now I seek information."

She tossed her head defiantly, making her thick mass of raven hair swirl around sleek shoulders left bare by the blouse. "We sell beer and tequila and whiskey, not information," she said.

"Not even for the right price?" Luke said.

"Not everything has a price, señor."

"I've never run across anything that didn't."

Her dark eyes flashed at him as she said, "And I am not for sale, either."

Luke felt a thousand years old. He let out a little grunt of laughter and told her, "That's good. Stick to it as long as you can. But for now, tell me if that slumbering gentleman over there in the corner is Jefferson Gillette."

The girl looked a little surprised, and genuinely puzzled. Luke supposed it was possible that no one here in this tiny settlement knew Gillette's real name. He might have given them one of his aliases, or no name at all.

"We call him Old Tiger. *Tigre.* That is all."

With his left hand—his right never strayed far from the butt of a gun—Luke took a folded piece of paper from his shirt pocket and held it out to the girl. By now, everyone in the cantina except the sleeping man was watching this conversation.

She unfolded the paper, revealing it to be a reward poster for one Jefferson Gillette, wanted for numerous armed robberies and murders across the southwest. The girl caught her breath when she saw the drawing of the man on the paper, and Luke knew she recognized him. Her eyes even darted toward the man in the corner.

"How old is this?" she asked.

"Twelve years," Luke said. "But the rewards have never been lifted. I'm sure he's changed some since then, but that man is the one you know as Old Tiger, isn't he?"

"You should go," the girl said as she thrust the wanted poster at Luke. When he didn't take it, she dropped it on the floor between them. "We want no trouble here."

"I don't want trouble either, but it's my job to bring lawbreakers to justice."

The two *vaqueros*—or *bandidos*—stood up from the table. One of them said, "Your job is to suck blood money from the bones of good men, *cabron*."

"I've no quarrel with you," Luke said.

"You should leave now, hombre," the second man said. "You do, and we let you live."

"No man *lets* me live," Luke said. "My life is mine, and anybody who tries to take it gets what's coming to him."

"Carmencita!" the fat man behind the bar blurted out. In rapid Spanish, he told the girl to come away from where she was. Her bare feet slapped the floor quickly as she obeyed the order.

Over at the bar, the two gringo cowboys edged away, putting themselves out of the line of fire as much as they could.

The man in the corner kept snoring.

Luke stood calmly where he was, waiting for the men who faced him to call the tune. He wasn't going to push them into a fight, and he wasn't going to let them prod him into drawing first, either.

The nerve of the man on Luke's right broke first. He snarled a curse and clawed at the gun on his hip.

Luke's arms flashed as he pulled both Remingtons from the cross-draw rig. Time had shaved the tiniest fraction of speed from his draw, but facing these two, it wasn't enough to matter. They were cruel, ruthless men, but they weren't really fast.

The right-hand Remington boomed and bucked against Luke's palm. The .44 slug bored into the man's chest and burst his heart. He had just cleared leather. His finger jerked the trigger involuntarily and he blew his right big toe off, but he was already too dead to feel it.

The gun in Luke's left hand went off so soon after the first shot that it was hard to tell them apart. Luke's aim was a little high—he had never been quite as good with his left hand—so the bullet ripped through the side of the man's throat. Blood spurted in a high arc from a severed artery.

The wound didn't kill the man instantly, though, and he was able to bring his gun up and trigger a round in Luke's direction. The bullet whined past Luke's ear. He didn't want to risk the man getting off a second shot, so he put a slug between the hombre's eyes. That knocked him down.

With all that gun thunder echoing from the cantina's low ceiling, Luke couldn't have heard the scrape of the chair's legs on the floor as Jefferson Gillette—Old Tiger—surged up and swept a sawed-off shotgun from under the filthy poncho he wore. It must have been instinct that warned Luke to twist and dive out of the way of the blast.

Gillette might have actually been asleep when Luke came in, but he had woken up at some point in the proceedings, enough to be aware that a day of reckoning had arrived at last. He wasn't completely drunk, either; otherwise he wouldn't have been able to react as quickly as he did now. He tracked the figure rolling swiftly across the floor and fired the sawed-off's second barrel.

Luke kicked an empty table over as he rolled. It absorbed the buckshot from the second blast. As he came up on one knee and tried to bring the Remingtons to bear on Gillette, the man slung the empty scattergun at his head. Luke had to duck.

When he did that, Gillette leaped onto a table with an agility that belied his years and dived at him.

The old outlaw's shoulder rammed into Luke's chest and drove him over backward. Luke's head hit the floor hard enough to make the cantina spin crazily around him.

The impact also caused the Remingtons to fly out of his hands. He lay there stunned for a second with Gillette's weight pinning him down, and when he got his wits back about him, he looked up to see that the man had pulled out a big knife and was about to plunge it into his chest.

As the deadly thrust fell, Luke grabbed Gillette's wrist just in time to keep the cold steel from ripping into his body. It took both hands to stop the knife.

That left Gillette's other hand free to hammer punches into Luke's face. He jerked his head from side to side, avoiding the blows as much as he could, but enough of them landed that he felt conscious- ness slipping away from him.

If he passed out, Gillette would gut him like a fish. Luke knew that. He brought his right leg up, bones and muscles creaking and resisting more than they used to, and hooked his ankle across Gillette's throat. When he swung his leg back, that ripped Gillette off of him.

Luke rolled over onto hands and knees and looked around for his Remingtons. He spotted one of the re- volvers lying on the floor nearby and made a grab for it.

He had to jerk his hand back as Gillette brought

the knife down and almost impaled it. The tip of the blade stuck in the floor, though, and Gillette couldn't wrench it free right away. He grunted with the effort as he tried to do so.

That gave Luke a chance to slide across the floor on his belly the other way and scoop up the second Remington, which he had just spotted. As he closed his left hand around the revolver, he rolled onto that side and thrust the barrel toward Gillette.

The outlaw had just pulled the knife loose from the floor and lifted it with a triumphant grin on his weather-beaten face when Luke pulled the trigger. The bullet smashed through the yellow stubs of teeth revealed by Gillette's expression and on out the back of his head, taking a good-sized chunk of skull with it.

Gillette stayed there on his knees for a second before he fell forward onto his face with a thump, the third dead man to hit the floor in not much more than a minute.

Breathing hard, Luke lay there hoping that his heart, which was racing a mile a minute, wouldn't burst. His pulse beat a loud, swift tattoo inside his head.

Over that racket, he heard the furious shout from the fat man behind the bar.

"You killed *El Tigre!*"

Luke saw the man come around the end of the bar holding a machete, of all things. A great weariness flooded through him. He didn't want to kill this cantina owner, who was probably an honest, hardworking man who felt sorry for the old outlaw and doubtless had no idea what a bloody-handed scoundrel Gillette had been.

He certainly didn't want to kill the man in front of his wife and daughter—or granddaughter, as the case might be.

Luckily, he didn't have to. The two cowboys caught hold of the fat man's arms and halted his charge toward Luke. One of them yelled, "Paco! Stop it! That hombre'll kill you, you damn fool!"

The other man told Luke, "Mister, you better get outta here while you got the chance."

"Not without . . . what I came for."

Luke climbed to his feet, holstered the Remington he held, picked up the other iron and pouched it as well. He found his hat and put it on.

Standing beside Gillette's body, he asked, "Does he have a horse?"

The girl—Carmencita, the fat man had called her—looked disgusted and said, "A horse? He has *nothing*. Only the pity of the people in this place."

"He had a sawed-off shotgun and a knife," Luke snapped. "And he used both of them to try to kill me." A cold edge came into his voice. "You're welcome to them, to settle his bar tab."

"Mister," one of the cowboys said, "Ol' Tiger rode in a year ago on a burro even more ancient than he was, and it died two days later. Since then he ain't had any kind of a horse or much of anything else, like Carmencita there said."

"What about the horses tied outside?"

"Two of 'em are ours. The other two belonged to those hombres."

"You know who they were?"

"I'm pretty sure they used to ride for Diego Ramirez." The cowboy leaned his head toward the border. "One of those so-called revolutionaries south of the line who's really just a bandit. Nobody around here's gonna miss 'em or try to settle the score for 'em, if that's what you're worried about."

"I wasn't worried," Luke said, "but I thought I might take one of the horses to carry Gillette."

The cantina owner had been sputtering in fury, but he regained control of his emotions enough to say, "Take them both, just get out, gringo. You killed two bad men here today, and one good one."

"He was trying to kill me," Luke said, "and his act might have fooled you, but he wasn't a good man. He was a very bad man, in fact, hiding out from the law."

The second cowboy said, "For God's sake, mister, don't argue. Just take him and go."

Irritated though he was, Luke knew that was good advice.

Five minutes later, he had Jefferson Gillette's body lashed facedown over the saddle on one of the horses belonging to the bandidos. He would take both horses; they would fetch a decent price in Tucson. He rode away from the little border settlement without looking back.

The next day, in the sheriff's office in Tucson, the lawman wrinkled his nose and said, "I hate the stink of a corpse that's started to get too ripe. Takes a long time for me to stop smellin' it." He pushed the stack of greenbacks across the desk to Luke. "There you go, Jensen. You should've hauled in Ramirez's boys, too. Might've been some dodgers out on them."

"A couple of pissant *bandidos* like that, I didn't figure the reward would be worth the trouble. Besides, I didn't have an extra horse."

"Well, there's that to consider," the sheriff admitted. "Mex bandits are a dime a dozen around these parts." He frowned. "Jensen, right? Luke Jensen?"

"I told you my name, Sheriff," Luke said. He was ready to go.

"Telegram came for you. They brought it over here, figurin' if you showed up in Tucson, you'd likely come here." The man added loftily, "Your reputation precedes you."

The news surprised Luke. His brother Smoke and Smoke's wife, Sally, knew he was down in this part of the country—he was headed for their place in Colorado next—but he wasn't sure who else would.

The sheriff dug out the telegram from the litter of papers on his desk and handed it over. Luke read it, then folded the paper and stuck it in his pocket.

"Bad news?" the sheriff asked.

"No. Just a change of plans. I was going to Colorado, but now I'm headed for Reno." It was none of the lawman's business, but Luke added anyway, "Going to see my brothers and my boys for Christmas."

CHAPTER 21

North of Laramie, Wyoming

Matt Jensen wasn't Smoke's brother by birth, but more than thirty years had passed since Smoke and the old mountain man Preacher took in a scared, orphaned youngster and turned him into a man. When Matt rode away to make his own way in the world, he had taken the name Jensen with him, and ever since, the bond between him and Smoke had been thicker than even blood could ever be.

Matt had had plenty of adventures of his own. He had worked as a lawman, scouted for the army, ridden shotgun on stagecoaches, been a troubleshooter for Wells Fargo, and roamed the West as a range detective, his current occupation. That only scratched the surface, because Matt had a wandering foot and never stayed any place for too long.

At the moment, he was in Wyoming, under a cold, leaden sky, lying on his belly at the crest of a ridge so he could keep an eye on a crudely built log cabin about two hundred yards away, on the other side of the creek at the bottom of the slope.

The man lying beside him asked quietly, "Are you sure they're in there?"

Matt hung on to his patience, which wasn't always an easy task. He said, "There are four horses tied up in front of the cabin. We tracked four men here with those stolen thoroughbreds that are now in the pole corral next to the cabin. I reckon there's not much doubt about this being the right place."

"Then why don't we go down and round them up now, instead of sittin' out here in the cold?"

"Because your boss is paying me to find out who's been *buying* the stock he's lost. That's what he really wants to know. Those men in the cabin are just common horse thieves."

"I reckon," Dab Newton said. "But it's still cold."

Newton was the foreman of Edison McKavett's M2 ranch. Along with half a dozen more punchers from McKavett's crew, he had accompanied Matt this morning on the trail of the thieves who had plundered McKavett's horse herd yet again during the night.

Matt had been on the job for a week, scouting around the rugged Wyoming countryside in search of a likely spot for the gang of horse thieves to be holed up. He had found this isolated cabin the day before and decided it was a perfect place for the gang's headquarters.

He had resolved to keep an eye on it, but before he could actually do that, the thieves had struck again, running off two dozen head of McKavett's fine, blooded stock.

Matt had taken a calculated risk, heading directly for this spot with the makeshift posse McKavett had provided for him, but along the way he had picked up the trail, confirming his suspicions.

Now they were just waiting to see who showed up to take possession of the stolen horses. Back in the trees, the rest of the cowboys waited. They were restless, but they weren't making too much noise . . . yet.

Matt hoped his quarry wouldn't take too much longer, though. He felt the same impatience the other men did.

Movement off to the left caught Matt's eye. He looked in that direction and saw four men riding along the creek toward the cabin. One was in front, with three horsebackers following him.

Matt nudged Newton and asked, "Do you recognize those fellas?"

The M2 foreman squinted at the riders for a long moment, then said, "Damn me if that ain't Walker Dixon."

"The one in front? That name's familiar. He owns another spread hereabouts, doesn't he?"

"He sure does. He's got the Crosshatch spread, over east a ways. Thing of it is, him and Mr. McKavett are good friends."

Matt grunted and said, "Maybe not as good as you or McKavett believe. Because he sure looks like he's here to dicker with those horse thieves. You know the men with him?"

"Seen 'em around," Newton said. "I reckon they must ride for the Crosshatch. Billy Hooper ain't with 'em, though. He's the ramrod over there. I'd sure hate to think ol' Billy was thick with them thieves.

Him and me rode for some o' the same spreads down in Texas."

The newcomers drew rein in front of the cabin. The leader, a thick-set man in nicer clothes and a cream-colored hat, dismounted and handed his reins to one of the other men. Those three remained mounted while the boss went into the cabin.

Newton sighed and said, "Well, I reckon that's plain enough. Ain't no other possible reason Dixon would be here. The boss is gonna be plumb mortified to find out his friend has been stealin' from him right along."

"That happens sometimes," Matt said. "Nobody is a perfect judge of other people's character."

Except maybe Smoke and Preacher, he thought. He had never known those two to be wrong in their instincts.

"What do we do now?" Newton asked. "Go back to headquarters and tell Mr. McKavett what we found out?"

Matt pondered that for a moment, then said, "That man you mentioned, Billy Hooper. He's Dixon's foreman?"

"Yep."

"And he's an honest man?"

"I'd stake my life on it."

"Then those men with Dixon won't drive the stolen horses back to the Crosshatch. There's too much of a chance Hooper would see them and recognize them as M2 stock, and then Dixon's operation would be ruined. No, they'll take them somewhere else and dispose of them. They probably have a regular buyer lined up in Laramie or Cheyenne who doesn't care where the horses come from. So if they leave here with the horses, there won't be any proof. It would be just our word against Dixon's."

"You don't reckon Mr. McKavett would believe us?"

"You know him better than I do," Matt said. "What do you think?"

Newton considered that question. "I reckon he'd be more inclined to believe us if we came back with them stolen horses . . . *and* Dixon."

Matt nodded and said, "That's what I was thinking."

"There's eight hombres down there right now, and eight of us. Them's even odds."

"I'll see if I can't tip them in our favor," Matt said. "Stay here for now, and if you see any gunplay, you'll know to charge down this hill and take cards."

"What're you gonna—"

Before Newton could finish the question, Matt had already slid back along the ridge and gotten up to head into the trees where the horses were.

He emerged a moment later riding a big gray gelding and loped off along the ridge, out of sight of the cabin. He left Newton and the other punchers behind and followed the ridge for half a mile, to a spot where he could circle around and cross the creek without being spotted.

Then he headed back along the stream toward the cabin where the horse thieves were holed up.

He rode at a nice, easy pace, ambling along like a man out for a jaunt. He didn't appear particularly threatening, just a tall, well-built man with sandy hair and a mustache, wearing a brown coat and trousers and a dark brown hat.

A gun belt was strapped around his waist, something that was less common these days but not really anything unusual.

The three men sitting their horses in front of the cabin couldn't help but see him coming. Matt kept his pace deliberate as he rode up and reined in about twenty feet from them. He gave the men a friendly nod and said, "Howdy, boys."

Now that he was closer, he could see that although these men might have jobs as cowboys on the Crosshatch spread, they weren't typical ranch hands. They had a rougher, more dangerous look about them. Matt had seen enough hardcases in his life to recognize the breed when he came across them.

"This is private property, mister," one of them said. "You'd best ride on now, and don't waste any time about it."

"I sure didn't mean any offense," Matt said.

A second hardcase jerked his head and ordered, "Get movin'."

"Well, I can't right do that," Matt said. "You see, I've got a dozen sharpshooting regulators up there on the ridge on the other side of the creek, and if you fellas make a move toward your guns, or if I raise a hand to my hat, they'll blow you right out of your saddles."

The three men had stiffened while he was talking. Hate burned in their eyes. But they didn't reach for their guns.

"You're just runnin' a damn bluff," one of the men said.

"It'd be easy enough for you to find out," Matt told him.

Still, they didn't move. Tension grew thick and heavy in the air.

"Mr. Dixon, you'd better come on out here!" Matt called.

Someone jerked the cabin door open. The well-dressed man Matt had seen earlier stomped out. His face was brick red with anger.

"What the hell is this?" he demanded. "Who in blazes are you?"

"Name's Matt Jensen," Matt drawled. "I'm the leader of a company of regulators who've got the drop on this place. Y'all might as well shuck your guns and surrender, because you're not getting out of here."

Dixon glared at his men and blustered, "What are you waiting for? Kill him!"

"He's got sharpshooters up on the ridge, Mr. Dixon," one of the hardcases said.

"No he doesn't! It's a damn bluff!"

Matt smiled and said, "I told my best shot to wait until you came outside, Dixon, and then put his sights right on you. He won't take them off until I signal him. All it'll take for him to put a bullet through you is a little more pressure on the trigger."

Dixon glared at him. "You wouldn't dare! My ranch is one of the biggest in this part of the country!"

"And you should have been satisfied with that, instead of stealing from your neighbors." Matt shook his head. "Some men are just born greedy, I reckon. No matter how much they have, it's never enough."

From inside the cabin, a harsh voice said, "Get out of the way, Dixon. I'll ventilate that son of a bitch!"

"I go down, all of you die," Matt said coolly. "The four of you out here will be dead before I hit the ground. Then my men have enough ammunition to shoot that cabin to pieces. They'll pour lead into it until it collapses, and there won't be anything left alive inside it."

The flush on Dixon's face began to fade to a frightened pallor. "My God," he said in a hollow voice. "You mean it, don't you?"

"Every damn word of it," Matt lied.

He could have left Newton and the others up there ready to bushwhack this bunch of horse thieves, but wholesale slaughter wasn't his way, not when there might be some other option. He wanted to take as many of them alive as possible.

That didn't mean he wasn't ready for gunplay. He had already figured out the order in which he would kill the men on horseback, if it came to that. He would probably take some lead himself, but he was confident that he could down all three hardcases and then put a bullet in Walker Dixon.

Suddenly, one of the hardcases said, "Hell. Now I remember why that name sounded familiar. This is Smoke Jensen's brother."

Matt smiled faintly. "You've heard of Smoke, have you?"

"And you, too, you loco sumbitch! Mr. Dixon, a few years back this man walked into a saloon and shot it out with ten men. Killers, every one of 'em, but Jensen put them all in the ground." The hardcase stared at Matt. "Hell, I heard they shot you to doll rags!"

"Those stories always get blown out of proportion. I was laid up for a little spell." It had been more like a month, and he had almost died, but they didn't have to know that.

The hardcase shook his head. "I don't want no part of this. If we kill this Jensen, his brother will track us down. And he's even worse!"

"Like I said, shuck your guns," Matt told them quietly. "Nobody has to die here today."

Dixon said, "If you men surrender, I'll see to it that you never work again!"

"We'll never work again if we're dead, either."

All three hardcases wore their guns on the right. Matt said, "Raise your right hands, then use your left to take your guns out and toss them on the ground."

"This . . . this is insane!" Dixon sputtered. "The man hasn't even drawn his gun!"

"Not this time. But he's drawn it plenty of times in the past . . . and plenty of men have died."

The man who had spoken lifted his right hand and reached across his body to his holster.

"Nice and easy," Matt said. "Use just two fingers."

The gunman did as he was told. So did the other two, although one of them cursed bitterly as he gingerly drew his Colt and tossed it on the ground.

"You men in the cabin," Matt called. "Throw your guns out first, then come out of there with your hands in the air."

Dixon watched, flabbergasted, as four revolvers sailed through the open doorway. Then their owners shuffled into view with their arms lifted and their hands held at shoulder level. They were the same sort of small-time owlhoots as the men Dixon had brought with him.

Only one of them still looked defiant, and something about him set off alarm bells in Matt's head.

With no warning, that man leaped behind Dixon

and looped his left arm around the portly rancher's throat. At the same time, he reached to the small of his back with his other hand and yanked out a gun he had hidden there before coming out of the cabin.

Matt's hand flashed to his Colt and drew it with blinding speed, but he couldn't fire without hitting Dixon, who let out a screech of fear before the arm around his throat tightened and turned the sound into a pathetic gurgle.

Matt kicked his feet free of the stirrups and went out of the saddle in a dive as the horse thief's gun cracked and sent a slug sizzling through the space where he had been a fraction of a heartbeat earlier.

Matt hit the ground and rolled. As he came up, he saw a lot of white around the pupils in Walker Dixon's eyes. Dixon fainted, and the sudden dead weight dragged the man who held him off balance. The man couldn't hold Dixon up.

That gave Matt a tiny opening, but it was all he needed. The gun in his hand roared. The bullet whipped past Dixon's right ear and shattered the outlaw's jaw, spraying blood and bone splinters onto the side of Dixon's head. The man groaned, dropped his gun, and collapsed. Dixon went down with him.

One of the other men from the cabin thought about making a grab for the guns they had tossed out, but he froze as the barrel of Matt's Colt swung swiftly toward him.

"Bad idea, mister," Matt said as the echoes of his shot rolled along the creek.

The man raised his hands again and backed away quickly.

Matt heard hoofbeats pounding nearby and knew

Dab Newton and the rest of the M2 hands were on their way. A moment later the cowboys splashed across the creek and surrounded all the prisoners. It was over, and only one man was wounded.

That one, the man with the bullet-shattered jaw, had passed out, but he was still alive. Dixon lay beside him, out cold.

While Newton and the others covered the captives, Matt holstered his gun and bent over Dixon. He lightly slapped the rancher's cheeks until Dixon sputtered awake.

"You're under arrest," Matt told him. "I'm sure it won't take these other fellas much time at all to figure out they'll do better with the law if they admit how you were behind this horse-stealing ring."

"You'll be sorry," Dixon said as he climbed slowly and awkwardly to his feet. "I'm a rich man. I won't go to prison."

"You might be right." Matt smiled. "In this part of the country, sometimes they still hang horse thieves."

Dixon looked sick.

"Almost certainly, he won't hang," Edison McKavett said that evening as he and Matt sat in the comfortably furnished living room of the M2 ranch house. "But the prosecutor in Laramie assures me that he *will* go to prison." McKavett shook his head. "Such a damn shame. I would have bet almost any amount that Walker Dixon was an honest man. I've considered him my friend ever since he came to this region five years ago."

"There's no telling how long he's been an outlaw," Matt said. "Some fellas are just really good at covering it up. 'A man may smile and smile, and be a villain.'"

"You've read the bard, I see."

"My brother Luke is a reading man. Always has books in his saddlebags. It's rubbed off some on me, over the years. It'll be good to see him, and his sons, too."

"You're going to visit them for Christmas, I take it?"

"We were all going to get together at my other brother's ranch in Colorado, but there's been some sort of hitch," Matt explained. "I got a telegram from his wife about it when I was in town yesterday. We're going to meet in Reno instead. So I'll need to be riding in that direction first thing tomorrow." He smiled. "I wanted to finish cleaning up this mess first, though, if I could."

"And clean it up you did," McKavett said as he raised the glass of brandy he held. "To Christmas and family."

"Christmas and family," Matt echoed as he lifted his own glass.

CHAPTER 22

Big Rock, Colorado

The two men riding along the main street of Big Rock, Colorado, were no longer young. Soon after the first of the year, they would celebrate—or maybe that wasn't exactly the right word—their fortieth birthday.

The very same day, in fact, since they were twins.

They didn't look all that much like twins, since they weren't identical, but there was a strong enough family resemblance to make it obvious they were brothers.

Nor did they appear to be as old as they actually were. There was an air of something eternally boyish about them, as if they had taken the prospect of growing old under advisement and decided against it.

William "Ace" Jensen was the bigger of the two, brawny and broad shouldered and dark haired. In his well-worn range clothes, he looked like a drifting cowpuncher, while his sandy-haired brother, Benjamin "Chance" Jensen, wore a brown suit, a tan planter's hat, and was something of a dandy.

Both of them still used the nicknames given to them by the man who'd raised them, the gambler Ennis "Doc" Monday, and had never considered going by their legal names. If they ever did that, somebody might take it to mean they were ready to settle down, and that held no appeal at all to these Jensen "boys."

"Big Rock hasn't changed too much since the last time we saw it," Ace commented as they rode.

"But it's changed a great deal from the *first* time," Chance said. "You remember that? It was at the same time of year."

Ace chuckled. "Be hard to forget it, the way all hell broke loose that Christmas."

Abruptly, a terrible racket rose into the air, causing the people in the street and on the boardwalks to look around hurriedly in surprise. Whatever it was continued popping and roaring and rumbling.

"Sounds like all hell's about to break loose now," Chance said wryly.

Somebody yelled in alarm, and a man ran out from one of the cross streets as if Satan himself were right behind him.

A moment later, the "devil" he was running from careened around the corner, throwing dust into the air and causing bystanders to leap out of its path. The thing lurched and jolted toward Ace and Chance, who sat on their horses in the middle of the street, staring at it in amazement.

"It's a horseless carriage!" Ace exclaimed.

"An automobile!" Chance said. "I've read about them."

A man sat atop the thing, on a seat that looked much like one found on a buckboard. He had a cap on his head and a pair of large, grotesque spectacles strapped over his eyes. He clutched a lever that he hauled back and forth with seemingly no effect on the horseless carriage's path.

The man took one gloved hand off the lever and waved it at Ace and Chance as he shouted, "Out of the way! Get out of the way, you fools!"

"Why doesn't he stop that blasted thing?" Ace said.

Chance's eyes grew wider as he said, "I don't think he *can!*"

With the horseless carriage bearing down on them, Ace and Chance hauled their mounts away from each other, Ace to the right and Chance to the left. The runaway contraption roared between them.

The terrible racket spooked both horses and made them rear up and dance around. For a minute, Ace and Chance had their hands full getting the animals under control again.

When they had done that, they turned to watch as the horseless carriage veered wildly back and forth across the street. It crashed into a hitch rail and knocked it down, then angled all the way to the other side and rammed its front end against a water trough.

That finally brought it to a halt. The terrible racket stopped.

The man slumped forward over the lever and didn't move. Ace saw that and exclaimed, "I think that fella's hurt!"

He heeled his horse into a run and pounded toward the now motionless machine.

Ace had heard about these horseless carriages but

had never seen one until now. As he came closer, he caught a whiff of the stink that came from it and grimaced.

A man could get used to the smell of horse manure, but Ace wasn't sure anyone would ever grow accustomed to the stench hanging over this thing.

He reined in and swung down from the saddle. By now the man had started moving again. He shook his head groggily as he tried to sit up straighter.

Ace gripped the man's shoulder through the long duster he wore and said, "Mister! Mister, are you all right?"

The man turned his head to look at Ace. Those odd spectacles made his eyes seem so big he reminded Ace of a giant insect. The things were attached to a strap that went around the man's head. He pulled them down so they hung around his neck. They left a bare pattern around his eyes in the dust-covered face.

"Good Lord!" the man said. "How thrilling! I haven't felt so exhilarated in years!"

Ace frowned. "Wait a minute. Are you saying you nearly ran over those folks and caused this damage on purpose?"

"What?" The man stared at him for a second, then laughed and went on, "Oh, no, not at all! I just built up too much speed, and then something snapped in the brake and steering linkages, and I couldn't stop the machine or control it to the necessary degree. But still, it was very exciting, don't you think?"

Chance had followed Ace over to the wrecked contraption. From horseback, he said, "This is a gasoline runabout, isn't it?"

"Indeed it is, my good man," the driver answered in an eastern accent that got on Ace's nerves. "A Haynes-Apperson Gasoline Runabout, to be precise. The finest automobile produced today." He looked at the machine's crumpled front end and added ruefully, "Well, perhaps not at the moment. I'll have to have the brakes and steering repaired, and the suspension straightened out as well, but then she'll be good as new. A competent blacksmith should be able to do the work. Do you know if such a person can be found in this hamlet?"

"Hamlet's not a very good word to describe Big Rock," Ace said. "This is a good-sized town."

The man smirked and said, "Perhaps by the primitive standards of the frontier. But to someone from New York, the greatest city in the world, this is a mere flyspeck of humanity."

"A lot of good people live here, mister," Ace began hotly, "and I don't reckon they'd appreciate—"

Chance interrupted him and asked the stranger, "When you get it fixed, you think I could try my hand at driving it?"

The man gave him a disdainful stare and arched one eyebrow. "Allow a mere cowboy to take the controls of a Haynes-Apperson? I think not!"

Chance frowned. The man's attitude rubbed him the wrong way, too. Now both of the Jensen brothers were angry.

Some of the townspeople had recovered from their shock and fear by now. A few of them curiously approached the runabout and stared at it in amazement.

A boy stepped forward and said, "Hey, mister, is

that critter really dead? Or is it gonna start growlin' and runnin' around again?"

One of his companions called, "Touch it, Alby! I dare you!" Some of the other boys took up the cry.

The one named Alby lifted a hand and stretched it tentatively toward the rear corner of the runabout.

"Here now," the driver exclaimed as he swung down from the seat. "Get away from there, you urchin! Keep your filthy paws away from this vehicle."

The boy jerked back.

"Take it easy," Ace told the man in a hard voice. "The boy wasn't trying to hurt anything."

"Yes, but in his stupidity, he might do so anyway."

One of the boys said, "I think that gent just called you stupid, Alby."

The gathering crowd moved back a little to let a man in late middle age through. He had a badge pinned to the vest under his coat. Ace and Chance both recognized him.

"What's going on here?" Sheriff Monte Carson asked. He stared at the wrecked automobile. "What in blazes is this thing?"

"It's a Haynes-Apperson Gasoline Runabout," Chance said dryly.

"A horseless carriage, Sheriff," Ace added.

"Yeah, I figured that out." Carson glanced again at the Jensen brothers, then grinned. "Ace and Chance! Good to see you, boys! The other day when Sally was in town, she mentioned that you were coming for Christmas." The lawman shook hands with both of them. "Matt and your pa, too, I think she said."

"That's right," Ace said. "A gathering of the whole Jensen clan."

"Except Preacher," Chance said.

"Yeah, except Preacher," Ace repeated solemnly.

"Well, nobody lives forever, not even that old scudder," Monte Carson said. "Nobody ever saw him again after he went off into the mountains by himself that last time, did they?"

"No. Smoke said that was the way Preacher wanted it."

"I hate to break up this little reunion," the stranger said, his sneering tone making it clear that he didn't hate it at all, "but is there a blacksmith in this town who can be trusted to repair my vehicle?"

The sheriff said, "Yeah, two blocks down and around the corner to the right. Patterson's Blacksmith Shop. He can fix that . . . whatever you call it . . . if anybody can."

"I thank you, Sheriff. I'll go see if he has a wagon with which he can retrieve my poor wounded steed."

"If he doesn't, his cousin will. He owns the wagon yard."

"My thanks." The stranger started to turn away.

"Hold on a minute," Carson said. "You knocked down a hitch rail and maybe damaged this water trough. You're responsible for what this contraption did—"

"Say no more," the man broke in. He unbuttoned the duster and reached inside it to take out a wallet. He extracted a greenback and extended it toward the lawman. "Will this be sufficient?"

"Uh . . . yeah, I reckon. But I really ought to charge you with disturbing the peace and let the judge set the fine—"

"It wouldn't be more than a hundred dollars, including the damages, would it?" the man said. That was the denomination of the bill he was holding out.

"No, I suppose not." Carson took the money. "I'm gonna talk to him, though, and you may get some of this back."

"No need," the stranger said with an airy wave of his hand.

"One more thing. What's your name, mister?"

"Collinsworth," the man replied. "Edward Collinsworth."

Chance said, "Of the New York City Collinsworths?"

"Why, yes, I'm surprised that you've heard of us, all the way out—" He stopped short and frowned at Chance. "You're having a bit of sport with me, aren't you, chum?"

Chance just shrugged.

"You may come to discover that's not a wise thing to do."

"Neither is driving a devilish contraption like this through streets where people are trying to walk," Ace said. "I still think you could've hurt somebody."

Collinsworth rested a hand on the runabout's frame. "People are going to have to get used to watching out for these. They're the coming thing, you know. Soon they'll be in the streets of every city in the country."

"Lord help us," Monte Carson muttered under his breath.

Collinsworth lifted his head slightly in a listening attitude, then said, "In fact, I believe I hear the rest of my party coming now."

Ace heard the popping and sputtering and rumbling growing louder in the distance and bit back a groan.

"There are more of you?" he asked.

"Yes. My automobile club is making a cross-country motor expedition."

"Lord help us, is right," Ace said, echoing the sheriff's words. He looked at his brother and went on, "Let's go to Longmont's and get a drink before we ride out to the Sugarloaf. The stink from this thing has put a bad taste in my mouth."

CHAPTER 23

Longmont's Saloon, owned and operated by Smoke's old friend Louis Longmont, was more than a drinking and gambling establishment. It was also one of the finest restaurants in Big Rock. Maybe *the* finest.

Smoke's son, Louis, was named after the dapper gambler/gunman, as well as for Preacher, whose real name was Arthur. Longmont had a lot of silver in his hair and mustache by now, but he still stood straight and his eyes were keen.

Those eyes lit up as Ace and Chance walked into the saloon. Longmont was standing at the end of the bar. He waved the brothers over and greeted them warmly.

"The Jensen boys," he said. "It's very good to see you."

Ace said, "You know, one of these days, people are going to have to stop calling us boys. We're going to be forty years old our next birthday!" He gripped Longmont's hand. "But it's mighty good to see you, too, sir."

"You're still mere lads compared to many of us," Longmont said. He shook hands with Chance. "And just look at you. With your roguish ways, people are always going to think of you as those Jensen boys."

"I don't mind," Chance said with a shrug. "I still feel like a frisky young colt." He paused. "Most of the time, anyway. Although I'll admit that some mornings when I climb out of bed, it's more of a chore than it used to be!"

"Sooner or later that comes to us all," Longmont said. "A drink?"

"A cold beer would sure be good," Ace agreed.

Longmont signaled to the bartender. When the three of them had foaming mugs of beer in front of them, he said, "Actually, I've been keeping an eye out for you fellows. Sally asked me to pass along a message if I saw you."

That news brought a frown to Ace's face. "Why would she do that? We're on our way out to the Sugarloaf, so we'll be seeing her soon."

"I'm afraid not," Longmont said. "Sally's not there. She left town on this morning's train."

"What?" Chance said. "We're all supposed to get together at the ranch for Christmas!"

Nodding, the saloonkeeper explained, "I know. But there's been a change in the plans for your holiday celebration. Sally is on her way to Reno, over in Nevada."

"We know where Reno is," Ace said. "Got in a little fracas there once, in fact."

"But where *haven't* we gotten into a little fracas at one time or another?" Chance said. He waved that comment away and went on, "Why is Sally going to Reno?"

"She plans to meet Smoke, Denise, and Louis there. She's sent word to Matt and Luke, asking them to rendezvous there as well. But she knew the two of you were due to arrive in Big Rock at any time, so she decided it would be more effective to leave the message with me. It seems that one of the passes in the Sierra Nevada Mountains has been closed by a blizzard, and Smoke can't get home by train."

Longmont continued with the explanation. It didn't take long. Ace nodded as he listened, and when Longmont was finished, he said, "I suppose Chance and I need to catch the next westbound, then."

"We ought to get there in plenty of time," Chance added. "Hope there'll be space to ship our horses, too."

They chatted for a few more minutes about the upcoming holiday, and then Longmont said, "A short time before you came in here, there was a horrible commotion in the street. Did either of you happen to see what that was about?"

"We both did," Ace said.

"It was a horseless carriage," Chance added. "A *runaway* horseless carriage."

They told Longmont about the dangerous encounter with Edward Collinsworth and his Haynes-Apperson Gasoline Runabout. Longmont nodded and said, "I saw some of those machines on my last trip back east. People claim they're going to become the primary means of transportation in this country."

"They'll never replace the railroad," Ace said as he shook his head.

"The railroad replaced the stagecoach, for the

most part," Longmont pointed out. "It's very difficult to halt the march of progress."

Ace grunted and said, "Depends on how you define progress, I reckon."

Before the discussion could continue, one of the saloon doors opened. They were closed because of the cold December weather. A gust of chilly air accompanied the man who hurried in.

"There's about to be a fight over at the Brown Dirt Cowboy," he reported excitedly. "Those gents who came into town on the noisemaker machines are tanglin' with some o' Ab Tuggle's men."

Ace glanced at Longmont. "Who's he talking about?"

"Abner Tuggle," Longmont replied with a sigh. "One of the local ranchers. His hands are a bit on the rowdy side. That's why they prefer the Brown Dirt Cowboy Saloon to here."

Ace recalled the Brown Dirt Cowboy Saloon, although he and Chance had been there only a few times. For two decades, it had been Big Rock's most notorious watering hole, and it hadn't changed since Claude Brown, the nephew of the original owner, had taken over the place.

"What happens in there is none of our look-out," Chance said as he picked up his beer.

Ace couldn't argue with that. He didn't know any of Tuggle's men, and Edward Collinsworth and his friends could look after themselves. If the rest of that bunch was like Collinsworth, he wasn't surprised that their arrogant attitudes had sparked a fight.

The man who had brought the news had reached the bar by now, and a number of curious customers flocked around him. Reveling in the attention, the man said, "I overheard Chet Lewis say that if Sheriff Carson gets in the middle of the ruckus, they'll whale the tar outta him, too."

Ace asked Longmont, "Who's Chet Lewis?"

"Tuggle's foreman. A vicious brute, I'm sad to say." Longmont shook his head. "He's the sort of man who's always glad for an excuse to hurt someone."

Ace looked at Chance. "You know Monte Carson. He'll try to break things up before they get too far out of hand."

"Yes, but he has deputies to help him," Chance pointed out. "That's no reason for *us* to get mixed up in any trouble."

"Sheriff Carson is one of Smoke's best friends, and Smoke is family."

"That doesn't mean Carson is."

"Doesn't matter." Ace turned away from the bar. "I'm not going to stand by and do nothing while he may be walking right into a buzz saw."

Chance gulped down the beer that was left in his mug and then complained, "I don't know why I have the reputation of being the reckless one. Most of the time it's you who gets us neck deep in trouble!"

Despite that, he waved farewell to Longmont and followed his brother out of the saloon.

Ace was already striding along the street toward the Brown Dirt Cowboy Saloon. As Chance came up beside him, he said, "I thought you figured we shouldn't get involved."

"You think I'm gonna let you go and have all the fun by yourself?" Chance laughed. "Besides, I want to get a look at the rest of those gasoline runabouts. I wouldn't mind having one of them someday."

"You can't take those things nearly as many places as you can a horse."

"Maybe not, but they can keep going all day without ever stopping to rest. They're faster than a horse, too."

"Well, you can have one of the infernal contraptions if you want. I'll stick with what I know."

The sight of half a dozen of the horseless carriages parked in the street in front of the saloon was pretty awe inspiring, though. Ace had to admit that much. They were covered with dust, but even so, there was enough shiny metal on them to make them gleam in the afternoon sun.

"Would you look at that?" Chance said, clearly impressed.

"I see 'em," Ace said. "I can smell 'em, too."

"That's gasoline. The fuel they run on. It comes from oil, the black stuff they've started pumping out of the ground down in Texas and out in California."

"I know what oil is, and I've heard of gasoline. You're not the only one who keeps up with modern things, you know."

They were close enough now that they began to hear loud voices and crashing sounds from inside the saloon. Ace's steps quickened.

"We're too late," he said. "The fight's already started."

"We can still pitch in to help Sheriff Carson."

Both brothers trotted toward the Brown Dirt Cowboy. Other people were converging on the saloon as well, drawn by the commotion.

Ace, the bigger of the two Jensens, shouldered

through the crowd and made a path for Chance to follow him. The batwings that normally hung across the entrance were fastened back at this time of year, and the double doors stood open.

Ace had just reached them when a man flew through the entrance backward, propelled by a punch. Ace exclaimed, "Whoa!" and got his legs braced just in time to catch the man under the arms without being knocked off his feet.

The man wore the same sort of long duster and silly-looking cap that Edward Collinsworth had sported, but he was skinny, with big sideburns and a close-cropped beard. He turned his head to see who had caught him and said, "Thanks terribly, old man. I was about to—"

He didn't get any farther than that. His eyes rolled up in their sockets and he turned to dead weight, sagging in Ace's grip as he passed out.

Ace lowered the man to the boardwalk and stepped around him.

A big knot of cursing, punching, kicking men filled the middle of the room. Chairs and tables had been knocked aside in the brawl. Debris from broken pieces of furniture was scattered around the floor.

The painted, scantily clad serving girls had retreated to the staircase that led up to the saloon's second floor. They stood there wide eyed, watching the battle.

Likewise the two bartenders hunkered behind the hardwood, lifting their heads just enough to see what was going on and ducking every time a wildly thrown chair leg came in their direction. The backbar was already in a shambles from all the broken bottles on it. The spilled liquor put a sharp reek in the air.

There didn't seem to be any customers in the saloon other than the men clashing in the fight, Ace noted. More than likely, everybody else in the place had scurried out when the hostilities commenced.

Ace looked around for Sheriff Carson and spotted the lawman sitting at one of the tables with a bloody handkerchief held to his head. He hurried over and asked, "Sheriff, are you all right?"

Carson looked up and said, "One of those idiots clouted me with a table leg! I'm lucky he didn't bust my head open. I damn near shot the son of a . . ."

His voice trailed off into a furious growl.

"I'm surprised you didn't shoot him," Chance said. "I might have."

"Ah, hell, I figured once I started shooting, I'd have to gun down all of them, and Brown'd never get all the bloodstains off the floor!"

"Where are your deputies?" Ace asked.

"All out of town on other law business," Carson replied. "I didn't think I'd need any help today. Most folks are plumb peaceful this close to Christmas. I just didn't figure on that bunch of crazy easterners coming into town!"

"Did they start it?"

"I don't know. Haven't had a chance to find out yet. I'm gonna lock up the whole bunch of 'em and sort it out then!"

Carson started to get up. Ace put a hand on his shoulder and said, "Stay there, Sheriff. Chance and I will round them up for you."

"There's more than a dozen of them!" Chance objected. "We'll be outnumbered AT LEAST five or six to one!"

"That's why I don't plan on fighting fair," Ace said.

He drew his Colt from its holster, reversed the gun, and gripped it tightly by the barrel and cylinder as he stepped up behind one of the combatants. This happened to be one of the duster-clad automobile enthusiasts who still had his cap on.

Ace brought the gun butt down sharply on the man's head, not hard enough to do any real damage but with sufficient force to stun him. The man was getting set to throw a punch, but when Ace hit him, his knees buckled and he collapsed.

The cowboy he had been about to hit looked surprised, but he said, "Thanks, pard—" before Ace rapped him on the head as well.

Ace had developed this skill while working as a deputy town marshal many years earlier, one of several occasions the Jensen brothers had worn law badges. The cowboy dropped just as swiftly as the man in the duster had.

That was two down right away. Ace continued working swiftly, and Chance did the same, taking the brawlers by surprise as he knocked them out.

Sooner or later, somebody was bound to notice what they were doing, though, and half the fighters were still on their feet when a man bawled, "Hey, look out for those two!"

A man whirled around and threw a punch at Ace's head. He had to duck and let the fist whip above him. As he came up, he backhanded the man using the Colt, and this one probably had a broken jaw when he went down.

Ace regretted that, but somebody in this ruckus might have easily killed Monte Carson with that table leg, so he wasn't in the mood to be too lenient.

One of the other men swept up a still intact chair and smashed it across Ace's back, knocking him forward as the chair came to pieces. Another man grabbed him and slung him against the bar. The small of his back hit the edge of the hardwood. He grimaced in pain.

A cowboy's face, twisted into ugliness with anger, loomed in front of him. He smacked the man in the forehead with the gun butt. The cowboy fell away, but one of the duster-clad easterners instantly took his place. He sank a fist in Ace's belly and doubled him over.

Before the man could take advantage of that, Chance appeared and knocked him off his feet with a slashing blow. Somewhere in the melee, Chance had lost his gun, but as he helped Ace straighten up, one of the bartenders nervously extended a bungstarter across the hardwood and said over the racket, "Here! Use this!"

"Thanks," Chance replied with a grin as he took the bungstarter. "I will!" He lingered at Ace's side for a second. "Are you all right?"

"Yeah," Ace assured him. "I think maybe we're getting a mite too old for hell-raising like this, though."

"Speak for yourself!" Chance told him with a fighting grin, then plunged back into the chaotic whirl of battling men.

Ace holstered his gun. He was more in the mood to use his fists now. He grabbed a man's shoulder, hauled him around, and slammed a punch into his face, feeling the hot spurt of blood across his knuckles as the hombre's nose flattened.

That was more like it, Ace thought as a grim ferocity surged through him.

For the next minute or so, he waded in with both fists flying. Chance had walloped several men with the bungstarter already, and the odds were rapidly growing even. When there were only two of the brawlers left upright, Chance rammed the bungstarter into one man's belly, then smacked him on the head and knocked him facedown on the floor, out cold.

That left Ace facing the lone easterner still upright, a big, dark-haired man with a cocky grin on his face despite being battered and bloody.

"You don't want any part of me, cowboy," he told Ace. "I was the middleweight boxing champion at Harvard for three years straight!"

"Well, I've survived on the frontier a lot longer than that, fella, and I reckon that's harder," Ace said.

"Don't claim I didn't warn you."

The man darted at him. Ace flung up his arm to block the man's right, only to realize too late that it was a feint. The man's left crashed into his jaw and knocked him back against the bar again, thankfully not as hard this time.

Ace caught himself and saw Chance moving in on the man from the side with the bungstarter. He motioned his brother back. Chance paused and then shrugged. He knew Ace wanted to settle this himself.

"Give up?" the easterner asked with his arrogant grin.

"Not hardly," Ace said. He cocked his fists and went to work.

The man was a boxer, but no pugilist, no matter how skilled, can defeat a man who can hit just as hard and absorb more punishment. Ace took the blows and returned his own, smashing his fists against the man's head and body time and time again.

Stung by the punches, the easterner lost his temper and wound up standing toe to toe with Ace as they slugged at each other. That was a fight he couldn't win. Eventually Ace caught him with a left to the sternum that rocked him and made him drop his arms.

A split second later, Ace's right exploded on the man's jaw, lifted him off his feet, and dropped him in a heap on top of several senseless former combatants.

Ace stood there, chest heaving a little, as Chance came over to him and asked, "Are you all right?"

"Reckon I will be once I catch my breath." Ace flexed his hands. "Don't think anything is broken."

"There better not be," Chance said. "You never know when you'll need to use a gun."

Ace stood there and watched as Sheriff Carson, now with his gun drawn and the handkerchief tied around his head as a crude bandage, moved in and started rounding up his prisoners as they began to regain consciousness.

"We're going to Reno to celebrate Christmas with our family," Ace said to his brother. "I don't expect there'll be any sort of pitched gun battle out there, do you?"

"No," Chance said, "but we're Jensens, so you can't ever rule it out!"

BOOK THREE

BOOK THREE

CHAPTER 24

Smoke had ridden on many stagecoaches in the past, but this was a new experience for Denny and Louis. As the coach's rocking, jolting gait made them sway back and forth, he could tell they didn't care much for it.

"This is a bit like being at sea, isn't it?" Louis said. His face had a greenish tinge to it.

"You're not going to get sick, are you?" Denny asked.

"I'm fine," her brother answered with a trace of annoyance in his voice. "Just worry about yourself."

Smoke, Denny, and Louis were sitting on the rear seat, which meant they were able to face forward, at least. Alma Lewiston, Melanie Buckner, and Jerome Kellerman had the front seat.

That left the bench in the middle of the coach for Frank Colbert, Bradley Buckner, and the reporter, Peter Stansfield. Leather straps hung from the ceiling. The passengers on the bench could hold on to those in order to brace themselves, if they wanted to.

Stansfield took advantage of that, but Colbert,

who seemed to be a westerner born and bred, rocked along easy enough, and Brad was too young to be anything but excited at being part of this stagecoach journey.

Fred Davis had furnished lap robes for the passengers to help ward off the cold that came in around the canvas covers over the windows. Melanie and Alma were huddled under one of the robes, but no one else was using them yet.

They would before this trip was over, Smoke thought. It was going to get mighty cold up there in the mountains. He remembered telling Denny and Louis about the Donner Party and hoped wryly that they wouldn't get stuck.

"If you think this is uncomfortable," he mused aloud, "you should have ridden one of these things down in Arizona or Texas during the summer. The heat would just about melt you, and so much dust got into the coach that it seemed like you were trying to breathe with your head in a bag full of dirt."

"And yet people rode them everywhere," Louis said.

"Well, sure. That was the only way to get anywhere, other than horseback or covered wagon, and not everybody was able to travel like that. It was the fastest way to cover long distances, too, until the train came along."

Brad said, "I like this better. The train really stunk of burning coal."

"I wish the train had been able to get through," his mother said. "We'd be most of the way to Reno by now."

Smoke nodded toward Brad and said, "The boy

will have an experience he'll never forget. Not many youngsters this day and age can claim to have crossed the Sierra Nevadas by stagecoach."

"I may be the only one!" Brad said.

Smoke grinned. "Yeah, you just might be."

The youngster reminded him a little of Billy and Bobby, the two orphans he and Sally had taken in at different times in the past, raising them until they had gone out on their own. Brad was younger than either of those two had been, but he had the same sort of enthusiasm for life.

However, there was no sign of enthusiasm on the faces of either Colbert or Kellerman. Both men appeared serious, even solemn. They weren't going to be very good company on the journey, Smoke thought.

He was sitting beside the window on the right-hand side of the stage, so he moved the canvas cover on the window just a little, enough for him to look out and see the mountains looming in the distance.

They were traveling through heavily wooded foothills at the moment, but soon the trail would begin to rise at a steeper slope. By the middle of the afternoon, they would reach the point where the Mc-Culley Cutoff veered away to the south and avoided the tallest of the peaks and passes.

Around midday, Salty reined the team to a halt so he and Smoke could put the fresh horses in harness. They would make frequent stops like that, in order to keep the teams as fresh as possible.

It was good for the passengers to have a chance to get out and stretch their legs, too, in spite of the chilly, overcast day.

Ever since leaving Sacramento, Peter Stansfield

had attempted from time to time to engage Smoke in conversation. Smoke knew good and well that the reporter was trying to interview him, in the guise of being friendly, so his answers were short and unresponsive, although he wasn't rude about it.

Stansfield tried again now, standing around while Smoke and Salty worked with the horses. He said, "I understand that you and our driver, Mr. Stevens, have been acquainted in the past, Mr. Jensen."

"We've crossed trails a few times and ridden a few miles together," Smoke said as he unhitched one of the horses and got ready to lead it to the back of the stagecoach.

"I'd love to hear about some of your adventures."

"I don't recall us ever having any adventures," Smoke said. "Do you, Salty?"

"Well, there was that time in Dakota Territory we run into them no-good—" the old-timer began. He stopped short as Smoke gave him a stern look. Then Salty went on, "Nope, nope, can't think of a derned thing. Life was always plumb peaceful whenever the two of us was together."

"You don't expect me to believe that!" Stansfield burst out. "Why, Smoke Jensen is known all across the West—no, all across the entire *country*—for the exciting life he's led. There are bound to have been all sorts of occasions on which the two of you faced danger."

Salty shook his head stubbornly and said, "Not so's you could speak of."

With exasperation showing on his face, Stansfield said, "Well, then, what about that other man you mentioned back in Sacramento? The gunfighter you claimed was a friend of yours. What was his name?

"Frank Morgan," Salty said. "But if you want to know anything about him, you'd best go hunt him up and ask him your own self. He ain't one to flap his gums, and I don't reckon he'd want me doin' that, neither."

"You westerners are so laconic it's disgusting." Stansfield shook his head and turned away, leaving Smoke and Salty to get on with the job of switching out the teams.

Under his breath, Salty said, "You're gettin' on that young fella's nerves, Smoke."

"And he's getting on mine. I didn't want him to come along in the first place."

Smoke didn't eavesdrop on purpose, but he could still hear as Stansfield went over to Frank Colbert, who was walking back and forth and clapping his hands together lightly to try to get warm.

"Mr. Colbert," the reporter said. "If I might have a word with you . . . ?"

"What do you want?" Colbert snapped.

"I've been thinking about it, and there's something vaguely familiar about your name, as if I've seen it somewhere. Might I ask, what line of work are you in?"

"You can ask, but you won't get an answer. It's none of your damn business."

"I'm sorry. I meant no offense—"

"I'm not offended. You don't matter enough for me to be offended, mister. Go peddle your papers somewhere else."

With that, Colbert turned away and walked over to join Alma Lewiston. They had been talking together quietly all morning as they rode in the stagecoach, confirming Smoke's hunch that a friendship—if not more—had sprung up between them.

Stansfield stood there for a moment with a look of defeat on his face, but then he squared his narrow shoulders and approached Jerome Kellerman. Smoke saw that and felt a moment of fleeting admiration for the reporter. Stansfield was determined to get a story, even though everyone kept turning him away.

His determination counted for little with Kellerman, though, who curtly informed Stansfield that he had no comment about the trip they were on or anything else.

Brad Buckner approached Smoke and said, "I'd be happy to help you and Mr. Stevens, Mr. Jensen, if there's anything I can do."

"Ever hitched up a stagecoach team before?" Smoke asked in apparent seriousness.

Brad stared at him for a second and then laughed. "No."

"Then the best way for you to help is to keep an eye on your ma and do anything that she needs done."

"She doesn't need anything. She's busy talking to your son."

That made Smoke look around. The boy was right. Louis was walking with Melanie Buckner, their shoes kicking up little white puffs from the thin layer of snow on the ground. The two of them were laughing and talking.

Denny stood near the stagecoach, watching Louis and Melanie and looking faintly disgusted.

Smoke told Brad, "Why don't you watch what Salty and I do, then, and you'll learn something about how to handle horses."

"I'd like that! I want to drive a stagecoach one day."

Salty said, "You may not get a chance to do that, sonny. By the time you're old enough, I reckon all the stagecoaches will be gone."

"Maybe not. I mean, there aren't many around anymore these days, but we're riding through the mountains in one, anyway, aren't we?"

"The boy's got a point," Smoke said with a grin.

After Stansfield's futile attempt to interview Colbert, he and Alma had walked around to the other side of the coach and drawn away from it a short distance. As they stood at the base of a wooded slope, Alma said, "You were kind of rough on that reporter, weren't you?"

"I don't have any use for those scavengers," Colbert said. "Always prying into other people's business and trying to make hay out of somebody else's bad luck."

"I suppose that's true. Speaking of other people's business . . . you've never told *me* what line of work you're in, either, Frank."

"That's because there's no need for you to know that."

"Maybe not, but I just thought that since we're traveling together—"

"We're not traveling together," Colbert interrupted her. "Oh, we're on the same stagecoach, heading for the same place . . . and I don't mind spending some time with you. I'll admit, I was surprised when you knocked on the door of my hotel room last night, but it turned out to be a pleasant surprise. None of that really means anything, though."

She looked at him for a long moment, then said, "God, you really are a cold-blooded, hard-hearted bastard, aren't you?"

"You'd do well to remember that. And if you decide to have anything to do with me, remember that it's your own choice, too."

"I'll remember," she said softly.

"Then we understand each other." Colbert batted his hands together some more. "Damn, it's chilly out here."

"Yeah, it is," Alma said.

"It must have been difficult for you, raising a child by yourself," Louis said to Melanie Buckner as they walked around on the other side of the coach.

"It has been trying, at times," she admitted. "But Bradley is a wonderful boy. He's very good-natured and friendly. He's just enthusiastic and curious about things."

"Most boys are."

For a moment, Melanie lightly rested gloved fingertips on Louis's forearm. "I'm sure you were, too," she said, "when you were young."

"Well, I was certainly curious, I suppose, but there

was a limit to how much actual enthusiasm I could muster. You see, my health wasn't very good."

"Oh, no! I'm so sorry. You must have gotten better. You look fine now." A warm flush spread across Melanie's cheeks. "I mean . . . you look healthy. . . ."

"My condition is one that's not readily apparent. I have a weak heart."

"That's terrible! I mean, are you . . . in any danger?"

He smiled. "Some would say that we're all in danger from one thing or another, especially our hearts. But as long as I'm careful and don't exert myself too much, I'll be fine for now and perhaps for a long time to come."

"That's good to know. Although it must be difficult at times to stay calm and, ah, not get too worked up about anything. . . ."

"Yes, very difficult," Louis said. "But I've managed so far."

"If you need any help, I've worked as a nurse in the past," Melanie said.

"You have?"

"Oh, yes. I've been a nurse and a seamstress, and I worked in a restaurant. . . . Actually, I've done any number of jobs to support Bradley and myself since my husband passed away."

"I'm sorry," Louis murmured. "I don't mean to bring up bad memories."

"That's all right. It's been several years. Tom's death was shocking. He was working on a ranch when he was thrown from a horse and broke his neck. Bradley and I were living there, too, and I'll never forget what it was like when the other men brought his body in. It was a complete accident, they said. Tom was a wonderful horseman. But they were working in a wooded area, and his horse almost stepped on a rattlesnake and panicked." She shook her head. "He never had a chance."

"Life is like that," Louis said. "Sometimes it strikes without warning."

"And it's unfair, too, when it comes to things like my husband's death and your affliction."

Somehow while they were walking, his right arm had gotten linked with her left. He reached over with his left hand and patted her arm, saying reassuringly, "Don't worry about me. I may not be the healthiest Jensen, but I'm still a Jensen."

"And that makes a difference?"

"It certainly does."

She smiled at him. "I'm glad you have such a wonderful family."

Louis glanced toward the stagecoach and saw Denny standing beside it, glaring at him. He just grinned back at her, well aware that it would make her more infuriated. He knew he ought to be ashamed of himself for deliberately annoying his sister, but he wasn't.

Really, it was none of her affair if he was interested in Melanie Buckner. And it wasn't as if anything serious would ever come from such a mild, innocent flirtation. He was just passing the time, that's all.

And the time for this brief stop was over. "Everybody back on board!" Smoke called. "We're ready to roll."

CHAPTER 25

Reno, Nevada

The blizzard that had closed Donner Pass in the Sierra Nevadas hadn't made it as far as Reno. In fact, the weather was chilly but otherwise fairly nice there, with no snow and weak, wintery sunshine washing over the settlement.

The storm clouds were visible over the mountains to the west, though, and a storm of a different kind was brewing here, too. Folks just didn't know it yet, Deke Mahoney reflected as he walked along the street with Warren Hopgood and Magnus Stevenson.

"Are you sure that telegrapher back in Staghorn didn't say nothin' about which bank it is that's expectin' the money shipment?" Mahoney asked Stevenson, and not for the first time, either.

"I told you, Deke, he didn't," Stevenson replied. "I didn't know there were two banks in Reno. I couldn't very well go up to him and ask him for more details, either."

"I know, I know." Mahoney rubbed his angular jaw and frowned in thought. "We got to figure it out. There ain't enough of us to hit both banks at once."

"That never works, anyway," Hopgood pointed out. "You remember what happened to the Daltons over there in Coffeyville."

Mahoney grimaced. Every rider of the owlhoot trail knew the story of the ferocious gun battle that had resulted in the death or capture of all the members of the Dalton gang. All because they had tried to rob both banks in Coffeyville, Kansas, at the same time.

"What we need is an inside man," Mahoney said. He came to a stop opposite one of Reno's banks and stared at it with a frown creasing his forehead. "It's near noontime. The tellers will be goin' out for lunch pretty soon. I'm gonna follow one of 'em and strike up a conversation with the fella."

"And just ask him if a big money shipment is coming in between now and Christmas?" Hopgood said with a dour expression. "What the hell kind of an idea is that?"

"Hold on, hold on," Stevenson said. "There might be something to what Deke says. Why don't you let me be the one to give it a try, though?"

"You don't reckon I can do it?" Mahoney demanded.

"It's not that, Deke. You've got to admit, though, I'm more of a smooth talker than you are."

"Magnus is right," Hopgood said. "And now that I think about it, he might find out something useful. It's worth a try."

"Yeah," Mahoney said grudgingly. "I reckon it is."

"Why don't you boys go on back down to the sa-loon where we left Otis and Jim Bob, and I'll find you there later?" Stevenson suggested.

"Just be careful," Hopgood cautioned. "You're try-ing to find out information, not letting anything slip about our plans."

A grin stretched across Stevenson's face. "Don't worry, I know what I'm doing. I'll wait right here until I see one of the tellers come out of the bank."

The day before, after arriving in Reno, he and Hopgood had scouted both banks, going inside and lingering long enough to get good looks at all the people who worked in each establishment. Steven-son would recognize any of the tellers when they left the bank.

If he didn't have any luck today, they still had a couple of days. He could try the plan with another teller, or at the other bank.

But maybe fortune would smile on his first try. That had been known to happen.

Mahoney and Hopgood walked off toward the Silver Queen Saloon, which they had quickly settled upon as their headquarters while they were in Reno. The whiskey was decent there, the card games seemed hon-est, and the girls who worked the upstairs rooms were attractive, at least for soiled doves.

Stevenson loitered in front of the hardware store across from the bank until he spotted a familiar face. The man who emerged from the building had a long, narrow face with a derby perched on top of his head. He wore a brown tweed suit that had seen bet-ter days but was still respectable.

The last time Stevenson had seen the man, he'd

been behind one of the tellers' windows in the bank. Now he tracked the man from across the street as the bank employee walked purposefully to the east.

In the next block, he turned in at a stone building with a red tile roof. RED TOP CAFÉ—GOOD EATS read the sign on the awning over the boardwalk.

Stevenson crossed the street and went inside as well.

Delicious smells filled the air in the place, and the warmth from the kitchen was pleasant as well. Stevenson spotted his quarry sitting on a leather-topped stool at the counter. The stool to the man's right was empty, although the café was starting to get busy because of the time of day, so Stevenson slid onto it and rested his elbows on the counter.

A stout woman with graying brown hair gave him a friendly smile and asked, "What will you be having today, sir?"

Stevenson pretended to study the menu chalked on a board on the wall behind the counter and said, "I don't know." He looked over at the man to his left. "What's good here, friend?"

"You can't go wrong with the Irish stew," the bank teller replied. He had taken off his derby, revealing thinning brown hair. "That's what I'm having."

"Sounds good to me," Stevenson said with a nod. "And coffee."

"Right away," the woman said.

Stevenson looked at the teller again and said, "I'm much obliged to you for the advice. I'm new in town and haven't been in here before."

"It's a good place to eat. And they're quick about

it, which is good because my boss doesn't allow me a great deal of time for lunch."

"Slave driver, eh?"

The teller laughed. "Oh, I wouldn't go that far!" He looked around quickly, and Stevenson guessed he didn't want it getting back to the bank president that he'd been complaining.

Stevenson turned on the stool and extended his hand. "Bob Stevens," he introduced himself, using a fake name he had used in the past.

The teller shook with him. "Carl Andrews."

"Pleased to meet you, Carl. What is it you do?"

"I work down at the bank. I'm one of the tellers. How about you?"

"I've been driving a freight wagon. Looking for something else right now. The railroads have been putting most of the freight lines out of business."

"Yes, I suppose that's one of the prices we pay for progress. Something new comes along, and somebody else gets put out of business."

Stevenson chuckled. "Don't worry about me. I'm the sort who always lands on his feet. Reckon your job is nice and steady, though. A growing town always needs a bank."

"Reno has two, in fact," Andrews commented. "Ours is the biggest, though."

"Is that a fact? Still and all, the banking business must be pretty slow this time of year. I don't imagine anybody would have any big deals brewing at Christmas."

"Ha! You'd think so, wouldn't you?"

That response was intriguing, and just what Stevenson wanted to hear. He was playing Andrews like an expert angler plays a fish. Now he just needed to pull him in.

Before he could do that, though, the woman came through the swinging door from the kitchen carrying two bowls of stew. She set them in front of Stevenson and Andrews and then picked up a coffeepot to add some to Andrews's cup and fill one for Stevenson.

The bank teller picked up his spoon, grinned, and said, "Smells great, just like always, Mrs. O'Leary."

"Go on with you, Carl," she said to him, then added to Stevenson, "Enjoy your lunch, sir."

"I intend to," he assured her.

The two men ate in silence for a few minutes, but the hum and buzz of conversation in the café continued around them. When Stevenson judged that enough time had passed, he resumed, "You were saying something about how it's busier at the bank than a person might expect?"

"Well, yes, but I can't really be specific, you know? Such matters are confidential. Have to protect the bank's customers, of course."

"Of course," Stevenson agreed. "I know if I had money in your bank—and I very well might, one of these days—I wouldn't want it being talked about. So let's change the subject. Are you a family man, Carl?"

A grin spread across Andrews's face. "Indeed I am. I have a very lovely wife named Rebecca and a daughter named Sadie. How about you, Bob?"

"My late wife and I had two sons. One's in the army, and the other rides for a spread up in Montana." That would deflect any further questions about his mythical offspring, Stevenson thought. And the bank teller wouldn't be too curious about a dead wife.

They continued eating. The Irish stew really was good, Stevenson found, and the coffee wasn't bad, either. He had accomplished his goals by following the bank teller in here, and he had gotten a good meal out of the deal, too.

Andrews scraped his bowl clean, paid the counter-woman, and said to Stevenson, "I'd better get back to work. Nice talking to you. Maybe I'll see you around town."

"Maybe so," Stevenson said.

He turned his attention to the last of his stew as the bank teller put on the derby and left the café.

Carl Andrews would be seeing him again, all right, he reflected with a faint smile, but it wouldn't be around town.

It wouldn't be a pleasant visit, either.

The Sierra Nevadas

Snow had begun to fall again by the time the stage-coach stopped that afternoon, but it was very light, just a flake swirling down here and there, every now and then. That wouldn't add a significant amount to the thin layer of white already covering the ground.

But it was a start, Smoke thought as he and Salty switched the teams again. They had reached a cru-cial point in the journey.

The railroad route was about half a mile to the north, Smoke knew. The main trail, the former wagon road, ran straight ahead, climbing part of the way up a long, fairly gentle slope. Thick growths of snow-mantled pines and firs stretched for a long distance on either side.

As the slope grew steeper, the road curved into a switchback that rose for several miles into the mountains. Then there were more straightaways, more ridges, and finally the climb to Donner Pass itself.

In contrast to the main trail, which was fairly wide and had been packed down rock hard by thousands of iron-rimmed wheels when this was still the Dutch Flats Wagon Road, a smaller trail angled off through the trees to the right. After years of disuse, this path was nothing more than a pair of shallow ruts that were still visible if a person knew where to look. The trees crowded in closely on both sides.

"There she be," Salty said. "The McCulley Cutoff. Reckon we can get through that way, Smoke?"

"We wouldn't be here if I didn't believe it was possible," Smoke replied. "You can still see the trail all right, can't you?"

"Sure. My eyes are as good as ever. I'm a mite worried that the trees and the underbrush might've grown in too close, though."

"There's an ax in the boot, isn't there?"

"Yep. I made sure Fred put one in, and a shovel, too. You never know when you might need somethin' like that."

Smoke nodded and said, "Then we'll chop our way through if we need to. That might slow us down some, but we'll do the best we can."

As before, the passengers had climbed out of the stage to move around while the teams were switched. Frank Colbert was close enough to listen to the conversation between Smoke and Salty. He asked, "How long does it take to go around the cutoff to Reno?"

"In the old days, in good weather, it'd take three, maybe four days from here to Reno," Salty said. "We don't know what the conditions'll be like along the trail these days, o' course, so it ain't easy to predict how long. If the weather slows us down, or if the trail's in such bad shape it'll take work to make it passable, that could add a day or two."

"Four days would put us into Reno on Christmas Eve," Smoke said. "That's what we're shooting for."

Colbert nodded. He pointed at the main trail and asked, "How long if we went that way?"

"We can't," Salty said. "The pass is blocked. That's why the train ain't runnin'."

"Yes, but if we could get through on that road, how long would it take?"

"Used to make it in two days," Salty said with a shrug.

"So you're talking about half the time."

"Yeah, but there ain't no use in worryin' about it, 'cause it can't be done."

"A stagecoach isn't like a train," Colbert insisted. "It doesn't have to follow the rails. It doesn't have to stick right on a trail, either, if there's another way through."

Colbert's sudden interest in the subject puzzled Smoke. He knew the man was anxious to get to Reno—all of them were—but Salty was right: this discussion was pointless.

"Let's finish swapping those teams," he said. "We can still make a good number of miles before dark."

Colbert pointed along the dimly marked cutoff. "Any stage stations left through there?" he asked.

"No, they've long since been abandoned," Smoke told him. "But don't worry. We've brought along plenty of supplies. We won't run out of food."

Louis added from where he stood beside the coach's open door, "Unless we get stranded for a long time. Then we'll have to worry about turning out like the Donner Party."

Brad had already climbed back into the coach. He asked, "What's the Donner Party, Louis?"

"Yes," Denny said dryly, "why don't you explain about the Donner Party to the child, Louis?"

"It's nothing you have to be concerned about," Louis told Brad. "Just some people who tried to travel through the mountains when they shouldn't have and got into trouble. But that won't happen to us."

"It's dangerous, though, isn't it," the youngster persisted, "traveling through here in the winter in a stagecoach, like we're doing?"

"You'll be fine," Louis said, looking now like he wished he hadn't brought up the subject. "We all will." He looked at Melanie and mouthed the word *Sorry.*

"Are we about ready to go?" Kellerman asked. The white-haired man had the same air of impatience he had displayed ever since the journey began early that morning.

"Just a few more minutes," Smoke said. He had the last of the fresh horses and was leading it to the front of the coach to be harnessed into the team.

Of course, these animals were only reasonably fresh, as compared to the ones that had been moved to the back of the stagecoach. A few hours of rest wasn't enough to refresh either team, especially when the horses not actually pulling the stagecoach had to keep moving behind it. This was a makeshift, less than ideal arrangement but the best Smoke could manage.

He hoped resting overnight, once they had stopped, would be enough to put some spring back in the horses' steps.

Salty climbed to the driver's box, making the coach sag a little to one side on its thoroughbraces, while Smoke backed the last of the horses into its place. Everyone else was back in the coach now except for Colbert, who stood nearby.

Smoke glanced at the man and frowned as he finished up the task. "Help you with something, Mr. Colbert?" he asked.

"I'm just trying to make sure I've got everything straight in my head. Going this way"—he pointed along the McCulley Cutoff—"we'll get to Reno on Christmas Eve at the earliest, and that's if we don't run into any major problems."

"Yep, that's right," Salty said from the box.

Colbert pointed at the main trail. "But that route might get us there two days earlier."

"I don't think you were listening," Smoke said. "The pass is closed."

"The pass is closed *for the train*," Colbert said. "Because an avalanche tore up the snowsheds and piled up tons of snow on the tracks. Back in Sacramento, that's what they told us the telegram from the hotel at the summit said."

Smoke gave a little shake of his head. "I don't get your point, mister."

"This road doesn't follow the same exact route as the train tracks, does it?"

Salty said, "It's pretty close, especially up yonder in the pass. The mountains come in close enough on the sides that there ain't much room for the old wagon road and the railroad right-of-way to be apart."

"But you don't *know* the road itself is blocked just because the train tracks are. And if you *could* get through that way, it would cut two days off the trip, at the very least."

Salty sounded like he was getting a little exasperated as he said, "Mister, you just ain't listenin'. I been through these parts durin' the winter, and Smoke has, too. The only way we're gettin' to Reno, whether before Christmas Day or not, is by takin' the cutoff." He waved a hand toward the peaks. "They's a storm still ragin' up there. Even if the road ain't completely blocked, you can't drive through a blizzard. It's too dang risky."

Smoke said, "I think you need to get back in the coach now, Mr. Colbert. It's time we were rolling again."

"I was just curious." Colbert reached for the door, which one of the other passengers had pulled closed after climbing into the stagecoach. He fumbled with the latch for a second and then said, "This seems to be stuck."

Smoke stepped past him and said, "Let me take a look at it."

As he reached up to take hold of the door latch, some instinct warned him, but the alarm came too late. Smoke started to twist around. As he did, from the corner of his eye he caught a flicker of movement as Colbert struck at him with a gun the man had produced from somewhere.

The next instant, the blow slammed into the side of Smoke's head with terrific force. The impact drove him against the side of the stagecoach and made bright red explosions go off inside his skull. He grabbed at the door, only vaguely aware that he needed to hold himself up and stay on his feet, but his hand slipped and he fell, landing with his face in the cold snow.

The last thing he knew was the roar of a gunshot.

CHAPTER 26

As Jensen went down under the vicious blow, the old man on the driver's box yelled, "Hey! What in tarnation—"

Stevens dropped the reins and surged to his feet. He reached under his coat to claw at the old revolver he wore, but just as the weapon came free, Colbert lifted his gun and shot him. The blast slammed Stevens off the box and dropped him on the snowy ground on the other side of the coach.

Colbert didn't know how badly he had wounded the man. He glanced at Jensen, saw that he appeared to be out cold, and then ran around the front of the team to check on the old-timer.

Stevens was sprawled on his back, still alive and trying to get up. Blood had left red splatters on the snow around him. The gun he had drawn a moment earlier lay about six feet away, where he had dropped it when he fell off the driver's box.

Colbert stalked forward and swung his gun up,

ready to finish off the old man. Jensen could handle the team. Stevens was just extra baggage.

Colbert wasn't worried about any of the others in the coach. Jensen and Stevens were the only real threats. He could keep an eye on one of them if the other was dead. His finger tightened on the trigger.

The coach door flew open and slammed against his hand as he fired, causing the bullet to fly off harmlessly into the woods beside the trail.

The next instant, a wildcat landed on Frank Colbert.

For a second, Denny couldn't believe her eyes when she saw the big, ugly man named Colbert clout her father with a gun.

But then he tilted the revolver up and fired, and the blast jolted Denny out of her shocked state. She knew the shot had to be directed at Salty, and when she heard a thump from the other side of the coach, she jerked her head around and saw the feisty old jehu lying on the ground where he had fallen.

Denny's first instinct was to go to Smoke and make sure he was all right, but Salty had been shot. She lunged across to the coach's other door, past Melanie Buckner, who had started screaming in fear at the sound of the shot.

Louis cried, "Denny, wait!," but any time trouble broke out, she wasn't in the habit of sitting around and waiting for things to get worse.

The canvas covers over the windows had been raised while the coach was stopped. Through the window in front on the left, she caught sight of Frank Colbert as he rushed around to that side, still brandishing the pistol he had used to hit Smoke and shoot Salty.

Colbert tried to bring the gun to bear on the fallen old-timer, but Denny flung the door open and whacked his arm with it, sending the shot whining off into the trees.

Denny was right behind the door, leaping out of the coach and tackling the man.

The impact made Colbert stagger to the side. Denny tried to wrap her legs around his waist but couldn't manage it because the skirt of her traveling outfit bound them too much. She got her arms around his neck and stuck a foot between his calves instead, tripping him. They both sprawled in the snow.

Denny landed on top. Colbert's right arm was out to the side with the gun still clutched in that hand. Denny grabbed his wrist with one hand to pin it down and tried to pry the gun free with the other. Colbert seemed a little stunned by the ferocity of her attack, but she knew that wouldn't last, so she didn't have long.

Not long enough. Colbert snarled a curse and clubbed at her head with his other hand. Denny had to duck. His fist raked the hat from her head and caused her blond curls to spill around her shoulders. He heaved his body up and threw her to the side. He was too strong for her to stop him.

But as Denny rolled on the ground, she caught a glimpse of her brother aiming a kick at Colbert's head. Louis was no fighter; even when they were kids, it had been her saving him from bullies instead of the other way around. But he didn't lack for courage and was trying to come to Denny's aid.

Colbert twisted and took the kick on his shoulder. As Denny came to a stop on her belly, she knew a second of terror because she thought Colbert would shoot Louis.

Instead, Colbert caught hold of Louis's ankle and heaved, throwing the younger man over on his back. Louis hit hard and rolled onto his side, gasping for breath because the landing had knocked all the air out of his lungs.

Denny scrambled up, ready to go after Colbert again, gun or no gun.

She had no idea why he had attacked Smoke and shot Salty. From what she had overheard of the conversation going on outside, they had been arguing about whether the coach should take the McCulley Cutoff as planned or try to make it over the mountains on the old wagon road. That didn't seem like anything to fight over.

Before Denny could do anything else, Melanie screamed, "Bradley, no!"

The boy leaped down from the coach and charged Colbert. "You leave Miss Denny alone!" he yelled.

Colbert backhanded him and knocked him flying, drawing more screams from Melanie. She dropped from the coach to the ground but didn't go after Colbert. She hurried to Brad's side instead. Denny couldn't blame her for that.

Reaching down, Denny scooped a handful of snow from the ground and threw it in Colbert's face as he turned back toward her. She knew it wasn't going to hurt him, but it might blind him for a second. He was on his knees, so she lowered her shoulder and tackled him again.

The gun went off right beside her head, the report slamming into her ear like a giant fist. She couldn't help crying out in shock and pain.

But Colbert went over backward, and as Denny landed on top of him again, she tried to dig a knee into his groin. A grunt exploded from him, so she hoped she had hit her target. She pulled herself up, laced her fingers together, and swung her clubbed fists at his jaw as hard as she could. The blow jerked his head to the side.

For a second, he was stunned, unable to fight back. Denny raised her arms, ready to hit him again and knock him out.

Before that blow could fall, another gun roared. Denny flinched involuntarily as she heard the slug whip through the air above her head.

"Stop it! Get away from him right now, or I'll kill you!"

The shrill voice was panicky, almost hysterical, but Denny knew a hysterical person could pull a trigger and kill just as easily as one who was calm. She looked over her shoulder and saw Alma Lewiston standing a few yards away with a heavy old Colt clutched in both hands as she pointed it toward Denny.

That had to be Salty's gun. Alma had gotten out of the coach, picked it up . . . and taken sides in this battle, whatever the hell it was about.

"Put that gun down, Mrs. Lewiston," Denny said. "You're going to hurt somebody."

"Damn right I am—the bitch daughter of the man

who made me a widow! Get away from him now or I'll shoot, I swear it!"

Denny hesitated, and as she did, Colbert recovered enough to smash a fist against her jaw and knock her off of him. With her head spinning from the punch, she slid through the snow and came to a stop a few feet away.

Colbert clambered up, still holding the pistol, and told Alma, "Keep her covered."

"Are you all right, Frank?" she asked.

"Just do what I told you!" he roared. He strode over to where Melanie had pulled a groggy Brad into her lap. She screamed again as he reached down with his free hand and grabbed the boy's arm. He jerked Brad away from her.

Denny lifted her head, still seeing stars, but her vision was clear enough to see Smoke come around the back of the coach with the Colt Lightning in his hand. Colbert saw him, too, and wheeled around, putting Brad in front of him. He had his left arm around the boy's neck and rammed the gun muzzle against Brad's head.

"Not another step, Jensen, or this little bastard's brains are gonna be splattered all over the snow!"

Smoke stopped in his tracks. Blood trickled down the side of his face from the cut on the side of his head he had suffered when Colbert hit him with the pistol.

"Take it easy, Colbert," he said. "You don't want to hurt that boy."

"I don't give a damn about this boy. But if *you* do, you'd better toss that gun away."

Denny looked around. Melanie was still screaming as she huddled on her knees. Louis had recovered a little from getting the breath knocked out of him and had pushed himself up on one elbow, but he wasn't in any position to do anything. Salty wasn't moving anymore, but Denny couldn't tell if he was dead or just had passed out from being shot.

Over at the coach, Peter Stansfield and Jerome Kellerman gaped from the windows, but neither of them appeared to be willing to take a hand.

That left Alma, her face pale but resolute as she pointed Salty's gun at Denny.

Colbert rasped, "If Jensen doesn't do what he's told, shoot that bitch, Alma."

Smoke said, "Mister, I'm gonna kill you."

A harsh laugh came from Colbert. "You may be some fancy gunfighter, but my thumb's the only thing holding back the hammer on this gun. You're not fast enough to keep me from killing the boy. And while you're shooting me, Alma will put a bullet in your daughter. What's it gonna be . . . *gunfighter*?"

For a couple of seconds that seemed longer, Smoke didn't respond. Then he lowered the gun in his hand and tossed it to the side.

"You'd better shoot me here and now, mister, because I'm telling you . . . you're making a mistake leaving me alive."

"For two bits, I'd do it," Colbert said. "Lucky for you, there's a lot more than two bits riding on me getting to Reno, and with that old bastard dead, I need somebody to drive the stagecoach."

Denny saw Smoke's eyes cut over to the fallen jehu. "Salty!" he exclaimed.

"I think he's alive, Pa," Denny said. "I think I saw him breathing."

Smoke nodded toward Denny and said to Colbert, "Let her go and check."

Colbert looked like he was going to refuse, but then he shrugged and said, "All right, go ahead. But if you see her about to try anything, blow a hole in her, Alma."

"You could thank me for helping you, Frank," Alma said tightly without taking her eyes—or the gun—away from Denny.

"Oh, I'm obliged to you," he said. "I'll show you how much by cutting you in on the loot when we get to Reno, how about that? You'll have more money than you've ever seen before."

Alma frowned, causing Denny to wonder if money was actually what the woman cared about. But Alma said, "Go ahead and see how bad he's hurt," so Denny didn't waste any time crawling over to Salty on hands and knees.

She put a hand on his bloody chest. It rose and fell in a ragged rhythm. He was alive, all right, but she wasn't sure how badly he was hurt.

She pulled aside the heavy coat and the buckskin jacket, saw the hole in the cowhide vest and the flannel shirt underneath it. The bullet had hit Salty high on the left side of his chest, missing the heart by a handful of inches.

Carefully, Denny took hold of his shoulder and raised him enough to see the exit wound on his back. The slug had gone clean through.

That was good. It meant the blood Salty had lost was the main danger, and probably the reason he had

passed out. His shoulder might be broken, too;
Denny couldn't tell about that. But she thought that
if the wounds were cleaned and bound up and the
arm put in a sling, Salty stood a good chance of surviving Colbert's savage attack.

She looked up at Smoke and said, "He'll be okay, Pa."

A cruel grin stretched across Colbert's face as he
continued to hang on to the squirming Brad. "Maybe
I don't need you after all, then, Jensen."

"Wait!" Denny said. "Salty can't handle the team, if
that's what you're thinking. Not with a bullet through
his shoulder, thanks to you."

"He's lucky. I was trying to kill him. How about
you? You tomboy enough to drive a stagecoach?"

"Me?" Denny forced herself to say. She swallowed
as she thought fast. "I . . . I'm just a girl."

Those words tasted bitter in her mouth, but she
said them anyway. Anything was worth it to keep both
her father and Salty alive, not to mention Louis and
everybody else.

"I guess it's up to you, then, Jensen," Colbert went
on. "I'm sure none of these other tenderfeet could
manage, especially in bad weather."

Smoke said, "You mean you want me to drive the
coach through the mountains, through Donner Pass,
and on to Reno?"

"You do that, and all these others live," Colbert
said. "I give you my word on that."

"I reckon we're past me putting much stock in
your word, mister," Smoke said. "But you don't give
me much choice."

"Damn right I don't."

"Whatever's in Reno must be mighty important."

"Never mind about that," Colbert snapped. "We've got a deal?"

Smoke looked at Denny and Louis and grimaced. "We've got a deal. Now you can let that boy go back to his mother."

Slowly, Colbert shook his head. "I don't think so. The brat stays with me. My gun's never going to be more than a few inches away from him. You'd better keep that in mind all the time, Jensen."

Things seemed to be settled for the moment, although not at all satisfactorily. Denny said, "I need some help with Salty."

Louis said, "Mrs. Buckner used to be a nurse."

Melanie had stopped screaming when it became obvious Colbert wasn't going to kill Brad right away, but she was still sobbing. Denny said sharply, to get through to her, "Mrs. Buckner! Melanie! I need some help here."

Louis asked Colbert, "Can I get up?"

"Don't try anything," the man warned.

Louis got to his feet and held up his hands, palms out. "No tricks, I promise." He went over to the crying woman and bent to put an arm around her shoulders. "Come on, Melanie," he urged. "Let's go give Denny a hand with poor Mr. Stevens."

Melanie sniffled and wiped the back of a gloved hand across her nose. "All . . . all right," she managed to say. She let Louis help her up. They walked slowly toward Denny and Salty.

Melanie's face was bright red from both the crying and the cold. She looked like she might fall down if not for Louis's support. She kept turning her head to look at Colbert and Brad.

Then Salty began to stir. He groaned and mut-tered, "Jehoshaphat! Wha . . . what in tarnation . . ."

Denny put a hand on his uninjured shoulder. "Just lie still, Mr. Stevens," she told him. "You've been shot."

"I . . . I remember! That no good skunk Colbert—"

"Shut him up and tend to him," Colbert barked. He looked at Smoke. "Climb up there on the driver's box. But don't even think about driving away with the coach. That won't stop me from killing this boy."

"You're the boss . . . for now," Smoke said, his face and voice grim.

Salty's obvious pain finally seemed to penetrate Melanie's fear for her son. She swallowed hard and said, "We need to get him to sit up. Can you do that, Mr. Stevens?"

"I . . . reckon I can," Salty said.

"I'll give you a hand," Louis offered.

They got Salty into a sitting position and pulled away his clothing enough to reveal both of the ugly wounds. He began shivering and his teeth chattered.

"M-mighty cold out here," he said.

"It is," Melanie agreed, "and the blood you lost makes it feel worse. But the cold helps keep the blood from flowing quite as freely, too, and that's good. We need something to clean the wounds. Maybe some hot water?" She looked at Louis. "Can you build a fire?"

Colbert said, "We don't have time for that, damn it. Get some handfuls of snow and use them, if you have to. Then bind up the wounds and let's get out of here."

"We'll have to stop when it gets dark," Louis said quietly. "I'll build a fire and we'll tend to Salty's injuries better then."

Melanie nodded. "If that's all we can do."

Smoke had climbed onto the driver's box, as Colbert had ordered. He sat there looking like a leashed tiger that wanted to break free and go on a rampage at any moment. Denny thought about what her father had said about Colbert making a mistake by leaving him alive.

The same thing held true for her. Colbert didn't have just one Jensen who wanted his hide.

Now there were two Jensens who had a score to settle.

CHAPTER 27

Smoke sat on the driver's box and seethed with anger as he watched Denny and Melanie clean the blood away from Salty's wounds as best they could. Denny tore strips of cloth from her petticoat to serve as makeshift bandages. Melanie bound up Salty's shoulder with them.

Alma Lewiston kept Salty's gun pointed at the women as they dealt with the wounded jehu. Louis had remained close by after helping Melanie over there, so he was under the gun as well.

Smoke was proud of the way both of his children had leaped into action without hesitation, even though they hadn't succeeded in stopping Colbert's rampage. That was just bad luck. They hadn't known that Alma would back Colbert's play.

Although what did she have to lose by doing so? Smoke asked himself. And the fact that she might be able to take some revenge on him for her husband's suicide was just a bonus for her.

Colbert had drawn off a short distance. He didn't

have a stranglehold on Brad's neck anymore, but his left hand was still clamped on the boy's shoulder and the gun wasn't far from Brad's head, as Colbert had threatened.

When Smoke first met Colbert, he had felt an instinctive dislike for the man, and now he knew why. Colbert was an outlaw; there was no doubt about that in Smoke's mind. He had some sort of crooked scheme brewing in Reno, and he had to be there before Christmas to pull it off. That was why he was willing to risk going through Donner Pass.

And quite a risk it would be. Colbert was right about the old wagon road not following the railroad tracks exactly. But the avalanche that had blocked the tracks probably had the entire pass closed off.

Throw in the blizzard still going on up there, and the chances of surviving such a trip and actually making it to Reno ranged from slim to none.

"That's enough," Colbert told Denny and Melanie. "Get the old bastard up. We've wasted plenty of time already. I should have just left him here to freeze . . . if he didn't bleed to death first."

Denny and Melanie positioned themselves on either side of Salty, grasped his arms, and lifted him to his feet. Louis made a move to help, but Denny waved him off.

Smoke frowned as he looked at his son's face. Louis's features had a gray cast to them. Smoke hoped that the brief flurry of action earlier hadn't further damaged Louis's heart.

As the women approached the stagecoach with Salty, Peter Stansfield climbed out and held the door open for them. From the corner of his mouth, Smoke said quietly to the reporter, "Stansfield, have you got a gun?"

Stansfield twisted his head around to look up at Smoke. "What? No. No, of course not. I . . . I'm not armed."

"What about Kellerman? Has he said anything about having a gun?"

"Not at all. We're not . . . notorious pistoleers . . . like you, Mr. Jensen."

Alma was coming closer as she covered Denny, Melanie, and Louis, so Smoke didn't say anything else. He hadn't really expected any help to be forthcoming from the reporter or the banker, so he wasn't disappointed.

He was just mad, mostly at himself for letting Colbert wallop him like that.

There had been a time when the fella never would have been fast enough to get away with such a thing. As the years had rolled past, Smoke hadn't been aware that he was slowing down, but maybe he was. The serious wound he had suffered earlier in the year hadn't helped matters any.[4]

His reflexes and reactions were still faster than those of at least nine out of ten normal men. He was convinced of that. But Colbert possessed unusual speed and strength, too. Life as an owlhoot had hardened the man, although Colbert's underlying pallor hinted that he had gotten out of prison only recently.

Well, prison was no walk in the park. A man who went in there as a deadly killer usually came out even more dangerous. That seemed to be true in Frank Colbert's case.

Smoke felt the stagecoach shift underneath him

as Salty climbed in, helped by Denny and Melanie. He heard the old man groan and knew Salty had settled down on one of the seats. The others followed him into the coach.

Colbert put the gun muzzle against Brad's head again. Melanie saw that and cried out in fear.

Colbert ignored her and said, "Get in the coach now, Alma. Nobody will try anything unless they want me to kill this boy."

"No, please, no," Melanie begged. "Everyone, please do what he says."

"Alma, sit on the backseat," Colbert went on. "Everybody else crowd onto the front, or sit in the floor between the front seat and the bench in the middle. Once you're inside, Alma, keep them covered while the boy and I join you."

"I understand, Frank," she said.

They got loaded up. Smoke couldn't see how everything was arranged inside the coach, but Colbert seemed satisfied as he looked in through the open door.

Then the outlaw looked up at him and said, "The boy's gonna be sitting between me and Alma, Jensen. If you or anybody else tries any tricks, one of us will kill him. You can count on that."

"No trouble," Smoke said flatly.

For now, he added to himself.

"You're going to drive at a nice, steady pace. You know the trail through Donner Pass?"

"I know it. It's been a long time since I went through there, but I can find my way."

"Good. You take the route that'll get us through the mountains and on to Reno the fastest. If I get even the smallest suspicion that you're trying to double-cross me, the boy dies."

"I'm getting mighty tired of that threat," Smoke said.

"It's not a threat," Colbert responded with a leering grin. "It's a promise. We clear about everything?"

"We're clear."

"Good. You know what to do."

Colbert pushed Brad into the coach and climbed in after him. Smoke's jaw was so tight as he took up the reins, it seemed like his teeth might crack.

But he got the team moving again and started the stagecoach up the slope, following the old wagon road between the thick growths of pine. As he looked at the snow-mantled trees, they were a reminder of the season and how close Christmas was.

It might be a bloody Christmas this year, he thought grimly.

Because he didn't believe for one second that Frank Colbert intended to leave any of them alive after he got what he wanted.

Inside the stagecoach, Denny and Melanie sat on the rearward-facing front seat with Salty propped up between them. They pressed in close against him so the coach's motion wouldn't jostle him around too much. Louis was crowded in next to Denny.

Stansfield and Kellerman were forced onto the floorboards in the cramped area between the front seat and the bench in the middle of the coach. The ones on the seat pulled their legs in close as much as possible, but it was still crowded and uncomfortable for the two men.

The heavyset banker had it the worst of them all. He didn't make the situation any better for himself by clutching the flat leather case. His carpetbag was back in the boot, but he had insisted on keeping the case with him.

"I'll never be able to get out of here," Kellerman complained as the coach rocked along. "I'm stuck!"

"The others can grease you up and use a horse and a rope to pull you out," Colbert joked. "You'll pop out of there like a seed out of a watermelon!"

Kellerman just glared at him.

Alma sat on the right side of the rear seat, Colbert on the left, with Brad between them. The youngster was pale and scared looking, but he was more composed than his mother was. Melanie still sobbed quietly from time to time.

"Don't worry, Ma," Brad told her. "It'll be all right."

"Sure it will," Colbert said. "I don't have anything against you folks. I just need to get to Reno, that's all. Once I'm there, you can go on about your business." He laughed. "Hell, you might even thank me for getting you there sooner than if we'd gone that other way."

Denny knew good and well Colbert was lying about letting them go. He had tried already to kill Smoke and Salty, and whatever his reason was for wanting to reach Reno, obviously he was up to no good. He was a criminal . . . and criminals didn't like to leave witnesses behind them.

Salty said, "If this shoulder o' mine didn't hurt so much . . . I'd be plumb tickled to be stuck betwixt two pretty gals like this. Derned near . . . the best stagecoach ride I ever had. Course, I ain't rode inside that many. I was always . . . up on the box, handlin' the team."

"Do you think my father will do all right with the driving?" Louis asked.

"Smoke?" Salty grunted. "Son, I don't reckon Smoke Jensen ever set his hand to anything without windin' up better at it than pert near ever'body else."

Colbert said, "You'd better hope he's good at it, old man; otherwise you'll be back up there, busted shoulder and all. I don't have time to waste."

Denny looked out the window at the gloomy day and said, "We'll have to stop in a couple of hours. It'll be too dark to go on."

Colbert gestured with the gun in his hand and asked, "How about that, old-timer? Stagecoaches sometimes keep going at night, don't they?"

"On a good road that the driver knows like the back of his hand, with lanterns on the coach to help light the way?" Salty said. "A fella might risk that, especially on a clear night with a big moon and a lot of stars. But with them clouds up there, there ain't *no* moon nor stars, and there ain't no bein' sure what sort of shape the road's in farther up. A fella would have to be a plumb fool to risk travelin' through these mountains after dark."

"What's the worst that could happen?" Colbert wanted to know.

"You mean besides drivin' off a cliff and fallin' two or

three hunnerd feet?" Salty shook his head. "Nothin', I reckon."

Colbert's lips drew back in a grimace. "All right," he said. "You've had your sport, old man. Quit your japing, or I'm liable to forget to respect my elders."

"I'd say it's a mite too late for that," Salty muttered.

A tense silence fell over the coach. The vehicle leaned slightly to the side as Smoke reached the first of the switchbacks and wheeled the coach around the sharp turn. The pace slowed even more as they spent the next hour ascending that steep, zigzag path up the side of a mountain.

Colbert's impatience grew visibly, but he seemed to understand there was nothing he could do other than put up with their progress.

Finally, the ground leveled off. Smoke slowed the stagecoach and gradually brought it to a halt.

Denny felt the vehicle shift on its thoroughbraces as her father leaned over to call through the windows, "We've reached a little bench that would be a good place to make camp for the night. There's only about half an hour of light left, so it doesn't make sense to go on. This'll give us a chance to build a fire and heat some food and coffee."

Colbert frowned and looked like he didn't agree with Smoke's suggestion, but Alma said, "Some hot coffee sounds awfully good, Frank. And a half hour won't make any difference."

"We don't know that," Colbert snapped, but a second later he shrugged. "All right, I suppose it won't hurt anything." He leaned closer to the window. "Stay where you are, Jensen, until the rest of us are out. Don't even move. This stagecoach bounces, and I shoot the boy."

That threat brought another muffled sob from Melanie. She had a handkerchief pressed to her face, and Denny thought it must be soaked with tears by now.

She shouldn't judge the woman, though, she told herself. She didn't have any kids, so she had no idea how she would react if one of her offspring was threatened.

But she hoped she would be looking for a way to fight back, and she had her doubts that was what was going through Melanie Buckner's mind right now.

"You get out first," Colbert told Alma, "and cover the others. The boy and I will get out last."

She opened the door and stepped down from the coach, then turned to face it and backed off with Salty's gun held in both hands.

"Be careful with that," Denny said. "They go off easier than you might think."

"I've been around guns," Alma said curtly. "Now get out here, you first, then the old man and Mrs. Buckner."

Denny knew she had no choice right now except to cooperate. She eased through the door and swung down to the ground, then turned back to help Salty. Getting him out of the coach wasn't easy with Louis in the way on that side.

That was the idea, Denny thought. Make things as awkward as possible, so the passengers would be less likely to try anything.

When Salty and the two women were standing in the snow, Colbert ordered, "All right, the rest of you get out now."

Louis emerged first and helped Kellerman. The banker wasn't stuck, as he had feared, but he had to struggle to get his bulk dislodged from the small space. When he finally succeeded, he stood there red faced, breathing heavily. Denny thought he looked like he was about to have an attack of apoplexy, but his discomfiture gradually subsided.

Stansfield came next, unfolding his gangling length from the coach. That just left Colbert and Brad, and the gunman kept a tight grip on the boy's collar as they got down from the vehicle.

"All right, Jensen, you can tend to the horses now," Colbert said. "You ladies see to the old man." He nodded to Louis. "Gather some wood and build a fire."

"Of course," Louis said. "A fire will feel good."

Smoke swung down from the driver's box and said, "I could use a hand with the team. It's an easier job with two men."

Colbert laughed and gestured with the gun toward Stansfield and Kellerman. "These two look like they barely know which end of a horse is which, but between them they might add up to one man. If you can get any use out of them, go ahead. Just don't try anything. The boy and I will be keeping an eye on you." He looked down at Brad. "Isn't that right, son?"

"I'm not your son," the youngster said. "And if I was, I'd never admit it."

Colbert let go of Brad's collar and cuffed him on

the side of the head, bringing a sharp cry from
Melanie as she and Denny helped Salty sit down on a
nearby log.

"Leave him alone!" she said, showing a spark of
real anger for the first time.

"Tell the little brat to watch his mouth, then," Colbert said.

Melanie swallowed hard and looked at her son.
"Bradley, don't give Mr. Colbert any trouble. Do you
hear me?"

"Yeah," Brad said with a surly pout. "I hear you."

"That's better," Colbert said. "Now, everybody get
busy."

"What do you want me to do, Frank?" Alma asked.

"Watch those three," he replied, nodding toward
the log where Salty sat with Denny and Melanie hov-
ering over him. "I'll keep an eye on the others."

"If any of them try anything . . . ?"

"Kill them."

Louis gathered up an armload of broken branches
that looked dry enough to burn. Since the temperature was below freezing, the snow hadn't gotten them
wet, so all he had to do was knock it off the branches.

He kicked a space clear of snow on the ground,
piled the wood on it, and cleared another space for
the fire.

Meanwhile, Smoke unhitched and picketed the
horses, with Stansfield and Kellerman able to help a
little as long as he told them exactly what to do. The
layer of snow on the ground was thin enough that
the horses would be able to snuffle their way through
it to the dry grass below, so they could graze.

When Louis had branches laid for the fire, he told Colbert, "I don't have any matches."

"I do," Smoke said. He paused in what he was doing, took a tin container from his pocket, and tossed it to his son. Louis had to use a couple of the matches to get the fire burning, but when he succeeded, the flames were soon dancing merrily in the cold air.

"Coffeepot's in the boot," Smoke said, "along with the supplies."

Denny said, "Heat some water by itself first, so we can do a better job of cleaning these bullet holes."

Everyone stayed busy setting up the camp for the next little while, but no one forgot about the menace of the guns held by Colbert and Alma.

The darkness began to settle down while that was going on. The light and heat from the fire were both very welcome. Louis fed branches into it to keep it burning brightly.

When Salty's wounds had been cleaned and bandaged properly, Colbert said to Denny and Melanie, "All right, you two rustle up a meal for us."

"You don't want me rustling up anything, mister," Denny said. "I'm a terrible cook."

"She is," Louis agreed, nodding solemnly.

Melanie said, "I can fix some food."

"We didn't bring along anything fancy," Smoke said. "But there's bacon and the makings for biscuits."

"It won't take long," Melanie promised.

She was as good as her word. Hot coffee, bacon, and fresh biscuits were all very much appreciated on a night like this. The food should have made for a spirit of camaraderie around the fire.

Instead there was only fear and anger.

When the meal was over, Colbert said to Alma, "See if you can find some rope or cord in the boot. Everybody in this bunch is going to have to be tied up for the night."

"Do you expect us to sleep on the ground?" Kellerman asked.

"No, we'll all get back in the coach."

Stansfield said, "That'll be even more uncomfortable than before, if we're tied up."

Colbert cocked his head a little to the side. "You seem to be forgetting that I really just need Jensen to drive the coach. I could kill the rest of you and leave you here for the wolves." He grinned. "Or maybe just leave you here alive in the morning, so you can give the wolves a little fight before they eat you."

"Just leave it alone, Stansfield," Smoke said to the reporter. "We're going to cooperate with what Colbert wants."

Denny frowned slightly. That was so unlike Smoke Jensen that it had to be tearing him up inside. There was only one reason he would *ever* cooperate with an outlaw and killer.

He was trying to protect the lives of his children and the other passengers.

And he was waiting for the right time to strike back at Frank Colbert.

One by one, Alma tied their hands behind their backs with rope she found in the boot. With the barrel of Colbert's gun pressed to Brad's head, there was nothing anyone could do except go along. Then they clambered into the coach and sort of piled up on one side under the lap robes. They probably wouldn't get much sleep, but at least they wouldn't freeze to death during the night.

Colbert and Alma were on the other side, again with Brad trapped between them. "You'll stand first watch," he told Alma. "I trust you more to stay awake now than I would later in the night. I'll take that shift."

"Don't worry about me, Frank," she told him. "Once I decided to back your play, I was in all the way. I won't let you down."

"I'm lucky you wanted to come along on this trip, then."

"Lucky that my husband killed himself, you mean."

"I didn't say that. But he was a weak man, Alma, and I have a feeling you need a strong man in your life. I'm strong. I take what I want. Always have."

That didn't make him strong, Denny thought. It just made him an outlaw.

But there was no point in saying that now. She told herself she might as well try to get some sleep.

It was liable to be a long night.

CHAPTER 28

Reno, Nevada

Carl Andrews shivered from the chilly wind sweeping across the valley of the Truckee as he walked toward his home. He ducked his head so the derby would keep it from blowing in his face quite so much.

Andrews lived with his wife, Rebecca, and twelve-year-old daughter, Sadie, in a neatly kept frame house on one of Reno's side streets. They had lived there, and Andrews had worked in the bank, since Sadie was a toddler.

It was a good life, although one not blessed with further children, which was something of a disappointment to Andrews and Rebecca, but he certainly had nothing to complain about.

That satisfaction was reflected in the Christmas carol that Andrews whistled as he opened the gate in the picket fence in front of his house and went up the walk to the porch. He was eager to get inside.

For one thing, it would be warm and cheerful, and for another, this evening was when he and his wife and daughter planned to decorate the small pine tree he had cut down a couple of days earlier. They had made a family outing of it, taking the buggy and driving into the foothills to let Sadie pick the tree.

Yellow lamplight glowed in the front window. Andrews opened the door and went inside, taking off his derby as he did so. He hung it on a hat rack in the foyer, then shrugged out of his topcoat and hung it up as well.

Smiling, he turned toward the parlor to greet his wife and daughter, both of whom normally greeted him with hugs and kisses.

Tonight he found himself staring down the barrel of a gun instead.

"Don't move, Carl," the man holding the revolver said. "I'd hate to have to shoot you."

"I reckon these two beauties would hate it, too," said another man, this one standing next to the sofa where Rebecca and Sadie sat, both of them pale and obviously terrified of the gun the stranger was pointing at them.

The man standing closer to the arched entrance between the foyer and the parlor said, "You remember me, don't you, Carl?"

In his shocked state, Andrews hadn't taken a good look at the man until now. When he did, there was something familiar about him, but Andrews couldn't quite remember. . . .

Then he did, and he said, "Bob Stevens! You were sitting next to me at the Red Top! I recommended the stew to you."

That was an awfully mundane thing to think about under these awful circumstances, but it was what came back to Carl Andrews in that moment.

"That's right," the man said. "I'm afraid I lied to you. My name's not Bob, and I never drove a freight wagon in my life."

Andrews's eyes opened wider as a possibility occurred to him. "You're a bank robber!"

That exclamation made the man smile behind the gun he aimed at Andrews.

"Now, see, that tells me you're a smart man, and that makes me happy. Because a smart man's not going to do anything that will get him—or his family—hurt."

"Leave them alone." Andrews tried to put some strength and courage into his voice, tried really hard, but he didn't think he succeeded very well. "If you hurt them, I . . . I'll—"

The man holding a gun on Rebecca and Sadie said, "Oh, hell, let's not waste time with that. You ain't gonna do nothin', mister, and we all know it. We can do whatever the hell we want, and there's nothin' you can do about it."

He was a lean man with a shock of dark, curly hair and an easy grin that should have been friendly. Instead, the expression was one of the most coldly horrifying things Andrews had ever seen, especially when the man stepped closer to Sadie and cupped his free hand under her chin.

"If I want, I can teach this little lady what it's like to be a woman," he went on. "You reckon she'd like that, Mister Bank Teller? I know I would."

"Don't," Andrews said in a choked voice.

The first man—Andrews couldn't help but still

think of him as Bob—said, "That's enough. For now. But if you don't cooperate with us, Carl, I can't make any promises about what my friend there might do to your wife . . . or your daughter."

Andrews's pulse pounded like a steam engine inside his head. Rebecca and Sadie were both fair-haired beauties, no doubt about that. Rebecca was so lovely that she could have done much better than him, and right now he wished that she had. Then she wouldn't be in danger from these two . . . animals.

A part of him wanted to fight back against them, but he knew it wouldn't do any good. They would just kill him or, worse, overpower him and force him to watch while they assaulted his wife and daughter.

His shoulders slumped, and he said in a defeated voice, "What is it you want?"

"That's better," Bob said with a smile. He gestured with the gun toward an ottoman. "Sit down. We're going to have a talk."

The other man said, "That's it? He's gonna give up that easy, before we have any fun?"

"We're not here to have fun," Bob snapped. "We're here to find out what we need to know." Again he told Andrews, "Sit down."

Andrews sank onto the ottoman and sat with his hands dangling between his knees.

"Whatever you want to know, I'll tell you," he said. "Whatever you want me to do, I'll do it. Just don't hurt them."

"That's exactly the way we want it," Bob said.

Andrews didn't believe that. He knew that from the way the other man looked at Rebecca and Sadie they would never be safe as long as these intruders were here. But maybe if he cooperated with them, they would go.

"Tell me about the money shipment that's coming in," Bob said.

Andrews couldn't keep from lifting his head in surprise. He said, "You know about that?"

"You practically told me about it while we were eating lunch."

"I . . . I just said that the bank was unusually busy for Christmastime. . . ."

"Well, what else could it be?" Bob said. He let out a curt laugh. "But don't worry too much, Carl. To tell you the truth, I already knew there was a big load of money coming into Reno. It was just a matter of finding out which bank."

"We'll be handling it."

"How much?"

"Four hundred thousand dollars."

Bob's breath hissed between his teeth as he inhaled sharply. He said, "That's a lot of money. What's it for?"

"Do you know who Cameron Coolidge is?"

Bob frowned in thought. He shook his head. "I don't reckon I do."

"He owns the Gullywasher mine."

"Never heard of it."

"That's because Coolidge keeps his operation quiet for the most part," Andrews said. "But it's a very lucrative silver mine. Coolidge is worth several million dollars. So he can afford to buy the Tabernacle mine from Thomas Nickerson."

"Haven't heard of that one, either."

"It's not worth what the Gullywasher is, but it's a

fine, steadily producing mine," Andrews explained. "Coolidge intends to buy it for his wife, Cassandra. As a . . . a Christmas present."

"Wait a minute," the other man said. "This hombre's gonna spend nearly half a million dollars to buy a mine and then give it to his wife for Christmas?"

Andrews nodded. "That's right."

"That's the craziest thing I've ever heard!"

Bob said, "Rich people do loco things like that, or at least so I've heard." He narrowed his eyes at Andrews. "You're sure about all this?"

"Positive. I'm the head teller at the bank, and Mr. Hopkins—he's the president—trusts me with such details."

The grinning man laughed. "Well, that wasn't very smart of him, was it? Just the threat of us havin' a little slap-and-tickle with this pretty little girl o' yours made you spill your guts right out."

"Like I said before, Carl's a smart man," Bob told him. "Now tell me, Carl . . . when's that money getting here?"

"It'll arrive on the train, a special express shipment, on the morning of Christmas Eve. As soon as it's here, Coolidge and Nickerson will come to the bank and conclude their arrangement. Nickerson, you see, insisted on a cash payment. He's an older man, very crusty. He says he prefers money he can hold, instead of numbers written on a piece of paper."

"Lucky for us he feels that way."

"I've told you what you want to know," Andrews said, allowing a note of hope to enter his voice. "Now, if you'll just go away and leave us alone, I promise that

I'll never say anything about you to anyone else. I won't do anything to jeopardize whatever you're planning. I swear to that."

"And I believe you," Bob said. "Problem is, your word, and me believing you . . . well, that's just not good enough."

He turned his head and nodded at his companion, who holstered his gun and drew a knife from a sheath attached to his belt.

For some reason, the blade was even more terrifying than the gun. Sadie shrank away from it, and Rebecca let out a soft, frightened cry.

The man's other hand shot out and grabbed Sadie by the back of the neck. He jerked her onto her feet and toward him.

Andrews started to lunge up off the ottoman. Bob thrust the gun closer to his face and eared back the hammer. The sinister, metallic click, plus the looming menace of the gun muzzle, which looked like a cannon from Andrews's perspective, forced the bank teller to freeze.

Rebecca cried, "No! Leave her alone!"

The man with the knife ignored her. He kept his hand clamped on the back of Sadie's neck, holding her still as he slid the tip of the blade under the top button of her dress. The knife was a Bowie, so the upper edge along that part held a keen edge, too.

An expert flick of the man's wrist cut the button loose and sent it spinning away to land on the floor and bounce across the parlor. He moved the knife down to the second button and did the same, followed by the third and fourth.

Then he used the knife to push back both sides of

the dress, revealing the shift Sadie wore underneath it that clung to her budding breasts. She trembled and tears ran down her cheeks as he slipped the knife just under the top of the shift.

"That's enough," Bob said without taking his eyes off Andrews. The gun in his hand hadn't budged.

"You sure?" the grinning man asked. "I wouldn't mind gettin' a look at what I might be samplin' later on."

"There's no need to scare these good folks any more than we already have. They're going to cooperate and do everything we say. Isn't that right, Carl?"

"I already told you I would," Andrews replied, his voice shaking a little from the depth of the emotions he was feeling.

"Here's how it's gonna be, then. My friend and I are going to stay right here and keep your wife and daughter company for the next couple of days. You'll go on to work and act like there's nothing wrong."

"I . . . I don't know if I can do that."

Bob's voice hardened. "You'd damn well better be able to, if you know what's good for your wife and daughter. My friend there is going to be nice and polite to them and they won't have to worry about a thing . . . as long as I say it's going to be that way. You don't do your part, Carl, and I'll just have to wash my hands of the whole deal and let whatever happens . . . happen. You understand what I mean?"

Andrews swallowed hard, looked down at the floor, and whispered, "I understand."

"Good. You'll go on to work, like I said, and come home in the evening, and nobody will be the wiser. Then, Christmas Eve morning, once that money has been delivered, you'll make sure the back door of the bank is unlocked. That's all you have to do. Well, that and stay out of our way. Then it'll all be over and you and these ladies will be safe."

"How . . . how do I know that?"

"Why, I give you my word. Isn't that enough?"

Andrews didn't answer that question. Instead he asked, "How will you keep them from warning anybody, that morning?"

"We'll have to tie them up and gag them. I regret any discomfort that'll cause, I truly do, but it can't be helped. When it's all over, though, you can come straight here and turn them loose. See? It's all worked out."

Slowly, Andrews nodded. "I understand. I'll do what you say."

"Carl—" his wife began.

"I know, Rebecca. It's terrible, but we don't have any choice." He sighed. "I'll be ruined. I'll probably be sent to jail for helping them. But it'll be worth it to keep you and Sadie safe."

"Well, hell," the grinning man said. "This is disappointin'. I was hopin' you'd take more persuadin' than that, mister." He laid the flat of the blade against Sadie's cheek, causing her to shudder again. "I was gonna enjoy the persuadin'."

Rage flared up inside Andrews again. He said, "You . . . you—"

"Settle down, both of you." Bob lowered the gun slightly and motioned with the barrel. "Carl, go over there to that table by the window and pick up the lamp."

"What?"

"Do what I told you."

With a look of confusion on his face, Andrews went to the table. When he had the base of the oil lamp in his hand, Bob went on, "Now push the curtain back. When you've done that, move the lamp back and forth three times in front of the window."

"A signal," Andrews said as realization hit him. "You have friends watching the house. You're letting them know I agreed to the plan."

"Smart, just like I said. Go ahead."

Andrews opened the curtain and gave the signal.

"All right, put it back down and close the curtain."

Andrews did so. "Now what?"

Bob chuckled and said, "Your wife's got what looks and smells like a good supper on the table, and I don't reckon it's gotten too cold while we were talking. Is there enough for all of us, Mrs. Andrews?"

Rebecca said, "I . . . I . . . Of course." She took a deep breath and squared her shoulders, visibly gathering her courage. "I'll have to set two more places."

"That's mighty accommodating of you. I'm looking forward to spending the next couple of days with you and getting to know you better. It'll be Christmas Eve before you know it."

"We gonna sit around singin' carols?" the other man leered.

"I'm sure we'll find ways to pass the time," Bob said.

CHAPTER 29

The Sierra Nevadas

Sometime during the night, the snow had started to fall more heavily.

The canvas covers over the windows were pulled down and fastened tightly to keep the wind out as much as possible, and also to keep the body heat from the passengers in. The thick lap robes helped, too, and as a result, while the temperature inside the coach had been plenty cold, no one had even come close to freezing to death.

But that meant they didn't know what was going on outside, either, until the next morning when Frank Colbert ordered Smoke to open one of the doors.

Smoke did so, and instantly a bone-chilling wind whipped into the coach, bringing with it swirls of snowflakes.

"What the hell!" Colbert exclaimed. "It's a damn blizzard out there!"

Smoke jerked the door closed, cutting off the

wind. He loosened the canvas over the window beside him and pulled it back enough to look out.

"No, not a blizzard," he said. "The wind's not blowing hard enough for that, and the snow isn't falling that heavily. This is just a fairly bad snowstorm."

"How deep is it going to get?" Colbert demanded to know.

Smoke shrugged. "That's hard to say. Eight or ten inches, maybe a foot. Could even be deeper. Depends on how long it goes on."

"How deep is it now?"

Smoke checked outside again. "Maybe three inches. There might be some deeper drifts in places."

"Well, that's not going to stop us," Colbert said. "You and your son get out there and see to the horses. Get a fire going again. We need some coffee."

They had left some bacon and biscuits from what Melanie had cooked the night before, so they would have food ready for breakfast this morning. But the coffeepot was cold and would require a fresh fire before more could be brewed.

Smoke looked at Louis. The young man still had a grayish look about his face, which was gaunt and hollow eyed from lack of sleep. All of them had passed a restless night and were weary this morning.

"Louis can stay in here," Smoke suggested. "Stansfield can help me."

Louis began, "I'll do my part—"

"You have been," Smoke interrupted him. "Come on, Stansfield."

Colbert smiled grimly. "Don't mind me," he said. "I'm just the man with the gun, giving the orders."

"You have any objection?" Smoke asked.

"As long as the work gets done and you don't try anything, I don't care who does what. Anyway, maybe it's better having both of your kids in here with me. You'll be less likely to try something that way."

"I told you I was going to cooperate, mister. You've got the upper hand."

Those words were bitter gall in Smoke's mouth.

"And don't forget it," Colbert snapped. "Now get busy."

Stansfield looked like he wanted to complain about being drafted to help out, but he didn't say anything. He followed Smoke out of the coach as quickly as possible so they could close the door behind them and keep the cold air and snow out of the vehicle.

"You're *not* going to try anything, are you?" the reporter asked quietly when they were both outside.

Smoke waved a gloved hand at the snow falling around them and piling up on the trees and ground. "All I could do is take one of the horses and run off, and where would I go in this? When a man starts wandering around in a snowstorm like this, he generally gets lost and freezes to death. Besides, my children are in the coach. Do you think I'd abandon them to that owlhoot?"

"You think Colbert is a criminal, then?"

Smoke tried not to look and sound disgusted as he replied, "I don't reckon there's any other explanation, do you?"

He didn't wait for Stansfield to answer. Instead he went to the back of the coach where the horses were picketed. The animals all stood with their heads down and their tails to the wind. Snow dusted their manes. They seemed to be all right.

Having checked on them, Smoke turned away and said, "Let's get the fire built first. Knock the snow off some of that wood Louis piled up."

While Stansfield was doing that, Smoke knelt by the remains of the previous night's fire and cleared the snow away from it. He took the branches Stansfield handed to him and arranged them in a conical shape, then crumbled some dry bark to serve as tinder.

Under his skilled, experienced hands, the fire was soon burning strongly enough that it wasn't in danger of the snow putting it out. The flakes sizzled and evaporated as they fell into the flames.

Smoke melted snow in the coffeepot and then dumped in coffee to boil. While it was doing that, he and Stansfield began getting the freshest of the draft horses into harness.

"I have to say, I'm a little disappointed," Stansfield commented as they worked.

"About what?"

"You're supposed to be the fastest, deadliest gunfighter alive. You take on entire armies of outlaws and killers single-handedly and gun them all down, one by one. You've never been defeated. You're a mythical figure, Jensen. And yet . . . you're just a man."

"Never claimed to be anything else," Smoke said, making an effort to control the irritation he felt.

"You know what I mean. My God, one man and one grieving widow are able to get the best of you? You should have been able to rescue all the prisoners and deal with those villains without making more than the slightest effort. You're not living up to the legend of Smoke Jensen!"

"If you're trying to rub me the wrong way, Stansfield, you're doing a good job of it." Smoke tightened the harness on one of the horses. "You've read too many of those blasted dime novels. The fellas who write those just make things up to suit themselves. They've got me wandering around having gunfight after gunfight, and that's not the way it was in real life. Sure, I've burned more than my share of powder, but I've always tried to do it so that innocent folks were protected . . . like the people Colbert has under his gun in there."

"So you're just biding your time, waiting for the proper moment to unleash all your righteous fury on him."

"You said that, not me. Can't you fellas who string words together for a living ever talk like normal people?"

Before Smoke or Stansfield could continue the conversation, the coach door opened and Melanie Buckner climbed out, obviously stiff from the night spent inside the vehicle, trying to sleep sitting up.

"Mr. Colbert wants me to get him some coffee," she said.

"It'll be ready in a few minutes," Smoke said. "He needs to let everybody get out so they can move around a little before we get started."

"I'm sure he will." Melanie looked around at the falling snow. "Can you drive the coach in this storm, Mr. Jensen?"

"The snow's not deep enough to cover up the trail . . . yet." Smoke shook his head. "No telling what the rest of the day will bring."

During the next hour, the passengers climbed out

of the coach, tended to their personal needs, and ate the sparse breakfast, all under the guns and the watchful eyes of Frank Colbert and Alma Lewiston.

Smoke saw the anger on Denny's face and worried that his daughter would try something foolish, but if Denny felt those urges, she kept them under control. Maybe she was beginning to understand that sometimes restraint was the best option.

Of course, when it came time to *stop* being restrained and cut loose your wolf, then the only thing to do was let that wolf go ahead and howl. . . .

The thick overcast and the white, swirling clouds of snow made it difficult to see for more than a few yards. It was also hard to tell what time it was. The sun was up, but that was all Smoke knew without hauling out his pocket watch to check the hour.

He figured it didn't really matter, anyway. When all the preparations were complete, Colbert ordered everyone except Smoke back into the stagecoach.

"Same as yesterday, Jensen," he said. "Get us up this mountain and through the pass before the storm gets too bad."

Smoke knew it was probably past that point already, but he didn't see any reason to say that to Colbert. The outlaw wouldn't believe him, anyway.

He climbed onto the driver's box, took up the reins, released the brakes, and got the team moving. The coach lurched ahead. Snow on the hard-packed trail crunched under the wheels.

Smoke had tied a bandanna over the lower half of his face to protect his nose and mouth from the cold.

His hat brim extended over his eyes and kept too much snow from blowing into them and sticking on his lashes.

The icy wind bit hard on every inch of exposed skin, though. He kept his head down so his hat shielded his face as much as possible. Even so, he knew he was at risk for frostbite before the day was over. Frequently, he reached up with one hand and rubbed his cheeks and around his eyes to keep the blood flowing in those areas.

The horses didn't like the snowflakes spinning and dancing around their heads, but they kept moving without spooking. For now, Smoke had no trouble telling where the trail was. The route it followed through the trees was pretty obvious. The snow would have to get pretty deep in order for him not to be able to see it . . . and if it was that deep, the stagecoach wouldn't be able to get through anyway.

Smoke had no doubt they were going to reach that point, and he wondered what Colbert would do when they did. Clearly, the man was ruthless enough to attempt anything necessary to get what he wanted, but no matter how merciless and cold blooded he was, he couldn't command the forces of nature. The snow wouldn't disappear just because he threatened to shoot one of his hostages.

If it came to that, Smoke knew he would take action. There wouldn't be any point in holding back any longer. The balance would have tipped so that it would be more dangerous *not* to do anything.

But maybe a chance would come along before then. If it did, Smoke would strike.

He wasn't even thinking anymore about reaching

Reno before Christmas. All that mattered to him was getting his children and those other innocent folks in the stagecoach out of these mountains alive. . . .

The slope grew steeper again and the trail entered another series of switchbacks. Before starting on that stretch, Smoke switched the teams again. Louis insisted on helping with the chore this time.

"How are you feeling?" Smoke asked him.

"I'm all right. A little short of breath and light-headed now and then, but it's nothing to worry about, Father. You heard what Dr. Katzendorf said. I have a long time left."

"*If* you take care and don't exert yourself too much," Smoke reminded him.

"Helping you with these horses isn't that much exertion." Louis lowered his voice so that, with the wind blowing the way it was, none of the others could hear him, only Smoke. "Colbert has figured out that my health is bad. That's going to make him think I'm not any sort of threat. He'll let his guard down, and I might be able to get close enough to take him by surprise and grab that gun away from him."

Smoke shook his head and said, "Forget about that idea. Colbert's tough and dangerous. Even taking him by surprise wouldn't give you enough of an advantage to overcome him. You'd just get yourself killed."

Louis looked like he wanted to argue, but after a moment he nodded and said, "All right. As long as he doesn't try to hurt Melanie or her son. But if that were to happen, I make no promises, Father."

Smoke paused in the work he was doing with the team. "You like that young woman, don't you?"

"I've talked to her enough to know that she's gone through quite a few difficulties over the past few years, after her husband died, and she's borne up under them as well as could be expected. And she loves the boy very much. I admire her."

Smoke nodded. He had a hunch that what Louis was feeling was more than simple admiration, but under the circumstances, they had more important things to worry about . . . such as staying alive.

Alma Lewiston pushed the canvas back on one of the windows, stuck her head out, and called, "Frank wants to know if you're done yet."

"Almost," Smoke told her. "We'll be rolling again in just a few minutes."

Alma nodded and closed the canvas again. Louis said, "I could take one of the saddle horses and ride for help, Father. Denny likes to tease me about my lack of riding ability, but I assure you, I can stay on a horse just fine, even bareback."

"You don't know this part of the country at all, son. Like I told Stansfield earlier, making a break would be a good way to get lost and freeze to death."

"I'm willing to risk it."

"I'm not," Smoke said emphatically. He gave a tug on the harness and made sure all the horses were hitched up properly. "Get back inside with the others."

"All right. But remember what I said. I won't sit by and allow Melanie or Bradley to be hurt."

"Neither will I," Smoke promised.

Louis nodded and then climbed back into the

coach. The door slammed shut as Smoke was climbing to the driver's box. He brushed aside the snow that had collected on the seat while he and Louis were switching the teams and sat down to unwind the reins from the brake lever.

The stagecoach started up the switchback trail.

The higher the elevation, the harder the wind blew and the thicker the blowing snow became. The white carpet was at least six inches deep on the trail now, but the team didn't have any trouble with that and the coach's wheels cut through it easily. The drifts would have to reach the coach's belly before they caused any real problems.

Smoke could still see the trail, but he couldn't see very far ahead or behind the stagecoach. Because of the trees and the swirling clouds of snow, he couldn't make out much to the sides, either. It was almost as if the rest of the world had receded into nothingness, leaving only this small area around the horses and the slowly moving vehicle.

The light, dim to start with, had begun to fade even more by the time the stagecoach reached the top of the switchbacks. It had been a long, cold, hungry, arduous day, and as the trail leveled out again, Smoke was ready to stop and make camp.

Under normal circumstances, they would have reached Donner Pass and the Summit Hotel by now, but Smoke estimated they still had a mile or more to go. With the way the weather was worsening, he didn't want to attempt it.

Then he saw something that made him even more convinced they needed to call a halt.

Something dark darted through the corner of his

vision. He turned his head quickly but didn't catch more than a glimpse of whatever it was. He could tell it was moving fast, and low to the ground.

There it was again, only in the other direction this time! Smoke peered into the blizzard—because by now it actually *was* a blizzard—and tried to locate whatever it was he had seen.

When he couldn't, he realized the things had been too far apart to be the same one. More than a single creature was out there, and as a long, shuddery wail drifted to him through the storm, he felt a new chill go through him, a chill that had nothing to do with the frigid temperature.

He hauled back on the reins and brought the team to an abrupt stop.

Colbert jerked back the canvas and yelled out the window, "What are you doing, Jensen? I didn't tell you to stop!"

"Got to," Smoke said as he put a hand on the seat and vaulted lithely to the ground.

Colbert flung the door open and hung out of the coach to point the gun at him. "Don't move, damn you! I'll kill you if you try anything!"

"Don't be a damn fool," Smoke said. "We need to get fires going right now, on both sides of the coach and in front and behind it, too."

"What the hell are you talking about? We don't need four fires to boil coffee and cook food!"

"No," Smoke agreed, "but we do need them to keep the wolf pack that's stalking us from closing in, killing the horses, and stranding us here to freeze or starve to death!"

CHAPTER 30

"C"olbert's features tightened in an alarmed frown. "Wolves!" he exclaimed.

"Remember you joked earlier about leaving us for them?" Smoke snapped. "Well, you may have to deal with them yourself now."

Colbert's head jerked from side to side as he peered around with a so-called civilized man's aversion to natural predators. It would never occur to him, Smoke thought, that to the peaceful, law-abiding folks of the West, men such as Frank Colbert were the real predators.

"Where are they? How many of them are there?"

"I've seen two," Smoke said. "Don't know how many more there are, but wolves usually travel in a pack of a dozen or so. Enough to take down all these horses . . . and all of us, to boot, if they feel like it."

Colbert leaped down from the stagecoach. Snow puffed up around his feet when he landed. He waved the gun at the coach and ordered, "Everybody out! Now!"

"Let Salty stay inside," Smoke suggested. "He's wounded and wouldn't be much help."

The old-timer heard that, and the words rankled him.

"I've fought off *lobos* many a time!" he insisted as he leaned forward between Denny and Melanie.

"We don't want to fight them unless we have to," Smoke said. "We want to keep them from getting too close."

The passengers were climbing out of the coach. Colbert said, "Alma, get hold of the kid and keep your gun to his head. I'm going to be busy and can't watch everybody." He raised his voice. "Listen! If anybody tries anything, she'll shoot the boy. So don't get foolish ideas."

Denny said, "We want to keep those wolves at bay as much as you do, Colbert. When it comes to us versus them, we're all on the same side."

That wasn't strictly true, Smoke thought. If a couple of the wolves wanted to pull Frank Colbert down and drag his carcass off, he wouldn't try too hard to stop them.

He would just feel sorry for the wolves, having to eat such a skunk.

When everybody was out of the coach, Denny said, "What do you want us to do, Pa?"

"You and I will light the fires. Louis, Mrs. Buckner, Stansfield, and Kellerman, start gathering wood. Get the dryest you can find. Each of you pick a side and start piling the wood there. Denny, we'll help with that until we get big enough piles to light." Smoke turned to the outlaw. "Colbert, you and Mrs. Lewiston are the only ones with guns. You'll have to stand guard and keep the wolves off us if they start closing in."

At that, Alma said in an unsteady voice, "Frank, I'm scared. I don't like wolves—"

"Nobody likes wolves, blast it," Colbert barked. "Now watch the kid, like I told you." He sighed. "And watch out for those beasts, too."

Colbert went to the other side of the coach as the others split up and began gathering firewood. He stood there with the pistol gripped tightly in his hand as his head swiveled back and forth, eyes wide with watchfulness . . . and more than a little nervousness, Smoke thought.

Colbert being spooked might give them an opening to turn the tables on him, Smoke mused. But right now there was a more immediate danger threatening all of them. He heard another howl from somewhere out there in the storm.

He thought it sounded hungry, but maybe that was just his imagination.

He was on the right of the coach, Denny to the left. Melanie was gathering broken branches over here, shaking snow off of them, and stacking them about fifteen feet from the stagecoach, where Smoke had kicked a spot relatively clear of snow.

More of the white stuff was falling all the time, though, so he knew his efforts wouldn't last long. He grabbed branches and tossed them onto the pile as well.

He could see how frightened and hollow eyed Melanie was, so he told her quietly, "Your boy's going to be all right. I've seen enough to know he's a smart, levelheaded youngster."

She swallowed and said, "He must be terrified, having a gun to his head like that."

"I reckon he's scared. We all are."

"Even you, Mr. Jensen?"

Smoke laughed softly. "Ma'am, my young'uns may be grown—mostly—but that doesn't mean I'll ever stop being scared for them. Having kids means being scared every day for the rest of your life. But that doesn't stop folks from having them, and it doesn't mean we love 'em any less. It's just part of being a parent . . . at least if you're a good one."

"I suppose you're right. You're saying it never gets any easier?"

"Oh, I expect it does, if you've raised them right. But it never goes away completely. From the looks of it, you're doing a fine job with Bradley."

She brushed snow from a branch and added it to the stack. "He doesn't like being called Bradley. He'd rather be called Brad. He says Brad Buckner sounds like a cowboy name."

"Well, it does, I suppose," Smoke said with a smile.

"If we . . . if we get out of this alive . . . I should try to remember to call him Brad. . . ."

Tears began to run down her cheeks. Smoke said gently, "Try not to cry, ma'am. Tears are liable to freeze in weather like this."

A few yards away, Colbert said, "Quit talking and keep working! I thought I just saw something moving out there. With all this snow blowing around, it's hard to tell."

"I imagine you did," Smoke said. "The varmints are out there, sure enough."

He told Melanie to continue gathering wood,

then hunkered on his heels and started arranging the branches for a fire. Crumbled bark was the only thing he had for tinder, and as he began trying to light it, shielding the match with his body, it stubbornly refused to catch.

He shoved a hand in his pocket and brought out the telegraph flimsy with Sally's reply to his wire printed on it. He tore it in half and put one piece back in his pocket in case he needed it later. The other half he crumpled a little and nested it down among the firewood and tinder.

The idea of burning up Sally's message bothered him a mite, but Smoke knew she would understand. He struck a match, held it to the paper, and watched in satisfaction as flames began to curl it. That was hot enough to catch the tinder on fire as well. The flames spread to the branches, which began to smolder and smoke and then burn.

It wasn't long before the fire was blazing brightly in the gathering gloom.

Smoke straightened from it, looked at the pile of firewood Melanie had stacked up, and told her, "Move back closer to the coach, with the fire between you and the woods. Throw a branch on there every now and then when it starts to burn down."

She nodded and said, "I understand."

Smoke looked through the coach's windows and saw smoke rising on the other side of the vehicle. Denny had gotten a suitable blaze going over there, too. He called to her and said, "Light the one in the back!"

"All right, Pa!"

Smoke went to the front, where Jerome Kellerman, huffing and puffing as usual, had a stack of broken branches. Smoke noted with a frown that the banker had that leather case tucked under his arm. The man sure didn't want to let go of it, and that made Smoke curious about what was in it.

"Let's get a good spot cleared for the fire," he said to Kellerman as he started kicking at the snow and bending over to brush it away with his hands. "Give me some of the branches."

In a few minutes, Smoke had the fire ready to light. From where he hunkered beside the branches, he looked up at Kellerman and asked, "Got anything that'll burn good to use as tinder?"

Kellerman clutched the case tighter to him and said, "No! I mean, ah . . . no, no, I don't."

Smoke didn't say anything. The thoughts going through his head were pure speculation, but he wondered if Kellerman had money or bonds or something like that in the case. Was the man an embezzler? That was a big leap, but Smoke found that he wasn't willing to rule it out.

It also didn't matter right now, so he tried again to light the fire using bark as tinder, and this time it worked. He fed more branches into the flames until the blaze was a good one.

When he straightened and looked around, he saw to his satisfaction that fires were burning on all four sides of the stagecoach. The passengers had drawn back closer to the vehicle.

The horses still hitched in the team, as well as the ones tied with lead ropes to the back of the coach, were restless, moving around and nickering and throwing their heads in the air. Smoke figured they could smell the wolves out there in the trees.

For now he intended to leave the team in harness and the others attached to the coach, rather than picketing them. If they panicked, they would be less likely to break free.

As daylight faded, the garish, flickering firelight washed over the coach and the travelers. Smoke joined the others and said to Colbert, "There are a couple of Winchesters in the boot. They'd come in handy if we have to fight off those wolves."

A harsh laugh came from Colbert. "What kind of fool do you take me for, Jensen? I'm not letting you get your hands on a gun, or any of these other people, either."

"Then maybe you'd better get one of the rifles out and carry it yourself," Smoke suggested. "They've got more stopping power than that pistol you're toting."

"Now that's not a bad idea. Alma, keep an eye on everybody while I check on that."

Smoke said, "The rest of these folks could get back into the coach, too. They'll be safer there."

"Fine. Go ahead. You stay out here, though, Jensen. I want you where I can keep an eye on you myself."

Smoke didn't mind. If he had a chance to jump Colbert and put the man out of action, he would take it. He thought he could handle Alma Lewiston.

Colbert proved to be too careful, however, keeping Smoke well away from him while he took one of the Winchesters from the boot and loaded it from a box of ammunition in the supplies.

The heat from the fires made the inside of the

coach more comfortable than it had been all day, Smoke supposed. He hoped the flames would keep the hungry wolves at bay, too. But he worried that they didn't have enough wood to keep the fires burning like that all night.

If the flames died down too much, the wolves might become daring enough to risk an attack.

Colbert worked the Winchester's lever to throw a round into the chamber and told Smoke, "All right, get a cook fire going. It's been a long day and we need coffee and food."

Smoke couldn't disagree with that. He built a smaller fire closer to the coach and got it lit with a burning branch he took from one of the other fires.

In the middle of the day, they had eaten the last of the bacon and biscuits from the night before, so Smoke had to cook fresh batches of both. He got the coffee started boiling, then worked on rustling the grub. He'd made many a night camp in his time and was a good trail cook. When Melanie called from one of the coach windows and offered to help, he told her it wasn't necessary.

When the meal was ready, the others climbed down from the coach, with Alma and Brad emerging last, as usual. Alma didn't have her gun pointed at the boy's head, but it was close and ready.

While everyone was eating, Colbert asked Smoke, "How far are we from Donner Pass?"

"In this weather, it's hard to say."

"You know this country," Colbert snapped. "Make a guess."

"I believe we're about a mile, maybe a mile and a half from the entrance to the pass."

"So we should be through it and on our way down the other side by the middle of the day tomorrow."

Smoke said, "You seem to think that just because you want something to be so, it will be. There's no guarantee we can even make it all the way to the pass, Colbert, let alone get through it."

Colbert's mouth twisted angrily. He said, "You'd damn well better get us through it, Jensen, if you don't want any of these people hurt."

"You reckon I can just wave my hand at drifts too deep for the stagecoach and make them disappear?"

Before Colbert could respond, a shrill, terrified scream cut through the snow-filled air.

CHAPTER 31

Smoke whirled around and saw a large dark shape darting through the firelight. One of the wolves had overcome its instinctive fear of the flames and was charging toward Melanie, who screamed again as the beast left its feet and lunged at her.

Before the wolf could clamp its jaws on the young woman's quivering flesh, Louis leaped toward her. He wrapped his arms around her and drove her off her feet, sending both of them sprawling headlong into the snow.

As the wolf sailed past, it twisted its head and snapped at Louis, but its teeth snapped together harmlessly.

An instant later, as the wolf landed on the ground, a shot blasted and the shaggy creature jackknifed from the force of the slug ripping through it. The wolf rolled across the snow. Blood spurted from the wound and painted a crimson spatter on the white.

The horses all fought against their harnesses and lead ropes as they tried to rear up and let out shrill whinnies. The combined smells of wolf and blood had them panic stricken.

Smoke had no chance to try to calm them. He saw another large, furry shape hurtling toward Louis and Melanie where they lay on the ground. He shouted, "Louis, look out!" as he charged toward them from the other direction.

Louis threw himself on top of Melanie to shield her from the attack with his own body. He kicked at the wolf and caught it under the chin, slowing it momentarily.

That gave Smoke a chance to tackle the beast. He wrapped both arms around its neck and let his momentum roll them over so he was lying on his back with the wolf on top of him. All four of the animal's legs flailed in the air as it tried to twist its head around enough to slash at him with its teeth.

The wolf was incredibly powerful, but Smoke's arms and shoulders bulged with muscle as he tightened his grip on the beast's throat. His lips drew back from his teeth in a grimace of effort. He squeezed harder and harder. The wolf's struggles became more and more frantic. Its teeth ripped the sleeve of Smoke's sheepskin jacket but didn't penetrate to the flesh underneath.

Smoke heaved and twisted. A sharp crack sounded, like a branch breaking.

Smoke knew it was the wolf's neck that had just snapped.

The animal went limp. He shoved it aside and sat up. His pulse hammered inside his head, but not so loudly that he couldn't hear the shots as Colbert fired several times, aiming into the woods as he levered the rifle.

"Get out of here, you bastards!" Colbert bellowed as the echoes of the shots rolled through the trees.

Smoke clambered to his feet. Colbert swung the rifle toward him. Flame spurted from the Winchester's muzzle. Smoke's first thought was that Colbert was trying to kill *him*.

Then a heavy weight slammed into his back. Smoke barely had time before crashing to the ground to realize that Colbert had been aiming at a wolf charging from behind him.

The shot must have missed, though, because the hairy predator was on top of him, pinning him to the ground and snapping and snarling.

Smoke drove an elbow up and back and connected solidly with the wolf's head. That slowed the fierce assault for a second. Smoke managed to writhe onto his back, and as teeth flashed mere inches from his face, his hands shot up and grabbed the wolf's thick coat just behind its head. Smoke steeled his muscles to keep the killer from ripping his face off.

Hot slaver drooled from the wolf's gaping jaws. Its claws ripped at Smoke's heavy clothing. A great shudder went through him as he strained, pitting his strength against that of the wolf with his life on the line.

Vaguely, as if it were happening miles away, he was aware of more screams and gunshots. Fear for the safety of his children coursed through him, but he knew if he took his attention away from the snarling, snapping wolf for even the merest instant, it would mean his death.

Then, suddenly, another dark, hairy shape loomed over the wolf. In the firelight, with the beast's hot breath in his face, Smoke couldn't see very well, but he knew the wolf's weight went away with no warning. The thick pelt was ripped out of his hands. He heard a howl of pain.

Smoke rolled onto his side and looked toward the stagecoach. Everyone huddled against it except for Frank Colbert, who stood with the Winchester hanging in his left hand while he fired his pistol with the right. A couple of shots slammed from the gun as Colbert aimed into the trees.

The panic-stricken horses hitched to the coach lunged forward, but the brake held and the coach only lurched a couple of feet.

That was enough to throw Alma Lewiston off balance, and as she stumbled away from Brad, Denny leaped at her and grappled for the gun. Smoke scrambled to his feet, intending to go to his daughter's aid, but Colbert swung the revolver toward him and yelled, "Hold it, Jensen, or I'll drill you!"

Alma jerked away from Denny and chopped at her head with the gun she held. Smoke heard the thud as the blow fell. Denny's knees buckled.

Louis tackled Alma from behind. She cried out as she went down. Colbert's head jerked back and forth from Smoke to the struggle beside the coach. Obviously, he was torn between holding Smoke at bay and trying to help Alma. He couldn't take a shot at Louis, though, without risking hitting his only ally instead.

Just the distraction was enough. Smoke leaped at Colbert, and as the outlaw tried to bring the gun to bear, Smoke swung his left arm and caught the wrist of Colbert's gun hand, knocking it upward. The revolver roared and geysered flame, but the barrel was pointing at the snow-laden sky.

Smoke crashed into Colbert and drove him backward off his feet.

Colbert landed on his back with Smoke on top of him. All of Smoke's anger from the past two days boiled up inside him. He rammed his knee into Colbert's stomach, then smashed a punch to his face. He banged Colbert's gun hand against the ground, trying to dislodge the weapon from the man's grip, but the snow cushioned it too much and ruined that effort.

Colbert wasn't going to give up easily, either. He hammered a short but powerful left-hand punch to Smoke's jaw. The blow rocked Smoke's head back. Colbert heaved up from the ground and threw him off to the side.

As Smoke landed on his back, Colbert tried again to bring the gun to bear on him. Smoke snapped a kick that caught Colbert's wrist and sent the revolver flying from his grip. Colbert had already dropped the Winchester when Smoke tackled him, so that left the two men on equal terms.

They surged up from the ground and came together like two titans slugging it out for control of the world.

Smoke whipped in a left-right combination that rocked Colbert's head far back, but the outlaw recovered quickly enough to smash a punch to his opponent's sternum before Smoke could step back. Smoke planted a foot to brace himself as Colbert bored in and looped a left at his head. Smoke blocked it and retaliated with a left hook of his own that buried his fist in Colbert's belly.

That caused Colbert to double over, but the outlaw tried to turn that to his advantage by lowering his head even more and ramming it into Smoke's chest. He grabbed Smoke in a bear hug and forced him backward. Smoke clubbed his fists together and pounded them down on Colbert's back, but it didn't break his hold.

Colbert rammed Smoke into the trunk of a pine tree. The back of Smoke's head banged sharply against the rough bark. The world spun crazily around him. The vibration from the impact shook snow from the heavily laden branches. The white stuff showered down around them.

Smoke caught hold of Colbert's hair and jerked his head up. He butted his forehead against Colbert's. Maybe not the smartest move, since he was already dizzy.

The impact stunned both of them, but Smoke had enough strength, and enough of his wits about him, to shove Colbert away from him when he felt the man's grip loosen.

Colbert recovered a split second sooner, which gave him a chance to charge at Smoke. Smoke twisted out of the way, though, and grabbed Colbert's coat to sling him to the ground. Colbert hooked Smoke's ankle with a reaching hand and upended him. The two battlers fell close enough together that within a heartbeat they were rolling across the snowy ground, wrestling desperately.

Colbert managed to get behind Smoke and wrap an arm around his neck. As Colbert's forearm clamped across his throat like an iron bar, Smoke jabbed his elbow backward into Colbert's body. Colbert's grip didn't slip even a little.

Smoke had had some air in his lungs when Colbert got hold of him, so he wasn't in danger of passing out from being choked just yet. But much more pressure would crush his windpipe, Smoke knew. If that happened, he wouldn't have a chance. He reached back and clawed at Colbert's face, searching for his eyes.

The old "no bitin', no gougin'," rule had no place in a life-or-death battle like this.

Colbert yelled hoarsely and jerked back as one of Smoke's fingers dug at his right eye. That gave Smoke an opening to lower his chin and force Colbert's arm away from his throat. With that terrible pressure eased, Smoke gulped down some air and twisted around enough to hit Colbert under the chin with the heel of his hand.

That left Colbert slow to respond. Smoke swung his right fist up, then brought it down like a mallet in Colbert's face. Teeth came loose and blood flew. Smoke hit him again, this time slugging him on the jaw. He got a knee in Colbert's belly and rocked his head to the side with a left. Anger kept Smoke hammering punches, even though Colbert had stopped fighting back and was only half conscious.

Smoke wasn't the sort of man to lose control of himself, though, even under the most trying circumstances, so he hit Colbert only three or four more times than he actually needed to. As Colbert lay there mostly senseless, blubbering incoherently through smashed, bloody lips, Smoke put a hand on the ground and pushed himself upright.

He didn't know what he would find when he turned toward the coach. Alma Lewiston might be just about ready to shoot him.

Instead, Alma lay facedown in the snow with Denny sitting on top of her. Salty was a few feet away with his old revolver back in his hand, where it belonged. Smoke could tell the old-timer was poised to shoot if it had been Colbert who got up.

Melanie was on her knees hugging Brad, who appeared to be all right but a little uncomfortable at all the attention. Louis stood protectively beside them. He was breathing hard, and Smoke didn't like the looks of his coloring, but it was hard to be sure about that in the firelight.

Stansfield and Kellerman stood off to the side. Smoke told them, "Go hang on to the team's harness. Talk quietly to them. That'll calm them down." He turned to Salty. "What about the wolves?"

"The rest of the pack seems to've lit a shuck. Four of 'em are dead. Colbert shot a couple, and you broke that one's neck."

Smoke frowned. "What about the fourth one?"

"We'd best talk about that later," Salty said. "How bad are you hurt, Smoke?"

"Me? I'm all right." Smoke looked down at the rips and tears in his jacket. "The wolf didn't get me, just did some damage to my clothes. Any blood on me is from Colbert."

He picked up Colbert's pistol and the Winchester and went straight to the opened boot to reload the rifle. As he thumbed cartridges through the loading gate, he said to Denny, "Is Mrs. Lewiston alive?"

"You don't think I'd be sitting on her if she wasn't, do you?" Denny replied. "She's fine, I just don't want her getting too rambunctious again."

"Are you all right? I saw her wallop you with that gun."

"It was just a glancing blow," Denny said contemptuously. "Addled me for a minute, that's all. As soon as I got my wits back, Louis and I took the gun away from her and gave it to Salty."

Smoke reached through the open door of the coach and picked up one of the lengths of rope Colbert had used to tie their hands. He tossed it to Denny, who pulled Alma's hands behind her back and lashed them together without being told to.

Then, when Denny stood up, Smoke handed the Winchester to her and said, "Keep an eye on Colbert. I'm going to tie him up, too."

Being careful to stay out of the line of fire, he got another piece of rope and approached the bloody outlaw, who was starting to come around. As Colbert lifted his head, Denny trained the rifle's sights on it and said, "I'm a crack shot, mister. Give me an excuse and I'll be happy to put a bullet right through that diseased brain of yours."

Colbert snarled but didn't put up a fight as Smoke tied his hands behind his back. Smoke hauled him upright and gave him a push that sent him stumbling toward the coach.

Alma had gotten to her feet by now. Her hat was gone and her hair had come loose, so it hung around her haggard face as she leaned against the coach and glared murderously at Smoke, Denny, and Louis.

Stansfield and Kellerman weren't very effective at calming the horses, but at least the team wasn't trying to bolt anymore. Smoke told them, "Grab one of those wolf carcasses and drag it out beyond the fire. We don't need them up here around the coach. They're probably still stirring up the horses."

"What if the others come back?" Stansfield asked. "Aren't they liable to attack us?"

"I'm coming with you, and I'll have the rifle." Smoke looked around at his son. "Louis, help Mrs. Buckner and Brad into the coach. You might as well stay in there, too, and start warming up again."

Colbert demanded, "What about us? Are you going to leave us out here to freeze?" The words were thick and slurred because of his smashed lips.

"Maybe I ought to, but I won't. You can stay outside for a few more minutes, though, until we get things squared away around the camp. Salty, keep an eye on them."

"Damn well betcha I will," the old-timer said.

Smoke didn't see or hear any signs of the survivors from the wolf pack, but he kept the Winchester handy as Stansfield and Kellerman dragged off the carcass. That reminded him of Salty's odd refusal to discuss what had happened to the fourth dead wolf. Smoke told Stansfield and Kellerman to get back in the coach, and when they had, Colbert and Alma climbed in awkwardly as well. They sat on the floor this time, which would make it more difficult for them to try anything if they managed to get free . . .

which Smoke didn't believe would happen, as securely as he and Denny had tied them.

That left Smoke, Denny, and Salty outside. Smoke told Denny to add some more branches to the fires and build them up again. While she was doing that, he said to Salty, "Now, what's all the mystery about that fourth wolf? What happened to it?"

"Well . . ." The old jehu scratched his beard and kept his voice pitched low as he went on, "You remember when that critter was tryin' to gobble up your face and you was barely holdin' him off?"

"It wasn't that long ago, and anyway, I'm not liable to forget something like that."

"Well, that was the fourth wolf," Salty said. "What did *you* see whilst you was tusslin' with it?"

Smoke recalled the large, dark, indistinct shape. "Somebody grabbed that wolf, tore it off me, and . . . did something to it. Is that right?"

"Flung it right into a tree and busted it to pieces like it didn't weigh no more than a rag doll. But it wasn't some*body*, Smoke. It was some*thing*."

Smoke frowned. "Blast it, what are you trying to say?"

"That it was another wolf that come along and saved your bacon, Smoke, the biggest, hairiest wolf I ever seen . . . only it walked on two legs, like a man."

CHAPTER 32

Smoke looked intently at his old friend for a long moment. Salty seemed completely serious, even though what he had just said clearly made him uncomfortable.

"I never saw a wolf that could walk on two legs, Salty," Smoke ventured. "Maybe one in a circus somewhere could do a trick like that."

"This weren't no circus animal," Salty said. "It was big and fast and strong. I never got a good look at it, mind you. But I could tell it weren't nothin' that ought to be walkin' around on this earth." He paused. "Smoke, did you ever hear tell of a critter called ... the Donner Devil?"

Until Salty asked that, the name hadn't cropped up in Smoke's thoughts. But once he heard the words, he *did* recall stories he had heard in the past. Crazy stories about a creature roaming Donner Pass and the mountainous area around it that was half bear, half man ... or half wolf and half man, depending on who was spinning the yarn.

Salty obviously came down on the half-wolf side.

"You don't put any stock in that tall tale, do you, Salty?"

The old-timer frowned. "Well, I never did until now. But I never seen anything like what I saw tonight, either."

"You say it ran off after it killed that wolf?"

"Yeah. Loped off through the trees. Didn't seem to be in a hurry, but it went out of sight mighty quick-like, let me tell you."

"And it was still moving on two legs?"

"It sure was."

Smoke nodded and said, "There's nothing we can do about it now, other than be grateful that it helped me, for whatever reason. I don't know how long I would've been able to hold off that wolf."

From behind him, Denny asked, "What are we going to do now?"

Smoke looked around at his daughter. "You heard what Salty was saying?"

"I heard."

Salty began, "You probably think I'm plumb loco, Miss Denny—"

She held up a hand to stop him. "You don't need to worry about that, Salty. Louis and I have spent a lot of time on the continent—in Europe, I mean—and there are places over there where you hear all kinds of strange stories. Why, we were touring through the Carpathian Mountains once, and we heard a story about some bloodthirsty count from hundreds of years ago—"

"We can swap stories later," Smoke said. "For now, Salty, why don't you get back in the coach and get some rest? Denny and I will take turns standing guard tonight."

Salty shook his head and said, "Let the gal rest. Ever since I got plugged, y'all have been makin' me take it easy, and I'm startin' to feel plumb useless. I'm rested up enough so's I can stand watch, and there ain't nothin' wrong with my right arm. That's my gun hand, you know."

Smoke thought about it and then nodded. "Good idea. Denny, you get in the coach. But before you do . . ." Smoke took the pistol Colbert had been carrying from behind his belt, where he had tucked it away, and held it out to her. "You'll be packing iron from now on. I know I can trust you to use it if you need to."

"That's the truth," she said. "But what if you need a handgun?"

Smoke reached under his jacket and brought out the Colt Lightning that Colbert had taken away from him the day before. "He had this one in his pocket when I tied him up. After I tackled him, he never had time to try to get it out." He hefted the Winchester. "Plus I have this rifle if I need it."

"And there's another o' them repeaters in the boot," Salty added. "What kind of a rifle shot is Louis?"

"He'll do," Denny said in a tone of grudging admiration. "But I'm better."

Smoke smiled. He wasn't sure his children would ever get completely over that sense of sibling rivalry. . . .

As Denny climbed into the coach, Smoke said, "You get some sleep now, too, Salty. I'll wake you later."

"I don't mind takin' the first turn," the old-timer said.

"No, I'm fine. Fact of the matter is, now that I've got a gun on my hip again, I feel pretty good."

He would feel better, though, he thought as snowflakes brushed his cheeks, if they weren't all still facing a very uncertain future here in these blizzard-swept mountains.

Smoke and then Salty, when the old jehu took his turn, were able to keep the fire blazing brightly all night. Smoke didn't see any sign of the wolves coming back, and Salty reported the same thing the next morning when Smoke climbed stiffly out of the coach.

A faint gray light hung in the heavens. With the thick overcast and the snow still falling heavily, the day might not get much brighter than it was right now.

Everyone else got out of the coach for the break-fast Melanie prepared. Now that Brad was no longer in imminent danger, she seemed much calmer and reserved.

She made sure that Brad stayed close to her, though, and began to look anxious whenever he strayed too far away.

Louis appointed himself to help Melanie with the meal. Denny was charged with guarding Alma Lewiston while the woman went off into the trees to tend to her personal business. Smoke handled the same chore with Colbert.

When he came back, he found that Stansfield and Kellerman had started switching the teams. He grinned and said, "We'll make stage station hostlers out of you fellas yet."

"Not likely," Kellerman snapped. "I just want to be

on our way as quickly as possible. The sooner we get back to civilization, the better."

That comment brought up something Smoke had been mulling over in his mind. He waited until everyone except Colbert and Alma had a cup of coffee and a tin plate of food. Those two would be fed their meals later, because Smoke didn't plan on untying them again.

"There's something we need to talk about," Smoke said as he stood beside the cook fire. "And that's where we go from here."

"Where we go?" Stansfield echoed. "I assume we go back to Sacramento. Surely you don't still intend to try to make it through the mountains in this terrible weather, even on that less hazardous trail farther down."

"That's just it," Smoke said. "I reckon we've gone past what they call the point of no return. The snow's already more than a foot deep, and it doesn't show any signs of slowing down, let alone stopping." He shook his head. "Under these conditions, I don't think we could make it back to Sacramento. We'd get stuck, and then we'd have to survive for who knows how long with a limited supply of food and nothing for shelter except the coach."

"You're saying we'd wind up like—" Denny began, but she stopped short at the look Smoke gave her. He knew she'd been about to say *Donner Party*.

"But . . . but if we can't go back, what can we do?" Kellerman asked. His normal bluster was heavily tinged with fear now.

Smoke looked around. They were all watching him with anxious expressions, except for Salty, who seemed to have figured out what was on Smoke's mind, and Colbert, who was still too filled with rage to be worried.

"If we can't go back, then we have to go on," Smoke said.

"Ha!" Colbert burst out. "Just like I wanted all along, and you told me we couldn't do it, Jensen!"

Stansfield said, "That's right, Mr. Jensen, but now you claim we can make it through Donner Pass after all?"

"I never said that," Smoke replied. "But we don't have to make it all the way through the pass and on down to Reno to reach a better place than this. I figure the Summit Hotel is less than two miles from here. If we can get that far, we can hole up there."

"For how long?" Melanie asked quietly.

Smoke shrugged. "Probably a week or two, to be honest. It may be that long before the railroad can get a work train up here to try to clear the pass."

"So we won't make it to Reno for Christmas."

"No, ma'am. But we'll all be alive. I'm betting they've laid in a good stock of supplies at the hotel, and it's a sturdy building, meant to stand up to mountain winters."

Denny asked, "Will the telegraph line still be up?"

"No way to tell until we get there, but I doubt it. As hard as the wind's been blowing the past twenty-four hours, and with all the snow piled on the trees, too, some of them have probably come down on the wires by now. But even if the hotel is out of touch with Sacramento and Reno, the railroad will send a relief train as soon as it's able to get through."

"Well, then, your suggestion makes good sense, Pa."

Salty chuckled. "Whatever your pa says usually does, Miss Denny."

Kellerman had overcome his nervousness enough to say, "This is unacceptable. I can't sit in some hotel in the middle of nowhere for two weeks."

"I think you can if the alternative is freezing to death," Stansfield said dryly.

"This is none of your business," Kellerman snapped at the reporter.

"I'd say I'm in the same boat as you are, Keller-man. Or stagecoach, as the case may be."

"We can't change the weather, Mr. Kellerman," Smoke said. "All we can do is try to stay as safe as possible, and that means making a try for the Summit Hotel."

Kellerman glared at him for a moment, then said, "Oh, very well. In that case, I suppose I vote yes."

Stansfield said, "The fact that you think it's up for a vote is rather amusing."

Kellerman looked like he wanted to make some angry retort, but Smoke cut it off by saying, "All of you finish your breakfast and get back in the coach. The sooner we get started, the better."

He left it at that and didn't say anything about how the speed with which the snow was piling up concerned him. It might get too deep for the horses and the stagecoach to break through before they even reached the Summit Hotel.

"Why don't I ride up on the box with you?" Salty suggested. "I know the trail mighty good, and I can help keep an eye out for wolves. Them varmints could still come back, you know."

Smoke nodded. "Thanks, Salty."

The others climbed in, Colbert and Alma first once they'd been fed a sparse breakfast. Stansfield and Kellerman took the front seat, while Denny got in the rear seat and watched the two prisoners. Brad scrambled aboard next, and then Louis started to help Melanie step up.

Before he could do so, his knees suddenly buckled, and he dropped to the snowy ground.

"Louis!" Melanie cried in alarm. His collapse had thrown her off balance since he was supporting part of her weight, but she caught herself and knelt beside him.

Smoke reached his son's other side in a heartbeat. He put his arm around Louis's shoulders and helped the young man sit up.

Louis's hat had fallen off. Melanie brushed away the snow that tried to collect on his fair hair. She leaned closer to him and said, "Louis, what's wrong?"

Through teeth gritted against obvious pain, he said, "It's just this . . . bum ticker of mine. Isn't that . . . what you'd call it, Father?"

"You're sure it's your heart?" Smoke asked.

"Yes, I've had . . . attacks like this before . . . when I exerted myself . . . too much."

"He . . . he wasn't really doing anything that hard," Melanie said.

"It adds up," Denny said as she knelt beside her brother, too. "The past few days have been rough on all of us." She put a hand on Louis's knee and squeezed in encouragement.

"I'll be fine," he said. "I just need to . . . rest a bit. You know what the doctors in Europe all said, Denny. It'll pass. . . ."

"They said the attacks will pass with rest . . . until the one that doesn't," Denny said with a grim note in her voice. "The one that—"

"That's enough," Smoke said. "Stansfield, give me a hand. We'll get him up and put him in the coach. Sorry you're going to have to be jolted around, son, but we need to get started."

Louis nodded and said, "Go ahead. I understand."

Denny got into the coach first, and then carefully, Smoke and Stansfield lifted Louis into the vehicle, where Denny helped lower him to the seat. Melanie got in then, and Brad crowded in beside her, next to the window.

Louis mustered up a smile. "Now I'm the one . . . sitting between a beautiful woman . . . and my sister."

"Shut up," Denny told him. "I know good and well you're just trying to make Melanie feel sorry for you."

The worry in her eyes made it clear she actually didn't feel that way, however.

A few minutes later, with Salty beside him on the driver's box, Smoke got the team moving. The horses didn't like forcing their way through the deep snow, which built up on the coach's undercarriage and weighed it down, making it even more difficult to pull.

"I hope you're right about how far it is to that hotel," Salty said quietly, so the passengers couldn't hear. "I ain't sure how far we can go in this."

"We have enough rope we can tie on the other eight horses in front and have them pull, too," Smoke said. "We'll have a fourteen-horse hitch."

"When I was workin' on the borax wagons down in Death Valley, sometimes we'd have twenty mules hitched in a team," Salty reminisced. "I sure remember them ol' Death Valley days."

Their progress up the mountain was agonizingly slow. Smoke and Salty could both still make out where the trail ran, but it was getting more difficult to follow. In some places snow had drifted deeply enough across the trail that Smoke had to climb down, get a shovel from the boot, and clear some of it before the stagecoach could go on.

They hit another switchback. Over the constant moaning of the wind, Salty said, "Best get them other horses. We ain't gonna make it up these slopes otherwise!"

Smoke agreed. He got Stansfield and Kellerman out of the coach to help. Both men complained bitterly as they worked in the flying snow, moving the horses from the rear of the coach to the front. Smoke ripped rope harnesses for them and tied some of them to the regular team while the others were tied directly to the coach.

"I can handle the reins, even with one hand," Salty said. "You get on one o' them lead horses. Otherwise I don't reckon they're gonna go."

Smoke agreed. He went to the front of the elongated team and swung up bareback on one of the leaders. He dug his boot heels into the animal's flanks and urged it to lean forward into the storm.

When Smoke glanced back over his shoulder, the snow was so thick in the air that it blurred the sight of the stagecoach with Salty on the driver's box.

"Come on!" he yelled at the horse underneath him.

Slowly, the coach lurched up the switchback trail. The only advantage to the steeper slope was that the snow didn't drift as deeply here.

Smoke hunched over against the wind and the

flakes that were pelting him so hard they almost felt like raindrops. He wouldn't have said that this was the coldest he had ever been in his life . . . but it was right up there.

He didn't know how many turns the trail made, but one by one, they fell behind the struggling horses and the coach. When they finally got to the top, he thought, they ought to stop and let the animals rest for a while.

Unfortunately, they couldn't. It was a race now, with the Summit Hotel as the finish line and the lives of everyone aboard that stagecoach as the stakes.

The trail turned, but not as much, and almost a minute went by before Smoke realized they were traveling over mostly level ground again. He thought the switchback they had just overcome was the last one on the approach to the pass. They ought to be in Donner Pass now.

Unless he had miscounted and there was another such ordeal ahead of them. If that was true, they were doomed. The horses couldn't make it.

The snow was even deeper here on the flatter ground, up to the horses' bellies, up to the bottom of the stagecoach, packed in around the wheels and the axles. Smoke heard a sudden crack, felt the lurch through the rope tied to the horse he was riding, and looked back in alarm. Something was wrong. The coach was tipped a little to one side.

The front axle had broken.

And with it, their chances of survival were crushed as well.

CHAPTER 33

Smoke dropped off the lead horse and fought his way through the deep snow toward the coach, kicking up the white stuff as he did so.

Salty was already climbing down from the box, hurrying despite the arm he still had in a sling. He shouted, "Everybody outta the coach! Now!" He turned to Smoke and went on, "The axle's just cracked. If we can bind it up with rope and get it to hold just a spell longer—"

With a splintering noise, the coach tipped even more to the left. Someone inside cried out in alarm. The vehicle lurched again, and something else broke.

"That does it," Salty said. His voice had turned grim and hollow. "It's busted plumb in two now. She ain't goin' nowhere."

The door on the right side opened. Denny looked out and said, "Pa?"

"You might as well stay in there," Smoke told her. "The damage is already done. At least you'll all be out of the wind, to a certain extent."

She nodded and pulled the door closed. The passengers might be uncomfortable because of the way the coach was tilted, but as Smoke had said, they were protected from the fierce bite of the wind as long as they were in there.

"How far you reckon we've come?" Salty asked quietly.

"From the spot where we spent last night? Half a mile. Maybe."

"Then the hotel could be just half a mile away. Maybe even less. It's mighty hard to be sure o' distances in weather like this."

"As long as it's snowing and the wind is blowing like this, the hotel might as well be a hundred miles away," Smoke said. "If a man set out in this blizzard, he'd be blind and lost within a hundred yards. Somebody would find his frozen carcass next spring . . . if he was lucky."

Salty reached under the bandanna tied over the lower half of his face and scratched at his beard. "Yeah, I reckon you're right. But we got to do *somethin'*, Smoke."

Smoke's brain was already working quickly. "We'll take the canvas off the boot and a couple of those lap robes and make a lean-to tent out of them, with the coach as one side of it. Once we've done that, I'll shovel the snow out of it and we can build a small fire for warmth. If everybody huddles around it, they won't freeze to death." He glanced up at the sky, which was still unleashing a torrent of snow, and muttered, "If this blizzard would just stop. . . ."

"That's a lot to count on."

"I'm not counting on it. We're still going to try to find the hotel."

Salty's weathered forehead creased in a frown under the turned-up brim of his old hat. "You just said it was too dangerous for a man to set out in this weather."

"I said he'd get lost. But if there was a way to keep that from happening, somebody could scout on ahead, maybe spot the hotel if it's not too far away."

"How do you figure on doin' that?"

"We'll take all the pieces of rope we have, plus we'll cut up the harness into lengths and tie them together, too, to make more rope. String it all together and a man could go a couple hundred yards and still have a lifeline to get back."

Salty thought about it and nodded slowly. "Might work," he said. "Don't know if that would be far enough to do any good."

"Only one way to find out," Smoke said, "but let's get that shelter built first."

Smoke cut the canvas cover loose from the boot at the back of the coach while Salty got two of the lap robes from inside the coach. They knotted corners together, then tied the makeshift tent to the trim around the top of the coach, on the left side since the vehicle was tipped that way and that side was closer to the ground. It took a third robe to make a large enough shelter to satisfy Smoke.

With that done, Stansfield and Kellerman got out of the coach and held the canvas and robes up while Smoke bent to get underneath them and work with the shovel. He cleared as much snow as he could off the area under the shelter and then put rocks on the corners to hold it in place.

There were gaps in the cover, but it would provide some protection from the snow and wind, especially after they hung robes over the openings at the sides.

The snow underneath the coach was deep enough that it served as a wind block on that side.

Denny had been gathering wood while the others were working on the shelter. When it was finished, she built a small fire. The wind snatched away some of the heat, but most of it reflected from the cover and kept it from being unbearably cold in the shelter.

"Somebody will have to crawl out every now and then and brush away the snow that collects on the canvas and the robes," Smoke told the group gathered next to the stagecoach. "Otherwise it'll melt and drip through and make things more miserable, not to mention making it harder to keep the fire going. I won't lie to you, it's going to be pretty miserable anyway, but we'll be all right until this blizzard stops, and then we'll figure out what to do next."

Kellerman said, "The blizzard has lasted for several days already. How do you know it's going to end anytime soon, Jensen? And by that, I mean before we freeze or starve to death!"

"Nobody's going to freeze or starve to death," Smoke snapped. "We have supplies."

He was a little more worried about firewood, although he didn't give voice to that thought. But he had been looking around, and since they were now in the pass, there weren't nearly as many trees around as there had been earlier. Denny might have already gathered up all the broken branches that were in the immediate vicinity.

Venturing out farther than that in search of firewood might turn out to be dangerous. As he had told Salty, it was easy to get lost in conditions like this. . . .

"Anyway, we may not have to wait for it to stop snowing," Smoke went on. "I'm going to see if I can find the hotel. If I can, I'll bring back help and we'll all be fine."

"Wait a minute, Pa," Denny said. "You don't need to be wandering around out there in this weather. You won't be able to find your way back."

"Salty and I have thought about that already. We're going to use the rope and some lengths of harness to make a lifeline. I'll tie one end to the coach, and all I'll have to do is follow it back."

"You should let me go," Denny volunteered without hesitation.

Smoke shook his head. None of them were what could be considered safe, by any stretch of the imagination, but he wasn't going to allow his daughter to run that extra risk.

"I'd rather you stay here and keep an eye on things," he said. He turned to Louis, who sat next to Melanie and Brad. It seemed to Smoke that Louis's color had improved slightly, although it was difficult to be sure in the shadowy, flame-lit, cave-like space under the lean-to. "How are you doing now, son?"

"I'm all right," Louis said, but Smoke could still hear some strain in his voice. "The pain isn't as bad."

"But it hasn't gone away."

Louis shrugged. "That takes time. But don't worry, Father. I have a good nurse on hand, after all."

He smiled at Melanie, who said, "I don't know how good I am. I never cared for a patient with a bad heart."

Louis took her hand. "You make me feel better just by being here, although I wish you and Brad were somewhere much safer right now."

"Good Lord, kid," Frank Colbert rasped. "We're freezing, and you're making calf eyes at a woman!"

"No one asked for your opinion," Louis responded with a glare.

Denny said, "Are you sure I can't come with you, Pa?"

"No, you stay here," Smoke told her. "Salty, let's get busy putting that lifeline together."

They left the shelter and went back out into the snowstorm. Smoke began tying the lengths of rope together while Salty cut the harness loose and used his knife to separate it into usable lengths. He could manage that one-handed, but it took two hands to tie secure knots.

Smoke added the pieces of harness to the rope. While he was doing that, Salty said, "There's one thing we didn't think about, Smoke. What if that . . . varmint . . . we both saw last night comes back?"

"You mean . . . ?"

"The Donner Devil." The old-timer nodded emphatically. "That's what I mean, all right. You don't want to run into that critter when you're out there by yourself."

"Whatever it was, he helped me," Smoke pointed out. "He grabbed that wolf and pulled it off me, then broke its back by throwing it against that tree. Sounds like he's on our side."

"You don't know that," Salty insisted. "Like I said, he looked like he was half wolf his own self. Maybe that one he killed was his enemy from the pack. Maybe he just didn't get around to attackin' us yet."

"He had his chance last night. Instead he ran off, according to what you told me."

Salty nodded. "He did. Didn't seem to take no interest in us at all. But that still don't mean he's friendly. Or *it*. Don't hardly seem right, somehow, callin' that thing a he."

"Well, I don't expect we'll find out one way or another. Whatever it was, it's probably long gone by now." Smoke touched the grip of his Colt through the sheepskin coat he wore. "But I'm packing iron if anything *does* give me trouble out there."

The makeshift rope was ready. Smoke tied one end to the stagecoach and then coiled the rest so he could play it out as he made his way through the snow. He told Salty, "Get back inside the shelter. You might as well be warm."

"No, sir," Salty replied. "I'm gonna hang on to this end of the rope. You run into trouble, give it three tugs, and I'll come and find you."

Smoke considered that suggestion and then nodded. "That's a good idea." He began trudging in the same direction the coach had been going before the axle broke, holding the rope in his gloved left hand and letting it play out from the coil in his right.

It was slow going because of the deep snow. Smoke didn't think he had gone very far when he looked back, but his eyes were able to follow the rope for only a short distance before it disappeared in a white void behind him. He peered intently toward the spot where the stagecoach should be, but he couldn't see any sign of it.

Smoke sighed, looked ahead of him again, and pressed on. He knew that the tall, rocky walls of the pass had to be rising somewhere on either side, but nobody could prove that by him, because he couldn't see a thing.

The snow got in his boots. There was no preventing it. He felt his feet getting colder and colder. He couldn't leave them like that for too long, or he'd risk losing his toes to frostbite.

Right now, though, that was the least of his worries. His breath fogged in the air before the wind snatched it away, along with seemingly every ounce of warmth in his body. His teeth began to chatter so hard he clamped his jaws together to keep them from breaking.

In this white hell, there was no way of knowing how far he had gone, so he wasn't really surprised when he came to the end of the tied-together lengths of harness.

That was it. His lifeline was stretched out behind him, and it was his only way of getting back to the stagecoach. Without it, he could pass within fifty feet of the vehicle and never see it, and his shouts might never be heard because of the wind's howling.

Smoke gripped the harness tightly in his left hand and peered ahead of him, searching for anything other than the whipping snow. A light, a glimpse of a building, any sign of the hotel.

Nothing.

He used his teeth to pull the glove off his right hand, then slid that hand between two buttons and under his coat. The fingers were so cold they felt like stiff, dead sticks, but after a few moments they began to warm up. When he could flex them again, he closed them around the Colt's grips and pulled out the .38. Pointing the gun into the air, he squeezed off two shots.

If somebody at the hotel heard those shots, they might come out to investigate, bringing their own lifeline with them. It was unlikely, Smoke knew, since the wind was so loud . . . but wind was capricious and did funny things. You never could tell when and where sound might carry.

He stood and listened.

After an unknowable time, Smoke sighed and looked around. No trees were in sight, but he saw an iron-gray rock jutting up from the snow about twenty feet to his left. He made his way over to it.

What he was contemplating amounted pretty much to suicide, and he knew it. But his children were back there, and despite what he had told them earlier, he wasn't confident that they and the others could survive in such a primitive shelter for four or five days or even longer, depending on when the blizzard ended. For one thing, he didn't think they could find enough wood to keep the fire burning for that long, and without it they would freeze. So he had to take a chance and trust his natural ability to find his way. That instinct had never let him down before.

He took a deep breath, feeling the cold air burn his lungs, then wrapped the lifeline around the rock and knotted it in place. It was high enough that it would keep it from being covered up with snow, at least for a while. He ought to be able to find it if he could get back here. As long as the lifeline remained taut, Salty would believe he was on this end of it.

Smoke took a good look around him, even though there wasn't anything to see except snow. He hoped the mere act would help keep him oriented and pointed in the right direction.

He started walking again, deeper into the pass. If he was able to keep going straight, he would find the Summit Hotel sooner or later. The trick would be to keep himself from veering off or even starting to go around in circles.

One foot in front of the other, he told himself. One foot in front of the other . . .

Damn Frank Colbert for getting us all into this predicament. That outlaw's greed might wind up killing all of us.

Smoke wasn't sure how long he had been walking when that thought crossed his mind. A long time, that was for sure. His legs felt like lead except for where they ended at his feet.

He couldn't feel his feet at all anymore.

He stopped, his arms hanging. Despair did not come naturally to Smoke Jensen. It wasn't just that he didn't like to give up. The thought of surrendering almost made him ill.

"Preacher would keep going," he muttered to himself. "You don't want to let Preacher down."

Sally wouldn't want him to quit, either, he thought suddenly. She had a core of steel stronger than any woman he had ever known. That was one reason he loved her so much. He hated to think that they would have to spend Christmas apart, but if he survived, he would make it up to her.

Not *if,* he corrected himself. He was going to survive, and so were Denny and Louis.

He took another step, then another and another.

Then stopped again to lift his head. He dragged in a deep breath of the frigid air, feeling the snowflakes against his face.

There it was again, the thing he thought he had smelled a moment earlier.

Wood smoke.

A fire meant people. More than likely, it meant the hotel.

Unless he had looped around despite his best efforts and was right back where he started from, smelling the fire underneath the makeshift lean-to beside the stagecoach. That possibility brought a bleak chuckle from him. There was only one way to find out, so he had to keep moving.

He had taken only a few steps when a large, dark shape loomed up in front of him. Not the hotel—it was too close to be the building, and shaped wrong, to boot. This was a vaguely human figure. . . .

That thought had just formed sufficiently in Smoke's mind to set off alarm bells when something whipped out of the snow, crashed against his head, and sent him pitching backward. The blizzard's whiteness faded into an enveloping black.

CHAPTER 34

Time meant nothing in a situation like this. Denny had no idea how long it had been since her father had left in search of help, trailing the makeshift lifeline behind him. It seemed as if hours had passed since then when she crawled out of the lean-to and stood up next to Salty. The old-timer waited next to the coach with his right hand on the rope.

"Anything?" she asked.

"Nope. But that's a good thing, I reckon. I told Smoke to tug on the rope three times if he got into trouble, and there ain't been no tugs at all. The rope's as steady as a rock and has been for a good long while."

Denny thought about that and frowned. "But that doesn't make sense," she said. "If he was still moving around out there, wouldn't you be able to feel it through the rope?"

Salty didn't reply for a long moment. Denny could tell that he was considering the idea, too. Finally he exclaimed, "Dadgummit! You're right. It shouldn't be *this* still. Grab hold of it yourself and see if you feel anything."

Salty let go of the rope. Denny wrapped her fingers around it and waited for several minutes. Every now and then, she felt a tiny shiver, but she thought that might have been caused by the wind. As worry welled up inside her, she looked over at Salty and said, "I don't think he has hold of it anymore."

"But he's gotta. It didn't go slack."

"Maybe he tied the other end to something," Denny suggested.

"Why in blazes would he do that?"

"So he could keep searching for the hotel without you knowing that he'd let go."

The more Denny thought about it, the more that sounded to her exactly like something Smoke might do. He had complete confidence in his ability to get himself out of whatever predicament he might get into . . . and so far in his life, that confidence had been completely justified.

"Smoke ain't that loco," Salty insisted. But even he didn't sound convinced.

"I'm going out there to have a look."

"Blast it, no!" Salty said. "I ain't gonna have two Jensens disappearin' while I'm supposed to be in charge."

"I'm not going to disappear," Denny said. "I'll just go out to the end of the lifeline and then back. I promise."

Salty grunted as if he would believe that when he saw it, but he seemed to understand the futility of arguing with Denny once she had her mind made up. That was one quality she shared with her father.

"All right," the jehu said reluctantly. "But you be mighty careful out there."

"There's one thing I want to do before I leave."

Denny went to the rear of the coach and rummaged in the snow-covered bags stored there. She found a pair of jeans and a flannel shirt among the range clothes she had brought along, as well as her Stetson and a pair of high-topped boots. She kept the coach between her and Salty as she changed clothes.

That was one of the most bone-chilling experiences she'd ever had, but the range garb was much more suited to trudging through snow than the traveling outfit she'd had on.

She tromped back around the coach to where Salty was standing. He nodded in approval when he saw how she was dressed.

"Got your gun?" he asked.

She moved the thick coat aside so he could see the holstered .38 on her hip. She had put that on, too, as well as changed clothes.

"If I run into any trouble, I'll be ready."

"Yeah, but there could be anything out there in that blizzard. You hang on tight to that rope and don't LET LOOSE."

Denny nodded, crammed her hat down tighter on her head, and pulled up the chin strap. She didn't want the wind blowing it off. If that happened, she would never find it again.

She grasped the rope in her left hand and started out. By now, Louis was probably wondering why she hadn't crawled back into the lean-to, but she hadn't wanted to tell him what she was doing because she knew he would argue about it. If he got curious enough to stick his head out, Salty could tell him what was going on.

Denny ducked her head against the wind as she plodded forward. The deep snow made every step an effort. She couldn't help but move the rope as she clung to it and trudged along, but there was no response from the other end, which made her more convinced than ever that Smoke no longer had hold of it.

When Denny reached the end of the rope section and slid her hand onto the first piece of harness, she stopped to listen. Nothing but the wind blowing. She lifted her voice and called, "Pa! Pa!" There was no response to that, either.

Well, that wasn't surprising, she told herself. With that howling wind, nobody could hear anything for more than a few yards. She and Salty had had to talk pretty loudly when they were standing only a few feet from each other.

Denny resumed the frozen trek and didn't stop until she came to a large rock jutting up from the ground. It was a couple of feet in diameter, and the lifeline was wrapped around it and tied in a hard knot.

When Denny saw that, she felt a hollow in the pit of her stomach that was even colder than the air whipping the snow through the air around her. Smoke wasn't here at the end of the lifeline, where he should have been. She looked desperately for tracks in the snow, but in this blizzard, even a few minutes would be enough to obliterate any sign of where someone had gone.

Denny's heart pounded hard as she called again, "Pa! Smoke! Where are you? Can you hear me?"

The wind mocked her.

Terrible indecision filled Denny as she stood there. She wanted to let go of the lifeline and search for her father, but she knew how hopeless that idea was. Stumbling over him would be sheer luck . . . and stumbling was the right word, Denny thought bleakly, because she knew there was a good chance he was lying out there somewhere, covered up with snow that would keep his body preserved until the spring thaw.

No! That was exactly the sort of thinking she had been raised to avoid. Smoke Jensen was a practical man, but he wasn't the sort who ever gave up, no matter what the odds against him. He was alive, Denny told herself. He was alive, and he was out there trying to get help for all of them, to save them from the danger into which Frank Colbert had led them.

And he was counting on her to keep the others safe, she recalled, so if she did anything else, no matter how strong the impulse was, she would be letting him down.

She went around the rock so she could continue holding the lifeline with her left hand and started back toward the stagecoach.

By the time she got there, she was chilled to the bone and ready to warm herself beside the fire. As she came in sight of the stagecoach, Salty came out to meet her, holding on to the rope himself.

"You didn't find him, did you?" the old-timer asked.

"No. He had tied the last section of harness around a rock."

"Damn it!" Salty burst out, then said, "Pardon my French, Miss Denny—"

"Don't worry about it, Salty. I promise you, what I was thinking when I saw that was worse."

"Why would he do such a thing?" Salty asked, then answered his own question by continuing, "He wasn't willin' to admit defeat, was he?"

"You've known my father for longer than I have, and honestly, I was never around him that much when I was growing up. What do you think?"

"I reckon that's exactly what Smoke Jensen'd do. He knew it was dangerous, but he figured he could keep looking for a while and still find his way back."

Denny nodded. "That's what I think, too. The question is, what do we do now?"

Salty didn't answer for a long moment. Then he said, "We can't go lookin' for him in this blizzard. He wouldn't want any of us to risk that."

"We should send Colbert to look for him," Denny said with a bitter edge in her voice. "It would serve him right."

"Smoke wouldn't even want that. He'd put a bullet in a fella quicker'n he'd send him out to freeze to death in a blizzard."

Denny sighed, which made a cloud of condensed breath appear in front of her for a second before the wind carried it away, then said, "You're right about that."

"We'll stay here and keep warm as best we can," Salty said. "And keep hopin' that Smoke finds his way back here and brings some help."

Denny nodded. "I don't like the idea of telling Louis that Pa has disappeared, but I reckon it's got to be done."

Louis was understandably upset.

"Why would Father have done such a thing?" he demanded. "He was supposed to go out there looking for help and then come back if he didn't find any."

"He *didn't* find any," Denny said, "and he didn't want to give up. You know how he is."

"Yes. Stubborn as a mule."

Denny held out her hands toward the small fire burning under the lean-to and flexed her fingers. They had been almost numb when she got back, but the warmth and the movement restored feeling to them. She looked across the fire at her brother and said, "Pa is determined. He doesn't know what it's like to give up." She paused, then added, "And he's never been wrong yet, has he?"

Louis shrugged. "His continued survival speaks volumes, that's true. But you can't gun down a blizzard, no matter how fast on the draw you are."

"We're doomed." The words came from Jerome Kellerman, who stared morosely into the small, leaping flames. "We'll never get out of here alive."

"Don't talk like that," Denny snapped at him. "When the blizzard stops, we'll find that hotel, and then everything will be fine."

Melanie said, "Do you really think so, Denny?" Her arm was tight around Brad's shoulders, holding him against her so he would be warmer.

Over the past couple of days, Melanie had become Denny's friend. She tended to be too protective where Brad was concerned, and she went to pieces easily, but Denny liked her anyway and knew she was the way she was because she'd had to survive plenty of hardships and make sure her son survived them, too. Denny didn't like lying to her.

But despite that, she said, "I'm absolutely sure of it. I don't blame anybody for being worried or upset, but you have to have faith."

Peter Stansfield said, "You'll have to pardon me, Miss Jensen, but I'm a reporter. That means I'm naturally cynical. I think you know our odds of survival are just about nonexistent, but you don't want to say that. Am I right?"

"If you were, I wouldn't admit it, would I? Just keep your mouth shut, save your energy, and try to stay warm." Denny looked around at the circle of anxious faces. "That last part is good advice for all of us."

She tried not to glare at Frank Colbert, but judging by the smirk on his face, he knew she was blaming him for what had happened and didn't give a damn. Alma Lewiston huddled against the outlaw's side as they tried to share what little body heat they had left.

Salty hunkered next to the fire and fed a small branch into the flames. "I hate to say it, Miss Denny, but we're gonna have to have some more firewood pretty soon."

Denny grimaced. She had just gotten warm . . . well, a little less cold, anyway . . . and now she would have to go back out and search for firewood. But she could tell that the others were all looking to her for leadership with Smoke gone, and with that came responsibility.

The worst part was, she had looked around outside while she was gathering the first pile of broken branches, and she didn't think there were many more to be found nearby. When the wagon road and then the railroad had come through Donner Pass, most of the trees had been cleared away.

"I'll go see what I can find," she said.

Brad sat up right away and said, "I'll come with you and help."

Melanie's arm tightened around his shoulders. "No! I mean . . ." She looked embarrassed. "I mean, Denny will have enough to do without keeping up with you, too, Brad."

"I can take care of myself," the boy insisted. "Nobody has to keep up with me."

Louis said, "You know that's not how it works. Denny, I can help you."

"There's no need for *anybody* to help me," she said sharply. "All of you just stay in here and keep as warm as you can. I'll be back in a little while."

"Don't go out of sight o' the coach," Salty warned.

"I don't intend to."

Denny crawled out of the lean-to, stood up, and brushed off the snow she had gotten on her. She looked around. No trees were in sight, but she thought she remembered where she had found most of the branches earlier. She headed for that spot and began rooting around in the snow.

She found half a dozen small branches and knocked the snow off of them. That was all she came up with. Those would help for a while but wouldn't last the night, when the temperature would drop even more . . . to killing levels of cold.

She took the branches back to the shelter and handed them in to Salty. "I'm going to look around some more," she told the old-timer through chattering teeth.

"Dadgum it, you come on back in here and warm up," Salty said. "We can hunt more firewood later."

Denny wanted to argue but was too cold to do so. Also, she was having to fight off an insistent feeling of despair. She knew Smoke wouldn't want her to ever give up hope, but sometimes maintaining it took a real effort.

As she settled down at the fire, sitting cross-legged on the ground between Brad and Salty, she said, "We may have to find other things to burn. The coach is blocking the wind, so I don't want to destroy it, but there might be parts of it we could break off and burn. We might find some things in our bags that would work as fuel, too." She gestured toward the case in Kellerman's lap. "All those business papers you're carrying around would make good tinder, Mr. Kellerman."

The man's eyes widened as he held the case to his chest. "These . . . these papers are irreplaceable, young lady. You can't burn them!"

"If it comes down to a choice between doing that and freezing to death, we dang sure will," Denny replied in a firm voice. Salty felt like he had been left in charge, but Denny knew that Smoke was actually counting on her to get them all through this ordeal safely. If that meant giving orders and imposing her will on the others, she was prepared to do it.

Kellerman just glared at her and clutched the case. Denny noticed how intently Frank Colbert was looking at the banker. Colbert was suspicious, and that made Denny suspicious.

Maybe what Kellerman had in the case that he considered so precious wasn't just a bunch of bank documents. Maybe it was something more valuable.

Although trapped out here in the middle of nowhere, in a blizzard, nothing had much value unless it could be burned for warmth to keep them alive.

Denny hoped help would arrive in time, and they wouldn't need to open Kellerman's case and use whatever was inside for fuel.

But if that time came, she would be mighty glad that she had a Colt on her hip and knew how to use it.

CHAPTER 35

The red flicker of flames was the first thing Smoke was aware of as consciousness seeped back into his brain. Immediately following that came a thundering ache that filled his skull. As seconds crept past like hours, he gradually became aware that he was hearing and feeling his pulse.

That realization told him he was alive . . . and a moment later he also realized that he was warm. Both of those things seemed unlikely but were true.

As his thoughts cleared, he figured out that he was lying on some hard surface. Cautiously, he moved one finger enough to tell that it was a rock floor of some sort. Until he knew more about where he was and what the circumstances were, he didn't want to announce that he was awake again.

So he kept his breathing deep and regular and didn't move or open his eyes. He just lay there and let his other senses do the work.

The smell was the next thing he noticed. Rank, like that of a wild animal. If not for the fact that he could see a fire through his closed eyelids, he might think he had been dragged into some predator's den.

No animal could build a fire, though. That required the human touch. And as Smoke listened, he heard an odd sound that he finally figured out was someone grunting and muttering to themselves.

The Donner Devil. Salty had seen something that appeared unnatural, and so had Smoke. Under the circumstances, it wasn't too far-fetched to believe that some sort of strange creature roamed this isolated pass, but the fire made Smoke believe it was a man, not an animal.

Or maybe . . . it had *been* a man.

He was going to have to take a chance eventually, and he felt stronger now. His wits had returned to him, and the pain in his head had subsided to a dull ache. The other members of his party were still in danger, so he couldn't afford to wait too long.

He opened his eyes; pressed his left hand against the hard, rocky surface underneath him; and pushed himself into a sitting position. His right hand slid under his coat in search of his gun, but he didn't find it.

The muttering got louder and sounded alarmed. It came from Smoke's left. He turned his head in that direction and the glare from a small fire made him grimace and squint after so long in the darkness of oblivion. But his eyes adjusted quickly and he saw a huge shape on the other side of the flames.

The scene was a lot to take in. Smoke had seen some strange things in his life, but few stranger than the giant of a man who stood across the fire from him in a cave with a rounded ceiling over their heads. The man was close to seven feet tall, with a wild mane of gray hair and a long beard that covered nearly all of his face. Smoke could barely make out the eyes and nose in all that growth, and he couldn't see the man's mouth at all.

The man was wrapped in some sort of fur garment, obviously crudely fashioned from animal pelts, probably bear and wolf. His feet were wrapped in fur as well. It was easy for Smoke to see how he could have been mistaken for a bear or a giant wolf.

But the stranger was a man, no doubt about that. The eyes told the story.

Smoke suspected that madness lurked in them.

But the man didn't sound loco as he rasped, "Don't . . . don't hurt me. Please."

His voice was rusty, as if it hadn't been used much for many years. Unarmed as he appeared to be, Smoke wasn't sure he was capable of hurting a giant like this, especially given the condition he himself was in, but the man's fear seemed genuine. Smoke sat up straighter, held out an empty hand, and said, "I won't hurt you. I promise."

The man had backed all the way to the far wall. He wasn't particularly burly, but the muscles were like clumps of rope. Smoke knew from the way the man had picked up the wolf and flung it against a tree that he possessed enormous strength.

The idea that this strange individual might not be the one who had saved him from the wolf never occurred to Smoke. For there to be two such creatures lurking around Donner Pass was just too much of a stretch for him to believe.

While the man watched him warily, Smoke looked around the cave. It was roughly circular, about twenty feet in diameter, and the arched ceiling twelve feet high at the most. Animal skins were scattered here and there, as were bones. Clearly, the man subsisted on what he could catch, but he didn't appear to have any traps or weapons. He made do with what he could run down and grab with his bare hands. No wonder there wasn't any extra fat on him.

A low tunnel led out one side of the cave. The opening was no more than three feet tall, so Smoke would have to crawl out through it when he left. Certainly, that was the only way his "host" could get through it.

Since the man understood English, Smoke figured it was time to communicate more with him. He put his hand against his chest and said, "Smoke Jensen." Then he asked, "What's your name?"

The giant made a sound like "Urrrr." Smoke couldn't tell if he was growling or trying to form some word.

"Smoke," he said again as he lightly tapped his chest. "I want to be friends with you. Can you tell me your name?"

The man looked back and forth quickly, then down at the floor of the cave. Without raising his eyes, he said again, "Urrr."

He was embarrassed about something, Smoke realized. A possibility occurred to him, and he said, "Are you trying to tell me your name is Earl?"

Still without raising his head or meeting Smoke's eyes, the giant nodded.

"I'm pleased to meet you, Earl," Smoke said, keeping his voice calm and steady. "You're the one who saved me from that wolf, aren't you?"

"Don't like . . . wolves." The voice rasped like a corroded hinge. "They take my food . . . chase me."

"I don't like them when they attack me, either. Thank you for helping me."

Earl ducked his head even more.

"You don't have to be afraid of me," Smoke said. "Like I told you, I won't hurt you." He was anxious to find out where he was and how much time had passed, but he sensed that rushing things with this eccentric giant could be disastrous. "Why won't you look at me?"

"Not fit."

"I'm not fit?"

Earl shook his head emphatically and pressed a closed, knobby fist against his chest. "Not fit . . . to be around people. Ashamed . . . so ashamed."

"Why? What have you done to be so ashamed of?"

"When the wagon train stopped . . . people got so cold . . . so hungry . . . I was so hungry . . . just a boy. . . ."

A stunning theory burst in Smoke's brain. He couldn't stop himself from exclaiming, "Were you one of the Donner Party?"

He knew the words were a mistake as soon as they were out of his mouth. Earl cringed like a whipped dog, bent down to hunker at the base of the wall, and turned away. Smoke saw his shoulders shaking with sobs.

"Earl, it's all right," he said quickly. "I'm sorry. I didn't mean to upset you. I didn't know anybody was left around here from that bunch. That would make you . . . what? Sixty or seventy years old?"

The giant didn't look that old, and the thought that someone of such advanced years could pick up a full-grown wolf and throw it through the air like a rag doll seemed beyond belief.

On the other hand, trying to survive alone in the wilderness would either kill a man . . . or hone away all the civilized weaknesses and harden him to the point that almost anything was possible. If he'd been a youngster when the Donner Party became trapped on the other side of the pass and had spent the past five and a half decades alone, ashamed of what he had done, the effects on his mind and body would be difficult to predict.

Such an ordeal might well result in the gigantic creature who crouched before him, Smoke mused.

He was a little surprised, though, that Earl could still speak after so many years of solitude. That thought led him to another question.

"Have you been by yourself all this time, Earl?"

At first he thought the giant wasn't going to answer, but then, as if every word had to be dragged out of him, Earl said, "My pa was with me . . . for a while. . . . He told me . . . we couldn't ever go back . . . around civilized folks again. . . . Said we weren't fittin'. . . . Said we weren't nothin' but . . . animals."

Anger welled up inside Smoke. He had a better picture now of what had happened. One of the survivors from the Donner Party, instead of going back to civilization after the spring thaw, had decided to remain in the mountains because he was ashamed of what he had done to survive. He had had his young son with him, and over the years of isolation, he had taught the boy to feel the same sort of crippling shame.

There was no telling how long ago the older man had died. Probably many, many years had passed since then. But at least Earl had had some human companionship for part of the exile his father had imposed upon him.

"I don't think you're an animal, Earl," Smoke said. "Why don't you come over here and sit down closer to the fire? That rock wall you're leaning against has to be pretty cold in weather like this."

Earl took a step, stopped, moved his fur-shod foot back where it had been. He lifted huge hands and raked his fingers through the long, tangled hair on his head. As he muttered something that Smoke couldn't understand, he started shaking his head.

After a moment, Smoke began to understand the words. Earl was saying over and over again, "Shouldn't have brought him here . . . shouldn't have brought him here."

"Why *did* you bring me here, Earl?" Smoke asked. "Why did you knock me out?"

Earl finally looked up again. He said plaintively, "You *scared* me. I heard you shooting. You came to hunt me, the way other men have hunted me in the past."

His voice had loosened up some while he was talking. He seemed to be getting more used to putting words together in sentences. Smoke didn't want to lose that bit of progress.

"I would never hunt you or try to hurt you, Earl."

He kept using the name to remind the giant of his humanity. "Other people may have done that, but not me. I try to help folks, not hurt them."

Earl shook his head. "You can't help me. I'm damned."

Again Smoke felt anger toward the man responsible for this, Earl's father. Allowing his shame and guilt to ruin the rest of his own life was one thing, but to put his son through a lifetime of self-torture and being alone . . . that was a terrible legacy.

Smoke got to his feet. Earl cringed again, which was ludicrous considering his size and strength.

"Listen to me, Earl," Smoke said firmly. "There's no need for you to be ashamed or to hide in the mountains like this. What happened was a long, long time ago, and nobody is mad about it anymore. Nobody blames you for what happened. You can live the rest of your life around people and try to find some happiness. I'll help you. I give you my word on that. I just want to be your friend."

And to get your help in rescuing the others, he thought as he stuck his hand out toward the giant. Earl had to know this area better than anyone else, having lived in it for so long. More than likely, he could find his way around even in a blizzard.

Earl stared at Smoke's hand as if he wanted to step forward and take it, but he couldn't summon up the courage to do so. Finally, after a couple more false starts, he moved closer to the fire and stretched out his right arm. His big paw closed around Smoke's hand. He clasped it just for a second, but that was long enough to seal the connection between them.

To emphasize that, Smoke said, "We're friends

now, Earl. I'll help you any way I can. And I hope you'll help me, too."

Earl frowned, or at least Smoke thought he did. It was hard to be sure with so much hair hanging over the giant's face.

"How can I . . . help anybody?"

"Do you know where the Summit Hotel is?"

Earl flinched visibly. "The big building, next to the steel rails?"

"That's right."

"I don't like it! Too big. Too many people during the summer! They should all go away and leave Earl alone!"

Smoke didn't want to make Earl pull away from him so soon after he had accepted their fledgling friendship, but he had no choice. He had pushed his worry about Denny, Louis, Salty, and the others to the back of his mind while he was trying to establish some sort of rapport with the giant, but now he had to start nudging Earl into helping him.

"I have other friends who've been stranded here in the pass by the blizzard, Earl, and they need help. I need to get all of them to the hotel where they'll be warm and safe, but I can't do it by myself. I'm not sure I can even find them again as long as it's snowing. But I'll bet you know the way."

Earl shook his head. "Can't go to the hotel!" he said. "People there will shoot at me, because they know I'm bad!"

"I told you, Earl, nobody is mad at you. Nobody will shoot at you. I'm your friend, and I won't let them. Just help me, and you'll see. Everything will be all right."

"Can't." Earl wouldn't meet Smoke's eyes again. His head drooped and he looked at the ground. "Can't go around other people."

Smoke took a deep breath. "Well, then, I reckon I'll have to go by myself."

This time, the sound that came from the giant was definitely a growl, not an attempt to say his name. He added, "No! You stay here!"

"My son and daughter are out there, as well as some other innocent people." *And a couple not so innocent*, Smoke added to himself as he thought about Frank Colbert and Alma Lewiston. "I have to help them."

"Too much snow! And it's night. If you go out in it, you'll die!"

Smoke's heart sunk for a moment at the news that another night had fallen. That meant his children and the others would have to survive in their crude shelter until morning. They might make it, if they were able to find enough firewood, but the odds against them were high.

He wasn't sure even Earl could find his way around in the snow-clogged darkness, though. He said, "I'm going to crawl through that tunnel and take a look outside."

Earl shook his shaggy head. "No!"

Smoke squared his shoulders, looked directly at the giant, and said, "You can't stop me. You won't stop me . . . if you're really my friend. And we shook on it, remember?"

Did Earl retain enough of his humanity for that symbol of their pact to mean anything to him? Smoke didn't know, and there was only one way to find out.

He swung around, crossed quickly to the tunnel, and dropped to hands and knees.

He halfway expected Earl to grab one of his legs from behind, but that didn't happen. Smoke glanced over his shoulder and saw the man standing there with his head hanging, obviously at a loss what he should do.

Smoke didn't waste any more time. He crawled into the tunnel.

An icy wind blew in his face. There were small openings in the cave ceiling to carry away the smoke from the fire, and those created a draft. The tunnel curved, and that cut off the glow from the flames and caused darkness to close in quickly around Smoke. He kept moving anyway.

After a few moments he felt more on his face than the wind. Tiny cold jabs against his skin were snowflakes being whipped into the tunnel. That meant he was getting close to the outside opening.

It was so dark in the tunnel—and so dark outside—that Smoke didn't realize he had reached the end until his head stuck out into the full force of the wind. He pulled back and stared into the void with the bleak realization that Earl was right. No one could find their way around in that, not even the exiled giant. Accepting that was a bitter pill for Smoke to follow, but he had no choice.

The tunnel was too narrow for him to turn around, so he backed up until he emerged once more into the cave.

Earl was sitting down now, on the other side of the fire with his back against the wall. His head lifted when Smoke crawled in and stood up.

"You came back."

"That's right. I don't desert my friends."

That seemed to have an effect on Earl. He frowned for a long moment, then said, "In the morning . . . we will find your friends. We will take them to the hotel. But I won't go there myself. I'll show you, and when you see where to go, I will leave and come back here." A pathetic note entered his voice as he added, "Please don't tell them where to find me. They will hunt me. They will hurt me."

Smoke shook his head. "I give you my word that won't happen, Earl. And thank you for agreeing to help me and my children and my friends."

Earl opened his mouth to say something, hesitated, and then said, "They may be frozen by morning."

"I know," Smoke said. "But I'll never give up hope."

CHAPTER 36

Denny was right: the branches she had found to use as firewood didn't last long. And as the flames began to die down, the heat they generated went with them.

"We'll tear out the bench in the middle of the coach," she decided. "If we can break it up, that'll last us for a while. Where's that ax?"

She noticed that Jerome Kellerman looked relieved that she hadn't brought up burning whatever was in his case. But it might still come to that, she thought as she fetched the ax from the boot.

"I can do that," Stansfield offered as Denny crawled back into the lean-to with the ax. He held out his hand for it.

Denny hesitated, then gave the tool to him. Might as well let the reporter try to be useful. She watched from the door as he climbed into the coach and started chopping away at the bench.

"We need to bust it into fairly small pieces," she told him. "It'll last longer that way."

"I understand. It's a good thing your father left you here with us, Miss Jensen. You seem . . . unusually competent."

"Ha! Competent for a woman, you mean?"

"That's not what I said. But you have to admit . . . you're not the sort of typical female that one usually meets."

"Nothing's typical about Jensens, mister. You'd do well to remember that."

Stansfield chopped through the bench, then started working on breaking off a smaller piece. In the light from the fire outside, Denny saw that his face was covered with sweat, despite the cold. Being a fellow who made his living with words, he probably wasn't used to such hard physical labor.

She pulled herself up into the coach, took hold of the ax handle, and said, "Here, let me work on it for a while."

"I'm all right," Stansfield insisted. He was pretty breathless, though.

"Just sit down and rest for a few minutes."

He did so, and Denny turned her efforts to the bench. She hacked off a piece of wood and leaned out of the door to hand it to Salty.

"That'll burn for a little while."

"It sure will," the old-timer agreed. "Hate to damage ol' Fred's stagecoach—the thing means a lot to him—but I reckon he wouldn't want us to freeze to death."

Denny went back to work, using the ax to cut partially through the bench in places. Then she and Stansfield were able to pry those pieces loose. The boards were fairly thick and would burn slowly.

Denny began to think they might make it through the night after all.

All day, the storm had made it seem like twilight outside. As actual night began to fall, the darkness thickened and closed in, the wind howled even harder, and the feeble spark of light and warmth from the fire inside the shelter seemed like a tiny flicker of life in an endless abyss of nothingness.

Denny kept feeding pieces of broken wood from the bench into the fire. She looked around, saw that everyone had dozed off except for Salty. Louis and Melanie lay with Brad between them, keeping the boy warm. Colbert and Alma were cuddled together, too. Stansfield and Kellerman were asleep, wrapped up in thick robes that hadn't been used for the shelter, but they shivered a little in their slumber.

"Smoke'd be proud of you, if he could see how you're keepin' these folks alive, Denny," Salty said quietly.

"You've done your share to help, too," she told him.

"Yeah, but you're the one who's willin' 'em not to give up. I reckon if not for that, some of 'em would've laid down and died before now, instead of layin' down and goin' to sleep."

"Speaking of that, we don't need to let any of them sleep for very long. It's too easy to freeze to death without even knowing it while you're asleep."

Salty nodded. "Good idea. I'll wake 'em in a bit." He paused. "You can get some rest if you want."

"I'm all right," Denny replied with a shake of her head. "I'd rather keep an eye on the fire."

Her eyelids were getting heavy, though, and the

drowsiness continued to steal over her. Realizing that, she looked around for something to keep her awake. Her gaze lit on the leather case Kellerman kept with him at all times. One end of it was sticking out from under the robe wrapped around the middle-aged banker.

Denny found herself wondering if he had hold of it right now. Could she reach over there and slide it out from under the robe without disturbing him? Maybe, she decided, but she had no right to do such a thing, and she knew it. Under normal circumstances, the thought wouldn't have crossed her mind. Right now, the main reason for it was that she wondered if what was inside would burn and help keep them warm.

While Denny was musing about that, she fell asleep without knowing it.

The sun was a rich, warm yellow as it flooded over the patio at the villa in Italy Louis's grandparents had rented for the summer. He sat in a comfortable chair and drank in the heat and the fragrance from thousands of flowers blooming in the gardens spread out on the hillside below. He felt wonderful, and at this moment, it seemed like nothing could ever go wrong with the world.

Then he woke up to cold, dark desperation and tried not to groan as he realized he'd been dreaming. He wanted to escape back to that Italian villa . . . but he wanted to take Melanie and Brad with him.

Louis lifted his head and looked around. The fire was still burning, but it had died down quite a bit and the flames might be in danger of going out. Brad's head was pillowed on his left arm, which had gone numb under the weight.

Carefully, so as not to disturb him, Louis shifted Brad just enough to slide his arm free. Then he sat up and flexed it to get some feeling back into it.

A couple of feet away, Denny slept as she leaned against the stagecoach's rear wheel on this side. Salty had dozed off, too, and the others all appeared to be sound asleep. Louis knew the fire needed to be fed.

Out of habit, he paid attention to the way his chest felt before he did anything. His parents and Denny probably had no idea he always did that, but he had learned to check his condition before proceeding. It only took a second.

No tightness or pain in his chest. He leaned forward and reached across Denny to pick up one of the pieces of broken board from the destroyed coach seat. He worked one end of it into the fire and watched as the flames danced around the wood. After a few moments, curls of smoke appeared, and then a tiny orange-red flame danced along the board's surface.

Louis watched until the board was burning well and the heat it was generating took a little of the edge off the chill in the lean-to. Then he pulled back the canvas to look out.

There was nothing to see but darkness. Cold air whipped in, and snowflakes whirled in its wake. Quickly, Louis closed the gap.

He stretched out again and looked past Brad at Melanie. Even under the strain of this harrowing ordeal, she was beautiful. He watched her sleeping and thought about how much he had come to care for her, even though he had known her only a few days. Melanie didn't have the obvious stubborn determination of his sister, Denny, the female he had been around more than any other, but he sensed that she had a core of strength, especially where her son was concerned.

Louis's gaze moved over to Frank Colbert. Anger welled up inside him. Colbert's actions were directly responsible for the deadly danger that threatened all of them, including Melanie and Brad, and Louis couldn't shake the image of Colbert holding a gun to the head of the frightened little boy. He wanted to smash a fist into the outlaw's face.

Of course, he was no match physically for Colbert. The man could break him in two. Not for the first time in his life, Louis wished he were as big and powerful and courageous as his father. If he were, he could give Colbert the good beating that the man deserved.

Such wishes were those of a child, Louis told himself. He was a grown man. Not much of one, maybe, but a grown man, regardless.

Time crawled on. Whenever Louis saw the fire burning down, he added another piece of board to it. The pile began to concern him as it dwindled.

He frowned as he looked at Jerome Kellerman's case. The man was a banker, on his way to Reno for business, so the case was almost certainly full of ledgers or something like that. Pages ripped out one at a time would make a nice fire, Louis thought, and their lives were more important than any numbers that might be entered on those pages.

Without thinking about what he was doing, he

reached over and took hold of the case where it was sticking out from under the robe Kellerman had wrapped around himself.

Kellerman came awake instantly, as if the mere act of Louis touching the case had sprung a trap of some kind. "Thief!" he bellowed. "Get away! Thief!"

The shouts jolted everyone else out of sleep. Stansfield let out a startled, incoherent yell. Kellerman reared up, tightened his grip on the case, and jerked it away from Louis, who had never really gotten a good hold on it. The lack of resistance caused Kellerman to fall over backward.

The case popped open. Bundles of cash fell out and scattered across Kellerman's lap, falling close to the flames. He gasped in horror and scrambled after them, his pudgy hands shooting out with frenzied speed to retrieve the money before it could catch fire. He gathered the bundles to him like they were precious children.

Something else fell out of the case. Louis's eyes followed it as it landed on the ground. He wasn't experienced enough with guns to recognize what make it was, but he knew a revolver when he saw one. A hand reached out and closed around the checkered, hard rubber grips.

The gun came up with Frank Colbert holding it.

Denny was groggy from sleep. She might not have intended to doze off, but she had descended into deep slumber despite that.

Now people were yelling and Kellerman was lunging around like some sort of white-haired lunatic and a gun skittered across the ground until somebody grabbed it up. . . .

Colbert!

That was crazy. His hands were supposed to be tied. But somehow he was loose, and he had the gun in his hand. That was enough to make Denny leap at him and grab his wrist with both hands. Time enough for questions later.

Denny shoved Colbert's arm up. The revolver roared and the bullet tore a hole in the lean-to's canvas cover. Colbert brought his left fist around and slammed a punch against Denny's jaw. The blow drove her against Alma Lewiston, whose hands appeared to be still tied behind her back. Alma tried to writhe around and get Denny beneath her so the younger woman would be pinned there.

Louis grabbed Alma and wrestled with her. Denny managed to hang on to Colbert's wrist. She tried to lift a knee into his groin, but he shoved her leg away and then caught her by the throat. He rammed her head against the coach wheel.

That stunned Denny. Her fingers slipped away from Colbert's wrist. He started to bring the gun to bear on her, but another shot blasted and splinters flew from the coach's body a few inches away from the outlaw. Colbert shoved Denny down, threw himself over her, and rolled out of the shelter, his foot catching on one of the robes and dragging it with him. The canvas landed in the flames and caught fire.

Colbert kicked free, lunged to his feet, and bolted away from the stagecoach. Denny was surprised to see by the gray light that dawn had come again, but it didn't really matter. The snow was still coming down so hard that Colbert was out of sight in a few steps.

Denny grabbed the burning shelter and threw it in the snow. The flames sizzled out. She didn't know if enough of it remained to salvage, but they would have to try. They needed the protection it had given them.

The fact that Colbert was out there—and armed—didn't escape her. He was a definite threat. But just as she couldn't see him, he couldn't see them to shoot at them, and she didn't believe he would waste the bullets in the gun by blazing away blindly.

"Damn it, girl, are you hurt?" Salty asked. He was the one who had taken that hurried shot at Colbert. Smoke still curled from the muzzle of the gun in his hand. He pouched the iron and came over to her.

"I'm fine," Denny said, although her jaw ached where Colbert had punched her. She'd have a good bruise there, she thought, but at least nothing was broken.

She turned to Alma Lewiston, who lay there glaring up at her, and said, "You untied him, didn't you? You just pretended to be asleep all night, but really you turned enough to get your hands on his ropes and worked on the knots the whole time!"

"That's right, I did, you bitch," Alma said through clenched teeth. "And I wish he'd shot you! He will when he comes back to get me."

Denny laughed. "Comes back to get you? Have you lost your mind? Colbert's not coming back. He's going to wander around out there in the blizzard until he freezes to death. He's probably completely lost already. And even if he isn't, he's not coming back for you. He's gotten what he wanted from you. You turned him loose, and that's all he cares about."

"You're wrong," Alma said. "You'll see."

"All I see is that we're in one hell of a mess." Denny turned from Alma to Jerome Kellerman, who was still gathering up bundles of bills and stuffing them back in the case. "You! You had a gun in there all the time. You could have shot Colbert when he took us all prisoner."

"Why would I do that?" Kellerman demanded with a scowl. "I'm no fast gun cowboy like your father. He would have killed me, and I just want to survive this trip, confound it!"

"And we all saw why you're so anxious to survive," Louis said dryly. "All those funds that were being kicked around the fire wouldn't happen to belong to the bank you used to work for, would they, Kellerman?"

"It's none of your business who they belong to."

"I ain't sure about that," Salty said. "Looks like we been travelin' with two crooks—we just didn't know it."

Denny said, "None of that is important right now. What matters is that those bills will burn, and they may be all that keeps us alive until my father gets back with some help."

Kellerman drew back with both arms crossed over the now-closed case, holding it tightly against him.

From her position leaning against one of the wheels, Alma said, "Jensen's never coming back, you little fool. You're so sure Frank's going to freeze to death. Well, your father has been a block of ice ever since last night!"

Brad surprised them all by saying, "You be quiet,

lady! Mr. Jensen can do anything he sets out to do. No ol' blizzard is enough to kill Smoke Jensen!"

"Bradley!" Melanie said. "You should be respectful to your elders—" She stopped short and looked at Alma, then went on, "No, wait, in this case I'm not sure you should be."

Denny picked up what was left of the shelter they had rigged from the canvas and the robes. "Let's put this up again and get the fire going before we all get too cold to move."

Everyone pitched in except Kellerman, who stood sullenly to one side, and Alma, who was still tied securely. Denny checked her bonds to be sure. Alma's fingers were bloody from broken fingernails she had suffered while struggling to untie Colbert's ropes.

The shelter was smaller when they got it back up again, and enough snow had fallen so that everyone was covered with it and had to shake it off their clothing before climbing in again. Denny gathered up what was left of the firewood, including the last two pieces of the broken bench from the coach.

"We're going to need some kindling," she said as she looked meaningfully at Kellerman.

"Then use some of your own damn money," he snapped back at her. "I'm sure you or your brother have some bills."

Stansfield laughed. "No reporter is ever going to get rich, so what do a few dollars matter?" He drew out a wallet and took a greenback from it. As he handed the money to Denny, he said, "There's more where that came from . . . although not a great deal."

Denny knelt beside the firewood and used a match to light the bill Stansfield had given her. She poked it into the stack and watched as flames consumed it without the wood catching.

"Damn it, Kellerman, give me a handful of that cash!"

Kellerman's face worked miserably as he considered the demand. Finally, he sighed and reached into the case to take out one bundle of bills. He handed it to Denny, who broke the paper seal around the money and poked that into the firewood. She crumpled several of the bills and worked them into place, then struck another match and held it to them.

This time, the "tinder" burned hotly enough to catch the wood on fire. As the flames began to jump up, warmth spread through the shelter, although it was fighting a losing battle against the storm raging outside.

The trick to surviving would be keeping the fight going on long enough for Smoke to get back. . . .

Because Denny was never going to give up on her father. Not until she knew for certain that he was dead.

CHAPTER 37

It didn't take Denny long to realize that she'd been wrong about the money in Jerome Kellerman's case. The bills made fine tinder, but they burned too quickly to substitute for firewood. She could dump the whole caseful of cash on the fire, and the money would be consumed so fast it wouldn't do much good.

They were going to have to chop off more pieces from the stagecoach.

Brad was trying to keep his spirits up by talking. He said to Louis, "I'm glad I got to ride in a real stagecoach. I read about them in books, but I didn't think I'd ever even see one."

"This is the real thing, all right," Louis said as he patted the side of the coach. "Listen, I have an idea. Salty, do you have a pocketknife?"

"Sure I do," the old-timer replied. "Never go anywhere without my trusty ol' Barlow knife."

"If we could borrow it for a minute . . . ?"

Salty dug the knife out of his pocket and handed it

to Louis, who said, "Brad, I think you ought to carve your name into the door so people will always know that you rode this stagecoach."

"Wait a minute," Melanie said. "The coach doesn't belong to us. It wouldn't be right for Brad to deface it like that. Doesn't the man who owns it set great store by it?"

"Fred Davis sure does, ma'am," Salty said, "but there's an old tradition in the West of folks carvin' their names or initials into trees and rocks and such-like to show where they've been. This stagecoach is what we got right now, so we'll have to make do with it." Salty paused, then went on, "I reckon it'd be a fine idea for all of us to put our names on it."

Denny had seen the quick look that passed between her brother and Salty, and it didn't take her long to figure out what they were doing. Carving their names into the stagecoach might seem like a lark to Brad, but if they didn't survive, that would also serve to identify them when the wrecked coach was found after the blizzard. Their remains might still be here, or the wolves might have scattered them by that time, but at least people would know what had happened to them.

Louis unfolded the knife and handed it to Brad. Melanie frowned and said, "Be careful with that. It looks sharp."

"Oh, it is, ma'am," Salty said. "No point in carryin' a knife that ain't sharp."

Louis said, "I'll lift you up, Brad, and you can carve your name right there on the side for everybody to see."

"Are you sure it's all right?" Brad asked. "I don't want to get in trouble."

Salty clapped a hand on the boy's shoulder. "Sure, it's fine, younker. Go ahead."

Louis bent and put his arms around Brad's waist. As he lifted the boy, Denny said, "Louis, are you feeling well enough to be doing that?"

"I'm fine," he insisted. "You don't have to worry about me at all, Denny."

Because they were all going to freeze to death before another morning dawned, she thought. That was what her brother was saying.

Brad scratched at the wood with the knife point and said, "It's hard. I don't know if I can do my whole name."

"You can put your initials," Louis told him. "I'll add your name when you're done."

Brad carved out *B.B.* on the door, then asked, "Should I put the date?"

Louis laughed and said, "I'm afraid I've lost track. Is it Christmas Eve, or just the twenty-third?"

"Just write December, Brad," Melanie said. "I still don't like you using that knife."

Brad frowned in concentration, stuck the tip of his tongue out the corner of his mouth, and scratched *December 1901* into the wood of the stagecoach door. Then Louis set him back on the ground and took the knife from him.

Melanie looked relieved. She said, "Maybe what we should do instead of carving up that stagecoach is sing a few Christmas carols. That would be a better way to pass the time at this season, wouldn't it?"

"That's a good idea," Denny said. "Let's start with 'God Rest Ye Merry, Gentlemen.' I always liked that one when we sang it in England."

She and Melanie started singing. Louis and Brad joined in, then Peter Stansfield added his baritone, and Salty warbled some scratchy notes as well. Alma just glared, and Jerome Kellerman sat there looking sullen, holding the case that was never far from him and refusing to join in.

They sang "The First Noel" and several other carols, and then Melanie launched into a heartbreakingly poignant "Silent Night." The others sat silently and listened, each thinking his or her own thoughts.

Melanie had just reached the final *Sleep in heavenly peace* when the canvas was yanked back suddenly. The song ended abruptly, and Melanie screamed as a monster peered into the shelter.

"Earl, wait," Smoke said as the giant yanked the canvas aside and looked curiously into the makeshift shelter. He heard the scream and knew it had to come from Melanie. Denny wasn't the sort to scream, even when confronted with such a shocking visage as Earl's.

Smoke raised his voice and called, "It's all right! Take it easy in there!"

Denny rushed out, ducking around an obviously startled Earl, and threw her arms around Smoke. "Pa!" she cried as she hugged him. "You're alive!"

Smoke was more than alive. He was doing fine this morning, now that he was reunited with his children

and the other travelers. Earl had returned his hat
and gun to him and then led him unerringly through
the blizzard to the stagecoach.

Smoke's hunch had been correct. Earl possessed
an almost supernatural ability to find his way around
in this pass, even under the worst conditions.

Earl stepped back, looking spooked now, as if he
wished he hadn't let his curiosity get the better of
him. Smoke heard him mutter, "Don't let them hurt
me. I'm sorry for what I did."

"No one's going to hurt you, Earl," Smoke said as
he patted Denny on the back. Relief that his daughter was still alive filled him, and then seeing Louis
emerge from the shelter made the feeling even
stronger. He turned to Louis, gripped the young man's
outstretched hand, and then pulled him into a hug.

"How are you doing, son?"

"A lot better now," Louis said with a relieved sigh.
"Nothing to worry about, Father."

Salty was next out and slapped Smoke on the
back, then pumped his hand. "I knew you wasn't
froze, Smoke," he declared. "But, uh, who's the big
varmint with you?" Salty's eyes suddenly widened.
"That ain't . . . ?"

"His name's Earl," Smoke replied. "I don't know
his last name yet. But he's the fella who saved me
from that wolf the other night, sure enough. The
one that folks have been calling the Donner Devil for
all these years. But he's no devil, Salty, just a man
who had a really bad break a long time ago and never
recovered from it."

Salty looked pretty leery, but he nodded, summoned up his gumption, and held out a hand to

Earl. "Howdy there," he said. "I'm pleased to make your acquaintance, old son."

Earl hesitated, but after shaking hands with Smoke in the cave the night before, he must have realized that not everyone was out to harm him. He clasped Salty's hand for a second, then ducked his head and backed up.

"Mighty shy, ain't he?" the old jehu commented.

"You probably would be, too, if you'd lived in these mountains for decades by yourself," Smoke said. "Is everybody else all right?"

"Hello, Mr. Jensen," Brad greeted him. "I knew you wouldn't freeze to death!"

Smoke grinned and said, "Well, I was beginning to wonder about that myself." He touched a finger to the brim of his hat as he nodded to Melanie. "Ma'am."

"By this point, I think I can give you a hug," she said, and then did just that.

"And I won't object," Smoke said. He patted her lightly on the back, then turned to Peter Stansfield and Jerome Kellerman, who had also come out into the falling snow. "Glad to see you fellas are all right. That just leaves Colbert and Mrs. Lewiston, and I reckon they're tied up."

"Mrs. Lewiston is," Denny said with a grim note coming into her voice. "But Colbert got away."

Smoke frowned. That frown deepened as Denny quickly sketched in what had happened.

"So Colbert's not only on the loose, he's armed, too."

Louis said, "Surely he's frozen to death by now, Father. He wasn't dressed for this sort of weather."

"Well, it seems likely he wouldn't have made it . . .

but you never know about things like that. We'll keep
an eye out for him on our way to the hotel."

"You found it?" Denny exclaimed.

"No . . . but Earl knows where it is and can take us
there."

Louis waved a hand at the thickly falling snow and
said, "In this blizzard?"

"He brought me right back here to you, didn't he?"

None of them could argue with that.

"Get what you need that you can carry," Smoke
went on. "Earl says it won't take us long to get there.
The hotel isn't very far away."

All of them except Alma Lewiston bustled around
getting ready to leave the stagecoach. Since she was
still tied and sitting on the ground, Smoke asked her,
"What do you need to take with you, ma'am?" Even
after everything she had done, he was going to be
courteous to her.

"I don't need anything," she answered sullenly
without looking up at him. "I'd rather you just leave
me here."

"You'd freeze to death," Smoke pointed out.

"Good. I don't have a damn thing to live for anymore. My husband's dead, and the next man I trusted
after that ran off and left me as soon as he got the
chance . . . and after I was the one who helped him get
away."

"Maybe throwing in with Colbert wasn't the best
thing you could have done," Smoke said, "but that's
no reason to give up on living. You're coming with us."

"So you can have me arrested when this is all
over?" Alma shook her head and laughed harshly. "I

don't want to go to prison any more than Gordon did, even if I don't have an opium habit. No thanks. I'll take freezing to death. It's just like dozing off, they say."

"I don't see any reason for you to be arrested," Smoke told her. "Sure, you pointed a gun at us for a while, but nobody got hurt except Salty, and Colbert's the one who ventilated him. I'll have to talk to the others to be sure, but I think there's a good chance nobody will insist on pressing any charges against you."

Alma looked like she didn't believe that, but at the same time, Smoke saw a flicker of hope in her eyes. No matter how bad things might appear to be, as long as a person was drawing breath, there was a chance to make things better.

After a moment, Alma said quietly, "Kellerman's a crook, you know. That case he's always hanging on to is full of cash. He's bound to have stolen it from the bank where he works."

"More than likely. My daughter said something about that to me. We'll deal with that, too, when the time comes. Now, do you want us to take your bag with us?"

"I suppose so," Alma said, then added grudgingly, "Thanks."

A short time later, they were ready to leave. With Earl and Smoke in the lead, they set off through the whirling, whipping snowfall. Denny, Stansfield, and Kellerman led the horses. They couldn't leave the animals in the snow to fend for themselves.

The lifeline Smoke had followed the day before,

then left to go ahead on his own, was still visible, and
the path Earl took went along the same route. That
told Smoke he had been going the right direction,
anyway. The blizzard had long since covered up the
tracks he had made, so once the rock with the harness tied to it was behind them, Smoke couldn't tell
if they were still going the same direction or not.

Within a quarter of an hour, he saw something up
ahead. At first it was just a barely glimpsed dark shape,
but as the group trudged on through the deep snow, it
took on form and definition and became a large
building.

The Summit Hotel. Smoke felt relief go through
him as he realized they had arrived at their destination. They had been close, very close, just as he'd suspected. Fate had prevented him from finding the
hotel himself, but his hunch had been right.

Earl stopped and pointed. "There," he rasped.
"The place where people come in the summer."

Smoke put a hand on his shoulder. "Thank you,
Earl. You've saved our lives. Now come on, let's get in
there and warm up."

Earl shook his head. "Not going. Don't want to.
Not fitting."

"Earl, don't be like that," Smoke said. "I told you,
nobody blames you for what happened a long time
ago. Anything you did, you more than made up for it
by rescuing us. Anyway, you didn't actually hurt any
of those people back then. Whatever happened to
them, their lives were already over and you had nothing to do with that."

Stubbornly, Earl shook his shaggy head. "Going
back to my cave, where I belong." Smoke thought he

smiled under the forest of beard, but it was difficult to be sure. "Not everybody is like you, Smoke. Some people would still hate me. I'll be better off alone."

"But Earl—"

Salty interrupted Smoke by saying, "Seems to me like the fella's got a right to live however he wants. Reckon he's earned it by now." He turned to Earl and went on, "I used to call you the Donner Devil, and I'm plumb sorry about that. You ain't no devil at all. You've been a mighty good friend to us."

Earl ducked his head and muttered something incomprehensible, probably thanking Salty for that sentiment.

Smoke wanted to argue, but at the same time, he knew Salty was right. He couldn't force Earl to reenter civilization; he didn't have that right.

Also, Earl might be correct about how other folks would regard him once the truth came out, as it inevitably would. Not everybody would be as willing to forgive what he had done, all those years ago, even though Smoke still didn't believe what had happened was Earl's fault.

"If you're sure that's the way you feel, Earl, then Salty is right. It's your decision to make, and I'll respect it. And I'll always be grateful to you for saving all of us."

Earl nodded, then surprised Smoke by drawing him into a quick, rough hug.

Then he turned and loped off into the blizzard, vanishing in a matter of moments.

Denny said, "It seems like there's quite a bit about Earl that you haven't told us, Pa, but I don't suppose it matters right now. We'd better go on to the hotel while we can still see it."

"You're right about that," Smoke said. "Come on, everybody."

The hotel became more distinct the closer they came to it. Seeing the sturdy walls and the lights glowing through the windows lifted everyone's spirits, even Alma's. Brad tried to run ahead, but Melanie called him back.

Smoke could see a long line of dark buildings off to his left and knew those were the snowsheds covering the railroad tracks coming in from the west. They ran close beside the hotel and then on out of sight. According to what they had been told in Sacramento, an avalanche deeper in the pass had demolished the sheds east of the hotel and covered the tracks.

They reached the hotel porch, tied the horses to it for the time being until they could be put in the stable, and climbed the steps, which had been swept clear of snow at some point this morning. The white stuff was beginning to collect on them again, of course, but for now it wasn't a problem. Snow had drifted onto the porch and was a foot deep in places, but a path had been shoveled from the door to the steps.

A festive attitude came over some of the travelers as they approached the door. Not only had they survived a terrible ordeal, but now, even though they wouldn't be with their families, they could celebrate Christmas somewhere warm and safe.

Alma didn't appear all that glad to be here, however, and neither did Kellerman, who had to be worrying about his future now that everyone was suspicious of the cash he'd been carrying around ever since the journey began.

This time when Brad ran ahead into the cavernous lobby, Melanie didn't try to stop him. Everyone hurried into the warmth coming from a blaze in a huge fireplace on the other side of the lobby. Two men were seated in armchairs near it, and both got to their feet in apparent surprise at the new arrivals.

Peter Stansfield was the last one through the door. Smoke heard the reporter close it against the wind, and then a startled exclamation came from Stansfield, followed by an ominous thud. Smoke started to turn. . . .

A gunshot roared, almost drowning out Melanie's scream. Then Smoke and all the others froze at the sight of Frank Colbert with his left arm around the young woman's neck and his right hand pressing the muzzle of Kellerman's Smith & Wesson against her head.

CHAPTER 38

For a long moment, everyone in the room stood silent and motionless.

Then Smoke said, "Don't you ever get tired of threatening innocent folks, Colbert? I almost felt sorry for you when I thought you'd died in the blizzard, but I reckon I won't be feeling that way anymore."

Colbert pressed the gun harder against Melanie's head, causing her to gasp in fear and pain. He had pulled her with him as he backed away from the others. Now he stood with his back against the closed door.

Stansfield lay a few feet away, moving around a little and groaning. Blood welled from the cut on his forehead he had suffered when Colbert hit him with the gun. Smoke realized that the outlaw had been hiding behind the open door, covering the two men by the fireplace, and had waited until everyone was inside and Stansfield had closed the door to make his move.

Smoke glanced at Louis and saw that his son was

trembling with the urge to jump Colbert. The way the outlaw was threatening Melanie had to fill Louis with rage.

But for a change, Denny had her hand closed tightly around her brother's arm and wasn't going to let him do anything foolish. Usually it was the other way around, with Louis urging caution on his headstrong sister.

Salty had his good hand on Brad's shoulder, keeping the boy under control, too. Once again, it appeared that Colbert had the upper hand.

But that wouldn't last. All Smoke needed was the tiniest opening. . . .

And if he got it, he would put a bullet through the outlaw's twisted brain.

In the meantime, he wanted to keep Colbert talking, figuring Melanie would be safer that way, so he continued, "How did you make it, anyway? The last time anybody saw you, you were running off into the blizzard without even a heavy coat."

Colbert grinned over Melanie's shoulder. "Luck was on my side, Jensen. Or call it fate or destiny or what have you. All I know is that I hadn't run through the snow for very long when I tripped over the steps of this hotel. My God, we were sitting there freezing to death when this place was that close!"

"There was no way for us to know that. All we could do was play the odds."

"Well, it looks like luck was with you, too . . . for a while, anyway. I figured *you* were dead when you never came back yesterday."

Smoke didn't say anything about his encounter with Earl, and neither did any of the others. Under the circumstances, it didn't really mean anything. Colbert could just be puzzled about how Smoke had survived.

"What is it you're planning to do now?" Smoke asked. "You're stuck here just as much as the rest of us are. There was no need to clout Stansfield, or to threaten Mrs. Buckner."

A savage grin appeared on Colbert's face. "I'm going to Reno," he said. "I might still be able to get there in time."

One of the men standing near the fireplace said, "He came in talking crazy like that and took over the place. There are only a few other employees on hand, and he herded all of them into the kitchen and tied them up. Herman and I told him the pass is blocked, but he wouldn't listen to us."

"Who are you, mister?" Smoke asked.

"Juniper Jones, the telegrapher here." Jones nodded to his companion. "This is Herman Painton, the manager of the hotel."

"I'd say I'm glad to meet you," Smoke told the men, "but I wish it was under different circumstances." He looked at Colbert again. "How do you think you're going to get to Reno? The best thing for you to do is turn Mrs. Buckner loose, put that gun down, and be reasonable."

"Is it reasonable to pass up a lot of money that's just sitting there for the taking?" Colbert laughed. "*That* would be crazy." He nodded toward Jones and Painton. "Those two told me the railroad has a maintenance shed farther up the pass, and there's a handcar stored in it. From that point, it's downhill all the way to Reno, so I can use the handcar to get there."

The man really was loco, Smoke thought, or else so hungry for the loot he was after that he just couldn't think straight.

At the same time, there was a slim possibility Colbert's plan might work . . . if he could reach the maintenance shed and the handcar.

"How do you plan on getting past the avalanche if it completely blocked off the pass?" Smoke asked. He hated to carry on this conversation while Melanie was in danger and obviously terrified, but if he pretended to play along with Colbert, he might get a chance to turn the tables on the outlaw.

Juniper Jones spoke up and answered that. "The pass *isn't* completely blocked. The snowsheds are wrecked and the railroad tracks are covered, but a man on snowshoes can get through. I was out taking a look at it this morning, not long before this man showed up."

"And you told him that?"

"We don't want him here, mister. I don't know why he wants to get to Reno, and I don't care. But if he's willing to pump a handcar that far, then more power to him, I say."

"Damn right I'm willing," Colbert said. "And I'm leaving now. Jones, bring two pairs of snowshoes."

The telegrapher frowned. "Why two?"

"Because Mrs. Buckner is going with me as far as that maintenance shed, just to make sure none of you get any funny ideas. I'm talking mostly to you, Jensen."

"If you want to take a hostage with you," Smoke said, "why not take me?"

"And give you a chance to jump me? I don't think

so." Colbert put his cheek next to Melanie's and leered. "The little lady will do fine. She'll be good company for a tramp through the snow."

Brad said, "You'd better not hurt my ma!"

"Then you'd better hope none of these fools tries anything, kid," Colbert said. "Jones! Move, damn you! Get those snowshoes."

The telegrapher went over to a closet and retrieved two sets of snowshoes. Colbert turned Melanie loose but kept the revolver pointed at her head as she put on one set of the shoes, tying them on with shaking fingers. Then he put the other set on himself.

"Kellerman, give me your coat," Colbert ordered then. "It looks like it'll fit me all right. And while you're at it, I'll take that case full of loot, too. You think I didn't notice when all those bills came tumbling out of it, back there at the stagecoach?"

Kellerman stepped back, clutching the case with his usual fervor. "No! I won't let you have—"

"The hell with this," Colbert snapped. He turned the gun away from Melanie and shot Kellerman in the head. Kellerman jerked and blood welled from the red-rimmed hole above his right eye. By the time his knees buckled and he hit the floor, dropping the case as he did so, Colbert had the gun pointed at Melanie again.

The others were shocked by the sudden violence, except for Smoke and Salty, who stood there impassively. Both men had seen plenty of death in their time. Smoke's biggest regret was that Colbert hadn't given him a chance for a shot. The outlaw was slick, though, and had kept Melanie between himself and Smoke the whole time.

The case hadn't come open this time, but it had slid across the hardwood floor a couple of feet from Kellerman's body. The pool of blood seeping from the man's head wound advanced steadily toward the case.

"You," Colbert said to Louis. "Young Jensen. Slide that over here with your foot. Don't try anything else."

Louis looked furious, but he didn't want to take any chances with Melanie's life. He did as Colbert ordered.

Colbert bent to pick up the case with his left hand while his right kept the revolver trained on Melanie. "Now get Kellerman's coat off of him."

Louis struggled to do that, but he managed to pull the coat off the dead man. Following Colbert's commands, he tossed it onto the floor next to the outlaw.

Colbert picked up the coat and got into it, all without taking the gun off Melanie.

"Come on," he told her when he had finished donning the garment. "We're going."

"Please," she said. "Please don't make me leave my son—"

"We can take him with us if you want," Colbert broke in.

"No! I mean, no, don't do that. I'll come with you. I'll do whatever you say. Just . . . just leave Brad here, where he'll be safe." She gazed at Louis. "Promise me you'll look after him."

"Of course, but nothing's going to happen to you," Louis told her. Salty still had hold of Brad's shoulder, so Louis gripped the boy's other shoulder. Brad was crying a little now, but they were tears of rage.

Colbert tucked the case under his arm for a moment and used that hand to open the door. Then, holding the gun close to Melanie's side, he put his other hand on her shoulder and backed out.

"If I see anybody coming after me, I'll kill her!" Colbert shouted as he and Melanie stepped out onto the porch. "You know I'll do it!"

After watching him gun down Kellerman in cold blood, there was no doubt in anybody's mind that Colbert meant exactly what he said.

Colbert put his arm around Melanie's neck again, this time holding the case so that it was in front of her. As the people in the hotel watched through the open door, the two of them backed away until the snow hid them from view.

Then Denny turned to Smoke and said, "You're going after them, aren't you?"

"Wait," Louis said. "If you do that, Father, he'll shoot Melanie."

"He's liable to shoot her anyway," Denny argued. "You saw him, Louis. He's a mad dog."

Smoke said, "Don't worry, I'm going after him. The man's a killer and needs to be brought to justice. But I don't want to risk Melanie's life, either." He turned to Jones and Painton, the two men who worked there at the hotel. "Are there more snowshoes?"

"We have plenty of them," Painton said.

"I need somebody to show me where that maintenance shed is."

"I can do that," Jones volunteered. "What are you going to do, mister? And just who are you, anyway?"

"Who is he?" Salty repeated. "Why, this here is Smoke Jensen!"

"The gunfighter?" Jones asked as his eyebrows rose. "I've read books about you!"

"Don't believe everything you read," Smoke told him. "Just fetch snowshoes for both of us."

"For three of us," Salty said. "I'm comin' along, too."

"And me," Denny said.

Smoke said, "Salty, you're wounded, and Denny, your mother would have my hide if I let you get shot up in a gunfight. You're all staying here except me. I can handle Colbert."

"I dunno, Smoke," Salty said as he shook his head. "That varmint seems to have the devil's own luck followin' him around."

"Well, it's run out now," Smoke said.

It didn't take long to get ready. Smoke and Jones put on snowshoes, and the telegrapher bundled himself in an overcoat and took a Winchester from another closet.

"Be careful you don't shoot me or Mrs. Buckner with that," Smoke warned him.

"I don't intend to use it unless I have to," Jones assured him. "But I'm a decent shot when I need to be."

Smoke and Jones were walking across the lobby when Alma Lewiston stepped up to them. Her hands had been untied by someone, and she was lightly rubbing her wrists where the bonds had been.

"You're going to kill him, aren't you?" she said to Smoke.

He paused. "I reckon that'll be up to him."

"You don't think he'll let you take him alive, do you? I've only known him for a few days, and I know that about him already. He's got his sights set on whatever big job is waiting for him in Reno, and now that he's got another chance at it, he won't let anything stop him . . . nothing short of a bullet, anyway."

"If that's the way it has to be," Smoke said bluntly.

"I hope he doesn't hurt that woman. She doesn't deserve it."

Smoke glanced across the lobby at the chairs where Louis was sitting with Brad, talking quietly with the boy and trying to keep him calm.

"No, she sure doesn't," he agreed, "and neither does her son."

Alma gave a small, defiant toss of her head. "Maybe I was wrong to do what I did, out there on the trail. But at the time, I didn't see that I had any choice." She shrugged. "Maybe things will be different from now on, or maybe they won't. Who can say? All I know is that some people seem to get everything they want, and some always seem to come up short. Why do you think that is?"

"Ask a philosopher," Smoke snapped. "I'm a rancher. Come on, Jones."

They left the hotel and went out into the blizzard.

"Colbert will follow the tracks as much as he can," Jones said, "but I know a quicker way to that maintenance shed. We can get there first and be ready for him."

Smoke peered into the white, rippling curtains of snow and said, "Am I mistaken, or is it actually letting up a little?"

"I think you're right. It's not snowing quite as hard as it was a little while ago. Good Lord, is this monster of a storm finally blowing itself out?"

"We can hope," Smoke said grimly.

"Speaking of monsters . . ." Jones hesitated, then went on, "You'll probably think I'm losing my mind, but there's been something strange wandering around here lately—"

"You're talking about the Donner Devil?" Smoke interrupted him.

Jones stared. "You know about the Donner Devil?"

"More than that." Despite the situation, Smoke chuckled. "I've met him. He's not nearly as threatening as most folks think he is."

"You've met . . . Wait a minute. You can't be serious."

"It's a long story," Smoke said, "but we wouldn't be here if it weren't for the man you call the Donner Devil."

"He's a man? Really?"

"A good man, I think."

Jones didn't press for details, but Smoke knew the people who worked at the Summit Hotel would want the whole story later. He would tell them about Earl, but only after he swore them to secrecy. He didn't want a bunch of people coming up here to hunt for the so-called Donner Devil, even any do-gooders who would claim they were going to help him. Earl just wanted to be left alone, and Smoke had realized that would be the best thing for him.

Jones led Smoke through a stand of trees, one of the few left here in the pass, and then up a steep slope. The deep snow made it even more difficult, but the snowshoes helped. Smoke had used snow-shoes before, but he was far from an expert at it. Jones was a lot more accustomed to them and gave Smoke several tips that made the going easier.

"There's a little gap along the edge of all that snow the avalanche brought down," Jones explained. "Col-bert will be able to follow it. The way we're going is harder but shorter. If we push, we can beat him."

"You know what you're doing," Smoke told him. "You set the pace. I'll keep up."

Maybe Salty should have come along after all, Smoke mused. The old-timer had been up in Alaska with Frank Morgan a while back. He might have got-ten some experience on snowshoes. Smoke was glad, though, that Salty was safe back at the hotel.

It was bad enough they had lost Fred Davis's stage-coach. Smoke wouldn't have wanted to lose the old jehu, too.

The wind was still blowing hard and whipping the snow around, but when Smoke looked up, he was surprised that he could see the mountains looming on both sides of the pass. The snow really wasn't falling as heavily now. This was the best visibility of the past couple of days.

A few moments later, they topped the crest and started down the other side of the little ridge. Up ahead, Smoke saw the line of snowsheds again, com-ing in from the east this time. The pass had a long curve to it, which made the shortcut possible.

The shelters over the tracks ended abruptly where the avalanche began. Jones pointed at a spot about a quarter of a mile east of there and said, "That's where the maintenance shed is. You can see it's wider than the others. That's because the railroad stores equipment there, including a couple of handcars."

"There's not just one handcar?"

"No, there are two."

That could be important information, Smoke thought. He didn't intend to let Colbert get away, but if that happened, at least Smoke would have a way of pursuing him.

First and most importantly, though, he needed to get Melanie Buckner away from the outlaw.

They crossed a little depression that was full of snow, but the special footgear kept them from sinking into it up to their necks. Knowing that the snow was over his head and might try to swallow him up if he wasn't careful was a little nerve wracking for Smoke.

Finally, they were across. Smoke looked behind them and saw that the wind and snow were already filling up the tracks they had left. Jones went up another small slope to a door that opened into the maintenance shed.

It was dim and shadowy inside the building. At each end, the tracks split to form a fifty-yard-long siding onto which cars could be pulled and uncoupled if work was needed on them or if a train had to drop them off for some other reason. There were also two short, curving spurs on which handcars rested. The far wall was covered with shelves and cabinets where various tools and equipment were stored.

"Colbert and Mrs. Buckner are bound to be here soon," Smoke said. "Let's take cover behind that second handcar."

They did so, crouching down and counting on the

shadows inside the shed to help conceal them. Many times over the years, Smoke had waited for a moment that might well bring with it gunplay and sudden death, so he was calm, but the imminent violence made Jones nervous and fidgety.

Then the door began to creak open. Smoke motioned for Jones to be still and quiet. They waited while Colbert forced Melanie into the shed and kicked the door closed behind them.

"You . . . you said you'd let me go back to the hotel when we got here," Melanie quavered as Colbert pushed her toward the nearest handcar.

"Yeah, but I got to thinking about it, and I'm liable to need help pumping this son of a bitch," the outlaw told her. "And that bastard Jones didn't tell me there was another handcar here. Probably trying to trick me. But if I take you along, Jensen and the others will be less likely to follow and give me trouble."

"You can't take me," Melanie pleaded. "My son needs me. Don't do this—"

Colbert set the case full of money on the other handcar. He turned sharply and backhanded Melanie, then grabbed her and pulled her against him.

"Listen to me, you little bitch. I'm tired of your whining. My men are waiting for me in Reno, and they've got a big job lined up. I don't know exactly what it is, but they told me that it's worth a fortune, and if I'm not there, they'll go ahead and steal it without me! I'm not going to let that happen. That's my gang, and I'm damned if I'm not going to be there leading them when they pull that job."

"You're . . . you're tired of me whining?" Melanie said. Something happened to her then, something that Smoke hadn't seen from her before. Her eyes flashed with anger as she cried, "I'm tired of you threatening me and my boy!"

Her hand shot up and clawed at Colbert's face.

He snarled a curse and smashed his fist against her jaw, knocking her back so that she sprawled on the railroad tracks. Spewing filthy names, he started to bring his gun to bear on her.

Until now, Smoke hadn't had a shot because Melanie was too close to Colbert. But with several feet of distance between them, Smoke seized the chance. He stood up and fired across both handcars. His Colt boomed like thunder as it echoed from the snowshed's walls and roof.

The slug crashed into Colbert's side and flung him back several steps. He twisted to meet this new and unexpected threat, but before his gun could come to bear, Smoke triggered his revolver again. This bullet drove into the outlaw's chest.

Colbert sagged, his eyes wide with shock and horror and disbelief. "Jensen!" he gasped. "You . . . you son of a—"

Smoke's third shot went through Colbert's forehead and blew out a good-sized chunk of skull, along with a grisly spray of blood and brains, as it came out the back of his head. Colbert rocked back again and then pitched forward, dead as he could be.

"Good Lord," Juniper Jones said in the hush that followed on the heels of that gun thunder. He hadn't needed to use the Winchester he had brought along. "Those dime novels about you didn't tell the half of it!"

Smoke started thumbing fresh cartridges into the Colt to replace the ones he had fired. As he was doing that, he said, "Go check on Mrs. Buckner, and then we need to get back to the hotel. I've got some figuring to do."

"Figuring? It's over, isn't it?"

"Not hardly," Smoke said as he pouched the reloaded iron. "You heard what Colbert said. His gang is in Reno and is about to pull some sort of big job. That means there's liable to be plenty of shooting. I have family there waiting for me who might wind up in danger, so I have to find a way to stop it!"

CHAPTER 39

Sally Jensen sat at a table in the dining room of the Riverside Hotel and lingered over a second cup of coffee. From where she sat in Reno's oldest and best hotel, she could see the large bridge spanning the Truckee River right beside the establishment, and beyond that in the distance the snow-capped peaks of the Sierra Nevadas.

She couldn't help but wonder where her husband was at this very moment. The last she had heard from Smoke, he had a plan for reaching Reno before Christmas despite the snow-blocked pass in the mountains. If there was one thing Sally knew about Smoke, it was that when he set out to do something, he always accomplished it.

Because of that, she expected to see him come strolling into the hotel at any moment.

Instead, four other men entered the dining room and started across it toward the table where Sally sat. Luke and Matt Jensen were in front, followed by

Luke's sons, Ace and Chance. The men were talking among themselves and laughing quietly over something.

Sally smiled at them. It would be hard to imagine a more formidable quartet. Each of them had lived a life packed with adventure and danger. Yet none of it had hardened them . . . well, not too much. Luke's profession as a bounty hunter had left him with some rough edges. But all the Jensens were gentlemanly and chivalrous around her and, in Sally's estimation, had genuinely good souls.

"That brother of mine hasn't shown up yet?" Matt asked as he pulled out a chair and sat down.

"If he had, he'd be right here," Luke said. "You know Smoke is never very far from Sally if he can help it."

Matt grinned. "He's the smartest of all the Jensens, you know. He's the only one who has a beautiful wife."

"Or a wife of any kind," Luke said dryly.

Chance said, "I'm not sure that makes him so smart. A married man doesn't have much choice except to settle down, and I'm not ready for that yet."

"You never will be," Ace muttered, while Matt laughed and said, "You try telling Smoke that he's settled down. I'd like to listen in on that conversation."

The others all sat down to order coffee and a late breakfast. The morning had dawned sunny but extremely cold in Reno. Off to the west, clouds still hung stubbornly over the peaks, but to Sally they looked like they were starting to break up at last.

Ace and Chance had reached Reno first, followed in fairly short order by their father and uncle. All of them had had a very pleasant family dinner with Sally the night before. Now they were just waiting for Smoke to show up, along with Louis and Denise.

Worry nagged at the back of Sally's mind. She knew the weather had been terrible up there in the mountains. The Donner Pass was blocked by snow. Smoke planned to take another route and travel by stagecoach, but it was quite possible that he had run into obstacles.

Her confidence in her husband's ability to handle whatever problems fate threw at him was almost boundless, but it wouldn't have been natural if she wasn't a little bit concerned.

All that would evaporate the instant Smoke strode in, gathered her in his arms, and kissed her.

Sally was more than ready for that to happen.

Two waiters were kept busy bringing out platters of flapjacks, biscuits, steaks, bacon, eggs, and hash browns for the Jensen men, along with pots of coffee. Best known for fast guns and quick fists, Jensens also had hearty appetites. When the meal was finally done, they leaned back in their chairs and stretched out their legs, letting the food digest in peace.

"I believe I'll walk down to the train station in a bit," Luke commented. "There's an eastbound coming in, and watching a train arrive is always a pleasant diversion."

"Might be somebody interesting getting off," Matt commented. "I'll come with you."

"It's something to do until Smoke gets here," Ace added.

Sally smiled at them. "None of you like to just sit around and take it easy, do you?"

"A fella likes to be up and doing something," Luke said. "That's just the natural way of things."

"Well, don't let me keep you. I'll be fine here at the hotel."

Chance said, "I'll stay, and we can play cards, Aunt Sally."

Ace frowned and told his brother, "Don't go trying to promote a poker game."

"Who said anything about poker?" Chance asked with an innocent look on his face. "I was thinking more of bridge. I'm sure we can get up a nice, enjoyable game of bridge with some of the other guests."

"All right," Ace said, "but no wagering."

Sally laughed and said, "I'll make sure we don't get involved in a shootout over cards."

"Don't sell my brother short," Ace warned her. "If there's a way to get in trouble over a game of bridge, Chance can find it!"

"At least watching a train come in ought to be nice and peaceful," Matt said.

Magnus Stevenson finished tying Sadie Andrews's hands behind the rungs on the back of the kitchen chair where the girl sat. Sadie had cried for the first couple of days Stevenson and Jim Bob Mitchell had held them hostage in the Andrews home, but now her tears had dried up and the gaze she turned toward Stevenson was cold and filled with hate.

Stevenson had to chuckle. Sadie looked like she would gladly take Mitchell's knife and carve the outlaws' cojones right off. He bet she'd do it if she got the chance, too. An adolescent girl was a bad enemy to have.

"There," Stevenson said. "I didn't tie you too tight, did I?"

"Why do you care about that?" Sadie asked. "You've been threatening to kill us for days. Why worry about making the ropes too tight?"

Mitchell was finishing up the job of tying Rebecca Andrews into another chair. He grinned and said, "Better go ahead and gag that one. She'll be cussin' your ears off in a minute."

"I'm not worried about that, but yeah, we'll have to gag them. Otherwise they might start yelling and somebody passing by could hear them."

"Best not waste any time. The others will be gettin' ready about now. These two pretty ladies better hope ol' Carl ain't thinkin' about tryin' any sort of double cross. 'Cause we'll be back to see 'em if he does."

Mitchell leaned over Rebecca's shoulder and ran his hands over her breasts, causing her to shudder. Stevenson frowned. He hadn't been able to keep Mitchell from pawing both of the prisoners at various times, but at least he had stopped there, despite his continued threats to molest them further. Stevenson didn't feel any real sympathy for the hostages, but he had never seen any point in evil for its own sake. Getting their hands on that four hundred grand was all that really mattered.

Stevenson cut a piece off the tablecloth, wadded it up, and shoved it into Sadie's mouth, being careful that she didn't bite him as he did it. She might take off a couple of fingers if he gave her the chance.

Then he tied the gag in place while Mitchell was doing the same with the girl's mother.

They left the Andrews house through the back door, after taking a good look through the kitchen window to make sure nobody was around. It would look suspicious if anyone spotted two strange men sneaking out of the house in the middle of the morning.

Once they had walked a short distance along the alley behind the houses, they cut through a narrow passage to the street. The air was crisp and very cold.

Stevenson said, "I sure thought Frank would be here by now."

"Could be something happened to him," Mitchell said. "We know he got Deke's telegram, but there's no telling about anything after that." He nodded toward the mountains. "I've heard folks talkin' about how bad the weather's been up there. Frank might be stuck somewhere, waitin' for it to clear up."

"Well, that's just too damn bad, because we can't wait for him. If he meets up with us later, he can take over for the next job. I've got to say, Deke's actually come up with a pretty good plan for this one . . . as long as Andrews cooperates."

"He ain't gonna double-cross us now," Mitchell said. "Not with those two honeys waitin' for him at home."

Up ahead was the bank where Carl Andrews worked. It was open for business, but on Christmas Eve not many people were going in and out of the place.

As Stevenson and Mitchell drew even with it, Mitchell sat down on a bench in front of a hardware store, drew his knife from its sheath, and took a piece of wood from his pocket. He had been whittling on it for a while and had fashioned it into the rudimentary figure of an Indian chief. He whistled a sprightly little tune as he resumed work on it.

Stevenson looked around, spotted Otis Harmon across the street, looking in the window of the store next to the bank. That happened to be a dress shop, and nobody was going to believe that the cold-eyed gunman was actually interested in the gowns displayed there, but Harmon didn't have to fool people for long. The cash was supposed to arrive on the train in less than half an hour.

Mahoney and Hopgood were nowhere in sight, but Stevenson wasn't worried about that. The plan called for the two of them to enter the bank through the rear door—which Carl Andrews would make sure was unlocked, if he knew what was good for him and his family—and they would get the drop on the guards. Then Stevenson, Mitchell, and Harmon would come in from the front to close the jaws of the trap.

Andrews had explained that Cameron and Nickerson, the two mine owners involved in the four hundred thousand–dollar transaction, had decided not to bring the cash in under heavy guard. That would be liable to draw attention, and they wanted to keep the deal as quiet as possible until the money had changed hands and was locked up safely in the bank's vault. So there would be only a couple of extra guards, as well as the two normally on duty in the bank.

The gang would have the guards outnumbered, and they didn't expect trouble from anyone else in the bank. As soon as the money showed up and was inside, Stevenson would signal Mahoney and Hopgood and the real job would begin.

When it was over, the five of them would be rich men. Earlier, talking to Mitchell, Stevenson had mentioned the gang's next job. Now, as he thought about it, he realized there might not *be* a next job. Each man's share would be eighty thousand dollars. That was plenty for them to live in comfort for the rest of their lives if they wanted to. No more trading shots with lawmen and outraged townspeople. No more running from posses. No more cold, hungry nights on the trail.

The others could do what they wanted, Stevenson thought, but as far as he was concerned, today would be the last day of his career as an outlaw.

Matt, Luke, and Ace turned up the collars on their sheepskin coats as they walked toward the railroad station. The wind blowing down from the mountains was cold enough to turn a fellow's cheeks red and take his breath away. Good weather for Christmas. Reno had streetlights, and decorated bells hung from the poles and swung back and forth, making festive music.

The sound of a train whistle blended with the ringing bells. Matt said, "Sounds like we're just in time. That westbound is about to roll in."

A few other people were walking toward the depot, intent on either boarding the train or greeting passengers who were disembarking. The westbound would be turned around in Reno's roundhouse and

become an eastbound, and that practice would continue as long as Donner Pass was closed.

The three Jensens went into the station lobby,
which seemed a little warm and stuffy after being
outside. They moved across the big, high-ceilinged
room to the doors that led out onto the platform.
The big Baldwin locomotive was already in sight
along the tracks, with black smoke billowing from
its diamond-shaped stack. Drivers clattered, brakes
squealed, and steam hissed as the locomotive rolled
past the platform and the train ground to a halt.

Ace leaned a shoulder against one of the posts
holding up the awning over the platform while Matt
and Luke sat down on one of the benches. The three
of them watched as porters put steps in place and
passengers began to climb down from the cars.

Idly, Ace glanced along the length of the train and
then frowned as he watched several men unloading a
small trunk from the express car. Two porters were
on the ground while two more lowered the trunk to
them so they could transfer it to a wheeled cart. From
the way they all handled the trunk, it was rather
heavy, although not so much that it was a real burden.

That wasn't particularly unusual, and it wasn't
what really caught Ace's eye. What made him look
twice were the two men standing by while the trunk
was unloaded. Both wore holstered pistols. One man
carried a Winchester while the other had a double-
barreled shotgun tucked under his arm. Ace didn't
see any badges on their coats or vests.

While it wasn't unusual to see armed men on the

streets in the early days of this new century—all the Jensens were packing iron—it wasn't nearly as common as it had been even a few years earlier. And men as heavily armed as these two seemed to be expecting trouble. The way they constantly turned their heads and regarded their surroundings in hawk-like fashion confirmed that.

"Matt, Luke," Ace said quietly. He always called Luke by his first name, rather than "Father" or "Pa," and so did Chance. When the brothers had first met Luke none of them had been aware of the relationship between them, so they still thought of him that way.

"What is it?" Matt asked as he looked around.

Ace straightened from his casual pose against the post. "See those two fellas down there by the express car? You notice anything about them?"

"They appear to be armed for bear," Luke said as he joined Matt in gazing along the train toward the men Ace had mentioned.

The porters began wheeling the cart around the end of the depot. The two armed men went with them.

"Whatever they're doing, it's none of our business," Luke said.

"Maybe not," Matt said, "but it's more interesting than watching family reunions and lonely traveling salesmen who are away from their families for the holidays." He came to his feet. "I say we go take a look."

"There's no profit in it."

"Maybe not, but there might be some fun."

Ace said, "I have a hunch your idea of fun is a lot like Chance's, Uncle Matt."

Matt just grinned at that and started along the platform. Luke shrugged, stood up, and followed him. Ace fell in alongside his father.

It was too bad Chance had decided to stay back at the hotel with Sally, he thought. On the other hand, there was still a possibility that bridge game would turn out to be more exciting.

Sally and Chance sat at a table in the hotel's opulent lobby, playing bridge with a middle-aged couple who had been on their way to San Francisco to see their daughter when the blizzard in the Sierra Nevadas had stymied their holiday plans. They hadn't completely given up on being able to continue, which was why they were lingering in Reno for a few days rather than returning to their home in Kansas City.

That story had come out while they were playing. Chance was beginning to wish he had gone with Ace, Luke, and Matt down to the train station. On the other hand, he was very fond of Sally, who had been a gracious hostess at the Sugarloaf for the Jensen brothers on many occasions, so it was nice to spend the time with her.

Then Smoke came in, and everything changed.

Everyone in the lobby looked toward the door as the cold wind whipped in. Smoke, tall, broad shouldered, sporting several days' worth of beard stubble, drew all eyes, including Sally's. She dropped her cards, the bridge game forgotten, and hurried to meet him. His arms went around her and drew her against him. He kissed her like a drowning man who had suddenly been delivered to fresh air again.

Chance noticed the man who came into the hotel

right behind Smoke. Tall and lanky, dark haired, with a somewhat angular face. He was dressed in a dark suit and overcoat and had a dark hat pulled down tightly on his head.

Smoke broke the kiss with Sally and gazed down into her eyes for a moment. "You're all right?" he said.

"Of course," she replied. "What about you?"

A grin stretched across his rugged face. "A lot better now that I've seen you again." He looked over at Chance and stuck out his hand. "Mighty good to see you again, son. Is your brother here, too?"

"He went down to the train station with Luke and Matt," Chance said as he shook hands with his uncle.

Smoke gave him a sharp, shrewd glance. "Everything quiet here in town?"

"Quiet?" Chance repeated. "Why wouldn't it be? It's Christmas Eve, after all."

Smoke rubbed his chin. "Is there a train coming in this morning? That's why the other boys went to the depot?"

"That's right. We're not expecting anybody else, since we're all here now, but it was something to do." Chance looked at the stranger. "Who's this?"

"Peter Stansfield is the name," the man introduced himself. "I take it you're one of the illustrious Jensens?"

Smoke said, "He's a reporter, so watch what you say around him. But I'll give him credit. He helped me pump a handcar all the way down here from Donner Pass. We stopped just outside of town because we weren't sure what we might find here. Might not have made it without him."

Stansfield beamed, as if that praise from Smoke meant a great deal to him. Chance shook hands with him, then asked Smoke, "Why did you want to know if there was any trouble here this morning?"

"Because there's a gang of outlaws here in town planning to pull a job on Christmas Eve. I don't know what it is, but there's a good chance hell's about to break loose!"

CHAPTER 40

Stevenson stood up straighter as he spotted the wagon coming along the street toward the bank. It was just an unassuming buckboard with two men on the seat. The one handling the reins of the two-horse team had a rifle leaning beside him, while the other man rode with a shotgun across his lap. In the back of the buckboard was a plain-looking wooden trunk with leather straps around it.

Every instinct in Magnus Stevenson's body told him there were four hundred thousand dollars in cash inside that trunk.

He nodded to Mitchell, said curtly, "Buckboard coming up the street," and moved along the boardwalk until he could look along the alley between the bank and the dress shop. He took off his hat and ran a finger around inside the brim. Either Deke Mahoney or Warren Hopgood would be watching from the rear corner of the bank, and they couldn't fail to see the signal.

Minutes now. Mere minutes until they were all rich.

Earlier, Stevenson had seen two groups of well-dressed businessmen enter the bank at different times, and none of them had come back out. At the center of each group had been an older man with an arrogant, imperious air about him. Those had to be the two mining tycoons, there to conclude their deal.

They would be in for a surprise.

The buckboard came to a stop in front of the bank. The two men on the seat climbed down but made no move to unload the trunk. Several of the men Stevenson had noticed earlier emerged from the building, however, and converged on the vehicle. Flunkies who worked for Cameron Coolidge and Thomas Nickerson, Stevenson thought. Mitchell moved up beside him as they watched the men lift the trunk from the buckboard and carry it into the bank.

Mitchell said quietly, "Maybe we ought to have grabbed the loot while it was still out here."

"We couldn't do that without attracting a lot of attention," Stevenson said. "The idea is to take over the bank and make sure nobody can give the alarm while we load the trunk again and drive off. If things go as planned, we'll be out of town before anybody knows what's happened except the people in the bank."

Mitchell hadn't sheathed his knife, although he'd put away the figurine he'd been carving. He ran the ball of his thumb along the blade and said, "There's one way of makin' sure ever'body in there stays nice an' quiet. You can't go to hollerin' when your throat's cut."

"You'd murder more than a dozen people?"

"For that kind of money," Mitchell said, "I'd kill a whole heap more than a dozen."

Stevenson realized suddenly that he felt the same way. This was the big payoff, the sort of job that not many who rode the owlhoot trail ever got to pull, and nothing was going to stop them from getting away with that fortune in cash.

"All right, here we go," Deke Mahoney said to Warren Hopgood after seeing the signal from Stevenson across the street. The two outlaws moved along the rear of the brick bank building toward a sturdy-looking door that was kept locked unless something had to be taken in or out that way.

Today was going to be different, though, if Carl Andrews had done what he was supposed to.

If the door was locked, Mahoney and Hopgood would have no choice but to back away and leave the area, collecting Stevenson, Mitchell, and Harmon along the way.

But as they were leaving town, they would stop at the Andrews house and take the teller's wife and daughter with them. Andrews would never see them alive again. That would be poor payment for the time the gang had spent here in Reno, but better than nothing, Mahoney supposed.

It wasn't going to come to that, he discovered as he tried the doorknob and felt it turn. He nodded to Hopgood, and both men pulled up bandannas over the lower halves of their faces. They drew their guns and Mahoney eased the door open.

Just inside was a short hall with a door on the left-hand side. Mahoney was surprised to see Carl Andrews standing in front of the door, as if he was waiting for them.

"I can't let you go through with this," he said in a quiet but desperate tone. "Please, just turn around and leave now, and I'll never say anything about what you tried to do. Rebecca and Sadie and I will act like we don't know anything about it."

Mahoney ignored the plea and rasped, "Where's the money?"

The way Andrews's eyes darted toward the door was all the answer Mahoney and Hopgood needed. As they moved in that direction, Andrews exclaimed, "That's Mr. Hopkins's private office—"

Mahoney didn't need to hear anything else. He slammed the gun in his hand against the teller's head. Andrews went down like a sack of rocks.

Mahoney opened the door and strode into the bank president's office. Hopgood was right behind him. They leveled their guns at the five men standing next to a table where a trunk sat. The trunk's lid was raised, and inside, visible to the outlaws, were bundles and bundles of greenbacks. The sight was almost enough to make Deke Mahoney stare.

But he couldn't afford to do that, because two of them in the room were armed guards, and they were trying to bring their weapons to bear. They froze as they found themselves staring down gun barrels.

"All right, boys," Mahoney drawled. "Get rid of all that iron you're packin'. We're here to ruin Christmas."

* * *

"Look at those two crossing the street," Luke said quietly to Ace and Matt as they approached the bank. "They have mighty intent looks on their faces, like they're after something."

"And there's another one on the boardwalk over there by the dress shop," Matt said. "He's a gunman if I've ever seen one."

Luke drew in a sharp breath. "You're right about that. I recognize him. That's Otis Harmon. As cold-blooded a snake as you'll ever find. I've seen reward dodgers on him. There's probably paper out on those other two, as well."

"What are we going to do?" Ace asked.

Luke increased his pace. "What I always do when I see a wanted fugitive with a reward on his head." He moved his hand toward the old, long-barreled Remington revolver he still carried after all these years. "Harmon! Elevate!"

"Watch the other two," Matt snapped at Ace. They turned toward the men crossing the street toward the bank.

Otis Harmon whirled around toward Luke. The man's face twisted as his hand flashed toward the gun on his hip. Luke pulled the Remington and cocked the .44 as the barrel came up. The crash of guns came so close together that they sounded like one shot, but Luke's was a fraction of a second earlier.

The bullet slammed into Harmon's chest and knocked him back just enough that his arm jerked and his shot went high in the air. Luke fired again and then again, driving Harmon off his feet with the smashing lead so the outlaw couldn't get off another shot.

The other two men had stopped and turned at Luke's challenge of Harmon. The older, stocky one looked startled, but that reaction lasted only a split second before he clawed for his gun. The younger man, a cocky grin on his face, was holding a knife in his left hand. He tossed it in the air, caught it by the blade, and whipped it in a vicious throw toward Ace, who flung himself forward off his feet as he was drawing. The knife missed him by inches.

Ace's Colt roared and bucked as he landed in the street. The bullet caught the knife thrower in the belly and doubled him over. He collapsed, clutching at himself as blood welled between his fingers.

The older man was faster than he looked but was no match for Matt's speed. Matt called, "Drop it!" as he pointed his gun at the outlaw. For a second it looked like the man was going to, but then he said something that sounded like, "So close," and tried to raise his gun and fire it.

Matt fired first, his bullet knocking the man off his feet. He lay there in the street and writhed for a second, then lay still.

"Is that all of them?" Ace asked as he pushed himself up on one knee. "Is it over?"

It wasn't.

Inside the bank president's office, the sudden and unexpected sound of gunfire from somewhere outside distracted Mahoney and Hopgood just enough that the hired guards decided to make a play. They had already been forced at gunpoint to put their rifle and shotgun aside, but they still had their handguns. Both men drew.

Mahoney and Hopgood fired and couldn't miss at such close range. Bullets ripped through flesh and sprayed blood in the air. Some of the flying crimson splattered on the money in the open trunk.

Snarling, Hopgood turned toward the banker and the two mine owners, and it was obvious from his face that he intended to cut them down, too, in his anger over the robbery being thwarted.

But Mahoney yelled, "Come on, let's get outta here!" With his free hand, he grabbed several bundles of cash from the trunk and then darted toward the door. With some reluctance, Hopgood followed him.

As they emerged into the hall, someone lunged at them. Carl Andrews had regained consciousness. With blood dripping from the cut on his head where Mahoney had pistol-whipped him, he tackled the outlaw and tried to hold him.

Mahoney's gun roared again, flinging Andrews away from him. Mahoney hurdled over the fallen teller and slammed out the rear door. Hopgood was close behind him.

"What the hell happened?" Hopgood asked. "What could have gone wrong?"

"I dunno, but let's get to the horses. We can still ride away from here, and we got a little money." Mahoney holstered his gun and started cramming the bundles of cash inside his coat. "Act like we don't know what's goin' on."

They turned along an alley and headed for the

main street. As they stepped out, Mahoney was distracted by a crowd gathering to his right, in front of the bank. He spotted three motionless shapes lying on the ground and knew those had to be his friends and fellow members of the gang.

He sure had let Frank down, he thought.

And as that was going through his head, he fumbled the last bundle of greenbacks as he tried to stash them inside his coat. They fell on the boardwalk in front of him. He started to bend over and pick them up when a man's voice, as hard as flint, said, "Leave it right there."

Smoke, Chance, and Stansfield were on their way to the train station when the shooting started in front of the bank. Any time guns roared like that, Jensens were usually involved, so Smoke wasn't surprised when he saw his brothers and his other nephew standing there as a crowd gathered around several bodies.

Then two men stepped out from an alley in front of them, and one of the men dropped what Smoke instantly saw was a bundle of money with a telltale red splash across it.

Somebody had spilled blood on those greenbacks, so whatever was going on, Smoke was sure these two hombres were part of it.

Both strangers had their guns holstered. So did Smoke, who stood facing them squarely, blocking Chance and Stansfield so that they were out of the line of fire. Smoke went on, "If you've been waiting for Frank Colbert . . . he's not going to make it."

The looks of surprise on the men's faces told him he had guessed right.

Their draws were fueled by hate and desperation, and they were fast. Faster than most, the kind of speed that meant life or death to men such as these who rode the dark trails.

But Smoke Jensen was faster. His arm was a blur as his Colt seemed to appear in his hand as if by magic. The revolver thundered twice, one bullet going into the chest of each man. The shots drove them back, but something kept them on their feet, snarling and cursing. Smoke triggered twice more.

The planks of the boardwalk vibrated a little as the two bodies came crashing down on them.

"Good Lord," Peter Stansfield said in an awed voice. "I never even saw him draw. I . . . I never saw anything like it. The legends are true."

Smoke glanced over his shoulder at the reporter, grunted, shook his head, and started reloading.

"Smoke!" Matt called as he, Luke, and Ace hurried toward them, drawn by the fresh burst of gunfire. "It's about time you got here. We thought you were going to miss Christmas!"

"No," Smoke said, "it looks like I got here just in time for the celebration."

The Summit Hotel, Donner Pass, New Year's Eve

The big main table in the hotel dining room was full tonight. Not everyone in the Jensen family had been able to spend Christmas together—Louis and Denny had remained at the hotel while Smoke and Stansfield took the handcar to Reno, something that

Denny had complained about loud and long—but now they were all together for New Year's Eve.

Melanie and Brad Buckner were here, too, Melanie sitting next to Louis with her son on her other side. Smoke had invited Salty to join them, of course, and even Peter Stansfield, with the provision that the reporter agreed not to write anything about this family get-together. Stansfield seemed quite taken with Denny, so maybe he could honor his pledge . . . although there was no chance in hell that Denny would ever return his interest, Smoke thought.

Even Alma Lewiston was still on hand, although not at this dinner tonight. Herman Painton, the manager of the hotel, had offered her a job here. She had taken it, with her usual glum assertion that she didn't have any other choice, but Smoke figured she had more options than she knew about. Both Painton and Juniper Jones had shown an interest in her. Maybe, if she could let go of her tragic past and the mistakes she had made, Alma might be able to fashion a decent life for herself here.

Getting everyone to the Summit Hotel hadn't been easy. It had involved taking the roundabout route by rail back to Sacramento and then chartering a special train to bring them to Donner Pass. Since the hotel was a short distance west of the avalanche site, the tracks were relatively clear to that point, although it would still be weeks before the entire pass was open again.

None of that mattered now, Smoke thought as he looked around the table at his family and friends. Their dinner this evening was a belated Christmas feast and New Year's celebration combined into one.

They weren't the only ones who had something to
be thankful for as one year ended and another
began. Back in Reno, Carl Andrews had survived
being shot by Deke Mahoney as he and Warren Hopgood tried to escape. The wounded bank teller had
spilled the whole plan and then been reunited with
his wife and daughter, who had survived their ordeal
unscathed. Smoke had spoken to the bank president
and asked him not to be too hard on Andrews. The
man had been afraid for the lives of his loved ones,
after all. No matter how that turned out, all three
members of the Andrews family were alive and together.

Amid the eating, drinking, talking, and laughing,
Brad said to Smoke, "Mr. Jensen, I was wondering
about something."

"What's that, Brad?"

"The stagecoach is still out there, isn't it?"

Smoke nodded. "Without a team of horses, it can't
get up and run off by itself."

"Are you going to get it, so you can return it to Mr.
Davis?"

Smoke folded his napkin, set it beside his plate,
and said, "Now that's a mighty fine idea. Once the
weather is better, we'll take some horses out there
and fetch it in. After the damage we did to it, we
ought to try to fix it up."

"And then I'll drive it back to Sacramento," Salty
spoke up. "Would've been nice to take it all the way to
Reno, but some things ain't meant to be, I reckon."

"What will Mr. Davis do with it?" Brad wanted to
know.

"Oh, I expect he'll keep it, like he'd been doin'

before we came along and borrowed it," the old-timer told him.

"But he just had it in a barn," Brad said. "Stage-coaches are part of history. People ought to be able to see them."

Louis said, "You mean like in a museum?"

"Yeah," Brad said, nodding excitedly. "That would be a good place for it."

"I'll talk to Fred," Smoke promised. "That old coach is pretty close to his heart, but we might be able to convince him to share it with folks."

"I'd like that." Brad grinned. "Especially since my initials are on it."

Louis laughed and said, "You want people to re-member you, is that it?"

Solemnly, Brad said, "I want people to remember what it was like to go through Donner Pass in a stage-coach, in the middle of a blizzard, at Christmastime, with badmen and wolves and the Donner Devil lurk-ing around."

"I don't reckon any of us around this table will ever forget, Brad," Smoke said.

"And none of us ever forgot," the tall, silver-haired man said as he rested his hand on the stagecoach and lightly traced a fingertip along the faint markings. "I know I never did."

Some of the visitors to the museum had gathered to listen to him. Among them was the little boy whose question about the stagecoach had started the whole thing. Wide eyed, he gazed up at the silver-haired man and said, "Are . . . are you—"

"Wait, wait, wait," the professor interrupted. "Seriously,

after spinning that ridiculous yarn, you're not going to claim that you're really Brad Buckner and that you lived through the whole unbelievable thing?"

"You want to see my driver's license, mister?" the silver-haired man asked coldly. "You can read the name on it for yourself."

"I don't care what your name is," the professor said, "you can't expect anybody to believe such a pile of utter hogwash. It's claptrap! I've never read about this in any of the history books, and I know everything there is to know about transportation in the Old West."

"Mister, you only know what you *think* you know." The older man dropped a slow wink to the little boy, who laughed.

The professor blew out a disgusted breath, shook his head, and turned away. "Hogwash," he muttered again as he stalked off.

The rest of the crowd began to break up. It would soon be closing time for the museum.

The little boy lingered, though, ignoring his mother's stern look. "Was it true?" he asked. "The story about the Jensens, and the Donner Devil, and how all of you almost froze to death at Christmastime?"

"What do you think?" the silver-haired man said with a smile.

"I think *I* want it to be true."

"Then that's all that matters." The man touched his chest over his heart. "If it's true in here."